Her Best Bo

A Picking Daisy Novel

By: Kimberly M. Miller

Copyright © 2020 By Kimberly M. Miller. All Rights Reserved.

This is a work of fiction. Names, characters, businesses, places, events, and incidents, are either the product of the author's imagination, or are used in a fictitious manner. Any resemblance to any actual persons, living or dead, or actual events, is purely coincidental.

No part of this book may be reproduced or used in any manner without the express written permission of the publisher, except the use of a brief quotation for a book review.

Dedicated to my precious mom.
Thank you for always being my biggest fan.

Chapter one

Marilyn Darby stared at the gas gauge, doing the weak mental calculation of a person who'd never been adept at story problems. She had no idea how to figure whether she could make it to work based on an estimate of how many miles she had to go versus how much gas she had versus how much money remained in her miniscule bank account.

An embarrassing number of minutes and finger-counting passed before she jammed the ornery vehicle into drive, grateful her mother didn't witness the 'wing and a prayer' life she lived.

As if on cue, Marilyn's cell phone rang. With a glance at the display she found the very woman she'd just been thinking of calling, yet again.

"Hey, Mom." Marilyn clicked the radio down a notch. Her mother would have a conniption if she heard her daughter listening to hip hop, rock, or anything else that might, unbidden, come blaring out if she wasn't careful.

"Marilyn. Where are you? Why did it take so many calls to finally get you to pick up? I do not like that one bit."

Marilyn paused at a stop sign, looked both ways, and started driving again. "I'm sure you don't. Sorry. I've been really busy with work."

Grace didn't appreciate that her daughter worked three jobs, sometimes more, to make ends meet. She struggled to understand how Marilyn could be almost twenty-three and still without a degree, husband, or a nine-to-five position her parents could brag about to their friends.

"I need to know if you'll be attending your sister's engagement party." She cleared her throat. "And whether you'll be bringing a plus one."

Rosemary's engagement party. To Mr. Perfect himself. A NASA engineer. It wasn't bad enough that Rosemary had been nominated for the Nobel Peace Prize for her work to end human trafficking, she had to also go and marry Mr. Perfect.

The family made it impossible for Marilyn to ever feel good about her own accomplishments, few though they might be.

Marilyn snorted. "I'm not sure, Ma. That's probably why I never sent in the RSVP."

"I worried you'd lost it."

While that would be something Marilyn might do, that didn't keep her from bristling at the accusation.

"I didn't lose it," she snapped. But for a moment she did wonder where she left the dumb thing. Oh, that's right. She used it as a bookmark in a dance magazine. She'd been in the midst of reading an article about shin splints and…

"Well, it's not an impossible question." Grace continued. "Yes? Or no?"

Marilyn pulled her car over short of her destination, wondering how to answer. She dumped her boyfriend ages ago and decided she wouldn't date again until or unless she found someone worth her time.

And by worth her time, Marilyn meant someone who shared her faith, someone with a stable job, and someone who would unequivocally support her still-floundering career aspirations. And most of all, someone who only had eyes for her—and would dance with her whether he enjoyed dancing or not.

That man, the superhero unicorn saint he would need to be, probably didn't exist. Still, Marilyn would wait, holding out for her impossible dream. She wouldn't be distracted by shiny things like a good attitude or musky cologne. Or glasses. Definitely not glasses, no matter how weak a man in glasses made her knees.

"I have an audition coming up, Mom. If I get the role, I can't say I'll be able to make it to the party because we'll be starting into rehearsals."

"So, you're saying no? When you haven't been home in so long?"

Marilyn beat her head on the steering wheel, praying to knock herself unconscious. Conversations with her brain surgeon mother always went like this.

Sadly, that wasn't a joke. Grace Darby actually made her living as a world-renowned brain surgeon while her embarrassment of a daughter struggled to start her car and keep it full of gas.

"OK, Mom. I'll find a way to make it. And go ahead and be wild and put me down for a plus one too." Why did she say that? What poor schmuck could she drag along to this painful event?

Might as well go for broke.

"I can hardly wait. Now, I need to go—I'm almost to work."

Marilyn hung up before her mom could say another word.

Now, she only needed to find a way out of going home. Again.

**

Bo Sutton descended the winding staircase, mentally ticking off all his day would entail. He worked as a personal assistant to songwriter Daisy Grant, who kept everyone on their toes, including her rock legend husband, Robby.

A year earlier Robby hired Bo as security for Daisy, who'd survived a car accident that left her in a wheelchair well before the couple even met. Now, as a songwriter to nearly every popular, successful musician in the business, in addition of course to being Robby's precious wife, the rocker would not take any chance of putting Daisy in harm's way just because of their fame. Their love story captivated the nation and culminated in a wedding like no other, where Daisy even mastered a standing wheelchair to out-rock-star her own husband.

While Bo hadn't been there himself, he'd seen the pictures and the videos. And now, knowing Daisy and Robby, he couldn't imagine two people more suited to one another. He could only hope one day to find the same kind of relationship for himself.

Fat chance given his terrible, pathetic history.

Still, one thing remained sure—Bo didn't doubt for a moment his ability to do the job he'd been hired for. With his training and experience working with disabled veterans and athletes, not only could he keep her safe, but he also intended to lead her in workouts too per her request.

Already the original job morphed into so much more. And with every addition to his daily tasks, Bo's love for his work only increased.

Today's agenda: breakfast, prepare the gym for Daisy's dance class, take care of the Grant's baby, Nicolette. After that, per Robby's specific instruction, Bo would make sure the bad-boy flirt Titus Black behaved while he worked with Daisy on a new song.

Having lived in the power couple's mansion for the better part of a year, Bo no longer noticed the gold and platinum records lining the walls of the foyer. His eye did, however, catch the crystal chandelier as he hustled under it. It would be cleaned next week. He made a mental note to call and confirm that appointment.

Bo's attention returned to the sweet baby in his arms, the one he promised to take care of overnight and through the morning until Daisy and Robby decided to get out of bed. The couple enjoyed a long date the night before—their first date without their youngest daughter, a one-and-a-half-month-old tiger who kept him up nearly all night with her fussing.

Not that Bo minded. No, he adored the baby and his ability to calm her when no one else could. He cradled her in one arm and carried her bouncy seat in the other as he entered the kitchen, not surprised to find Robby's teenaged daughter, Alice, at the table with three friends waiting for him.

"What took you so long?" she demanded, jumping to her feet to steal the baby.

As usual, Bo didn't miss a beat. "She didn't like the first outfit." He'd already become so fond of Alice that he could scarcely imagine his life without the teen in it. Most days he took her to school and picked her up, and lately he helped with her homework nearly every night.

Being needed satisfied Bo as nothing else could. Secretly, he read a book every week or two and loved learning. Helping Alice with her homework meant he got to revisit the lessons he forgot from high school that at the time seemed so pointless but now he realized were actually important.

Alice's friends stared at him as he set the seat on the counter and tied on his apron. "You ladies need some snacks?"

The girls giggled, which didn't surprise him. A man who stood nearly six-five didn't usually nanny for a rock star couple, he usually didn't cook, and he definitely didn't wear frilly aprons designed for women. One day he'd find an appropriate apron. Or maybe he could make one.

Bo didn't care. He'd never been much for convention.

Alice didn't lift her eyes from the baby as she spoke, the girls now leaning over to look at Nicolette too.

"What do you want? Bo makes everything."

"How about crepes?" one of the girls asked.

Bo winked. "Crepes it is." He got to work tugging everything he needed from the cabinets and tossing it across the counter.

"Who's having crepes?" Robby's voice boomed as he entered the kitchen, followed closely by his wife.

"Move it, Robby, I need my baby." Daisy swatted him out of her way and stopped beside Alice, peering with the girls at the sweet, sleeping infant.

The teens turned in Robby's direction, jaws dropped. They moved silently away from Daisy, eyes wide. Neither the husband nor wife appeared to notice the impact of their arrival on their guests.

Bo continued working on the snack. Over the last year he got used to people's reactions to his employers who, truth be told, still intimidated and fascinated him too sometimes, regardless how normal they actually were.

For his fans, Robby Grant embodied swagger and a supremely cocky attitude. And at just over six feet two inches tall, he stood as a formidable presence of wild hair, piercings, and tattoos. All of that did nothing to diminish his musical genius. So far, Bo had seen him play the piano, shred a guitar, and even beat around on the drums a time or two, not to mention of course that gravelly, sultry voice of his. No wonder women swooned.

In private, the man himself could still be cocky, demanding, and confident, but he also spent a lot of time in Bible study, insisted on weekly dates with his bride, and had become an amazing stepfather to Alice. Bo liked and respected him, even if there were times Robby deliberately pushed the bodyguard's buttons for his own strange entertainment.

The musician pecked his stunning wife's head before resting one arm around Alice's shoulders as he gazed down at his baby. "How're my girls?"

Alice looked up at him, eyes softening in admiration and love. How quickly she and Robby went from strangers to an easy companionship of father-daughter. Years ago, at a time when Robby struggled with his own demons that included the stereotypical manifestations in partying, drinking, and otherwise making a menace of himself, he agreed to help one of his stylists, Mindy, by claiming her baby as his own.

So, when Mindy died just after Robby and Daisy's wedding, Alice appeared at the couple's mansion door. As a newlywed intent on building a life with his wife, Robby didn't want to take responsibility for the teen, but Daisy brought everyone together and helped them form a patchwork family of friends and relations tighter than most bound by blood.

"Better introduce us before their eyes bug out." Robby scooped Nicolette out of Alice's arms and cradled her against him. "Didn't tell your friends I'm so handsome, huh?"

Alice whacked him playfully before engaging in all the introductions, ending with, "And that's Daisy."

Daisy moved her wheelchair to the center of the group to greet the girls, warm and welcoming as always. "I'm so glad you could come today. Alice has been itching to invite you over since school started."

As the kids talked, Robby made his way into the living room, still fussing over the baby.

Bo finished the crepes and set them on plates around the kitchen island as Daisy turned to him.

"Did Nicolette keep you up long?"

Bo chuckled. He understood Daisy's concerns, and that they heightened because Nicolette didn't take kindly to most people. Bo, of course, would be an exception. "No longer than usual. No longer than she does anyone else." He minimized the truth of the matter. Nicolette only stopped fussing for him, Daisy, and sometimes Robby. Otherwise, a person had their work cut out getting the baby to calm.

Daisy watched the girls giggle their way out of the room carrying their plates.

"Do not drop crumbs everywhere!"

"We won't!" Alice's words were barely out before a door slammed and they likely headed outside to the enormous patio.

"What's the week look like?"

Bo set a crepe near Daisy and began cleaning up. "I synced it to your phone."

She took a bite of breakfast. "Excellent."

Robby entered the room, leaning down to kiss his wife's head before placing their daughter in her arms.

"Dang, you're gorgeous. And I adore you." His lips found hers this time. Bo turned his back on them. While their behavior no longer shocked him, it didn't make him less uncomfortable. He gave up on finding a spouse years ago, but that didn't mean the desire fizzled out completely.

Bo reminded himself to be grateful for what he had. This job was a lifeline, and he wouldn't forget it.

"You're a lucky man. I adore you too." The love in Daisy's voice couldn't be missed.

Bo tossed the last of the dishes into the dishwasher and headed over to Daisy with the baby carrier. "Want me to take her?"

Reluctantly, Daisy pressed her lips to Nicolette's soft head again and Bo set her back in her seat.

"I'll make sure the gym's ready." Bo started for the door to give the couple privacy before their busy days took over.

"You're the best, Bo."

Robby grunted. "That's all I hire, babe."

The couple started bantering as Bo made his way out the door. He'd need to be quick in this next job if he wanted to avoid running into his least favorite person on the planet,

Daisy's dancing instructor and his nemesis, the one and only Marilyn Darby.

**

Marilyn shoved out of her car and slammed its temperamental door. She stared up at the mansion belonging to Robby and Daisy Grant, still in awe that she got to come here a few times a week to teach Daisy how to dance again. While Marilyn hadn't yet been inside the sprawling estate, she wondered if the tour came with maps, or if every so often there might be a 'you are here' arrow on a kiosk to keep guests from getting lost.

The dance teacher let herself into the gym, tossed her bag aside, and slipped her light sweatshirt off, leaving her in tights, workout shorts, and a shirt with 'Dance!' blaring across it in colorful, capital letters. She kicked off her shoes and rolled her neck from side to side. Only minutes remained before Daisy would come through the doors, and Marilyn intended to be ready to hit the ground running.

After completing her stretches, Marilyn plugged her phone into the sound system and began to dance to the playlist she prepared specifically with Daisy in mind.

The movement and emotion came easily and made the dancer free again. As she neared the end of her for-fun practice routine, Marilyn leapt through the air, right as the music abruptly halted. Shocked, she barely managed to right herself and land without incident.

Cheeks flaming, she turned toward the offender, already certain of who it would be.

Bo Sutton. All two-hundred and fifty pounds of muscle, attitude, and those comments that made her crazy.

The only good thing about her hiatus from teaching Daisy while she took time off to have her baby, was that Marilyn hadn't had to contend with Bo or his ridiculous insinuations and judgements for her brief relationship with Zeke Fullerton, a man she'd not seen or heard from in over a year.

Good riddance to the last relationship she intended to have for a while. Zeke convinced the naïve twenty-year-old he would be the man she needed, when in reality all he wanted were things she refused to give, which meant he dumped her unceremoniously in the middle of a date, forcing her to walk nearly two miles home in the middle of New York.

Idiot.

Bo didn't know any of it, nor did he care. He assumed Marilyn to be beneath him, a woman looking to take Zeke for whatever she could, because apparently those were the women he cheated on Marilyn with, the ones who liked his money and attention, the ones who crowded the gym looking for him. Bo didn't care that Marilyn had pride, a work ethic, and enough confidence to move on from all of it.

And she never asked Zeke for a thing because she honestly cared for him, or at one time she thought she did.

While the break-up meant the loss of the gym space Zeke promised her for a dance studio, and a depleted bank account as she tried to make ends meet while finding a new job and apartment far away from him, Marilyn didn't care. She survived, and by God's good grace she realized she could get along without help from anyone, especially a man who'd only want her innocence in return.

Things finally started looking up when Robby's agent Lily found Marilyn teaching at a small dance studio. As these things often go, a friend of a friend recommended her. Once Lily met Marilyn, she hired her on the spot.

Weeks later the dancer discovered Bo's place in the Grant hierarchy. While it turned her stomach, she refused to lose out on the first good thing to happen to her in months.

She and Bo, the bodyguard/ assistant, and now manny, would never be friends. And the more time she spent with him, the more certain Marilyn became of her dislike for Bo Sutton.

Her eyes narrowed as she drank him in, folding her arms over her chest to remind him she couldn't care less about his clout in Daisy's life. She knew the songwriter liked her too and would never fire her just because Bo couldn't stand her.

In fact, Daisy appeared to be amused by the two of them fighting all the time.

Bo frowned, his legs spread wide, arms folded over his chest as if to remind her of his power position. So what? Marilyn refused to be intimidated.

Bo's almost-black hair looked shorter than she remembered, and his dark eyes glittered, not in amusement, but in complete, utter annoyance.

Getting under his skin was entirely too easy. Did it make her a sadist to enjoy it so much? One thing seemed sure, Marilyn shoved aside her Christian upbringing in the way she treated Bo.

She ignored that convicting thought as she waited for his first snip of the day.

"You would dance to this garbage." Bo's deep voice grated on the dancer's last, weak nerve. She wanted to sucker punch him.

But she would be an adult if at all possible.

Did adults stick their tongues out at one another?

Marilyn narrowed her eyes. "Every day, Beauregard. Why? Want to join me?"

He didn't turn the music back on. "That's not my name. And no. I'm never dancing with you. No telling what I'd catch."

"You say that like you believe I'd really want to touch you. No thanks." She rolled her neck again, trying to ignore his dark eyes and even worse, those blasted shoulders. He could lift her easily.

Bo raised one eyebrow. "Daisy said to tell you she'll be over in a few minutes."

Marilyn paused in stretching her quad as her gaze fell on the baby he carried in a car seat. She'd been so focused on those stupid shoulders and irritating attitude that she never even mentioned the baby!

She went to him, eyes focused on the tiny bundle who probably looked even smaller because her seat dangled from his monstrous hand.

"Oh… she's precious!" she cooed.

Bo shifted so the baby moved farther away from her prying eyes. "Don't breathe on her. She'll get your germs."

Marilyn put her hands on her hips as she rose to her full height to challenge him. "I'm not germy, you freak." She elbowed him in the gut, causing him to heave a low groan.

"Unless you count cooties." She wiggled her eyebrows. "I definitely got some girl-cooties."

Bo remained stoic. "What are you? Ten?" He focused on the baby as he continued. "Besides, I could already make a fair guess of what cooties you caught from Fullerton."

Marilyn stared up at him, a crick forming in her neck from the effort this took. "You delivered your message, manny-cake. Now get back to the kitchen."

He sneered. "Gone."

Bo started for the door, pausing as he turned back. "Beauregard means handsome and highly regarded." His forehead wrinkled as he appeared to be thinking this over.

Marilyn gagged. "Probably only to your mother." Without her cell phone to google it, she had no idea if he might be right. She allowed herself the pleasure of studying him because she could tell it made him uncomfortable.

As if on cue, he squirmed, one shaking hand reaching for the door.

Marilyn grinned. "You ever dance?"

Bo shifted the baby carrier. "Heck no. Why would I do that?" He nudged the door with his elbow as if intent on an escape.

Marilyn couldn't help herself. She went to him, took the baby, and set her gently on the floor nearby. The door closed with a soft click, so she grabbed his hand before he could protest, put it on her waist, and slowly lifted to her toes, which left her woefully, and a bit surprisingly, short of looking straight into his eyes.

Standing so close to him for the first time left Marilyn tingling and breathless as she inhaled his musky cologne. "See? No cooties yet, you big oaf."

She would have tried to meet his gaze, but his eyes were trained somewhere on the wall behind her, his cheeks flaming red. His lips in a firm line, in complete defiance of her hostile takeover.

Marilyn ignored all of that and clung to her spontaneous nature as well as the mantra that she could teach anyone to dance.

Even ornery old Bo Sutton. And even if he had no intention of playing nice or making an effort to try dancing with her, let alone treating her as an equal.

"You can pretend I'm wearing heels." She started swaying, closing her eyes and humming a sweet tune she imagined would be perfect for a waltz. Eventually she would get him into swing dancing, but with someone like this, Marilyn would need to start slowly, carefully so she didn't scare him off.

And beyond that, so she could convince him to help her prepare for her upcoming audition. The idea took wonderful root as she swayed in an effort to get his body in sync with hers.

Had she lost her mind? Probably. But it wouldn't be the first or last time Marilyn acted before thinking.

Bo didn't even shift his feet, a mountain unmoved.

Marilyn kept swaying anyway, dreaming of a beautiful, choreographed partner dance with someone who actually might enjoy the experience.

"This would be easier if you left the music on, Bo."

His feet must be broken because they were like chunks of cement stuck to the floor. Marilyn stepped back reluctantly, her hands still in place on him as she looked down between their bodies and back up at him again.

"Don't be scared. We can start off slow and eventually you'll be lifting me over your head—like in Dirty Dancing. You know, 'nobody puts Baby in a corner'?" She cackled at her own joke. "Boy, would Daisy be impressed!"

Bo tried to shrug her away from him. "Knock it off!" he grumbled, finally disentangling himself and stepping free.

Marilyn giggled again. "We'd be a perfect team. Come on. Think what a ladies' man you could be if you could dance. Women love a man who can dance, Buford."

His cheeks grew impossibly darker. "I don't need a woman."

She stifled a victorious smirk as he grabbed the baby and yanked the door open.

"And I don't dance. I already told you that."

Marilyn went to her phone and turned the music back on. "Funny how you're always over here like you want to. Or maybe you like me and need a friend." She winked. "Gimme a call if you change your mind. I'd teach you. For free even. Because I'm nice like that."

Bo held the door open with his backside as he faced her. Marilyn didn't think she imagined the steam coming out of his ears.

"Do you actually try to annoy me?" he snapped. "I don't need a friend—and if I did, it wouldn't be you." Bo exhaled on a groan. "There hasn't been one time yet since we met that you've done anything but drive me nuts."

Marilyn pressed her hand to her chest, feigning innocence. "I'm playing you like a violin." She winked. "I guess big tough guys make the easiest targets." She pointed to her heart. "You got a big, fat, red circle right here. Bull's eye!"

Bo squinted and shook his head before slamming the door closed so hard, she wondered how he didn't shatter the glass.

**

Bo stalked toward the house, nearly steamrolling Daisy on the sidewalk as he passed, intent on getting as far as possible from that infuriating woman and her electric touch and mentions of his lifting her over his head as they danced together.

Unfortunately, as soon as she mentioned that famous dance scene, Bo easily imagined it all. He never before had such an inclination. She was stark, raving mad!

And he, sadly, must be too.

Normally, Bo epitomized calm, cool, and collected any other day of the week. But when Marilyn Darby appeared, he went completely off the rails and became someone he hardly recognized.

Bo rubbed his free hand on his pants as if to remove any remnants of that woman's cooties.

If only getting rid of that sunshine she oozed could be as easy. Being in Marilyn's presence made things rise to the surface of Bo's consciousness. Strange, uninvited, annoying things.

Things that reeked of interest, dating, handholding, and lips made for… Bo squelched this ridiculous line of thinking. He did not want to date Marilyn Darby.

The woman represented everything he never wanted. He saw the way she laughed with that disgusting Zeke as they planned to take his section of the gym—the space he worked for months to clear to start Pilates and weight training for veterans.

But Marilyn waltzed in and poof! Zeke said she needed the space and gave it right over.

Then he made Bo listen to all the ways he'd encourage her to thank him for it later.

No. Bo did not want to be with a woman like her.

"Hey!" Daisy squeaked. "What's wrong?"

The bodyguard inhaled and exhaled, balling a fist as he turned to her.

"That woman is certifiable. There must be another dance teacher we could hire. Just say the word and she's good as gone." Bo pointed toward the gym, grateful that from this vantage point there'd be no way Marilyn could sense his frustration and pounce. He didn't want her to get the pleasure of watching him squirm beyond what he'd done already.

He blushed when she touched him. He would never look at her again.

He'd been on battlefields across the world, trained some of the toughest athletes, and now he worked for arguably the most famous couple in the United States and he blushed at a brief moment of contact with some annoying dancer who deliberately and insultingly pushed his buttons at every turn?

He needed to call his mom.

"Marilyn?" Daisy's features softened. She peered into the carrier and made faces at the baby before looking up at him again. "Really, Bo." She looked him over. "She's all of five foot three and a hundred pounds. What could she possibly do that makes you so crazy?"

"She exists." He didn't need to elaborate any further. Daisy already enjoyed this too much. "Buzz me when you're ready for our workout. I'm taking Nicolette for a run so we both get some fresh air. That way she'll go down for her nap easier and I won't need to worry about escorting old Twinkle Toes over there off the premises."

He turned and started for the house.

"Bo!"

The bodyguard inhaled again, closing his eyes momentarily as he pivoted to look back.

"I can put in a good word for you." Daisy winked. "Maybe write you two a song to dance to at your wedding. That would get her to lighten up."

Bo growled and stomped away, unamused at his boss's idea of humor.

**

Marilyn grinned as she watched Bo's receding back when he stomped out of the gym, likely to tattle on her. What did she care? Daisy wouldn't fire her because her bodyguard acted as mature as a three-year-old and had no sense of humor. At least

Marilyn hoped she wouldn't get fired for giving Bo a hard time. Besides, she rather enjoyed getting the man all riled up. He made it so darn easy, how could she stop herself?

She turned the music back up and started dancing, thinking of all the neat things she and Daisy would accomplish.

The sound of the door closing alerted her to her student's arrival. Marilyn slowed and turned.

"Yea! I missed you!" she exclaimed, hustling over to Daisy. The women hugged.

"I missed you too!" Daisy exclaimed. "I can't tell you how glad I am to be back here. It felt like forever before the doctor cleared me."

Marilyn flopped onto a weight bench. "I can imagine. So, how hard are we going to go? Do you remember where we left off? I figured we'd review first."

"That sounds perfect." Daisy moved to the center of the space. "But first, what on earth happened before I got here? Bo's the most mild-mannered person in the entire world, except when it comes to you. I've never seen anything like it. Either he really can't stand you or he's going to toss you over his shoulder and run away with you."

Marilyn howled. "Pretty sure it's not the last one. I'm not sure a man has ever been so turned off by yours truly."

Daisy already knew Marilyn's side of the history between her and Bo, but the fact that his anger toward her held firm remained curious. Sure, she nearly stole his precious gym space, but he must have gotten it back when Zeke dumped her! You'd think he'd revel in her humiliation, not continue holding it against her.

Marilyn wouldn't bring it up or it might seem like she wanted to be friends.

Teasing him and keeping him angry seemed a better plan than rehashing the past.

"I'm harmless, Daisy, I swear."

Daisy fell into a fit of her own laughter. "I trust you." She paused. "But do you think he's into you?" Her eyes sparkled as if this idea brought untold piles of joy.

Careful to keep her smile intact despite the unsettled feeling in her stomach, Marilyn turned the music off. "I doubt that."

She never considered it before, even if she'd need to be blind not to notice the man's strong, chiseled jaw or his deep, soulful eyes. And if he might by some miracle be interested in her, that didn't mean the feeling was at all mutual.

Not by a mile. He couldn't possibly meet her recently-established criteria for dating. Besides, Marilyn refused to be side-tracked on her quest of owning her own studio. She socked away nearly three thousand dollars already from her various jobs and meant to use that as a solid down-payment when the right studio space became available.

Daisy began stretching her neck, followed by her arms. "I hate to admit I don't really know a thing about Bo's personal life. He works like a dog for us but never says much about himself. Doesn't even leave the house much, honestly. It's a wonder he doesn't get sick of us."

Marilyn snorted. "He's probably a gigolo in his spare time. Or he's got some dirty secret like he's into mixed martial arts at night." She paused, trying to remain serious. "Does he get unexplained cuts on his face? Black eyes?"

This sent Daisy into a fresh fit of laughter. "I'm pretty sure that's not it. He's worked here a year and hasn't taken even one day off. And Carli Cross took one look at him and has been begging ever since to get him in one of her videos. He wants nothing to do with it."

Since singer Carli Cross represented the epitome of most men's dreams, Marilyn struggled to imagine Bo telling her no.

"Really? Well, maybe he's not into the spotlight. Or beautiful women. Or maybe relationships?"

Daisy shrugged. "Maybe shy. He tries to avoid pictures and paparazzi like the plague."

"Ever look at him from the side? Maybe he has a hunchback."

Daisy snickered. "All right, enough speculation. Let's get started so I don't waste your time. Then we'll make manny bring the baby over so you can officially meet her."

"Yeah... Bo's too ornery to share her with me." Marilyn groaned. "He didn't want me breathing on her."

"Oh goodness. He gets really weird about germs." Daisy rolled her eyes as Marilyn messed with the music and finally settled on a fun dance tune.

"I realized you don't talk much about your personal life either. You're not dating anyone, are you? Where do you work when you aren't here with me? Tell me everything!"

Marilyn snickered. "You must be spending too much time alone with the baby or something. I'm not that interesting. No boyfriend—black sheep of the family, yada yada. I waitress at an Italian restaurant when I'm not here, and I teach dance classes for some friends a few times a week in between auditions."

She shrugged, finding it unnecessary to get into too many specifics and so waste Daisy's time. "I'm boring." She paused. "But I do have a pretty big audition coming up. I'm hoping I can kill this one and finally get a good role."

Daisy glanced around the space. "Well, if you ever need someplace to rehearse, we don't mind you coming here. It's no problem."

Marilyn stood straighter, surprised. "Really? I might take you up on that."

"Good." Daisy lifted her eyebrows. "And if you do decide you're looking for love, I can recommend a lot of eligible guys. You can take me up on that too."

Marilyn stifled any sign of her interest. "Probably not a great time for me to get involved with anyone."

Daisy nodded. "Fair enough." She winked. "But in case—what's your type?"

Marilyn coughed, covering her embarrassment with a half-hearted cackle. "Bookish. Glasses. I like a guy in glasses. Fun and funny. Someone who likes to dance." She would do anything to get her student away from her current line of thinking.

Bo Sutton would never be boyfriend material. Except even as she tried convincing herself of this, she wondered what it would be like to date someone like him. He was handsome and intriguing for sure. She never dated anyone that tall and muscular before either.

Thank goodness he didn't wear glasses, or she might be in real trouble.

Daisy's eyes twinkled in amusement. "Sure."

Marilyn might as well put an end to this before it even started. "I'll keep picking on Bo for amusement, and going home to my tiny apartment, working my tail off, and eventually—hopefully—starting my own studio."

Daisy grinned. "Well, that sounds like a fine plan to me. But if you ever change your mind- let me know. I really do know a lot of solid guys you might be interested in."

Marilyn wished she wasn't curious about this list and who Daisy might pair her with. She reminded herself of her goal.

Eyes on the prize, Darby.

"I'll remember that."

"OK, let's dance before Nicolette needs me, or worse, Titus shows up and that will be the end of it. He's impatient."

Marilyn's eyes lit up at the mention of the musician's name. She'd seen him several times at the Grant house, but they'd not officially been introduced yet.

"Do you think he would help me? Or better yet go with me to my sister's engagement party? That promises to be an event in desperate need of a rock star's interruption." Marilyn couldn't imagine meeting rock's latest superstar, but she wouldn't be intimidated by him either if she got the chance.

Daisy howled. "I doubt Titus is the kind of guy you want to take home to mom, and yet, somehow, I'm kind of sure he'd go. Watch yourself. He's a bigger flirt than Robby. And I can't even imagine him serious—as in what he'd be like if he settled down with someone."

This surprised Marilyn. "I can't imagine anyone being a bigger flirt than Robby."

Daisy moved to the center of the space. "He's terrible—it drives Bo nuts too. He can't stand him."

"As if Bo can stand anyone." Marilyn snickered. "No worries, sweetie. I'm a flirt too—and Bo can't stand me either. So, maybe I will keep ole Titus Black in mind. After all, someone besides me needs to drive my mom crazy for a while."

Chapter two

Bo finished his run and hustled up the winding staircase to Nicolette's room, hoping to get enough time to get a quick shower before Daisy needed him in the gym. He took the monitor with him to his room down the hall, aware that he probably didn't need to bother. Nicolette had serious lungs, likely from her musical, singing parents, and could wail with the best, or worst, of them, monitor or no.

As the bodyguard entered his room and shut the door, his cell phone vibrated. Without looking, he expected his mom would be returning his earlier, frustrated message, probably hoping this meant things Bo intended to assure her it didn't mean at all.

"Hey, Ma." Bo toed off his tennis shoes, nudging them toward their place in the closet before heading toward the bathroom.

"Bennett Oliver. I don't remember the last time you've been so upset. Your passion is, well, I dare say—refreshing."

Bo's cheeks flushed at the tender sound of his mom's voice. He dipped his head as if she stood before him, hands on her hips, demanding an explanation for his juvenile behavior.

"Sorry about that." He went back to the closet and found clean clothes, then returned to the bathroom. "I only got a few minutes before I need to get back to work."

"Oh, something important going on?"

Bo squirmed. "I can't talk about my work, Ma. It's top secret." He tossed his clothes aside and sat on the edge of the tub. One day he'd come clean with his parents, but today would not be that day.

The lie started three years earlier. It began easily and without planning. Well, at least not any deliberate planning on Bo's part. When he didn't reenlist in the army, a hard line he drew against his father's wishes, his parents made it plain they wouldn't settle for anything less than his proving his own stability.

Bo didn't bother trying to form a solid plan because he let others figure things out for him instead of pursuing his own passions. He had the name of a gym owner he got from a buddy in his unit and the hope that the man would give him a job, even temporarily until he found something solid.

To buy time, he told his parents he had a government job with high security clearance that meant he couldn't talk specifics with anyone, even family. Bo hated himself. He'd never been a liar and couldn't imagine how he started this except out of sheer desperation.

But here he stood, three years and five gym-management jobs later, finally in a place he adored, and completely incapable of speaking the truth.

His parents had been so proud of this respectable, important job they never asked another question.

"I ran into Aunt Twila at the grocery store Sunday. She mentioned they didn't get your rsvp yet for Ricky's wedding."

Bo groaned. His cousin and the rest of the family had been relentless. Calls, texts, and even emails assailed him almost daily asking whether he'd be attending the wedding in a few weeks.

"It's too hard for me to get away."

"And you realize, Bennett, that it's been forever since we've seen you in person. Please. Put in whatever requests you need to." Robin paused, likely hoping to guilt her son into doing her bidding.

"I realize your work is important. And your father and I couldn't possibly be prouder. But we miss you. Emma's been begging to visit you if you don't come here. And I can tell you at fifteen years old she is not travelling alone."

Bo glanced at the monitor, grateful Nicolette remained asleep.

"I'm aware." The idea of asking Daisy and Robby for a few days off so he could go to the wedding in New Jersey made his stomach roll. He missed his family but understood the visit would come with questions. And his guilt would eat at him if he didn't tell them the truth. Keeping his distance let this thing continue.

Still, maybe the time had come.

"I'll ask, Ma. That's all I can promise."

"Good. Do it today and let me or your aunt know by the end of the week. They need a head count."

"Sure."

Bo glanced at the clock.

"Good. Now, about that message."

He could get out of this. Turn the conversation around, Bo!

"Forget the message. I need to get back to work." Again, he glanced at the monitor. Nicolette hadn't budged. He smiled. Fresh air always knocked the kid out. Next time she tried keeping him up all night they were taking a moonlit walk for sure.

Robin snorted at her son's attempt to end the call. "You don't leave a message like that and blow me off. Nope. We're going to talk about it. Your work can wait five minutes."

Again, Bo groaned. "OK. Fine. I think I met someone but she's off the charts wrong for me."

What was he doing? Could he seriously count that pain-in-the-backside dancer as 'someone'?

"Oh, for goodness' sake, Bennett. Does she go to church?"

Leave it to his mother to ask that. If only he could lie and say his preconceived notions about Marilyn having too many boyfriends and acting like a certain someone from his past were accurate. Unfortunately, he recently spotted her attending the very same church he did each week with Robby, Daisy, and the rest of the crew.

"I don't know if she goes to church." And now he lied to his mother yet again. Marilyn Darby might be the death of him.

"Bennett Oliver."

Bo huffed as he yanked a towel off the rack and hung it next to the shower. "Yes, all right? I've seen her in church."

"Really?" his mom's voice lifted. "Well, now. I figured I could be wrong, and we'd be talking job-change again. This is much better."

Oh, how easily he fell into this trap, tangled himself up, and struggled against the straight jacket of lies.

Bo neither confirmed nor denied anything. He already gave away entirely too much for his own good. Less was more with his mom. Like any good parent, she could see through the smoke and put pieces together, whether they were steeped in reality or fantasy, it didn't matter.

As long as it led to his being married and making her a grandma again, in the same tradition his brother and sister had gone before him.

"Where did you meet her? What does she do? Is her family nice?"

Leave it to his mom. She meant well and she sure loved him, as she did all her children, but she also had a way of drilling to the truth, making this charade even worse.

Bo's gut clenched. He learned young how to avoid this.

"Ma. I'm not ready to get serious. But I'm settled here, so I wondered if it might be a good time to think about things outside of work."

"Like visiting your family?"

"Ma…"

She refused to buy it. "Bennett. I'm not a fool. I want to hear about her, so start talking."

Bo wished he could ignore the amusement in his mom's voice.

"She's a train wreck. I'm not seriously interested." Like a kid, he crossed his fingers behind his back.

Robin Sutton always was too insightful for her own good. And bold. She started laughing so hard Bo had to hold the phone away from his ear.

"And yet you called me for the first time in months. I can't help but be amused, son."

Bo frowned. "I gotta get back to work."

"OK, OK. I'm sorry, but really, you haven't even gone on a date that I've heard about in... well, when was the last time?"

"Two years." He stood and looked at himself in the mirror. "And at this rate it might be two more. Forget I called and don't you dare say a word to anyone else." He imagined Lincoln, Asher, and Emma all having a field day at his expense.

Not to mention his father.

Ugh.

"Oh, settle yourself down, hon. What's her name?"

Bo rolled his eyes to the ceiling. "Nope. Like I said, she's a train wreck."

"Well, I can't pray for her if you don't tell me her name." She would want to pray for someone she never met simply because Bo brought her up. Robin was a prayer warrior like few others.

"You don't need her name." Bo tugged his shirt over his head. "I don't want to date her. She's a pest. Wanted me to dance with her if you can imagine that. I mean like not at a party- but dance like we were professionals." He paused, annoyed at all of this spilling out.

"I only called because... I wondered if it might be time. Not with her. But maybe someone else. Or maybe I need a hobby. I started cooking. Maybe I can get into that again. Or, you know what? I need an apron that actually fits me. Maybe I'll take up sewing."

"Mmm-hmmm..." Bo imagined his mom tipping her head to the side as she made this familiar assessment of his protest. "Cooking's not going to solve your problems, sweetie."

Bo groaned, but said nothing.

"Not every girl is Frannie. She's gone—not that you'd want her. She married that Stockett boy. Couldn't bring myself to tell you at the time but maybe that's the push you need to ask this girl you aren't interested in on a date."

Before Bo could respond to this news-bomb, Robin continued digging in. "Two years, Bennett? Really? Your father will be callin' when he finds out about that."

Bo's stomach turned over. His mom seriously played dirty.

"I gotta go."

"I'm praying for you and… remind me of her name again."

Before Bo could think, the word "Marilyn" fell out. He groaned.

"Good. That wasn't so hard. I'll put you down for the wedding with a guest. We'll be looking forward to meeting her. Maybe you two can dance for us." She giggled at her own joke.

"No! Dang it, Ma. I never said… ugh! I'll call you tomorrow."

He hung up to the sound of her laughter.

**

Marilyn laughed along with Daisy as they ended their third run through a new routine. Today they'd been at it two hours, but the time flew so she hardly believed it.

Daisy wiped the sweat from her forehead with a small towel as Marilyn turned off the music and stowed her phone in her bag.

"You're so good at working with someone like me. Ever considered making this your thing?" Daisy asked. "I can't be the only one who misses dancing, or maybe wishes she had a chance no one wants to give."

Marilyn slipped off her jazz shoes and stuffed them into her bag as she mulled this over. "I'm still saving to get my own studio space. But, when that time comes, I'll work with anyone who's as fun as you are."

"I appreciate it. I can't promise that, but I can say you make me so fun and free again, like I'm back to dancing like I used to. Think about it. That's a whole group of people who never get considered for anything – especially fitness."

Marilyn filed the idea away with every other idea to keep her planted in New York and still capable of chasing her dreams. It could make her a good amount of money, make people happy, and be a client base few considered. The idea had merit.

"I'll think about it." She slipped her shoes on and stood, rubbing her hands together. "Now, do I get to officially meet your little sweetheart?"

Daisy yanked her phone out and began typing. "I'll ask Bo what they're up to. My sweetheart can be, well, a diva sometimes."

But before Daisy even put her phone back down the door opened and Bo entered, the baby snuggled into his chest, his opposite hand carrying a diaper bag.

He grinned at Daisy as he urged the door closed with his hip. "Jazz and Robby are running late, and Alice's friends are still here, so I'm still on duty. I figured we could get your workout in if you want. Nico doesn't mind."

Marilyn hated that her heart fluttered at the sight of the bodyguard sweetly carrying the baby so protectively.

He changed his clothes and now wore workout shorts and a tee shirt, as well as a pair of glasses.

Oh heavens. He wore glasses!

Marilyn gulped. Had he been listening in on her conversation? She shouldn't have been so stupid. Of course, the place probably had an intercom or something!

Like this, with his mouth shut, Bo might even be a walking dream come true. If only he could keep his attitude in check.

If only he didn't hate Marilyn.

Daisy squinted at him as he leaned over to place the baby in her arms. "What's with the glasses?"

"What?" He nudged them higher on his nose. "Oh, I couldn't find my contacts and Nicolette started squawking…" He glanced at Marilyn, who zipped her bag shut as she tried to look busy and disinterested.

Bo scowled before turning away to put the diaper bag aside.

"Come on and meet the baby, Mar." Daisy moved the baby's blanket as Marilyn leaned over to look at her. Her insides turned gooey in an instant. She never considered herself interested in motherhood, but in that moment wondered why. Marilyn would wager Daisy changed her mind too when the right man entered the picture.

Maybe Marilyn acted hasty too.

The baby cooed softly as Daisy leaned down to rub her nose against her daughter's head.

"She's perfect…" Marilyn breathed.

"I didn't even realize he wore glasses. Didn't you say…?" Daisy's voice trailed off as they both glanced in Bo's direction.

Marilyn frowned, grateful he moved to the opposite side of the gym. "I was kidding."

"Sure, you were." Daisy held her daughter up. "You can hold her."

"What? Oh…" Marilyn gently took the baby and held her close, suddenly overcome by the gesture. "Wow. I don't think I've ever held a baby in my life."

"Nothing to it. Keep her head supported and you're good to go." Daisy leaned over to look at Bo who'd started doing something across the gym with one of the machines. She leaned back as her phone buzzed.

"Sorry." She held the phone to her ear. "Hey, Titus."

As Daisy dropped into what sounded like an important conversation about her work, the baby yawned and started to whimper, making Marilyn freeze. She had no idea what to do as Nicolette started winding up for a real scream.

The dance teacher gently patted her and tried doing what she watched parents do, but her efforts only made the baby's cries increase.

"Shh…" Marilyn prayed the kid would stop before she embarrassed herself. "It's OK, Nicolette, your mommy's right here. Shh…"

"At least her good taste is confirmed." Bo deftly stole the baby, lifted her to his shoulder and gently patted her back with his huge hands.

Nicolette sniffed and cuddled into him, turned her cheek, and fell asleep. Like magic.

Who was this superhero?

In three seconds, Marilyn forgot why he annoyed her as something strange and frightening stirred inside her.

It was the same, stupid thing she felt every time she thought a man might be worth the trouble. He never was. Not once. Surely Bo Sutton couldn't be different.

No matter how he looked holding a baby.

Marilyn grabbed her bag and hefted it onto her shoulder as she reminded herself not to be stupid. She only had to think of her last relationship to find the resolve to say, firmly, "I gotta go."

Bo didn't even look at her. He kept one paw on the baby and with the other he fussed with the sound system.

"Right. You got all those important dance lessons. Go save the world one waltz at a time, Twinkle Toes." Bo finished messing with the stereo and headed for the weight bench where he sat, dismissing her as nothing beyond a frustrating part of his day.

Marilyn pursed her lips. Twinkle Toes? At least now she remembered why he annoyed her. The fuzzy feelings from moments ago dissolved and she frowned at him, trying to think of something to say.

Finding nothing, she turned on her heel and left the gym, slamming the door behind her to punctuate exactly what she thought about Bo's assessment of her life's passion.

That would show him.

**

Marilyn stormed out of the gym, intent on getting to her car and away from Bo as quickly as possible. She tossed her bag into the backseat and tried to yank open the driver's door but to no avail. Sadly, the next firm tug too proved fruitless.

She gritted her teeth. She already had to climb numerous times through the backseat, so if this thing didn't give way soon, she'd do the same humiliating thing—and in the driveway of two of the richest people in the world. What choice did she have? She refused to spend any additional money on this crappy vehicle when her savings finally looked better than it had in ages.

"Need some help there, sweetheart?" A deep voice interrupted Marilyn as she whacked the door to punish it, kicking the stupid tire for good measure.

She stepped back and nearly fell when she looked up into the eyes of music's latest sensation, Titus Black. His half-smirk oozed with confidence that made Marilyn want to smile too. That swagger she recognized on her television screen didn't hold a candle to the man in front of her now.

He smelled amazing.

"How 'bout you let me give it a try?" Titus tucked his cell phone into his back pocket, and only then did Marilyn realize he must have been sitting in his tricked-out truck across the driveway, watching her the entire time.

She stepped away from the car, no longer caring about her humiliation. This would be fun. "Go for it." She gestured to the finicky handle.

How did Daisy live in a place like this? Surrounded every day by handsome, sexy musicians? One thing remained sure—she meant it when she said she could hook Marilyn up with a solid date.

She also warned of this one in particular.

Marilyn didn't worry. She could handle herself even against the likes of Titus Black or any man for that matter. She proved her worth in the way she handled Zeke, whether her parents, Bo, or anyone else knew it or not.

The musician yanked on the door, clearly trying to make it look easy, but struggling just the same. Marilyn pressed her lips together even as she worried whether he hurt his hand, the one used for strumming his electric guitar with such finesse.

"It's been giving me trouble for weeks."

Titus nodded, his dark, wavy hair catching the afternoon light. With a grunt he muscled the door open, gesturing with a slight wave and a bow that he satisfied his duty as a gentleman.

Marilyn smiled. "Much appreciated."

He tipped his head at her, a twinkle in his eye. "My pleasure, darlin'. I'd probably get it to a good mechanic. Before you break something doing it my way."

"Yeah. I'll remember that." Marilyn slipped by him and stood behind the door but stopped short of getting in.

"Daisy's in the gym. We just finished her dance lesson." She pointed. "If you follow the walkway, you'll run right into it."

Titus winked. "Got it, sweetheart." He extended his hand. "I'm Titus Black."

Marilyn couldn't fight her amusement as she shook his hand. "I'm sure everyone who's still breathing knows who you are." She reluctantly removed her hand from his, noting the extra squeeze he added for punctuation on his flirting.

With a smile she stepped back, needing the space for her own sake. "Marilyn Darby."

He nodded, his intense gaze holding hers. "You're a dancer?"

"Yep. I'm working with Daisy." What an idiot! She already said that!

Titus' grin widened. "Nice. So, I'll catch you around. I like the sound of that."

Marilyn hated that this kindness, after Bo's easy dismissal of her career, made her knees weak.

He nodded again. "You call if you'd be interested in choreographing my shows. Got some back-up singers who need training before we go on the road. Nothing fancy." He winked and tipped his head at her.

"Catch ya later."

Marilyn's mouth hung open when he strolled out of her view, his hands tucked into his pockets.

Did Titus Black offer her a job?

**

"You're going to burn the onions." Mrs. Fernsby stole the spatula from Bo and stirred the mess in the pan herself, huffing loudly at his incompetence. She'd only been back on the job a few weeks and already made plain her ideas about Bo's cooking skills. Forget that he kept everyone fed and happy for so long without her.

"Sorry." He stepped back and stuffed his hands into his pockets. "I better go check on Daisy. I'll be back."

"Don't hurry." Mrs. Fernsby didn't look at him. "Alice is better help because she stays out of my way."

The teen giggled from her spot at the table doing her homework. Bo rolled his eyes in her direction before making his way from the room and upstairs to find his boss.

"Hey." He tapped on the bedroom door.

"I'm in the baby's room!"

Bo headed in that direction. He leaned in the doorway as she worked on changing the baby, wondering if he had time to read another chapter in the book he started while up all night with the baby.

"Need anything?"

Daisy glanced in his direction but kept fussing with Nicolette's outfit.

"Robby and Jazz will be back shortly so we can head over to Warren's for dinner. You're off for the night but I need you to grab my phone and restock the diaper bag. I know Daphne has extras with her little guy around, but I hate to mooch off them because I forgot something."

Bo dug around in the pouch attached to Daisy's wheelchair until he came up with the phone. He held it out to her, but she shook her head as she lifted the baby for a closer cuddle.

"Send Marilyn a text with Titus's contact information." She wiggled her eyebrows at him. "Apparently they had quite a conversation in the driveway the other day. He kept asking me about her ever since. I'd just as soon get out of the way and let them figure it out."

Bo saw red. He couldn't stand the flirty, touchy Titus even if Daisy insisted he meant nothing by it. While he continued wrestling with his strange reactions to Marilyn, he didn't want to think of her falling for a guy like that. The man probably had thirty girlfriends if his behavior with Daisy meant anything.

Then again, Marilyn did date Zeke, so anything might be possible as far as her taste in men. What business was it of his?

But for whatever reason, Bo had to say something. "You're going to throw your friend to the big bad wolf?" He opened a message and started to do as he'd been told. "He flirts with you and gets all handsy and you're married! I've watched him do it. I hope you at least warned her."

Daisy rolled her eyes. "You almost sound jealous. Steal her contact information too if you like. You and Titus can fight it out."

Bo's jaw snapped shut when he realized it dropped open. He lowered his head and finished the text, sent it and stuffed her phone back into her bag.

He grabbed the diaper bag from the shelf and started refilling it with diapers and wipes.

"Anything else?"

Bo opened a drawer and grabbed an extra onesie and change of clothes for Nicolette. He'd been on the receiving end of a diaper explosion or two and understood well that one could never be too prepared.

"Yes. Confirm the time for Carli Cross later this week and tell that designer… what's her name…?"

"Justine Mirelle." Bo folded the extra clothes carefully and set them in the diaper bag.

"Right. Tell her I'll take a look at the dresses when she sends them. But nothing in pink. I've been wearing that too much lately thanks to the little squirt here."

Bo made a note on his phone list to follow up with the woman Daisy mentioned. "Sure. That all?"

Daisy snickered. "In a hurry for your big night off? All by yourself at the library?" she pursed her lips. "Didn't you buy ten books last week when we were out?"

She was a bit too observant sometimes. Bo grabbed the hand sanitizer and stuffed it into the diaper bag too.

"There's no need to be rude about it. So what if I like reading?" He followed her to the hallway, embarrassed he actually couldn't find anything better to do with this surprise night off. He wondered what Jazz might be up to.

"Do you want me to take the baby so you can get ready?"

"We're fine." Daisy smiled up at him. "You can take the diaper bag downstairs. Put it on the kitchen table and we'll get it on the way out." She paused. "I appreciate all of your help. You're truly a Godsend. I should say that more."

Bo often heard this sentiment from both Daisy and Robby, but he appreciated it the same, especially given his recent frame of mind. "I'm happy to be here."

Daisy's forehead wrinkled as her eyebrows lifted. "But all you do is work. Don't you want any time off?" She snuggled the baby close with one arm and reached out to him with the other. She squeezed his hand.

Bo swallowed, waiting for criticism that didn't come. She continued. "I'd rather not lose you. Who has the time to train an assistant? I sure don't. Besides, you already know my secrets."

The bodyguard patted her shoulder. "I appreciate it. I love it here. I don't plan to leave you and your family high and dry, so don't worry about it, all right?"

She affirmed with a nod, her expression soft and kind as usual. "Well, at least leave the house when you aren't working."

Bo couldn't imagine where to go, but he nodded. "About taking time off… my cousin's getting married and my mom's been hounding me about it. I wondered if it would be a big deal if I took the weekend of the seventeenth off. I checked the schedules and ran it by Jazz and things look clear."

He hated this. Would one weekend ruin his life? Probably not.

At least he hoped not. But his mom's nagging got to him. He put this off long enough, and at least New Jersey was closer for him than Alabama. In the grand scheme he could do this, and it would be fine.

Probably.

Daisy didn't hide her surprise. "There's no reason you shouldn't go to your cousin's wedding. Jazz can handle us for a long weekend." She paused. "I'm glad you asked. I think you should go. It's good for you to get away some."

Bo nodded again. He watched as Daisy set the baby on the bed and began fussing with her purse.

"Have fun tonight."

Daisy glanced at him. "You too. I'll expect a full report of all the debauchery in the morning."

Bo rolled his eyes. "Prepare for disappointment, boss. I'd imagine the most trouble I'll get into is eating a few too many chicken wings for dinner and reading past a reasonable hour."

**

Marilyn let herself into the dark gym, fumbling for several minutes with her cell as a flashlight until she got the overhead lights going. She grinned as she drank in the empty space.

Perfection.

No lamps to knock over, no ornery roommate to annoy, excellent acoustics, and all night to get this routine down so she'd nail the audition and get back on track.

Once Marilyn got the music ready, she stretched and mentally ticked off the trouble spots where she might falter or felt weakest. One failed turnout and she would be toast at this level of competition. There would be no room for error.

Even if she never believed she'd take Daisy up on the offer, Marilyn was glad she confirmed her friend meant it. She figured she couldn't be too careful with all the security Robby employed to keep the place safe.

Of course, Daisy agreed since no one was home anyway save for the evening security crew who knew enough to let her in.

With a few quick kicks and stretches, Marilyn let the music play and got to work.

**

Bo parked in his usual spot in the driveway, grabbed the filled bags from the backseat, and made his way toward the house as his eyes landed on a beat-up compact car that could only belong to one person.

He frowned. Why would Marilyn be here?

Bo started toward the gym, annoyed and wanting answers exactly at the same moment he remembered he should apologize for his earlier behavior, not to mention find some kind of common ground where they could live in this work world together. He slowed his pace as he rounded the house.

Whether he liked her or not remained irrelevant. She worked for Daisy and he'd be a decent human being, professional and all that, if that's what it took.

Or he could bolt. That seemed viable too.

Theoretically he could hop back into his car and pretend he never even noticed her. Talking to her with witnesses was bad enough. But alone? He'd be asking for trouble. That woman radiated danger.

Then again, apologizing without an audience would be easier than doing so with one.

Bo raised his eyes to the darkening sky, his lips drawn tightly together as he begged for help. Maybe he'd find her doing something she shouldn't be so he could really get rid of her.

A pit began to grow in his stomach. His loneliness and relationship fears weren't her fault. And he didn't have to like her or the way she constantly teased him, but he did need to do the right thing. And he would, if for no other reason than to get his mother off his back.

With that same resolve, Bo tightened his grip on the bags of books he purchased and went to the gym.

He stared at the building, feet firmly planted for several long moments before he summoned the courage to go to the door, open it, and slip inside, still not sure what he'd say when he saw her, but praying he could spit out an apology of some sort and run off to the safety of his room where he could spend the rest of his night cursing himself and praying for guidance.

What a sad lot for a man of his age. Maybe they'd get ready for the next tour soon and he could jump with both feet into full-work-immersion. That would be perfect.

It was a wonder he didn't enjoy the military, given the way it could take over your whole life if you let it.

After this Bo would avoid Marilyn with all he had while he also figured out a way to tell his family he would be coming to the wedding alone, if at all.

Why couldn't melting and disappearing be an option?

Bo stood frozen at the front door. He couldn't have prepared for the dancer, eyes closed, embracing every bit of the music as she moved—one with whatever emotions stirred her to pursue this passion.

And he faced this without the armor of a baby on his chest? He was in so much trouble.

Surely Bo imagined the foreign sensations of interest and desire that stirred in his gut as he watched Marilyn while he stood, still clutching his books, the same loser he'd been for years. He exhaled, wondering what to say, when at the same time she turned and leaped right toward him, squealing when she saw him, but unable to stop what she started.

Because for every action there is, after all, an equal and opposite reaction. In this case, it left Bo with only one real option.

He opened his arms, dropped the books, and did the only thing he could.

He caught Marilyn and held on tight.

Chapter three

Holy moly!

Marilyn's heart nearly stopped when she opened her eyes, turned, and leapt straight into Bo's arms, the momentum making him step back with an 'oof' when she knocked at least some of the wind out of him as he caught her without hesitation.

What was he made of?

She'd been caught by many dancers before and while solid, none had felt like she hit a wall made of bricks. Her ribs would remember that hit tomorrow.

Obviously, Bo hadn't expected to walk into this situation either because he dropped a stack of books with a loud thud on his own feet to keep her from being hurt.

Even as she gasped for breath, Marilyn looked into his eyes and winked, desperate to squelch the quivering in her limbs. Did he notice the electricity too?

"Told you we'd make the perfect dance team," she whispered, struggling to catch her breath.

Bo frowned and set her gently on her feet, as if she might be fragile and not a strong dancer built of muscle and sweat, leaving her wondering that he didn't drop her like the books.

"What are you doing in here?" He sank to his knees, turning his focus to gathering his things, probably so he wouldn't be forced to look at her.

Was she really that disgusting in his eyes?

Marilyn dropped beside him and lifted a book. "My apartment's really small and I've got an important audition coming up and Daisy said I could…" Her voice drifted off as she read the title on the book and coughed, her cheeks warming as she held it out to him, wishing she could stop the shock that made the words come tumbling out.

"Dating for dummies?" She flipped it over, her voice catching. "Sorry."

Bo snatched the book away and stuffed it back into the bag, eyebrows knit together, lips pursed as if he might throw up.

Marilyn searched for some way to change the course of this interaction as she picked up another book. "The collected works of Shakespeare? You sure got eclectic taste."

Bo grabbed the book. "Shakespeare is classic. The language is… I'm helping Alice get ready for a test next week." He grabbed two books and put those in the bag as well, though Marilyn couldn't make out their titles.

"I didn't mean I'm sorry about you reading a book about dating. I meant I'm sorry I jumped at you. You surprised me. That's all." She looked away, embarrassed. "I didn't mean to land on you."

Bo raised to his feet, extending one hand to help her up, a gentleman's move that brought no small amount of surprise. Coupled with the way he tenderly ensured her safety moments earlier, Marilyn struggled to move back to her earlier view of this puzzling and annoying man.

"I understood your meaning." He waited to continue as she dusted off her backside.

"You always dance with your eyes closed? You're asking for trouble- can't see where you'll land." He laid the bag on a bench nearby and stuck his hands in his pockets.

Marilyn snickered. "That's a good description of me."

Bo looked away. "I had the night off and when I came back and saw your car…" He lowered his head and spoke to his feet. He exhaled, changing the subject entirely.

"I want to apologize for being rude. And for being condescending and belittling what you do. I feel even worse about it now that I saw you…"

Before Marilyn could speak—even if she had no idea what to say—Bo coughed and grabbed his bag. "Anyway. I'm sorry." He turned and started for the door, but Marilyn rode his heels.

"Hey!" She grabbed his arm and tried to turn him around, but a man his size didn't budge unless he wanted to. And apparently, he didn't want to.

"What? You need to gloat now? Bo Sutton apologized and it made your day?" While he stood firmly in profile, refusing to look at her, Marilyn noticed his nostrils flaring.

She groaned. "Don't be stupid."

He turned slowly, waiting, but still not looking at her.

"You didn't even give me a chance to say thank you. For the apology. And for saving me from hurting myself."

Bo lifted his eyes. "Don't mention it." He reached for the door, but she, again, grabbed his arm.

"If you're not busy, you could help me. I mean, with rehearsing for my audition."

The bodyguard only grunted as he reached for the door again.

"For a guy the size of my car you sure are scared of something as simple as dancing. It doesn't make sense. It's easy. Just moving your body to music. You'd think working for Daisy and Robby, you must like music."

Marilyn couldn't help but notice his jaw working as he considered her words. "Just because I don't want to dance with you doesn't mean I'm scared. I'm not interested." He paused, gesturing toward the fuse box.

"Make sure you turn off all the lights and lock up when you're done. Good luck with your audition. But you don't need anyone's help- least of all mine. You'll get the part. Good night."

"Yeah… good night," Marilyn whispered as the door closed. He probably hadn't heard her, but it didn't matter.

She couldn't remember the last time anyone encouraged her. It felt so good she wondered if getting extra practice in would be possible now that her concentration had been so broken.

Bo Sutton might be a terrible distraction, but he could be a beautiful one too.

**

Days later Bo still stewed over what happened in the gym.

How could one person make him so crazy and at the same time make him want so badly to say he'd help her when he couldn't think of a reason he should, except maybe they could trade favors.

His dancing for her pretend girlfriending.

Bo snorted. That wasn't a word, nor would it be an option—even if his mother had already text him three times about what Marilyn might like to eat or if they'd mind sitting with his siblings at the reception.

He'd gone mad. He couldn't forget the justified fear that Titus Black might be interested in her. Bo couldn't compete with that!

Nor did he want to. Zeke and then Titus? Any woman who'd be interested in either man should have her head examined.

And the man who might be interested in her probably shouldn't be far behind on that trip.

Bo clenched and unclenched a fist as his mind worked all of this over. His cell phone buzzed, interrupting his runaway mind.

His sister, Emma.

"Hey squirt." He flopped onto his bed, aware he'd be needed shortly but had a few minutes to spare.

"Mom said you found a girlfriend and I'm kind of ticked I had to hear it from her first. Geez. She better be nice, not like stupid Frannie."

He lifted the dating book from its drawer, hidden in his nightstand. Maybe it would say something about his messed-up mind. "Ma has a big mouth." He flipped to the table of contents as he waited for his sister's reply.

"Bo…" The fifteen-year-old's whine reminded him of Alice. He grinned in spite of himself and this stupid conversation.

"Yeah, Ems."

She giggled. "You're bringing her to Ricky's wedding?"

He snorted right back, frowning as he answered. "Not sure yet." Bo shut the book and put it back in the drawer. "How's school?"

Emma rattled on for several minutes about her friends, her babysitting job, and their parents and siblings—especially Asher who still lived at home and Lincoln who lived there too while he went to a trade school or community college, Bo couldn't remember which. Wyatt got married and moved two hours away, so he didn't come home much, same with Haley who had two kids, a husband and a house to worry over.

"Sounds like things are good, huh?"

"I guess. I miss you. Mom doesn't make scones like yours."

Bo's heart constricted. "I miss you too, sis."

"I doubt you'll believe me, but I swear Dad's actually softening up. You really need to see it for yourself."

This caught Bo's attention. "Really?" Joe Sutton had always been hard edges and manly opinions. His personality stood in stark contrast to Bo's sensitivity and generosity and it was the reason Bo entered the military in the first place. He'd not been into sports in school and that needled his father. The son wanted desperately to prove to his father he might be worthy of the 'manly' status he dangled in front of him at every turn.

To discover he might better understand, or at least make an effort to relate to his son, would be tough to swallow.

"It's hard to explain. Like Asher quit soccer and he didn't pitch a fit. And I wanted to go on a date and… I mean, he didn't let me, but he said Sawyer could come over for dinner. He didn't even yell about it."

Joe's bark could be much worse than his bite, but that didn't mean it hadn't been a struggle to sit through his tirades. Bo silently gave his sister mental props for even asking if she could go on a date before her seventeenth birthday. Years ago, this would have meant a good deal of yelling.

"Good deal. Tell Marilyn we can't wait to meet her. And I'll slug her if she's mean to you."

"Ems." Bo made his voice as stern as possible.

She giggled. "What's she like? You can at least tell me that."

Bo sighed. What could it hurt?

"She's a dancer and I guess is auditioning for a pretty big show or something soon. She's really good."

"Wow. How did you meet a dancer?"

Bo flinched as his lies grew. "We, uh, know some of the same people."

Emma grunted. "That's super unspecific."

"There's not much to tell." He paused. "I'm still trying to figure all of this out."

He wondered whether he should be talking this way with his younger sister, but he didn't have many options either. And with all he kept from his family, little kernels of truth seemed acceptable. Maybe the full-impact of the whole truth would hurt less later if he sprinkled in some little truths now.

"Bo…." Emma dragged his name out again. "Send me a picture. I need to see what we're up against here. That way I'll know what kind of tactics you should use."

"Tactics?" Bo couldn't imagine how his sister knew more about relationships than he did—except for the fact he'd been teased and manipulated in the few relationships he'd had so far, not one of them even coming close to what anyone would call 'normal'. That likely explained his fascination over the way Daisy and Robby engaged on a daily basis.

Maybe they weren't weird. Maybe what they had was what any loving couple did. Bo wondered if his dating book would explain some of it so he could understand.

"I don't have a picture. And even if I did, I'm not sure what good it's going to do. We argue a lot."

"You're so dumb," Emma muttered. "That means you like her and she likes you. Didn't you ever want to kick someone when you were in elementary school?"

"What?"

His sister groaned. "You're a hot mess, Bennett. What does Marilyn look like?"

"Huh? She's tiny, but really strong. She has dark hair, but it's usually pulled back." He scratched his head as he tried to remember if he'd seen her hair loose. "I think it's curly. She's pretty. I guess."

He left out the part where he noticed she smelled like a cool breeze on a summer day and that her eyes made him want to stare forever.

"Is she prettier than Frannie?"

Bo's gut tightened as an image of the stunning, heartless blond popped into his mind. "I haven't seen Frannie in years."

And I haven't wanted to either.

"She moved." Emma paused. "I think you should give yourself a chance with her. It's not wrong to be happy. And send me a picture."

Bo pushed from his bed and glanced toward the window that looked over the gym. Marilyn would be coming for Daisy's lesson in hours and he'd either need to decide to avoid her or go over and deal with the annoying woman head-on.

He leaned toward avoiding her.

"I gotta go, squirt." He paused. "Love you."

"Love you too."

Bo stuffed the phone into his pocket and stood by the window, surprised to find Marilyn getting out of her car at the same time Titus's flashy truck rolled in. He hopped out and went to her, all winks and flirty smiles as he held out one hand to her and shoved her car door closed with the other.

Whatever the musician said made Marilyn toss her head back as she gasped for breath in her easy laughter.

Nausea rolled through Bo's stomach so fast he leaned closer to the window for a better view, certain he'd imagined the whole thing.

But when they hugged, Bo's fists automatically clenched. That man had no right to have his sleezy paws all over Marilyn and the bodyguard intended to say something about it before this insane situation got any further out of hand.

But then Bo drew a breath, exhaling slowly as he reminded himself this was par for the course with Marilyn. She drew this kind of attention, and from his experience, reveled in it.

Bo would leave the whole thing where it belonged, outside the realm of his influence.

Because if Marilyn wanted to date a flirt like Titus, the bodyguard had no say in the matter. None at all.

**

Marilyn beamed as she led Titus to the gym. Daisy told her when she called that she didn't care if Marilyn came early to try using Titus to help during her rehearsal. And of course the big flirt would be game for anything that meant one-on-one attention from a female, so he bit immediately, saying this would be her audition for him too so he could decide if she knew what she was doing before he hired her to help with his back-up singers.

A likely story.

Marilyn fussed with the door as she glanced over her shoulder at him. "You ever danced before?"

Titus stuffed his hands into his pockets. "Heck no. But I can move, don't you worry yourself over it." He winked. "Besides, don't I just need to catch you a few times and spin you around? Not much more to dancing, right?"

"Well, that's the bulk of it, but it takes some skill. And I need to trust you'll catch me and not drop me. If I get hurt there won't be an audition at all, Titus."

This cracked him up. "We're good. I work out." He strutted into the gym and waited as she flicked on the lights and set her things down.

"We better stretch first." Marilyn paused as she began stretching. "Do you want me to audition for you first so we can work on my piece?"

Titus shrugged. "Whatever." He glanced around. "How long do you and Daisy usually work? I'm hoping maybe I can wait and get her to tweak some things on a song we started a few weeks ago."

Marilyn motioned for him to begin stretching with her. He followed half-heartedly, but it beat starting completely cold.

"Your schedule with Daisy is your business. We usually work anywhere from one to sometimes two hours if she's really into it."

Titus grinned. "I got an idea that with two gorgeous ladies dancing, I'm going to be joining this class."

Marilyn didn't care to overthink his intentions. She'd treat it as serious and let him back out if he wanted. "I'm game if Daisy is. Sometimes Alice joins us, sometimes Robby does."

Titus whooped at this information. "Next you're going to tell me that bodyguard who follows us around like a rabid dog dances with you too."

Marilyn snorted as she recalled her botched interaction with Bo days earlier. "No. I don't imagine I'll ever see that man's dancing shoes." She went to the sound system and fussed with the volume before starting the music.

"Ready for me to audition?"

Titus leaned against the wall, folded his arms over his chest and grinned. "Sure thing, sweetheart. Show me what you got."

**

"Did you call that designer? What's her name again?" Daisy followed Bo down to the kitchen as she prattled on about their day. But her bodyguard's mind remained on the situation in the gym. He'd not mentioned it yet and couldn't decide if he should.

"Mirelle. Justine Mirelle." Bo pecked his lips to Nicolette's head, earning a sweet sigh and yawn from her. He grinned.

"And yes, I talked to her assistant yesterday."

Daisy looked him over, studying him in a way that made Bo squirm. "I didn't realize you wore glasses. Why didn't I know that?"

Bo handed off the baby, turning his attention to getting Daisy's coffee. "It never came up, I guess. Does it matter?"

"What else aren't you telling me?"

Bo grunted, still trying to forget that Marilyn and Titus were alone in his gym. Probably griming up the place. He made a mental note to take the heavy-duty cleanser for his gym equipment. No telling what that greaseball singer brought along with him.

"I imagine there's a lot you don't know, Daisy. Why? What is this?" He didn't wait for her answer. "You want pancakes?"

"Just yogurt." Daisy fussed over the baby's spikey hair. "You're from Alabama, right?"

"That's right." Bo reached into the fridge and found Daisy's favorite yogurt exactly where it should be thanks to Mrs. Fernsby's masterful organization.

"Why all these questions?" He grabbed a spoon and set everything at the table along with a banana because sometimes Daisy got so focused on conversation, she didn't eat enough and got hungry twenty minutes later.

She moved to the table while Bo took the baby carrier and set it next to her before securing Nicolette inside.

"You've spent all your time so far worried about me, Robby, and the girls. Last night I realized you've hardly mentioned your family, where you came from, if you have any hobbies. I mean… I notice things but we don't get into the nitty gritty."

Bo gently rocked the baby's carrier so Daisy could eat. "I don't do nitty gritty."

Daisy exhaled loudly. "Everyone's got nitty gritty." Daisy lifted the yogurt but didn't open it. "What's yours?"

Bo went back to the counter to get his coffee, deliberately turning his back to her. "You're my boss. This is weird."

Daisy pursed her lips. "You live in my house. You eat our food and don't go out with friends. You don't date or even go to the singles group at church—which I did sign you up for and you ignored."

Bo grinned as he looked away, only slightly embarrassed she noticed he'd done as he pleased rather than be bullied into friending some random group of desperate people he had nothing in common with.

"What about your friends? Girlfriends?" Daisy waved her spoon at him. "I'm not weird. You need to talk to someone." She cracked open the yogurt. "Might as well be me. You know too much about me already. It's fair I know something about you."

Bo dribbled the last of the cream into his mug and tossed the empty container. "Not that I don't find you interesting and pleasant to work for, but remember it's my job to know about you, Daisy." He tipped his cup toward the back of the house, ready for a change in subject. "Marilyn's in the gym with Titus. Are they working on something?"

Daisy paused, her spoonful of yogurt not quite getting to her mouth as she smiled, lowering it again. "How do you know they're out there?"

"Don't go getting ideas," Bo moaned. "It's my job. Jazz took Alice to school and Robby had some interview or something. I know everything around here." He paused. "Fernsby is at the farmer's market and the cleaning crew comes at three. The chandelier people come Thursday. And your schedule is in here too." He tapped his head.

"I can recite it if you want."

Daisy raised an eyebrow. Bo sipped his coffee, hoping he shut her down and didn't invite additional commentary and questions.

"Go ahead and scope out the situation in the gym. I'm fine here." Daisy took a bite of yogurt, but Bo didn't miss the amusement sparkling in her eyes.

He sipped his coffee again. "Nope. Those two make me cringe."

Why did his voice crack? Bo flinched, trying to forget the way Marilyn leapt into his arms.

"You'd go if I told you to. It's your job."

Bo turned. "I suppose that's true." He hoped his voice sounded disinterested. He wanted to be disinterested. His heart, unfortunately, appeared to be making different plans.

"Sure. Tell your bff Titus when he's done with Marilyn, he can use the studio to work. I'll be down an hour after."

Bo set his coffee mug down. "You can't tell him that later? When you go for your dance lesson?"

"Nope. Go." She waved her hand before turning her attention back to the baby.

Bo did as instructed, hating that his boss believed he had some sort of interest in the dance teacher, because sadly, he did.

And worse, he would surely ruin this.

**

Marilyn grabbed Titus's hand and, not for the first time, dragged him back to the center of their dance space. He laughed the entire time, likely aware how much work it would take for him to build up any dance game at all.

"Aww, come on, darlin'. I'm trying. I swear. Maybe I should stand around and look pretty. Maybe that's all I'm good for. Unless you need me to sing or strum my guitar. I got that down pretty good."

Marilyn ignored his weak explanation. "I guess I'll think about it when I need a singer or a pretty boy." She shook her head. "I've never seen a worse dancer in my life." She playfully yanked on a strand of his hair.

"At least you got good hair. That's something."

He chuckled as he reached for her. She evaded his grasp, annoyed. Titus groaned. "So, I need practice?"

She turned him so his body, again, faced the right direction. "Or you need to let your back-up singers handle the dancing and you handle the singing and flirting. You can work the crowd without dancing. A little hip action goes a long way." Marilyn placed one hand on his shoulder and gripped his large palm as she looked into his eyes.

He winked and pulled her closer. "Singing and flirting I can handle, sweetheart." He spun her until she squeaked and squealed along with him.

"Titus! Knock it off!" A giggle escaped as she realized she was having fun, even if his flirting failed to make her feel anything more than the warmth of friendship. At this point, at least it was something.

The gym door slammed, making Marilyn jump, but she didn't lose her grip on Titus, who remained a bit too close and offered a light chuckle, but made no effort to move.

Bo's jaw worked as he glared at them.

"Daisy said to tell you that when she's dancing you can set up shop in the studio."

Marilyn's stomach flopped even as she wondered why the bodyguard never knocked or made his presence known until he freaked her out first. She glared back at him, but kept herself comfortably in Titus's arms.

Might as well start messing with the dimwit again.

"And that couldn't wait because…?"

Bo shrugged. "Because Daisy's the boss."

Marilyn lifted an eyebrow. "Right." She dismissed him by turning back to Titus. "Ready?"

But the singer surprised her by lifting his chin toward Bo. "Is he going to watch?"

Marilyn didn't bite, making no effort to do anything but gaze up at Titus. "You'll be doing this in front of an audience of thousands of screaming fans, babe. Get used to it."

Titus didn't look convinced. "But this is your routine. I'm not going to be dancing like this."

Marilyn tried to ignore Bo's presence as she looked back up at her partner. "You promised to help!"

Titus winked. "That I did. So, let's continue this humiliation so I can get back to things I'm better at." He playfully swatted her backside in a way that probably made Bo think...

Marilyn winked back at the singer, hoping to dig the impression even further into the bodyguard's mind since she knew he couldn't stand Titus.

"Fair enough. Remember, keep your space until the big leap and stay strong, lock your arms. I'll count us off."

Before she could say anything else, the door slammed. Titus whistled before erupting into hysterics. "That man is jealous enough for me to write an awfully good song about. He's wound tight!"

Marilyn rolled her eyes. "Serves him right for refusing to help me."

"Shoot, dang." Titus shook his head. "Let's get this over with before he comes back in here to pound my face." He shook out his hair and rubbed one hand against his stubbled cheek. "I kind of like it the way it is."

"Your face will be fine," Marilyn assured him. "From my experience, he's all bark and no bite."

**

Marilyn tossed her clothes into the washing machine. She intended to use the time during her required weekly call to her mother to her advantage. Not a moment wasted, not a moment to spare.

"Did I mention I got an audition?" She closed the lid and started the clothes cycling. "I'm working my tail off to be ready."

"That's wonderful!" Grace exclaimed. "Maybe your name will finally appear on a marquis. That would be something to talk about at Rosemary's party."

Marilyn rummaged in the refrigerator for the leftovers she brought home from the restaurant. The Italian food would hit the spot after all the dancing she'd been doing.

She wondered why she needed to preplan her conversation subjects before her sister's party, but reminded herself few of her family's crowd appreciated her sassy humor. She sighed, disinterested in having to be on her best behavior.

"You did say you're bringing someone with you. Right?"

Marilyn yanked the container from the refrigerator and popped it in the microwave, grateful Sonya went to class, so she had the place to herself. Her roommate hated the incessant opening and closing of the microwave door, not to mention its beeping. And Marilyn could be loud at everything she did. It was a wonder they hadn't yet tried to kill one another.

"I'll let you know." Marilyn wondered how to get out of that one. She could say her boyfriend had to work, then she could make up a decent job for this imaginary man—one that would blow her family away. So, her sister planned to marry a NASA engineer? Marilyn could say she started dating a...

Her mom gasped. "If you get this role, you'll be well on your way, won't you?"

"I don't want to get my hopes up, but it would be amazing." Marilyn stirred the pasta and reset the timer before starting the microwave again. She prayed she'd make her parents as proud as they were of her brother and sisters. But so far, she'd only been one big worry and embarrassment.

"Any other options? I mean, one audition is fine, but you've been down this road before."

Did Marilyn tell her about Titus? Doctor Grace Darby was unlikely to recognize the name, let alone care about his clout in entertainment.

"I'm still working at the restaurant to make ends meet, I've got two students taking private lessons and I'm auditioning in between."

The microwaved dinged. Marilyn yanked out her meal, suddenly not as hungry as she'd been.

"I'm doing everything I can."

"Are you? Marilyn, it's only a matter of time before you hit twenty-three…" Grace didn't need to elaborate. They already decided, years earlier when she begged off going to college in favor of trying to make it on her own in New York, that the family would be behind her for the time college would have taken her. But if, after that time, she hadn't settled into a remotely lucrative full-time position, Marilyn agreed to consider college, a trade school, or something else.

Four years seemed reasonable four years earlier. Now, the time had flown and while she had a nest egg in her savings account, no one would be tempted to call her successful or impressive.

"I know when my birthday is, Mom. And I remember what we talked about. This place and this career don't just happen. It takes work and experience and you need to know people." She refused to be defeated even as the deep, dark ideas set in.

"I'm doing everything right, everything I'm supposed to. I'm doing everything I can."

Including whining.

Marilyn bit her lip.

Grace exhaled. She probably wished she could throw in the towel on this one, but at the same time, Dr. Darby didn't give up or give in. Ever. On anything.

"Well. Keep me posted, OK? There's an incoming call that I need to take."

"Sure. Love you, Mom."

"I love you too."

Marilyn tossed her phone aside, grateful Titus's manager already advanced her a good sum of money for the work she started. She'd be meeting with his back-up singers the following week and by then she'd know if she got the part in the play.

She prayed she would. Her name in lights, or at least in a legitimate Broadway production program, would validate all these years of work, all the struggle she endured for her dreams to come true.

And maybe her parents would see her as they did the twins, David and Donna, and of course, pure and perfect Rosemary. But more importantly, she'd see herself as fitting into a family that consistently and yet unintentionally made her think she came from Mars.

**

Hours later, Marilyn slipped into the gym to rehearse. Since her earlier conversation with her mother, the dancer struggled in a deepening battle with her confidence. Because of waitressing, she'd not been able to practice for a few days and now worried that the audition—just three days away—would be lost if she didn't hit it hard.

She couldn't risk it.

With a flick of the lights and soft music playing, Marilyn began to warm up. She considered her family, her failings, and her dreams, wondering all the while if she wasted her time. Maybe this marked the end. Maybe she shouldn't keep fighting.

With a jolt, she made the decision.

If she didn't get this role, she'd go home for her birthday and do as her parents wished. She'd do as she once, foolishly and optimistically, promised. She'd go to college and do something worthwhile. Dance could always be a hobby. Right? No one could take that from her. Maybe she could even teach a class here and there to stay fresh. In case.

The idea stole all the wind from her. She slowed and sank to the floor, biting her lip against the tears that began to fall. How could four years go by so fast without any kind of progress? With only one role, and her most stable job as a waitress?

Her parents must be mortified.

She'd been positive for so long, the notion of accepting failure crushed her spirit. Marilyn's shoulders shook as she cried, head on her knees, now unable to even fathom rehearsing, let alone driving home. She could sit on this gym floor and cry for all the disappointment she pushed her way through for entirely too long.

Maybe she could move and not tell anyone—start a new life under a new name, so her family could forget her altogether.

Hey, if a girl's going to throw her own pity party, why not make it a humdinger of an affair?

"Hey." A warm, reassuring hand squeezed her shoulder and Marilyn slowly raised her head, hating that she recognized that voice.

But even through her tears, Marilyn could see Bo wasn't looking at her with contempt for a change. His dark eyes were liquid chocolate, warm, inviting, reassuring. And most of all, they were sympathetic, as if he understood exactly where her pain came from.

"Oh, geez…" She shoved away from him. "I'm not in the mood to deal with you right now," she muttered, swiping at her cheeks. She pushed to her feet as he stepped back too, stuffing his hands into his pockets.

Of course, he'd be wearing the glasses on top of it. Like she needed this embarrassing episode to be any worse. Figures.

"I saw the lights and wondered if I left them on," he began. "I'm, uh, are you OK? Can I get you anything? Tea? Water?"

Marilyn sniffed, turning her back to him. "I'm fine. Daisy said I could rehearse."

He made a noise that told her he didn't care.

"Do you need in here? I can leave." She shut off the music and tossed her phone into her bag.

"Titus dump you already? Daisy said she tried to warn you."

Marilyn's lips pressed together, hating that she'd been the topic of conversation between Daisy and Bo. She went to him and slugged him as hard as she could in that massive arm of his.

Of course, he didn't give her any satisfaction in that act. He didn't move or even wince. He simply stared at her.

"That's a good start. Do it again."

Her mouth dropped open. "What?"

He planted his feet wide, lowering himself a bit. He tipped his head. "Do it again. Get it out. I don't mind." He pointed to his bicep. "You're not going to hurt me no matter how hard you punch. Not with those skinny arms."

Marilyn raised an eyebrow. She reared back and punched him, this time earning a slight frown.

"Who taught you how to punch?"

Her lip quivered. She did not need him critiquing her ability to punch.

"I'm a dancer, not a fighter."

Bo looked away briefly, exhaling.

Marilyn struggled to find energy for a battle. "Look. I'm having a day, all right? I don't want to do this with you." She started to step away, but gasped when Bo grabbed her arm and pulled her back.

He made a fist and held it up. "You need to act like you mean it. When you pull back to hit someone, you aren't hitting them with your hand, you're hitting them with the full force of your entire body. The power isn't in your arm. It's here."

He pointed to his chest and abdomen.

"And most of all –here." He pointed to his legs. "You get that, and you can take someone out."

He moved to the bag on the far side of the room. Marilyn followed as he demonstrated.

"Watch."

He punched the bag twice while she wondered over this bizarre turn in her night.

"Your turn." He held the bag. "Get it out. Whatever had you crying, punch the living daylights out of it. Go."

Marilyn folded her arms over her chest. "This is stupid."

Bo leaned around the bag and looked into her eyes. "What would be stupid is me trying to cheer you up when we can't stand each other. So, I'm going to help you deal with it so you can get out of my gym and stop scuffing up the floor with your stupid dance shoes!"

Despite the serious tone in his voice, Marilyn understood he meant to bait her, and through baiting her, he recognized that her fighting spirit would return.

The pain began to dissolve in her chest.

Still, she played it up as if his request put her out. "Fine." She stepped back and tried to hit the bag as he showed her.

"Good. Again. Harder. Use all those muscles in your legs. You can do it."

You can do it.

Those words weaseled their way into her chest and rooted until she started to believe them. She could do it.

Marilyn punched with everything she had and actually managed to move the bag and make Bo take a step back. She raised her eyes to find him smiling.

"Atta girl."

Chapter four

Bo could hardly believe what he'd done.

He meant to give Marilyn a piece of his mind to rid himself of the weird feelings she kept stirring up inside him. Instead he started giving her boxing lessons and loved every minute of it.

All because he couldn't stand to watch anyone cry.

"You're a quick study." He stepped away from the bag. "Better? Or do you need to keep going?"

She shook her head, averting her eyes. "I'm good."

Finally, Marilyn looked up and Bo's breath caught in his chest. "Sure." He extended a hand to her. "How about we just stop baiting each other and stay out of each other's way so we can do our jobs?"

She shook his hand. "Sure. Truce."

He gulped when she held his hand longer than necessary, squeezing his fingers for extra measure before letting go.

"I might still give you a hard time anyway. I mean, you're so easy and right now it's about the only joy I get."

Bo sighed. "Right back at ya, Twinkle Toes."

She glanced away. "Well, um, I think I'm going to go. I'm not much for rehearsing now."

He jerked his head in the direction of the door. "I can leave."

She waved her hand. "Nah. I'm, um, dealing with some things."

Bo watched as she packed her bag and hefted it onto her shoulder. Against his better judgment, he said, "Can I help?"

She froze, eyes wide. "Can you help what?"

He shrugged as a knot formed in his stomach. He tried not to do it, but whatever was happening felt too big to handle on his own. He stood outside himself watching this insanity unfold.

"Can I help with… whatever. I can listen or…" Bo shuddered. "I can dance."

The corners of her lips curled as her bag slipped down her shoulder. "You can dance?"

He shrugged again. "If you don't think it would upset Titus. I'm not about breaking up someone's relationship, even if I think you can do better."

Marilyn's eyes sparkled. "I'm not dating Titus. Give me some credit."

The bodyguard appreciated that she had the decency to at least look the tiniest bit ashamed as she spoke.

She'd been tormenting him all along. It should have upset him, instead it amused him.

"He wants me to teach his back-up singers to dance. And I conned him into trying to help me practice. It didn't go very well."

Hope sprang in Bo's chest. If she started making deals with that flirtatious idiot, maybe she'd consider one with him too.

Marilyn lowered her bag. "Would you really help me? Or are you only being nice? And if you're being nice- why?"

Bo couldn't decide which question to answer first.

"I'm being nice to help you, to make up for being a jerk. And yes, I'll help you but I'm not making any promises. I'll probably stink."

"You can't be any worse than Titus." She hustled across the gym to where he stood, now aware that he helped her get her pep back. She lifted to her toes and hugged him, sparking a fire inside his chest that nearly made him stumble.

"I owe you, big guy."

Bo met her eyes, forcing himself to be honest for a change.

"I'm going to ask you for a favor too. You'll earn your keep."

She stepped away, looking a mixture of confused and maybe a bit hurt.

Bo understood what he said, and what it sounded like. Maybe he thought that sort of thing of Marilyn at one time, with Zeke, but not now, not when he found her crying. It encouraged him that the very thought of that kind of loose behavior appeared to turn her stomach.

Perhaps she changed since he first met her. Or maybe he completely misjudged her in the first place.

"I didn't mean something weird," Bo muttered. "I mean, I need help too. Maybe we could trade?"

She mulled this over. "Let's dance first. We'll talk later."

Bo still didn't think he could get the words out, so he nodded, wondering how pathetic he'd sound asking her to pretend to be his girlfriend for his family's sake. Not to mention she'd be forced to lie about everything from his job to their first date and who knew what else.

Maybe he wouldn't ask at all. He would never hear the end of it.

"Fair enough. We'll dance, then talk."

**

Marilyn got the music ready while Bo stretched nearby as she instructed him.

"Do you have any experience at all with dancing?"

She couldn't help but wonder what his end of this would be. What could Bo Sutton, perfect manny, need from her? She couldn't focus on her dancing and teaching him well enough to ignore that conversation for the next hour.

"Nope. Never even tapped a toe."

She turned and found him smiling. "OK. I've tapped a toe," he muttered. "But I'm sure my rhythm was off."

"Well tapping is something. We can work on the rhythm. I'll pick an easy song, and an easy routine to start." She circled him, assessing the situation. "You might be a titch too tall but let me give you the story we're working with and I'll show you some of the routine. All you'll really need to do is take the lead in twirling me a few times and then the lift and catch."

Marilyn exhaled. "And we already established that you can catch me."

Bo mulled this over. "How are you going to audition this without me there? I'm not dancing in public. I gotta draw a line."

Obviously, he understood nothing of how auditions worked. "I'll be auditioning with the male lead—he's already cast. He's smaller than you but you'll at least give me a frame of reference so I'm ready."

Bo's eyebrows lifted. "OK."

"Nervous?"

He snorted. "I don't care if I'm bad at this. It will only prove my point."

"You caught me before."

"Reflex. Pity."

Marilyn went to change the music to avoid acknowledging the weird sensation in her chest as she tried not to let her amusement show.

"Ready?"

He shrugged.

Marilyn started the music, keeping her back to him so she could concentrate, show him the routine, and hopefully get this rehearsal back on track.

**

Bo wore the wrong shoes for this. He already tripped over his feet a thousand times and yet Marilyn never once belittled him or made fun of his lacking skills. Instead she kept encouraging and thanking him for helping her.

He wished he hated dancing, or that he could say she got on his nerves. But he only kept warming to her as he now noticed her grace, skill, and passion for dancing. She was good. And she deserved this chance.

Marilyn snapped off the music and turned to him. "You're tremendous. I can't thank you enough."

Bo yanked his glasses off and cleaned them. "You could have kicked me ten or fifteen times already and somehow you've refrained. Even if I deserve it."

She waved her hand and winked. "Don't be so sure I won't eventually."

He grunted and she playfully punched his arm. "It's getting late. I should get home."

"We can do it again if you want."

She looked up at him in surprise. He turned away, hoping to squelch the nerves in his stomach.

"OK."

He turned back and waited as she started the music again.

This time, he focused on her moves and how they suited the music, as if she felt the emotion deep into her soul. Her passion for this couldn't be denied.

Bo tried to think how he might do better, his muscles now accustomed to and expecting the movements and reactions that complemented Marilyn's. What he could do might loosely be referred to as dancing, but at least he could try.

So, as he caught her for the final leap, Bo embraced the story Marilyn shared- about lovers denied their relationship by forces outside of their control. He met her eyes, not as himself but as the character she described—loving and kind but scared of something that would mean he'd need courage he'd never shown or known.

Marilyn's arm wrapped around his shoulders and remained there, her gaze still locked with his as her right hand held softly against his chest.

He should have set her down by now but for inexplicable reasons he froze, relishing the feel of her in his arms. Maybe he'd been hasty in swearing off relationships.

For the first time since he could remember, Bo felt a spark. He wanted to kiss her.

That it was Marilyn Darby gave him so much pause he couldn't dream of moving.

"Daaannng!" Her exclamation shocked him back to life. Slowly, and with too much reluctance, he lowered her to the ground, their gaze holding.

"You're better than you gave yourself credit for." She patted his chest and stepped back, obviously overcome too.

"I'm glad I could help."

Marilyn's expression remained sincere. "You helped beyond what you probably meant to. I really appreciate it." She hugged him. "So, what's your end of the deal? Now that I sucked the life out of you?"

Bo's mouth went dry. "My…?"

Marilyn started fussing with the sound system as she removed her phone from it and turned everything off. "Yeah. You mentioned that I could do something to repay you."

How did one explain this craziness? Bo bit his lip as he struggled with the appropriate angle. "Oh… Uh. Hm. You might want to sit down for this."

**

Marilyn did as he asked, waiting as Bo leaned against the weight machine nearby, one hand slung over it as if he needed help standing.

"Well?" She prayed he wasn't some kind of freak, but dismissed the idea quickly. She already noticed the way he treated everyone in Robby and Daisy's house and inner circle. And even if he might not have seen her, Marilyn saw him in church every Sunday with the family, keeping right along in his Bible and taking detailed notes during sermons.

If he was a freak, he also was a fine actor.

Bo closed his eyes briefly, pain passing over his face. "Right." He opened his eyes and looked at her directly, his dark eyes signaling an intensity she'd never seen before in him.

"I am not used to asking for help," he began.

Marilyn nodded, biting her tongue against the jokes and teasing that so badly wanted to come out.

"But right now, I'm not sure what else to do." He raked one hand over his head. "And remember, I'm only telling you the minimum. You're on a need-to-know basis and that's it. Got it?"

Again, Marilyn nodded. "Geez, did you kill someone or something?"

"What?" Bo stopped pacing. "Don't be stupid."

"Trying…"

He exhaled loudly on a groan and looked into her eyes. "I've got a family wedding and I can't go alone. I'll pay for everything and I swear I'm not going to do anything weird like expect you to sleep in my room or whatever. It would be go to the wedding, pretend we're together, and get back home again."

Oh. My.

Marilyn's jaw dropped as she tried to keep up, barely processing his words as she worked on an appropriate reply.

Bo's cheeks flushed and he looked away.

She didn't expect this at all. Marilyn stared at him, not realizing her mouth hung open until Bo put his hands on his hips.

"Put your mouth back with the rest of your face. I'm not a horrible person."

"I don't think you're a horrible person. I… have so many questions."

Bo leaned against the wall. "Fire away. I'll answer some. Probably not all."

Marilyn racked her brain, starting with the most obvious. "Why me?"

Bo grimaced. "Pickings are slim, Twinkles. And if I can help you practice, I figure you owe me something."

But she only shook her head. "A few dances does not equal a romantic trip to visit your family for a wedding."

The bodyguard pursed his lips. "I never said it would be romantic. It won't." Bo pushed away from the wall and started a methodical process of cleaning off a piece of equipment that already sparkled.

"I'm not an actress. I don't know anything about you. How would I pull this off?"

Bo shrugged but didn't look at her as he continued working. "I told my mom we just started dating. That leaves it explainable why we aren't all over each other and why you might not know some basics." He paused. "I can fill you in on the way."

Marilyn pondered this. "Wait—you already told your family? That's presumptuous." She shook her head. "You actually told your family you're dating me? Like, by name?" Her knee bounced up and down as she absorbed the magnitude of this strange scenario. Could she pretend to date someone who drove her as nuts as Bo did? Probably not.

"This is ridiculous."

Bo snorted. "You're telling me."

The poor man looked wrecked, so Marilyn chose to bite back every single tease that tried to escape her mouth. Instead, she'd ask direct questions, saving the jokes for later.

"When? I'm not missing my audition for this garbage."

If Bo cared that she referred to his plight as garbage, he didn't show it. "It's in three weeks."

Her eyes widened. "Really?"

He raised to his full height and rolled his shoulders. "Yeah. Why?"

Marilyn chuckled. "Because if I do this for you, you're coming to my sister's engagement party with me. It's Sunday. And fancy that—it's even in New Jersey, so we could swing by on the way out of your wedding thing if it's not too far." She paused, thinking. "And if it is, I'll have the perfect excuse to skip."

Bo's eyes narrowed and he threw the rag across the room and turned to her. "No dice. The deal is I help you rehearse, and you go to this wedding. Tit for tat."

Marilyn planted her hands on her hips.

"That is not tit for tat. That is…" When she couldn't think of anything, she sprung to her feet and grabbed her bag. "I'm not sure what to call it, but that is not tit for tat. And you don't get a deal otherwise."

She went for the door and yanked it open, stopping when Bo cleared his throat. Slowly she turned to him, biting back the amusement she predicted would come out when he caved.

"Fine. I'll help you, and you come to the wedding and I'll go to your sister's stupid engagement party. I only hope we don't kill each other."

Marilyn met his eyes.

"Deal." She winked at him and blew a kiss. "And I hope you don't fall in love with me. It's going to be tempting, Bo."

He pursed his lips. "Not a problem. But I should be promising that I won't scream at you either. That's much more likely."

Marilyn winked, free for the first time in ages. "Sure it is. We'll talk later, manny-cakes. Nice doing business with you."

**

"I need three specials!" Marilyn called as she sailed through the kitchen to get a basket of bread.

"You got a private party, Mar. I'll go back and take care of the drinks if you're too swamped."

Marilyn smiled at Corinne, her favorite hostess by far because she always jumped in to help the waitstaff beyond simply seating customers. It probably helped that her grandparents owned the restaurant, but whatever the reason, Marilyn adored her. "I got it. I'll head over after I take care of the family in D9."

Corinne hesitated as Marilyn filled the basket, leaning toward her conspiratorially. "I don't want to freak you out, but your private party is Robby Grant and his family." She bounced up and down on her toes. "Oh my word, he's even better in person! He has this tattoo…"

Marilyn's breath caught in her throat. "What?" She'd been careful to keep quiet her good fortune and connections, especially at the restaurant where they would do her no good, and in fact might even make for more trouble than such information would be worth. She'd refuse to ask her employers for autographs or anything else—unwilling to lose the opportunity the relationship presented her.

She ventured a look at her friend who continued smiling, though it melted quickly. "What? Even if you aren't a fan of his music you gotta admit that love story and all is so romantic! And his wife! Yeesh- she's stunning! No wonder they're nuts for each other. That much beauty in one relationship? It's insane!"

Marilyn smoothed her apron and swung in the opposite direction to look in the cracked and grimy kitchen mirror before turning back to Corinne.

"Do I look OK? Is there a huge guy with them? Dark hair? Maybe or maybe not wearing glasses? Huge arms? I mean, HUGE arms."

Corinne's mouth opened. "There were two guys like that. One dark hair, one bald. No glasses." She yanked Marilyn closer, nearly sending the bread flying.

"You know them?!"

"What? No! I, uh…" She looked away, grimacing. "Well, sort of. Please don't say anything. I don't want to make it public."

Corinne took her by both shoulders and moved a stray curl from her forehead. "Oh, girl, I won't say a word. But that man is heaven. Go get him. You can tell me the rest later."

Marilyn hoped she wasn't a fool for trusting her co-worker. "What? Oh, um, sure. I gotta go."

She hustled off, wondering why they'd show up now. She'd not seen Bo since they danced together a few days earlier, but he had text her once to establish he had her number. He also wrote, in the most professional manner possible, that they'd talk when she next came to work with Daisy. Nothing to read into. No promises, no flirting, nothing.

Did she scare him? She badly wanted to talk to Daisy because she probably knew Bo better than anyone, but Marilyn didn't want to drag her friend into the drama, or risk losing a prized position in the Grant household.

Was there drama? Heck, Marilyn didn't even know that much. But she remained certain something happened that night and that she couldn't wait to dance with Bo Sutton again.

Or at least talk to him about their ridiculous deal.

**

Bo followed Robby, Daisy, and Jazz into the restaurant, a diaper bag over his shoulder and Alice next to him, giving him a detailed rundown of her Shakespeare class.

He grinned. "Sure sounds like you're ready for the test."

The teen exhaled. "I hope so. It's like I've been studying for it for weeks."

"That's because you have. And so have I. I definitely didn't do this much work when I took Shakespeare in high school." Bo followed the family to a semi-private room where they could be noticed by the astute eye but wouldn't cause chaos for the rest of the diners. This also made his job much easier.

While Daisy and Robby didn't really need to do much to garner attention, since they recently came off a tour and been home for six months and as-yet hadn't released any music, they had to work to keep themselves at the top of their fans' minds. Even if Bo understood this, he personally didn't enjoy the limelight the way they appeared to. Alice was acclimating but she tended to prefer hanging with him and Jazz at a separate table, away from the speculation and cameras.

Ever the over-protective father, Robby preferred it that way too.

"Bo…" Daisy lifted Nicolette for him. He swiped the baby in one arm, the carrier in his other hand and moved discreetly out of the way as everyone got settled.

Bo turned his back to them as he bounced the baby, hoping she'd stay asleep and that he'd get her into the carrier that same way. The less attention they drew to themselves, the better.

"Daisy!" The female voice sounded vaguely familiar and as Bo turned his stomach dropped.

Marilyn?

He gulped and turned away as Jazz grinned and Alice bit her lip in an attempt to hide her own amusement.

Traitors. He hated being transparent.

Please don't let her say anything. Please don't let her say anything.

While he established contact with her after their dancing session and mutually convenient agreement, Bo hadn't been able to decide what to say next or how to proceed, so he said nothing, hoping the whole thing would go away.

Unfortunately, that might have been a stupid move.

"Look Bo, it's your girlfriend." Alice giggled again.

The bodyguard pierced her with laser beams. She didn't look frightened.

"Hey Marilyn!" Alice hopped out of her seat and gave the woman a hug. "What are you doing here?"

"Well, when you're an actress or dancer, you wait tables to pay the bills while you're auditioning for roles. So, here I am!" she paused. "I didn't expect you guys! This is a nice surprise."

Daisy laughed. "You mentioned this place once and I thought we all needed to get out of the house. I'm glad we could surprise you!"

Against everything in him, Bo finally turned and took in the scene, grateful his arms and attention were occupied at least partially by the baby. How did Marilyn glow like that? He shook himself, wondering if he hurt her if he backed out of their deal. He couldn't be sure he could spend a weekend one on one with her and not make a complete fool of himself.

Or worse, rip her head off for pushing his buttons.

Marilyn beamed. "I'm so glad I got to be here to see you!" She hugged Daisy again, followed by Robby too. Her cheeks reddened when her eyes landed on him.

She drew a deep breath. Had she told them anything? He didn't think she and Daisy talked outside of their lessons, but he also couldn't be entirely sure what his boss did when she left his sight.

His stomach quaked. If anyone ever had the means or courage to humiliate him, it would be Marilyn Darby.

Play it cool.

"Beauregard." Her teasing tone signaled that she agreed to keep whatever happened between them private.

This urged Bo on, filling him with the slightest bit of confidence.

"Marilyn." He barely stifled his grin and slowly sat as Marilyn went on to do her job, taking drink orders, saving him for last.

She tapped her pen against her waitress pad.

"Well?"

Bo lowered his eyes back to the baby. "Iced tea."

"Sweetened or no?"

"Unsweetened." He looked at her and a silent something passed between them. Marilyn caught her lip with her teeth and exhaled.

"Of course."

She turned back to the opposite table. "I'll be right back with your drinks and I'll answer any questions about the menu." She rattled off the specials, but her eyes never again found Bo.

As she walked away, the bodyguard realized he'd been staring, and worse, everyone stared at him staring at her. He lowered his eyes and pretended to check on the baby who, regrettably chose to stay quiet exactly when he needed her to be riled up and distracting.

He hadn't told anyone what happened in the gym because he still needed to work it out himself. But man, if he didn't think about that woman being in his arms nearly every moment of every day!

And for as much as he never wanted to dance before, now he couldn't think about anything else.

His mom became relentless. She already called twice today to ask about Marilyn. Bo feared he'd soon come unglued.

Before he could consider running from all of his fears, Jazz interrupted with a low whistle.

"Ouch." He kicked Bo's foot. "No one ever teach you how to flirt, boy?"

Bo ignored him. "Is she asleep?"

"Marilyn or Nicolette? I think you put them both out." Jazz chuckled. "That was painful, dude."

Bo glanced at Robby and Daisy who were lost in their own romantic conversation of love and laughter, as usual. He turned his attention back to his own table where Alice pretended to study the menu and Jazz waited for his reply.

"Is Nicolette asleep?"

"Yeah, man, she's out."

Alice put her menu down as Bo struggled to get the baby into her car seat. She waited until he sat up.

"Do you like Marilyn?" Her voice wasn't teasing, it was hopeful. "I love Marilyn! Please say you like her!"

Ahh, the sweet innocence of youth that made it sound like he only needed to check a box on a note passed in study hall and all would be well. That stupid naivety got him all those years ago and nearly ruined him. Relationships were entirely too complex and all of it confused and frustrated him beyond measure.

Bo shifted uncomfortably. "No. I mean, she's fine. She makes Daisy happy."

Alice rolled her eyes and punched him. "I mean do you want to send her sweet texts and tell her you like her hair and take her on a date like her?"

Bo looked away. "No."

"You guys would be so cute!" Alice bounced in her seat. "Bo! Please let me help you! Please?! I swear I won't even embarrass you or anything. I want to help- I can be in your wedding and…"

Jazz chuckled, shaking his head.

He scoffed at them both, wondering how to shut this down.

"What? No. If I wanted to ask her out- which I do not- I could handle it by myself."

"Says who?"

Bo lifted his arm and flexed one huge muscle before turning it and flexing again with his tricep. "Says these."

"You're full of it." She picked up her menu and pursed her lips.

Bo looked at Jazz for back-up, but he only lifted his menu and shook his head. "I'm with her. You're full of it."

**

Marilyn hustled to get the family's drinks, delivered them with a promise to be back shortly, and then rushed to get her tables in order.

"Shoooot he's hot." Corinne fanned herself when Marilyn finally made it back to the kitchen. She'd stolen enough glances in Bo's direction that she moved beyond wondering to hoping they'd get it out soon between them.

Would she lose her job if she dated him and it failed? Was he worth that kind of risk when she had such a golden opportunity with Daisy, Titus, and who knew who else they might introduce her to?

Marilyn couldn't imagine it. And at the same time, she could hardly get Bo out of her mind. Whatever he meant of their 'fake' weekend relationship, she feared she'd ruin it with her sass, jokes, and the many differences between them.

"He is nice to look at. Only, I'm not sure it's worth it."

Corinne nudged her. "Well if you decide it's not, come find me and I'll talk you into changing your mind."

Marilyn grinned as she hustled back to the table to get their orders, again, saving the bodyguard for last. As she took the rest of the orders, the baby started fussing and he went back to walking again, so Marilyn trailed to the opposite end of the room after him, pen poised over her notepad, hoping the rest of the entourage didn't listen in.

"What can I get for you, sir?"

Bo continued bouncing as he talked to her, not quite looking at her but not quite looking away either.

Did she have something on her nose? Why wouldn't he look?

Her stomach turned. Maybe he regretted what happened. Maybe she imagined it. He probably wanted to back out of their deal.

"Yeah, uh, I'd like the salmon special with broccoli and rice."

"And your salad dressing?"

"Italian."

Marilyn nudged him so he'd look at her.

His eyes widened. "What?" He looked away again.

She grinned. "Nothing. I wanted to be sure you're still alive."

Bo growled. "I'm alive. Knock it off. This isn't the place or time."

Marilyn grinned as he moved to the opposite side of the room, his back to her. She glanced at Daisy who winked and Robby who didn't stifle his grin.

Poor Bo. Everyone but him enjoyed this immensely.

Chapter five

Bo wondered how he'd manage to eat his dinner with Marilyn flitting around the restaurant in that tiny black skirt and apron, taunting him when he couldn't even get two decent words out of his mouth in her presence since they danced together.

What could be wrong with him?

"You think the 'rents will let you drop me off at Julie's on the way home?" Alice interrupted Bo's musings.

He wiped his mouth with a napkin before placing it back in his lap. "It's a school night so I doubt it."

She slumped back in her chair, annoyed. "For having rock star parents, I sure don't live a very rock and roll life."

Jazz snickered. "Be glad you don't. Robby still acts like a five-year-old—but I imagine you plan to actually grow up someday." He tipped his head toward the next table where the singer tapped out a rhythm against his water glass as his head bobbed.

Of course, Daisy watched him adoringly as she held Nicolette.

Bo ignored them as he tried to look beyond the small windows to the rest of the restaurant in case Marilyn happened to be going by. He tossed his napkin and stood.

"I'll be back."

Alice stood with him and brushed something imaginary off his shirt before urging him toward the door. "Go get her, tiger."

Bo glared. "I'm going to the restroom."

"Sure you are."

If Bo didn't have a younger sister, he might have wanted to hit her, but instead he ruffled her hair, appreciating the teasing for what it might be—sadly based in truth and her observations. Bo hated transparency, but apparently he showed it anyway.

He made his way from the room in search of the waitress who now deserved another apology and maybe an explanation.

Before Bo got very far, he spotted Marilyn heading straight for him, her eyes dancing and her lips smiling as if she hid some kind of secret he now wanted in on.

"Need something? Directions to anger management?"

Bo felt his cheeks warm.

"Funny." He cleared his throat. "Any chance you can slip outside for a second?"

Marilyn's mouth opened in surprise.

"Sure. This way."

Bo followed, wondering what he should say.

"Shoot." Marilyn turned to face him as he stepped into the parking lot. The night air held a hint of a chill and Marilyn shivered as she waited for him to speak.

"I, uh, wanted to apologize. Again."

Her tiny frame struck Bo hard as he stewed over catching her and holding her. She inspected her nails, her confidence oozing out of the gesture.

"You sure need to apologize a lot where I'm concerned. What for now?" She looked at him. Waiting.

Man, she intimidated him! Bo looked away. He exhaled, keeping his eyes down. "I wasn't sure how I should act around you after. I mean…" He cursed under his breath before continuing.

"In front of them, you and I never got along. Now, we're kind of getting along and…"

Marilyn folded her arms over her chest. "Are you seriously this much of a wimp?" She whacked him on the shoulder. "You like me. Admit it. It's killing you, but you like me."

She winked and that pushed him over.

Bo rolled his shoulders back and looked down his nose at her. He leaned forward, the mess of emotions tangling up as he spat, "So what if I like you? That still doesn't mean anything."

Her mouth opened. Bo waited for her retort as he folded his arms over his chest.

"It doesn't?" Her eyes went wide in surprise. Bo wondered if he also imagined the flash of disappointment. "I mean, it will make our deal easier. Won't it? We wouldn't be able to fool everyone otherwise."

And that only served to ignite a spark of hope in his chest, one he quickly squelched. No sense moving in that direction.

"Right. Except ourselves. This is ridiculous." He narrowed his eyes at her. "From where I'm standing, we both like our jobs and don't want to lose them. They could find ten people to do what we do. Even if you're willing to gamble, I like a sure thing." He lowered his voice to a whisper. "Honestly, I need a sure thing. If I like you, and we do this and it gets messy—or even if it doesn't, it's going to make everything harder, not easier."

Marilyn held his gaze. "We should probably talk about this. I mean, what will happen, the details…"

Bo rubbed one hand over his head, overwhelmed by the weight of his idiocy. "Yep."

But his partner in crime appeared to be nonplussed. She tossed her head. "Good. So, would you rather call me later or…?" And yet, for all her bravado, Marilyn didn't seem sure where to look. Bo couldn't blame her, he didn't either, and the alley held painfully few options, so he ended up looking back into her eyes. Again.

"When are you done tonight?"

Her eyes sparkled in the dim lights. "I should be home by nine."

"I'll call you." He paused. "Thank you for agreeing to do this. My dad's pretty awful but the rest of the family should be fine. I mean, they won't be a problem. I… haven't been home in a few years so it's hard to say for sure."

Marilyn nodded. "Mine's bad too. And I haven't been home in a few years either." She grinned. "At least it will be eventful."

Bo's stomach churned but he didn't speak. Marilyn's pleased expression melted.

"So, um, I better get back to work."

Bo reached for the door, but she stopped him, grabbing his arm and blurting, "I can't decide if this makes everything better or worse, but when we danced it might have been one of the top ten most magical moments of my life."

Bo's mind went blank. He exhaled, stuffing his hands into his pockets as he searched fruitlessly for the right words and fought to keep himself upright. He would not fall into her arms or press his needy lips to hers.

"Wow. Um, thank you?"

Tension radiated from her. "But I've been at this four years, trying to convince my parents, and maybe myself, that I'm talented enough to make it." She squared her shoulders.

"So, the other day, I was crying it out because my parents are right, and if I don't get the part, I'm going home at Thanksgiving- and I'm not sure I'm coming back."

Bo's mouth opened as she turned slightly away. He couldn't imagine Marilyn not dancing. But he didn't get a vote. It would be hers to wrestle through.

She looked up at him. "They wanted me to go to college. I said they should give me some time to try this my way." She shrugged. "But I think I'm just stubborn and stupid."

Bo couldn't take listening to her convince herself she failed somehow by not meeting her parent's definition of success. He grabbed her by the shoulders, making her gasp.

"You can't give up! You're an incredible dancer!" He squeezed her shoulders to punctuate his statement. "This takes time. There's no overnight success."

Bo couldn't fathom how to get across to her that giving up meant giving in to her parents' perceptions of her. Maybe he'd been too entrenched in his own problems to be giving Marilyn an honest assessment of hers, but he had to say something.

And at the same time, he wondered if he spoke out of selfish ambition. After all, he meant to use her for his own gain, all the while hoping it might turn into something and he wouldn't lose his job.

"You're sweet." That precious assessment warmed Bo deep in places he'd long forgotten.

"I'm going to the audition," she continued. "But I should really start thinking long-term. I'm tired of being on the brink. I'm tired of disappointing everyone."

Bo exhaled, his hands still on her shoulders. He closed his eyes and asked the most foolish, ridiculous thing in the world.

"When's the audition? I'm going with you."

**

Laughter bubbled up inside Marilyn's chest. "You realize you've gone from being a huge jerk to a bit too nice in like ten seconds?"

Bo opened his eyes and met her gaze. He lifted an eyebrow.

"You prefer the jerk?" He dropped his hands. "That explains so much."

While she wanted to question that statement, Marilyn chose a different angle. "I prefer you being you."

He stepped away, running one hand over his head. "I doubt that."

She went to him and nudged him. "I've gone to a thousand auditions myself. I can do it."

"I never said you couldn't."

She held his gaze. "I'll text you the details. And then, Muscles, I seriously need to get back to work."

"Fair."

She poked him. "See? You like me."

Bo rolled his eyes. "Don't get a big head about it or I'll change my mind."

She playfully punched him, and he grinned stupidly at her. Marilyn's heart gave a weak flutter.

"I, um, better get back in case Daisy needs me. I'll call you later."

Her heart fluttered again. He'd begun to undermine every assumption she had about him. As a huge, muscular man he didn't only focus on working out. He wasn't, so far anyway, completely self-absorbed, and his gentle concern for others rattled her.

And honestly if she saw him carrying that baby again, she might explode for all the feelings it brought out.

"Thanks, Bo."

He held her gaze for a long moment, looking for all the world like he'd rather do anything else but end their conversation. Finally, he nodded and headed back inside.

**

Daisy and Robby were so loud getting Nicolette through her tubby and into bed, Bo wondered how the kid would fall asleep. All that singing and fun sure sounded wonderful, but it also made it impossible for him to consider calling Marilyn. He left his room, intent on finding some quiet space in the mansion where he could hold a serious conversation about how to handle their ridiculous situation.

Maybe he'd also figure out if he ought to abort this mission altogether before one of them got hurt.

Bo slipped into his office, put his feet up on the desk, and worked to summon the courage to press the button to make the call.

He waited only seconds for her to pick up.

"Hey stranger." Her friendly tone immediately set him at ease.

"Hey. Is now a good time?"

"Good as any. I just got home. Things good on your end?"

Bo shrugged. "I suppose so." He cleared his throat. "Is this weird? I feel like this whole idea is weird. Should I explain?"

Marilyn laughed. "It's a little weird, I guess. An explanation might be nice." She paused. "So, tell me, Bo, why do you need to convince your family you have a girlfriend? Or do you generally have something against going to a wedding alone?"

He wondered how to say it without really saying anything at all. He exhaled and did what he could.

"I haven't been home in years and they worry about me. If they think I'm at least committing to a solid relationship with a good job to boot, they'll be happy. Stop asking questions." He closed his eyes briefly. "And maybe it will make them a little bit proud of me for moving on."

"From?" Her tone held a note of curiosity. "I mean, if you want to tell me. Maybe I should understand the dynamic I'm walking into."

Bo ran one hand over his head as his ex-girlfriend popped into his head. Nothing like that image to make his stomach sour.

"I'm not sure I want to get into that."

Marilyn remained silent for a long moment. "OK. Fair enough."

He let her question and understanding lie before turning things in a different direction, intending to make her comfortable with the weekend looming in front of them. "My mom is the sweetest woman you'll ever meet. Pushy and confident, but sweet. I've got a younger sister, Alice's age—her name's Emma, and she's dying to meet you."

"Oh goodness. That should be fun."

Bo chuckled. "Yeah." He continued with the family picture. "Wyatt and Hailey are both older, out of the house, and married. Lincoln and Asher are still at home- Linc's in college and Asher is a senior in high school. Emma's a sophomore, like Alice."

"Big family."

"Yep."

"You said your dad's rough…? Should we practice my boxing?"

Bo appreciated her concern, but he refused to cave to his father. "Nah. Dad only gives me trouble. You'll be fine."

Marilyn stayed silent for a long moment. "I hope you're prepared to clear the dancefloor at the reception. Might as well show off your mad skills."

Bo laughed, afraid to give her too much encouragement. "I don't like being the center of attention. Besides, I might embarrass you."

"No way. Impossible. Let's make this trip worthwhile, Muscles."

Bo considered this. "OK."

"OK? Wow. You're easy. I need a thousand dollars. Write me a check. Or I guess cash will be fine."

Again, Bo chuckled. "What questions do you have?" He wanted to keep this conversation on track as much as possible, but at the same time, Bo was definitely encouraged so far.

Maybe taking Marilyn to the wedding wouldn't be so bad after all.

**

Marilyn no longer bothered trying to stifle her yawn.

"I should probably let you go." Bo's voice sounded reluctant. She understood. For the last hour and a half, they'd been enjoying a surprisingly pleasant conversation and Marilyn didn't want it to end.

"I hate to hang up," she said honestly. "But I'm teaching an early class, then I'll be out to work with Daisy. And I hoped you and I could get in some practice. I'm free after our dance lesson."

"Yeah. Sure." Bo cleared his throat. "Probably later in the day is better for me."

"Sure. OK. Um, before I go…" Marilyn struggled over how to ask. "What did you tell your family about me? About us?"

Loaded questions. Bad idea.

"I didn't say much. Just that you're a dancer and we met through mutual friends." As always, Bo remained professional and cagey.

Marilyn pushed off her bed and made her way to the kitchen where she started rooting through the refrigerator, ignoring Sonya as she studied, books spread across every inch of their small table.

"That's fair, but it's not entirely the truth."

"I guess not, but that part is messy, so I figured I'd skip it."

"Mmm…" Marilyn wasn't sure how she felt about that one, but she only pushed far enough to say, "Well, we probably ought to talk about that at some point. I know you had some serious opinions about me when I dated Zeke."

Bo coughed but didn't deny it, instead he changed the subject. "What did you tell your family?"

Marilyn snickered. "Nothing yet."

"Are you going to tell them the truth or make something up?"

She grinned at the worry in his voice. "Who do you want to be, Bo Sutton?"

Sonya gagged, which made Marilyn roll her eyes as she walked out of the room.

"I'm pretty happy with who I am, actually. But I'll be whatever or whoever you want for the sake of your family. Only make sure you tell me so I can play along."

Marilyn slowly closed the door to her room. She knew the truth made sense but having some fun with a few lies could be tempting too. "I appreciate that. I guess I'll get back to you."

"I guess you will. Good-night, Marilyn."

"No Twinkle Toes?"

He laughed. "Good-night, Twinkle Toes."

"Good night, manny-cakes. See you tomorrow."

Marilyn tossed her phone aside, but looked at it for a long time, worried. She would be pretending to date someone she suddenly realized she could actually envision herself dating.

What a tangled web she managed to weave.

**

As Bo finished his morning workout and headed into the house to make breakfast for Daisy and help her with the baby, his cell phone buzzed in his pocket. He hardly slept the night before, still thinking about his long conversation with Marilyn.

He liked her. Too much. He couldn't let anyone figure it out— most of all Marilyn herself, or she might think too much of the trip they'd soon take together.

So, Bo could only really keep praying Marilyn got the role, making her too busy to work for Daisy, thus freeing him from at least some of these worries. Then he'd be able to see her all the time, but at the same time, he'd also be free to actually date her if he so chose.

He pulled his phone out, pausing on the walkway as he opened the text.

Hey- the audition is at 9am. Any chance you can practice today?

She ended the text with the address of the audition.

Sure, TT. Tonight.

Her reply came immediately.

Ok, Muscles. I'll stop over tonight after work. Around 7?
Sure thing

Bo made his way into the house, anxious for a shower, but meeting chaos the minute he walked inside. It stole his attention away from being all warm and fuzzy about dancing with Marilyn again. He squelched his amusement and assessed the situation.

"There you are!" Robby shrieked as he threw up his hands. "Would you tell my wife she's insane?"

Bo turned his attention to Daisy, who nuzzled the baby, looking completely at ease with whatever might be happening even as her frantic husband paced the kitchen, still waving his hands around.

The bodyguard never got into the middle of anything between the husband and wife. He took a different approach.

"How about a few details?"

Robby grunted as he reached for a coffee mug he prepared exactly as Daisy liked. He took it to her and set it on the table before loudly and dramatically smooching her head.

"I'm only trying to help, Angel. I don't like people taking advantage of my girl."

Bo patted Robby on the back, confident this would be another non-issue, with Robby being overdramatic as usual. He walked through the kitchen and upstairs, nearly making it to his room when Alice threw open her door.

"Oh good, you're back!" She jumped in front of him, grabbed his hand and pulled him into her room. "I need help." She pointed to the clothes on her bed.

"Which one of these outfits says 'responsible'?"

Bo squirmed. "Uh... I'm not exactly a fashion consultant." He surveyed the options, pointing to a pair of jeans and a button-down shirt.

"That looks good. Matches and everything." He glanced at her. "What's this for?"

She whacked his arm. "I told you yesterday! It's for student council elections. I need to make a speech." She picked up the outfit. "You don't think jeans are too casual?"

Bo shrugged. "It says you're an ambassador of the people. You relate to everyone." He raised his eyebrows. "Good?"

She didn't look convinced, glancing up at him before stepping away.

"You stink."

He tousled her hair. "I just finished working out."

"Go shower before Daisy smells you. You're gross."

Bo moved toward the door. "Ask Daisy about your clothes. She lives for this stuff."

"No, I mean, I will, but I wanted a guy's perspective because I need everyone's votes. You and Robby both picked the jeans." She shook her head, clearly not believing the men in her life. "Maybe I should look again."

Bo chuckled as he left the room, only to hear Daisy yell, "Bo! Where did you go?"

He hustled back to the kitchen. "Right here. What's up?"

Robby left for the day and Daisy remained, holding Nicolette and cooing over her. "Can you get her down? Carli will be here shortly, and I need to be ready."

Bo didn't groan or flinch. He scooped up the baby and held her with one hand to his shoulder. "You got Titus later too. And isn't Marilyn coming?"

"What do you think Robby's freaking out about?" She snickered. "Thanks for knowing what to say so he'd figure it out."

Bo shrugged, not sure he'd done anything, but glad Daisy saw it different.

"He's afraid I'm taking on too much with the baby. But I love the writing sessions. I can't say no." She took her breakfast dishes to the sink.

"When I'm done with Carli, maybe you can take Alice for some tennis shoes and I'll stay here with the baby. By the time you get back Titus will be here so you can babysit all of us."

Bo raised his eyebrows. Robby did not want his wife alone with the flirtatious singer. Not because he didn't trust Daisy, but because he didn't trust the human-hormone named Titus.

"Sure." Bo started for the door, recalling Alice shopping online for black shoes a few days earlier. He knew exactly where she'd want to go.

"What are the plans for tonight? Am I on duty?"

Daisy shrugged. "I think we're staying home and having pizza and movies in the game room. You're welcome to join…"

He grinned, hating himself for acting like a stupid teenager. "I might have plans. Just wanted to make sure I wasn't needed here."

Daisy narrowed her eyes. "What plans? With who?"

Bo couldn't imagine how he'd say it out loud and not face ramifications in the form of teasing and questions.

"I'm not sure yet. I can keep you posted if you really want me to."

A strange look passed over Daisy's face. "No. I don't need in on every part of your life. Unless you want to tell me." She winked. "And especially if it involves you and Marilyn—because everyone's rooting for that."

Bo stopped and turned, still not sure what to say. His mouth went dry, but Daisy only wrinkled her nose, lifting one finger to point at him in accusation.

"You disappeared with her for over twenty minutes last night. Kind of hard not to notice."

Bo winced. "We're trying to make peace." He refused to tell Daisy the mess he made in his personal life. She, of all people, needed to trust he could do his job. If she knew what he'd done she might wonder if he would screw up her life too.

Thankfully she didn't press the issue. "Good. I'm going to get ready for Carli. Do you mind listening for the door?"

Before she could say anything further, the doorbell rang.

Bo went in that direction, reminding himself that this chaos was the reason he wouldn't jeopardize his job.

**

Marilyn let herself into the gym, surprised to find it dark and empty. She flicked on the lights and checked the time. Seven-twenty. She was later than she planned to be but figured not so late that Bo would have considered himself stood-up. She checked her phone, but finding no texts, set about getting the music ready and checked her phone again.

It rang, but sadly it was her mom, not her dance partner. Marilyn answered, intending to keep it as short as possible.

"Hey, Mom."

"Hello, Marilyn. I wondered how your audition went."

Probably so she could 'put in a good word' with her college friends that much sooner. Marilyn began stretching.

"It's not till Tuesday. I'm actually about to rehearse now."

"Oh. Good. Well, good luck to you. Break a leg! But don't really, of course."

Unsure of a proper response, Marilyn didn't speak.

Neither did her mother.

The silence would be deadly. Something was up.

"Anything else?"

"No. Well, it's just that we wanted to plan your visit. We can celebrate your birthday when you're here for the engagement party."

Marilyn nearly choked. How long did they think she'd be staying? The plan never included an extended stay so they could find creative ways to torture her. Heck, no!

"Mom. There's enough to do with the engagement party. And I'm only staying one day. I'll need to get back for work."

Grace sighed. "You haven't been home in so long."

Marilyn's stomach tightened. "I'm aware of that."

"And we were hoping to spend some time with your friend. We only want to be sure you're OK. What does your boyfriend do for a living?"

"Mom…" Marilyn looked up as Bo entered the gym, mouthing the word 'sorry' with a grimace. She waved him in, ignoring the way his casual attire made her heart flutter. His legs were just legs, after all. Big, powerful legs. And his arms… Marilyn swallowed and turned her attention back to the conversation.

Bo moved beside her, tipping his head in question toward her phone. She covered the speaker and whispered. "My mom."

The bodyguard winked, nodding in understanding.

"Marilyn."

"I need to practice, Mom. I'll call you later." She couldn't focus with Bo practically breathing down her neck, his cologne threatening to make her forget dancing altogether so they could go out for a night on the town.

Better stop those thoughts before they go any further.

Marilyn elbowed him, making him chuckle and move away, hands up in surrender.

"A name. I'll let it rest if I get a name. And profession. A job is very important. He needs to be stable, after all, especially if you continue pursuing dance."

Marilyn stuck out her leg and resumed stretching. No point wasting too much energy on this repeat performance.

"I realize a job is important. I probably understand that better than anyone in this whole world."

A set of weights crashed loudly, and Marilyn jumped with a loud shriek, spinning to find Bo grinning sheepishly.

"Oh, man. I'm so sorry." His voice sounded so sincere her heart melted as she looked at him trying to explain. "I tried to move this so we could…"

"Marilyn!" Grace snapped her daughter back to their conversation. "What's that noise? Where are you? Is it safe?"

"Of course, it's safe. Bo just moved a weight bench… Mom, I really need to go."

"Wait a second. I heard a man's voice. Who's Bo? Is that his real name? Is he your dance partner? Or your boyfriend?"

"Yes, both." Ugh, how did she admit that so fast? Marilyn lifted her eyes to heaven. "Bo is his real name and he's Daisy's assistant."

"Well, that's probably a good job. Isn't it? I imagine they pay well."

"It is a good job. And we haven't been dating long enough for me to ask what he makes."

Bo approached her, carrying two monstrous weights, one in each hand.

"You can tell her that my real name is actually Bennett Oliver, Twinkle Toes. And yes, the Grants pay me very well for my work."

Marilyn's heart skidded. She didn't want to know his real name because that would only make it harder to pretend he meant nothing to her.

To be fair, she probably lost that battle already.

Bo winked. "And I'm looking forward to meeting your mom."

"Oh, he sounds lovely, Marilyn. Put him on the phone." Grace's voice lifted, likely both in interest and curiosity.

Marilyn was done.

"I'm going now, Mom. I'll call you later."

She hung up the phone and turned to him, hands on hips.

"Is your name really Bennett Oliver?"

Bo set the weights down and rose to his full height. He shrugged easily. "Yeah. My younger sister and brothers started calling me Bo and it stuck. I don't mind."

Oh, goodness. Why did he have to be so adorable?

She studied him for a long moment. "All right, Bennett Oliver, pretend boyfriend, and mysterious dancing partner, let's get to work."

**

As he danced with Marilyn, repeating their routine for the fifth time, Bo struggled with why he did such a stupid thing as insert himself into her family business. He had no clue about handling his own family. Why would he think he knew what to do about hers?

They were on a fast-track to disaster with this ill-prepared scheme. Lying from a distance was one thing, but how would he fake being a boyfriend when he'd only been one in real life once, years ago in a place he could only remember in whispers and humiliation? And with the way that ended, Bo could scarcely call it a success.

To convince his family, he only really needed to show up with Marilyn at his side. Even without any outward appearances of a relationship, the family would be so thrilled he put himself in the regular presence of a woman, they wouldn't question a thing. The trouble was, he couldn't be sure her family would be so easily fooled.

And if things went further, even for the sake of pretending— whether it be hand-holding, or even an innocent smooch on the cheek—Bo worried he'd become over-invested, falling into an emotional pit that would likely ruin him.

And what of Marilyn?

"Break." The dancer waited as he set her back on her feet before turning to look up at him with those gooey doe-eyes that made his heart flop.

"So, what did Daisy and Robby say about this?" She waved her hands between them.

Bo tried to keep up, still half-focused on his own worries. "This?"

"This!" she exclaimed. "Us dancing. Are they teasing you? I can only assume you told them."

"You assumed wrong." He turned away as he went to the punching bag and hit it a few times. "I didn't tell them. I don't say much about myself and didn't think it anyone's business but ours. We're only dancing."

He turned back to her, disappointed when her expression faltered. "No, I mean, right. That's all. Just dancing. But… where do they think you are? It looked like everyone was home. They could come out here and…"

Bo turned back to the bag and gave it a firm punch, eager to work out his frustration in some physical way. "They won't. They're all in the game room watching movies. I told them I was busy."

She snorted. "Busy? And that's all it took?"

"Yeah." He stood to his full height, his feet apart. "Did you want me to say something different? I figured we kind of need to be careful with the weekend coming up and everything. I mean, that we need to be on the same page about it."

"Oh." Marilyn squinted at him. "No, right. Of course." She paused. "You don't need to come to the audition."

"I realize that." He punched the bag again. "You don't want me to?"

"I didn't say that."

He stopped punching the bag and approached her, that ever-present female fear making his stomach clench. "So, what are you saying? I'll be honest. Sometimes I'm not very adept at communicating clearly so it will help if you tell me where you are with this."

Marilyn looked away. "I… don't know. No one ever wants to come to an audition and sit there waiting."

"I'm not everyone." He playfully nudged her. "Just figured you might want moral support. I'll take you for ice cream after. Ice cream is good luck."

Marilyn laughed. "Not if you're lactose intolerant."

Bo would do something so stupid. "Are you?" His voice faltered.

She didn't suppress a giggle. "No."

Bo groaned. "You're never going to stop being difficult, are you?"

She grabbed his hand and twirled herself away from him and back again. "It's highly unlikely."

Bo's entire body tingled at their nearness, at the ease with which she toyed with him. He cleared his throat, reminded of another beautiful woman who'd once done the same thing, and how long it took him to recover.

"I figured as much." He let go of her. Being serious and touching her at the same time were simply too rough on his warring mind and heart. Reason and emotion would battle for who knew how long in this whole thing.

Keep it professional. As if they were business partners. Otherwise, he might start obsessing over how good it felt to hold her while they danced.

Reason told him to stop being stupid.

Emotion told him this woman might change his life.

Bo pulled himself back together. "All right. A few more passes over this thing and you better believe you're ready." He leaned down to look into her eyes. "Because, tiny dancer, you are so ready."

They were nearly nose to nose.

Marilyn's lips parted but she didn't speak as a look of doubt passed over her features, darkening them in a way that made Bo want to pull her close and hold her until she believed. He squeezed her arms.

"You're ready. This is simply the cherries on top."

She nodded stupidly.

Bo forced a smile, and they started the routine again, as he tried to convince himself he could do this and get them both out unscathed.

Chapter six

Bo finished his last lap, his attention caught on Jazz who flopped next to the pool in a lounge chair.

"Hey." He didn't hesitate to lift himself from the pool and grab a towel to wipe his eyes clear. "What's up?"

Jazz propped his feet on a nearby chair. "Got some changes to the schedule I figured we better go over. I updated the calendar and sent it to you but wanted to make sure you saw."

Bo rubbed the towel over his dripping hair. "I'll take a look when I change." He glanced toward the house. "We're good today, right? Daisy put Nicolette down for a nap and Titus is in the studio with her and Robby?"

Jazz nodded. "All present and accounted for. Alice should be home in an hour or so. Fernsby got dinner going. Smells good."

"Pot roast?" Bo asked, grinning.

Jazz pointed at his nose, indicating that Bo guessed perfectly. "Yeah. So, we moved the dance lesson from Wednesday to Tuesday because they got an interview they can't miss Wednesday."

Bo sat up straighter. "Did you clear that with Marilyn?" He didn't mention that Tuesday was her audition.

"Daisy text her. So, if there's any change we'll hear shortly."

Jazz narrowed his eyes at the younger man. "You were out here with her last night."

"Yeah." Bo didn't look at him but saw no reason to elaborate beyond his confirmation.

"It looked like you two were dancing. And you weren't half bad." Jazz chuckled. "Who knew you could move those boats to the music?"

Bo glanced down at his huge feet before turning his attention to Jazz. "You didn't say anything, did you? I mean, to Daisy or Robby."

"No." Jazz leaned back in his chair. "Why?"

"Well, I don't want to lose my job because they think I'm hitting on another employee."

Jazz jerked his thumb over his shoulder toward the house. "You think Mr. and Mrs. Romance themselves would fire you for dancing and flirting?"

"I'm not flirting… I'm… helping her."

Jazz grinned. "They already figure something's up." He paused. "You sure looked like you were helping her with that dopey grin."

"I did not… How long did you watch us?" Bo's cheeks warmed. He beamed so much when they were dancing, he probably looked every bit the enamored schoolboy.

He groaned to himself. Even if Robby and Daisy never got wind of his interludes with Marilyn, Jazz would tease him mercilessly.

"Long enough." Jazz glanced over his shoulder before turning his attention back to Bo. "They only ever encouraged me and Sadie, and now since we can't get our crap together, they stay out of the way. I guess that's probably best."

He exhaled as he stood and came to Bo.

"Point is, I don't think they care." He nudged Bo. "You into her?"

Against his better judgment, Bo finally spoke the words out loud. "Maybe. I mean, I... I'm not sure how I feel. I don't want to mess with her head right before this audition. It's too important to her." He paused. "Besides, if she gets the role, she might quit here, and I wouldn't need to worry."

Jazz put his hands in the air as if freeing himself from any responsibility in the conversation. "Whatever," he muttered. "But if you want the advice of someone who's watched at least a few successful couples make it to the altar, I'd say you're better off not waiting around to tell her how you feel. Otherwise, a million things get in the way and you never get around to it. Then it's gone before you can even have fun."

Bo nodded, his mouth suddenly dry.

"Then again," Jazz chuckled. "I still can't convince Sadie I'm worth the gamble, so I might be way off."

Bo watched as he went into the house before grabbing the towel from around his neck so he could finish drying off.

Daisy might be the sweetest person on the planet. While she probably did worry about losing Bo because they got along so well, he couldn't imagine she would fire him over having a relationship with Marilyn. Even if it did go sour, they could theoretically avoid each other most of the time. But that could put Daisy and Robby in an awkward position.

And what if the relationship went well? How would they really move forward to any kind of long term anything?

The whole thing made Bo's head swim.

This was why he didn't date. It all got so dang messy.

Too messy for a straight-shooter like him.

**

Marilyn wrapped up her shift at the restaurant and went straight home, not surprised to find her phone buzzing relentlessly when she turned it back on.

"I'm going to my study group, so I'll be late." Sonya paused at the door as if this should mean something to Marilyn. She aimed for an expression that revealed minor interest in her roommate's life.

"OK. Um, have fun."

"Fun. As if advanced cellular biology is fun." The med student shook her head and disappeared before Marilyn could respond.

She looked down at her phone and quickly told Daisy that she could change the next lesson to Tuesday afternoon, and then noted Bo had text her too.

Don't forget. You're ready, TT.

She smiled, encouraged by the cheerleader she never asked for.

Thanks, Muscles. It means a lot you're in my corner.

She moved on to the voicemail icon blinking to indicate her sister called and left a message too. Marilyn nearly groaned. She avoided her siblings at all cost. Her parents deserved her respect, but her siblings distanced themselves from her—especially when she declared she would be a success in New York City with or without them.

So far, her success hadn't been found at all and she managed that completely on her own.

Rock on.

"Hi Marilyn, it's Rosemary. Mom said she told you about my engagement, but I felt it would be wise of me to also call personally. I put you down for a 'plus-one' since Mom mentioned you started dating someone. I'll look forward to seeing you at the party."

No 'love you' or even a good-bye. Rosemary was too practical for emotion. For a brief second, Marilyn wondered how she snagged a boyfriend let alone a fiancé.

She deleted the voicemail with no intention of calling her sister back. What would be the point?

Seconds later her phone buzzed again as she flopped on the bed.

"What?" she nearly screamed as she opened the text.

Titus: *My girls need practice. Meet you at the gym? Robby said it's fine. OK, Daisy did. 8?*

Marilyn quickly text him back and hopped off her bed to change clothes.

Her phone dinged again with another text from Titus.

Just make sure you tell your boyfriend to back off. I'm not looking to get my face bashed in.

Marilyn didn't respond. Let both those goofy men stew over each other.

**

Bo finished cleaning the dinner dishes and tried to ignore the force pulling him toward the gym.

Marilyn and Titus were in there with five women Bo assumed were the back-up singers. Every so often he caught a loud piece of music or raucous laughter that made him go back to the window, curious.

He could make up an excuse to slip in for a few minutes and it wouldn't be suspect. After all, he did live here and largely took care of the building and everything inside, leaving Jazz to manage the overall scheduling of the security team.

And he did want to see Marilyn again, if only to wish her luck on her audition the next morning.

But he couldn't make his feet move. Not because he was scared what she would think, but because he couldn't imagine having witnesses to any of their conversations.

"Hey." Robby bumped hard into Bo's shoulder, trying to bait him into a response the bodyguard would never give.

Bo turned and leaned against the counter. "What's up?"

The singer reached into the refrigerator and yanked out two iced teas. "Can you make sure that leather-wearing idiot is out of my gym before ten? Alice needs to get to bed and if they wake up Nicolette after we put her down, so help me…" He set the drinks on the counter and pounded a fist into his opposite hand.

"Understood?"

Bo grimaced. For all Robby's bravado, the bodyguard couldn't imagine him actually hitting anyone outside of his brother, Warren. "Yeah. Sure."

Robby started toward the door. "Oh, and Dais said she needs to talk to you about dresses or something. Whatever- that garbage all runs together."

Bo pushed away from the counter. "Now, or…?"

Robby rolled his eyes to heaven. "No, idiot. Not now. We're going to watch a movie and we'd like to be alone. Talk to her tomorrow when you take Alice to school. Speaking of which, good job on that Shakespeare test. She'd be screwed if I had to help with that stuff."

Bo chuckled as Robby left the room.

And then he hustled to the mirror, raked his fingers through his hair, and made his way over the gym, prepared to deliver his message.

**

"This looks fantastic!" Titus hugged Marilyn with one arm, his pleasure clear as he did the same with all his singers.

"I'm glad you're happy." Marilyn turned off the music. "We should, uh, probably get moving." They'd been at it for over an hour and she didn't want to overstay her welcome.

Titus snickered, running one hand over his tousled hair. "No worries. We can roll. Thanks for doing this so spur of the moment." Titus grabbed his guitar and started for the door after his singers, all of whom shouted good-byes and thank-you over their shoulders.

"You're amazing, Mar." He gave her another hug, grimacing when he backed up and saw Bo heading his way.

Titus's hands shot straight up into the air. "I swear she made me hug her, man. I didn't even want to come over!"

Bo rolled his eyes but said nothing as Titus continued in his laughter as he hustled by him, grabbing one of his back-up singers and twirling her around and around until she squealed.

Marilyn hefted her bag onto her shoulder before looking at Bo. "It's all locked up."

He stuffed his hands into his pockets. "Robby asked me to come over and make sure you guys were out of here by ten."

The professional bodyguard might be huge, but his slouched shoulders and his inability to hold her gaze made Marilyn wonder whether he ever talked to women before. She wished she could tell him she didn't intend to bite him.

"Right. Well, I guess I better go."

"Yeah." Bo stepped out of her way.

Reluctantly, Marilyn started to pass, stopping when he spoke.

"You ready for tomorrow?"

She stifled her amusement as she turned back to him, encouraged he made an effort at talking to her. "Ready as I can be."

Bo lowered his head, shifting his weight from one foot to the other. "Good."

He reminded Marilyn of a schoolboy afraid of his first crush. Her heart fluttered in compassion and a bit of worry. She didn't want that kind of power over anyone.

And yet, the sweet innocence of his shuffling feet gave her a glimpse of hope. Marilyn never considered herself special, but the way Bo acted in her presence made her feel incredible. She didn't want to like it, but she couldn't help herself.

"Do you think they'd mind if we gave it one last go?" she whispered. "Or are you busy right now?"

He raised his head, mouth lifting in a half-smile. "Nah."

Before she could think about what they were doing, Bo grabbed her hand and opened the door to the gym.

**

Bo offered to drop Alice off at school because he'd only have a ten-minute drive after that to make it to Marilyn's audition. He didn't tell Daisy where he'd be, only that he had an errand to run. To his delight, she didn't ask any questions.

Since Jazz and Robby would be gone for the morning, Bo had no choice but to stoop to the level of asking Mrs. Fernsby to be available should Daisy need anything in his absence. To his surprise the curmudgeon readily agreed- probably because getting Bo out of her kitchen was of utmost importance—especially when she made her famous cinnamon rolls which he tended to scarf down as quickly as they came out of the oven.

Once he parked the car, Bo found the building easily and made his way to the correct floor, following Marilyn's directions closely. He nudged the door, pausing when every woman in the place turned and stared at him.

A light giggle caught his ear. "Hey, Muscles, over here."

Relief filled Bo's chest, warming him at the sight of the dancer stretching as she prepared for her audition. "Hey." He nudged her, leaning close to whisper, "How are you doing?"

Marilyn nudged him back as she continued her routine. "Normal. Like I want to throw up."

Bo took her hand and squeezed as he looked into her eyes. "You are meant for this."

She inhaled sharply, her hand squeezing his in return. "Why do you say this kind of stuff?" She stole her hand back and resumed stretching on the floor in front of him.

He shrugged as he watched her. "Because it's true."

But she only snorted. "Well, your vast experience in dance doesn't make me confident because I'm still nervous." She paused. "And you don't need to lay it on so thick—you're only a pretend boyfriend and there aren't even family witnesses."

Bo didn't flinch at her sass, figuring her nerves were getting the best of her. He understood that well enough as he watched Daisy and Robby prepare to go on stage for the last tour. For as wonderful and easygoing as the couple could be, pre-show jitters often made them difficult to bear.

He glanced around, grateful that the rest of the dancers had gone back to stretching. "How much time do you have?"

Marilyn stopped stretching as she glanced at the clock. "Probably ten minutes. Why?"

Bo didn't need to hear anything else. He stood, grabbed her arm, and tugged her out into the hallway. "Punch me. Get it out so you can go in there and nail it."

She looked at him, eyebrows knitting together as she considered it. "Punch you? Like I did the bag? Seriously, I'm not doing that."

He grinned. "Sure you are." He held up his bicep and flexed. "You think you…" he let his eyes roam over her and dismissed her with a shake of his head. "You think that you, with that piddly little dancer's body, can hurt this?"

Marilyn's eyes narrowed at the challenge. "You're pushing me."

Bo chuckled as he leaned toward her, arm still flexed. "That's the point, Twinkles. Come on."

"All right." Her eyes met his. "You're sure?"

While Bo appreciated her concern, he couldn't fathom how the one-hundred-pound woman would bring him any physical pain. He nodded, flexing again. "Go for it."

Marilyn hauled back as he taught her and punched him with everything she had. Bo beamed at her. "That's it. Again, Twinkles."

She followed his instruction, this time with increased power and thrust.

Bo put his hands on her shoulders. "Atta girl. You got this. Come on." He nudged her back into the room, satisfied that when this ended, she'd get the part and he could say all he'd been stuffing down deep, waiting for the moment when it wouldn't matter what his feelings for her might be.

**

Marilyn noticed the ice cream dribbling down her arm, but she'd gotten herself too wound up to bother wiping it.

"I haven't felt this good about an audition in forever."

Bo reached over and caught the drip for her, tossing the napkin in a nearby trash can. He grinned as he swiped at his own cone.

"I'm so proud of you. Seriously. It takes guts to go out there and do something like that."

She held his gaze as she reached over to grab his arm and squeeze it, wishing she could somehow explain the good he'd done for her in simply being there to support her. Marilyn couldn't remember the last time anyone stood with her that way.

"Thanks for coming today. And for the ice cream." She licked at her cone as he did the same.

For a long moment they watched the traffic pass in front of them as they ate.

"So, do you have any idea why your parents would think you should go to college instead of going after your dance career? I mean, even I can tell you were made for that."

Marilyn licked at her cone again. "Who says I'm made for it? Maybe I'm terrible and painfully slow on the uptake."

"That's not true. And I swear I'm going to throw you over my shoulder and punish you if you keep saying it." Bo poked her before going back to his cone.

Marilyn sighed, grateful he cared but hating to admit the truth to anyone. But as a friend, he could bear it. She made it clear enough, and so had he, that they wouldn't be much beyond friends, so even if she could imagine herself falling into his arms for more than a hold in their routine, she wouldn't push for something that perhaps wasn't meant to be.

"Come on…" he nudged her again.

As she licked her cone, Marilyn decided to go for broke. "My mom is a brain surgeon, my dad is a lawyer. My brother is a lawyer, and his twin sister owns her own design business and shop. And sweet Rosemary is involved in some kind of scholarly technological development to stop human trafficking that means she's actually up for the Nobel Peace prize."

She finally summoned the courage to look up at Bo. "Any other questions?"

He whistled. "That's gotta be hugely intimidating." His forehead wrinkled as he pondered this information while at the same time finishing off his ice cream. He wiped his hands on a napkin and tossed it aside.

"OK so your parents expect you to follow in the footsteps of being academic. But that's not you…" He shook his head. "And before you get defensive, I don't mean because you aren't smart- you are."

Marilyn laughed. "Boy you must know some women if you think that would bug me." She leaned close and whispered. "I'm not offended, so you can keep going."

"Good- just proves my point you do have a brain up there- even if you did date Zeke." He tapped her head, making Marilyn tingle and chuckle all at once as he continued.

"I mean, surely they've watched you dance. They'd have to admit you're amazing."

"You keep using that word." She made a face. "They only agreed to accept my decision to move to New York because they probably figured I'd fail. I mean, how many dancers actually make a career of it? Without waiting tables and having ten side-jobs, that is."

Bo tilted his head. "Not sure of the stats on that, but what does it matter? You're auditioning for the big time, but you seem like what you really want is the studio. Right?"

"No. I mean, right." Marilyn mulled this over as she finished her cone.

"So, why are you wasting your time with the auditions if that's not really what you want?"

She wondered this herself. But the answer always became abundantly clear when one of her siblings grabbed the spotlight, or her parents were recognized with yet another award, while Marilyn celebrated the mundane. Paying off her car or having enough in her account to get an extra sack of her favorite cookies were achievements her family would never understand.

"I'm auditioning because it's tangible. It's the only way they'll think I've made it." She stood and gestured to the marquis not far from them.

"If they can see my name on that sign, or on the show's program, that's the award. That's the closest I'll get to the same accolades they all get." She sank down beside him. "A studio is a daily grind. And just because I'd love it, they would think I settled or that it's all I can do. It wouldn't be enough."

Bo nodded but didn't say anything for a long time. Marilyn wondered if he struggled, trying to decide how pathetic she was on a scale of one to ten, or maybe how to get away from her without hurting her.

He stood and tucked his hands into his pockets.

"I should probably get back home before Daisy wonders what happened to me."

Marilyn stood. "Where did you say you went?"

He shrugged as they started walking. "I took Alice to school and said I had an errand to run. She's busy so as long as I'm back in the next hour or so it's fine. I'm always there. I imagine she's grateful for some time without me."

Marilyn appreciated his effort. "Well, thanks for coming. And for the ice cream."

"Sure. So, promise you'll call or text as soon as you hear something?"

She nodded. "You'll be the first one I tell." She watched him walk away and get into his car. He waved as he drove off, leaving Marilyn with her thoughts.

She spilled her guts so easily about her hang-ups with her family but learned nothing about him or his family.

As she started off toward her own car, Marilyn made a mental note to not let that happen again. Next time she saw Bennett Oliver Sutton, she intended to begin unravelling him.

**

Bo increased the weight by five pounds and raised his eyebrows at Daisy.

"Are you sure?"

She pursed her lips. "I need to get back to where I left off before Nicolette if we think we'll be back on tour in a year."

He smirked. "Fair enough." He gestured for her to start lifting on the machine he altered to suit her needs.

"You're doing great. We can start on some triceps work after this."

"Awesome." Daisy ground out the word, finishing the set with a final grunt. "You're awful. And mean, and…"

"Want me to fire him?" Robby entered the gym, carrying Nicolette in her baby seat, as well as her diaper bag.

"No." Daisy moved toward him to peer in at the baby, who slept peacefully with a blanket tucked in around her.

She lifted her eyes to her husband. "You did that?"

Robby puffed out his chest. "Course I did. She adores her father." He glanced at Bo. "And if either of you even think of waking her, I'm out—because that masterpiece took nearly an hour."

Bo put his hands up and stepped back to avoid any chance of waking the sleeping tiger. Robby leaned over his wife.

"I gotta go, Angel." His rough voice remained low, private, as he whispered something that made Daisy's cheeks go red.

Bo turned away and busied himself with setting the elastics to help Daisy work her tricep muscles next.

"Hey."

Robby rammed into him. "We're going on a date later and Jazz has plans so you're coming with."

Bo understood the drill. He'd drive them, keep the press back because surely their agent, Lily, tipped them off to where the couple would be and when, and then he'd sit stupidly alone at a table not far away and watch them and the surroundings to ensure their safety.

He nodded. "What time?"

"I'll be back around six." He kissed his wife again, likely as much for the show of making Bo uncomfortable as for the passion he felt for Daisy.

Robby winked as he raised to his full height and turned his attention back to the bodyguard. "Don't think I'm stupid about what's been going on over here every night either. But you could try taking her on an actual date and figure out if that doesn't suit her better than a few spins around the gym."

Bo's mouth fell open.

Robby left, which gave Bo no option but to pretend he hadn't finished rigging the elastics for Daisy. He deliberately kept his back to her as he spoke.

"Let's get this finished so I can pick up Alice from school in two hours."

When she didn't respond, Bo reluctantly turned around. He jerked his head in his own direction and turned back around. "Come on, Daisy, before the baby wakes up."

"I'm not moving one centimeter until you tell me what Robby meant."

Bo gulped. He could do this.

"I helped Marilyn get ready for her audition today. She needed a male lead and Titus is terrible, so I said I'd…"

But he never finished his sentence because Daisy cracked up until tears fell down her cheeks. "You were dancing?" she gasped as she swiped at her face. "I will suffer with flabby arms. I need to hear this story."

Bo flopped onto the bench nearby. "There's not a story. Get over here. She needed help. I help people. That's all. Come on."

Daisy moved slowly toward him, clearly with intentions of satisfying her curiosity, not of exercising any further.

"Bo…"

Exasperated, the bodyguard raised his eyes to the ceiling. "What, Daisy?"

"I want more than you're telling me. Please?"

Bo frowned. "I thought we agreed I get a private life." He cringed at the way this came out. "Not that I have anything to hide. I swear. That's it. Just dancing and me being a nice guy."

Daisy couldn't be fooled. "You're allowed to be interested in her. She's a beautiful, talented woman."

Bo ignored that he agreed wholeheartedly with her assessment, completing the sentence for her instead. "Who gets on my nerves."

Daisy laughed. "You protest too much."

He shrugged and set her up with the equipment. "Five reps."

She growled but did as instructed.

"Keep your arms closer against your body so you feel that here." He touched the back of her upper arms. "That way you get the nice cut. Like this." He showed her his arm.

"I don't want to look like a bodybuilder."

Bo resumed his position spotting her. "You won't look like a bodybuilder," he muttered.

"Five." Daisy handed the elastics back to Bo. "Do you think Marilyn is pretty?"

Bo handed the elastics back to her. "Five more."

Daisy groaned as she started again. "Do you think she's pretty?"

"Does it matter what I think?"

Now his boss glared at him. "Stop answering my questions with questions. I want to slug you when you do that."

Bo bit his lip. "Why would you want to slug me? I'm doing my job." He nudged her. "Arms in tight, there, noodles."

Daisy growled at him again but did as he instructed.

"It matters what you think if you want to date her. And I think you do." She paused. "She's gorgeous. And smart and so talented."

Bo didn't acknowledge her words, feigning interest in her form instead. "Good. Now give me a few more reps."

Daisy finished three reps. "You haven't been on a date since you moved in here."

"That you know of." Bo took the elastics and set them aside. "Let's work on your core. Are you up for it?"

"So, you have been on dates? Or you are dating someone?"

"Maybe you can read my autobiography and we'll talk about it later."

Daisy whacked his arm. "I am not moving until you answer my questions!"

Bo put his finger to his lips when Nicolette began to stir. "You're going to wake the baby. And I am not about to deal with that right now."

Daisy rolled her eyes. "Question one- do you think she's pretty?"

Bo exhaled. "Yes. Of course, she is. I'm not blind."

Daisy smirked. "Question two- are you dating anyone?"

"No." Bo raised to his full height and rolled his shoulders back. "I'm done with this game."

But of course, Daisy wasn't finished at all. "Question three- why are you being so stinking difficult?"

Bo lifted his eyebrows. "Because my opinion of Marilyn Darby is that we're friends and I'm glad I could help her. That's the story. That's the whole story. And that is the end of the story."

Daisy grunted. "I want you to trust me."

Bo patted her shoulder. "I do trust you. But trust me, Daisy. I'm here to work for you and do an exceptional job. And I think I'm doing that. Don't worry about me. I got my crappy, barren personal life under control."

Daisy laughed. "Sure, sounds like it. Hey- maybe Robby and I can go on a double date with you and Marilyn sometime."

"How did we go from working out to this?"

Bo urged her to the next machine. He wished he could pummel Robby for bringing this up in front of his wife.

But the bodyguard wouldn't say anything. Because now, no matter what he said, Daisy would believe he only wanted to date the dance instructor.

Marilyn told him she'd hear about the call back within twenty-four hours.

Bo prayed that time would pass quickly so he could either fully decide to let his infatuation go or embark on the terror of his first date in two years.

Why did neither option sound tempting?

**

Marilyn stared at the wall as minutes ticked by. The call should have come in by now telling her she got the role. They'd sworn she'd hear by three o'clock. It was well past five already.

She shouldn't be surprised. She should be used to this.

But rejection stung every time, and the same questions arose again as she accepted gaining no ground toward her goals. What did she do wrong? Was she too short, too tall, too thin? Did she have curly hair when they wanted straight?

Even if she knew, it wouldn't change anything. Marilyn lost another role, probably for something out of her direct control. When would luck find her?

Her phone buzzed, but she didn't give it a glance.

It buzzed again even as she wondered what to do now. Could she honestly walk away from all she swore she wanted? Her earlier resolve faltered as badly as a teenager in her first pair of heels.

Marilyn had always been steady, strong, confident. Lately she wondered where those attributes were hiding because she only seemed afraid and off-balance.

Her phone buzzed again.

Reluctantly she lowered her eyes to find a message from Bo.

Any word yet, TT? Daisy and Robby left for the day so I'm free. Can we meet?

Despite her disappointment, Marilyn's heart fluttered with hope. Did he want a date?

Her phone buzzed again.

Not like a date. I only want to hear your news. Hope I didn't freak you out

Well that answers that.

Marilyn opened her reply, stewing for several minutes before she typed

I can meet in an hour at the park by Scooters

Bo didn't hesitate to respond.

See you soon

Marilyn closed her eyes, mulling over how to tell her new friend what happened, that she failed. Again. She didn't want to imagine his disappointment. He'd realize how dumb he'd been to bet on a loser.

And then Marilyn considered how to tell her parents that when she came home for her birthday, she'd need a place to stay until she got accepted into college.

Chapter seven

Bo sat on a bench near the entrance to the park, his eyes roving over the people in an effort to spot Marilyn before she spotted him. He teased out at least ten different scenarios and how to respond to each.

Maybe he'd guess what happened as soon as he saw her. But more likely she'd make him work for it. So far, that appeared to be where she shined best, never giving him a thing until she wanted him to have it. For whatever reason, Bo enjoyed that chase tremendously.

"Hey!" Marilyn's exclamation from the opposite direction shocked him so he jumped and turned toward her.

"Yeesh," he muttered. "I was looking that way."

She sank onto the bench beside him, bringing a teasing, light breath of her perfume with her. "Yeah. But that way." She pointed. "Is where my apartment is, so…"

Bo nodded, wondering if he should remove his arm from the back of the bench or if that would call attention to the fact that it currently rested around her.

He didn't move. Might as well enjoy their closeness.

"So?" he asked. "Am I looking at the lead dancer in One Time With the Fox?"

Marilyn offered a weak effort at a smile. "Nope." Her voice cracked, making her upset clear. "I guess not. My phone hasn't rung all day." She scooted back so her feet lifted just above the ground where she began swinging them back and forth, her eyes glued to them, probably so she wouldn't be forced to look at him.

Maybe she still needed to absorb the disappointment. To his surprise, Bo needed a moment as well. She'd been amazing. Not that he knew a thing about dancing, but he couldn't fathom that there might be anyone more deserving of the role than Marilyn.

He exhaled, deciding not to push her to say anything beyond what she wanted to share. He used the arm around her shoulders to press her closer, an effort to bring comfort and share her disappointment. "I'm sorry."

To Bo's surprise, she turned her head into him and sniffed, the tears wetting his shirt. "I wish I could explain why this one is so much worse than the rest." She sat up and looked away, creating an obvious distance between them.

Bo missed her warmth. He put one hand on her shoulder. "I'm sorry," he stupidly repeated.

She shrugged. "I guess this is worse because I swore if I didn't get it that this would be it."

The defeat in her tone hit Bo square in the chest. He met her eyes. "It?"

"Yeah." Marilyn looked away. "I'll still go to the wedding with you but that will probably be my last hoorah." She paused. "You don't need to go to the stupid engagement party. Between now and when I head home, I'll pick a stupid college and make my parents happy for a change."

Bo couldn't suppress his grin, grateful to find her spunk returning. "That's a lot of stupidity."

She picked at a spot on her pants, still careful to avoid his gaze. "Yeah, well…"

"Marilyn." Bo squeezed her shoulder again. "Why would you make such a life-changing decision based on one instance of not getting a part? Especially when there are a million parts out there for you to audition for? Maybe ones you'd be better-suited to getting?"

While he couldn't be sure whether his efforts would help or not, Bo determined to try his best to make her see reality. Just because this audition didn't pan out didn't seem to be a reason for her to give up entirely. He'd been kicked around enough times in life to know that you keep going because eventually that hard work will be rewarded.

He'd never have gotten to his perfect job with Daisy and Robby if he gave up after a few knocks.

But Marilyn wasn't on the same page yet. She threw her hands into the air. "It's a thousand instances of not getting the part. I think the universe made itself clear. I'm not meant to dance. I get it now, that's all." She slumped back on the bench, shoulders sagging, defeated.

Bo refused to let her wallow.

"Doesn't sound to me like you get anything."

"What?" She jumped away from him and pointed her finger in his direction. "Like you understand anything about what I'm dealing with."

Bo snorted. "I know exactly what you're dealing with on multiple levels. My family thinks I work for the government as a spy or something. And I let them think it and don't go to any family functions because that's easier than listening to my father gripe about how a man should get a stable job and a wife and ten kids."

He looked away, hating how he sounded, hating that Marilyn now realized some of the truth of his pathetic life. He leaned forward, resting his elbows on his knees as he held his palms together and looked at the ground in front of his feet.

"When Joe Sutton finds out I'm working—happily—as a personal assistant and 'manny', he'll flip his lid that I'm doing what he'll think is a 'woman's' job. He'll think I've humiliated myself, thumbed my nose at the size God made me, and the stability I should have sought out by staying in the Army. He's still bitter I didn't sign on as a 'lifer' even if I was honorably discharged after serving my time."

Marilyn's jaw dropped and she scooted closer, leaning her head into his shoulder. She fit perfectly against him, her warmth bringing deep comfort.

"You realize that's probably the first personal thing you've told me since we met?"

Bo knew it full well and hated that he dumped so much word vomit at once. He supposed that's what happened after stuffing it all inside for years.

But Marilyn refused to let this golden nugget go. She squeezed his arm.

"Why don't you tell them the truth?" She made it sound so reasonable, Bo wondered how he could not follow through. But this wasn't about him right now even if he unintentionally hijacked the conversation.

"Why don't you?" He glanced in her direction. "Own who you are, Marilyn."

She snorted. "OK, pot."

Bo winked. "After you then, kettle. At least I admit what I need to do. I don't think I've heard you say it yet."

"I don't want to disappoint them. That's all I do."

Bo couldn't help but laugh. "Same reason I'm sitting here owning it and doing nothing to change it." He paused. "I get you, Twinkles."

They sat in amicable silence until Marilyn nudged him with her elbow. "Well, we're a pair, aren't we?"

Bo frowned. "Looks that way."

They watched people walking by, lost in their own sorrows as they absorbed the tranquil park. Bo couldn't imagine what he'd say to encourage her, so he hoped his presence would be enough.

She finally nudged him again. "Thanks for being here."

He grinned. "No problem. Glad I can be."

She held his gaze for a brief second before looking down at her hands. "I was thinking…"

Bo waited for her to continue, fearing she would back out of their weekend together, steeling himself for exactly that.

"I like you, hanging out with you. I'll miss dancing together."

Bo wasn't sure where this would go. Maybe it didn't sound like she meant to back out. "I like hanging out with you too," he said carefully. "I don't mind if you need a dancing partner sometime."

Marilyn exhaled. "That's actually what I meant. Sort of."

Bo forced his knee to stop bouncing, his nerves going crazy all through his body. "Yeah?" he asked, hoping she'd spit it out before he exploded.

"What would you think... I mean about us... going out on a date? I mean, before the wedding stuff. Who knows? Maybe we wouldn't need to do so much pretending if we already... I don't know. Like each other."

Bo watched as she bit her lip, averting her eyes. "If this is super weird or you're not interested, forget I asked."

He so badly wanted to say yes, but that scared him silly. The last time—the only time, really—he dated someone she asked him first and it turned into a pathetic joke. Would this be the same? Whether Marilyn admitted it or not, Titus definitely appeared to be interested in her, and Bo still wondered—almost daily—what went on between her and Zeke.

Maybe he should ask. Or maybe he should keep his mouth shut and play along to get through the wedding. He could guard his heart that long.

Besides, she'd just been rejected. How could he say no? A nice guy didn't say no. Bo prided himself on being a nice guy.

His cell phone buzzed.

Bo held up one finger and reached into his pocket. "I'm sorry..." He glanced at his phone and saw a text from Daisy

We're back early. If you can babysit tonight, Robby and I are going out.

Right.

That's how he could say no.

**

Marilyn felt as if she might explode.

She was so incredibly stupid for asking Bo on a date. He'd be sure to refuse, and things would be weird between them. She didn't have many friends and she blew it with one she really wanted to keep.

Darn her spontaneous nature!

Bo shoved his phone into his pocket as he pushed to his feet. "Sorry. Looks like I'm babysitting tonight."

She drew a calming breath. "Look, it's stupid. Forget I asked."

Bo met her eyes. "I'm not sure I can. I'm too flattered you'd think of it."

Her pulse quickened. "Really?"

His amusement sparkled in his eyes. "Yeah. Of course, really. For goodness' sake, you're an amazing person!"

"But…?" Marilyn's voice trailed off and the whisper of hope she felt went with it.

Bo looked away for a moment.

"But if you're leaving, I don't get why we'd…" He turned back to her. "I'd need to talk to Daisy and Robby. Not for permission but because I wouldn't want this to interfere with the job. I can't lose it."

"Of course."

Bo held her gaze, but from the corner of her eye she caught his knee bouncing. "I considered asking you out but I wondered if it would be weird, I mean, because of everything. I never in a million years expected you to want to date me." He laughed. "So, I am flattered."

She nodded. "Me too. That you'd want to ask me—especially after we went so many rounds." She paused. "Still…" She raised her eyes to meet Bo's. "It might be wise for us to go out before the trip. When are we planning to leave?"

"Oh. Uh, it's only a few hours, so I figured we'd leave on Friday morning so we could get settled at the hotel, maybe visit with my family, then we'll do the wedding Saturday and Sunday morning go to church and head over to your family thing."

Bo rubbed his hand over his face. "Anyway, do you think it's a good idea?" He gestured between them. "It could get messy. I'll say you couldn't make it or something."

Marilyn tipped her head to the side. It could get messy but for some reason she didn't care. Or maybe she didn't want to worry about it. Bo felt like the first good thing in so long she couldn't imagine missing this chance. He didn't seem like Zeke or any of the other men who convinced her trusting another man would be foolish.

Still, she jumped in too quickly so many times before and been burned, what made her think this would be any different?

"How about we try one date? No one needs to know and if it looks like it could lead to a second date, we'll see if there's anything to figure out. In the meantime, I'll tell my parents that you might need to work. Maybe you do the same in case we decide we really do get on each other's nerves."

Bo chuckled. "OK, Twinkle Toes, but the longer I'm with you, the less you're making me crazy. For now, anyway."

On a whim, Marilyn leaned her head against his arm. "Feeling's mutual, Muscles." Her stomach flipped and she prayed she didn't just make a huge, painful mistake for both of them.

**

Jazz punched Bo as he entered the office.

Daisy's bodyguard didn't look up from his work, scheduling his boss for her next hair appointment and dress fitting before an event she and Robby would attend in a few weeks.

"What's up?" He confirmed his work before turning to the other man, wondering if they had something to do that he'd forgotten since Jazz rarely bothered him when he handled the business side of Daisy's life.

Jazz flopped into a plush chair across the room. "They want to start recording for the next album in a few months."

Bo lifted his eyebrows. "Really? That fast?" While Daisy mentioned they might be ready, he hadn't believed her, given the baby and that they'd just come off a tour a short time ago.

"Yeah, it surprised me too. You haven't been through all of that- the schedule changes a lot and they've never been through it together since they got married—it was already set when Daisy went last time. You'll probably need to reel her in on doing so much writing for everyone else."

Bo grinned. "Is this you or Robby talking?"

Jazz chuckled. "Both. Probably more reality than anything. He's going to need her constantly and there will be rehearsals and Lil and probably the band will be here all the time. Not sure if he's serious, but Robby mentioned hiring a nanny, like a real one for Nicolette and Alice, so you'd be available for running Daisy around and taking care of her."

While Bo understood, he didn't like it. He loved handling the kids and their schedules and figured as Nicolette got older it would only be even more fun for him because by then Alice would either be in college or off in her own career. And who knew? Maybe Daisy and Robby would have another baby. The couple never expected to have children at all and now enjoyed it so much Bo already heard talk of adding kids to the mix—either naturally or through adoption.

Bo opened the calendar on his computer. "So, do we want to schedule a time to talk over all this?"

"I don't think we're there yet, but I wanted it on your radar. Once Lily sets some things up and Robby and Daisy talk to the band, we'll probably get a better idea on timeline and if it's serious."

"Sure. Got it."

Jazz pushed to his feet. "Oh, and Robby and Warren want a guys' night. So, hope you didn't make any plans. The ladies will be at Warren's with the kids and we'll be here. I'll drop off, you pick up."

Bo's eyebrows met in the middle of his forehead as he mulled over this information.

"That's... different."

Jazz chuckled. "Used to do it all the time, but with the tour and baby and whatnot it fell off. Those brothers go at it, I break it up, they both come at me, yada yada."

Bo wondered what the men did on these 'guys nights'. Robby didn't drink and he and Warren seemed to alternately love and hate each other. Still, he didn't have any plans.

He shrugged. "Sounds like a good time."

Jazz winked and lifted himself to his feet. "It's a good time if you like smoking cigars, playing video games, and listening to Robby sing and Warren yell. But it's entertaining, I'll give it that."

He left and Bo sat back, thinking.

He grabbed his phone and text Marilyn before he lost his nerve again.

How's Saturday strike you for our date?

Within seconds she replied

I'll text you my address. Six o'clock?

You got it, twinkles.

**

Marilyn avoided three calls from her mom and two from her dad before she finally summoned the courage to all them back. Calling the house instead of one of their cell phones meant she stood a good chance of getting the maid or having to leave a message which would prolong the inevitable, but would also hurt less.

She opted for this approach.

Unfortunately, both of her parents were home and the maid put it on speaker for them as they ate dinner.

"So, tell us, Marilyn, did you get the role you were so excited about?"

"Sadly, no, mom. I'll be trying out for the circus next week."

Her father grunted. "That's not funny. The circus is a dying form of entertainment. They're getting sued all the time. Working conditions, the treatment of the animals. It's a sorry prospect. You'd be better off doing nearly anything else."

Thank goodness her parents had no sense of humor between the two of them. She made a mental note to buy them one to share when she had some extra funds.

"Yes, Dad. I figured as much."

Did she tell them now or save it for when she came to the engagement party? Marilyn couldn't make the words come.

"Your mother says you're dating someone. Will you tell us about him before bringing him home?"

Marilyn opened her mouth but never got a chance to speak because Grace butted in. "You mentioned he's an assistant. What does he make per year? Is there any chance of advancement?"

Marilyn didn't even try to keep up. Her parents would banter back and forth with the details for several minutes before she could even begin to get in a word.

She definitely couldn't quit on Daisy. Her stomach lurched as she shoved that thought aside. She loved the job and did consider trying to reach out to some facilities and services for the handicapped to find out if she might be of service to teach a class or two. Maybe at the YMCA or a club of some kind. When Daisy mentioned that she might have a whole new customer base others had yet to invest in, Marilyn couldn't ignore the idea had merit.

In that case, maybe she wouldn't even need a studio. She could take her show on the road and…

"Marilyn?" Her father's voice caught her attention. "Are you listening?"

"What? Oh, yeah. Sure, I'm listening."

"Your boyfriend's name is Bo? Is he French?"

Marilyn snorted. "No. He's from Alabama."

"Oh, heaven help us. You did say, Alabama?"

Marilyn winced. "Yes." Why did her voice squeak?

"His name isn't really Bo, that's a nickname his family gave him when his little sister- or maybe it was his brother— couldn't say his name."

Her father cleared his throat. "And what is his name?"

"Bennett Oliver Sutton." Marilyn paused. "But we only started…"

"Well, bring him along if you can. I realize how much of a bore we are to you. You deserve some kind of entertainment while you're visiting."

Marilyn hadn't even been on one date with the man yet and already her parents wanted to decide if he might be good enough to take care of their flaky daughter so they could cut their ties of responsibility.

"He probably has to work."

"I'm sure a personal assistant, even to a celebrity, gets days off, Marilyn. It really would mean the world to us if you'd take this seriously."

What did it matter? Even if there wasn't much time, Marilyn did have a few days to come up with some reason or way to avoid this trip.

So, she did what any good, wimpy daughter would do.

She agreed.

**

"Here." Robby shoved a cigar into Bo's hand and lit it for him. "You never smoked anything this good in your life."

Bo lifted his eyebrows. "Daisy's going to kill us for smoking in here." He inhaled anyway, savoring the richness of a cigar that probably cost as much as his weekly salary.

And he'd never complained about his salary.

Robby groaned. "Let me take care of my wife. Just enjoy the cigar."

"I will." Bo chuckled, wondering how he could be this fortunate. Even two years ago, he never would have imagined himself kicking back with a rock legend and his family, in the inner circle with Robby Grant.

And Bo could safely say he felt wanted right where he sat.

Warren flopped onto the couch next to him. "Ignore him. He likes to pick fights with her because he enjoys the making up so much."

"I do… not!" Robby dropped his elbow into Warren's arm as he hit the couch next to him.

Warren grunted and the brothers began their usual tussle. Bo puffed away, exchanging a glance with Jazz.

"Told you." Even with Warren's size and Robby's passion, the bodyguard easily separated the men.

"Enough."

Warren glowered for not getting to finish what his brother started, while Robby stuck his tongue out.

"Let's play Frogger." Warren whacked Bo on the arm and jerked his head toward the machines.

"You'll never knock me off the top spot." Robby puffed away on his cigar, one foot resting casually on the coffee table.

"That sounded like the perfect challenge. Let's go, Bo. Us against them."

For two hours the men went from one video game to the next until Bo's sides hurt from laughing. Despite all of Robby's cockiness and bravado, it occurred to Bo that the rocker appreciated home and family more than almost anyone else he knew.

That he brought Bo into his fold meant the world, and made him not miss his family so much.

Jazz's phone buzzed. "Pizza's here. I'll go grab it." He hustled toward the stairs to get the snacks the men ordered from the security guards manning their posts outside the mansion.

Robby headed behind the bar and came back with an armful of drinks. "You want anything?" He set the bottles across the coffee table. Bo reached for an iced tea as his phone buzzed in his pocket.

Robby cursed under his breath. "What's my wife need now? You'd think she could at least give you one night to yourself." Robby leaned over in an attempt to look at the phone.

Before Bo could shield the screen, the singer grinned.

"Twinkle Toes?"

"Leave the man alone, Rob." Warren grabbed a drink and kicked his feet up onto the table. "He's allowed a life outside of you and Daisy."

"If only he wanted one." Robby looked back at Bo. "So? Who's texting you about your date? And where and when did you manage to meet someone?"

He whacked Bo's arm. "Don't tell me- it's that single mom at drop-off. Not bad, bud. Not bad at all. She's cute."

Now Warren's eyebrows raised in interest. "Do tell."

"It's not the single mom from school drop-off." After the way he left things with Marilyn, Bo didn't think he ought to say anything to Daisy, and definitely not to Robby, about their date until he could figure whether it might go anywhere.

Robby snickered. "Let me give you some advice. Don't tell her you bake, garden, and change diapers for a living. She'll think that's weird and run the opposite direction."

Warren slugged his brother. "Or she'll want to marry you immediately. Not many men willing to admit they like those things and do them well."

Bo smirked. "I'm not ashamed of what I do. I love it."

"So, where are you taking twinkle toes on this date?"

Bo exhaled. "I'm open to suggestions. I haven't decided."

Warren tipped his root beer bottle in Bo's direction. "There's a place over off Sunset where they do dinner and a movie. It's fantastic. Daphne loves it—super romantic."

Robby scoffed before Bo could respond. He wasn't sure he wanted to go too romantic. After all, what kind of vibe would that send? Desperate? Needy?

"You can't talk during a movie. That's a terrible first date." The rock star sipped his iced tea. "Dinner definitely, maybe a romantic walk or take her somewhere you can look at stuff and talk about it—a museum, a zoo, a butterfly sanctuary."

Warren howled. "A butterfly sanctuary? My word, Rob, I think they kick guys out of the rock and roll hall of fame for that kind of talk."

The singer shrugged unapologetically. "What? Daisy loved it."

As the men howled over Robby's romantic streak, Jazz appeared with a stack of pizza boxes, plates, napkins and more. "I can hear you fools all the way upstairs."

Robby shrugged. "So? No baby to worry about."

Warren nudged Bo. "Our boy here has a date and we're giving him ideas where to take her."

Bo wished he could disappear into the couch cushions. Jazz set the pizzas and other goodies on the bar. As Robby and Warren dug in, the other bodyguard looked at Bo and grinned.

"You finally asked Marilyn out? Good for you, man!"

The whole room stopped then and all eyes turned on Bo, who wondered if there would be anywhere to run.

**

Marilyn finished her shift at the restaurant and trudged toward her car, grateful for the generous tips, but also aware she had to work on a routine and plan for her time with Daisy the next day.

Not to mention what she'd say if Bo poked his head into the gym during their lesson. The idea brought nervous excitement.

They hadn't discussed how they'd handle their interactions in front of Daisy, and even if she noticed Marilyn's interest in Bo, it seemed they entered a phase of a strange relationship that began with bickering and somewhere, quickly, moved into mutual admiration.

She still couldn't get over that he so easily and skillfully danced with her.

And now they were going on a date! Saturday couldn't come fast enough.

She text Bo during her brief break earlier in the evening and he'd not responded, but she didn't give it any mind. After all, he worked twenty-four-seven for two of the most famous people in the world. He likely didn't get much time to himself.

Marilyn finally got to her car and fussed and struggled with the door, considering whether she should hop in through the back—again—when it finally opened.

She really had to get the stupid thing fixed.

As she slipped behind the wheel and inserted the key in the ignition, Marilyn prayed for the conversation with her parents in a few weeks. She still couldn't get their last talk off her mind.

Would she go home and stay and keep her word? Would her parents expect her to? Going to college for four years still sounded about as enticing as never dancing again. But her parents stopped directly bringing up her promise months ago. Maybe they'd finally given up hope of ever having their daughter do something worthwhile and productive. Marilyn wondered how long she could keep at this without it coming up again.

She flicked her wrist to start her car, but nothing happened. With a deep, exasperated roll of her eyes she tried again.

Again, nothing.

Marilyn rested her head on her steering wheel, heaving an annoyed moan in the process.

She was ten minutes from her apartment. In New York, just outside the city. Walking was not an option.

Her roommate didn't have a car because they lived so close to her school she walked everywhere.

Marilyn glanced around the parking lot and to her chagrin noticed the last cook getting into his fiancee's vehicle. She tried to push open the driver's door but wasn't fast enough as the taillights glimmered as the couple drove off.

Her phone buzzed. Marilyn glanced at it and found a text from Bo.

I'm excited for our date too. I'll try to call you later.

Marilyn stared at the text. Could she call him? Should she?

Seeing no choice, Marilyn pushed the button, squeezing her eyes closed and hating herself the entire time as she prayed Bo wouldn't feel the same way.

**

Warren and Robby turned to look at Bo, who felt his cheeks warm.

Robby, of course, recovered first. He grinned.

"You dog! Now I get it." He cackled, grabbing his sides. "Twinkle Toes! So, I was right?" He howled. "I told Daisy you were going down like a house of cards!"

Bo pushed himself from the couch, glaring at Jazz the entire time.

"Sorry, man." Jazz clapped him on the back and snagged a few slices of pizza he tossed onto a plate and held out to Bo, who shook his head.

"Why wouldn't you say something?" Warren asked. "We don't care. She's OK."

"She's fine." Robby stole a plate of pizza. "Cute even. I get it. Daisy loves her." He poked Bo. "And now all that after-hours dancing in the gym makes sense. No self-respecting guy would be out there only trying to be nice."

Bo took a drink and paced to the opposite side of the room. Robby knew about Marilyn, which meant Daisy would soon know too. Did that number his days working for them? If things didn't work out, it seemed a sure bet they'd pick sides. He couldn't prioritize his job over hers, that wouldn't be fair.

But Bo also couldn't imagine doing anything else for anyone else. He gulped as he tried to sort the mess he made.

"I, uh, can call the date off. I wasn't sure how you guys feel about employees dating." Bo let the question drop off, waiting as Robby scarfed down half a slice of pizza.

The singer shrugged as he wiped his mouth. "I don't need to approve of what you do in your life because you live here. But if you treat her like garbage, I won't be quiet about it either. She's a decent person- you better treat her like it."

Bo couldn't imagine it would be this easy. His father lost his first job because he got involved with his future wife, Bo's mom, who, at the time, had been a secretary at the company. That it worked out between them remained of little consequence apparently as the warning had always been there for the kids.

If you get a good job, be careful. Quit if you want to fraternize with other employees, don't get fired. It looks bad to future employers.

"As long as you're doing your job, why should anyone here care?" Warren asked. "From what I can tell Alice and Daisy both love you." He nudged Robby roughly as he sat next to him.

"And if this one isn't griping about you that means he's satisfied with you too." Warren waved his hand. "Go on your date. Godspeed."

Bo's phone buzzed. He slipped it out of his pocket enough to look at the screen, surprised to find the buzzing meant a call, not a text.

From Marilyn.

This might be the worst timing ever.

Chapter eight

"Try again."

Bo wasn't much of a mechanic but when Marilyn called, he couldn't very well leave her stranded in the middle of a parking lot so late at night and so close to the city.

This time when Marilyn turned the key, the car roared to life. She squealed in victory and Bo slammed the hood shut. He went to her door and leaned down.

"I'll follow you to make sure it gets you home OK, but you'll probably want to get a real mechanic to take a look at it sooner rather than later." He wiped his hands on his pants, leaving a light grease stain down the side.

"You…" She pointed.

He glanced down, grimacing, but covered quickly with a shrug. "Don't worry about it."

Even in the dim glow of the streetlight Bo could see her discomfort. "I'm sorry I interrupted you on your guys' night."

Bo waved her off. "I'm glad you did. I'm glad you're OK." He held her gaze as he tried to make himself stand up. He couldn't move.

"Me too." She clasped his hand. He squeezed hers back.

"Let's get you home. I'll call you tomorrow?"

Marilyn winked. "Or you can see me. Daisy has a dance lesson."

Bo's stomach knotted. "Oh. Sure." He raised to his full height. He didn't want to tell her, but he couldn't very well let her be surprised either.

"I said something to Jazz and he didn't realize Robby didn't know, so the long and short of it is, this came out with them tonight. I was actually in the middle of that conversation when you called."

Marilyn looked away and leaned back in her seat, her hands on the steering wheel. "Oh, boy. And I bet my calling and you having to come and rescue me made it worse."

Bo didn't doubt it, but he also didn't want her to worry.

"I only wanted to tell you in case it came up."

She turned back to him. "We haven't even been on one date yet. It could be awful, you know. You could chew with your mouth open and I could talk all about my old boyfriends, and we could be in completely different places spiritually and politically." She lifted one shoulder. "So, this could still be a huge disaster."

Bo's racing heart calmed at her words and he even smiled. "It's true. We could be completely incompatible."

Marilyn laughed with him.

They both slowly sobered and by the lights of the nearby businesses, Bo noticed her cheeks flush.

"It could also be wonderful." Marilyn's whispered words made Bo's heart skip a beat.

He gulped. "It could."

She raised her eyes to meet his. "So, I guess we'll see."

He nodded. "I'm a Christian. But I don't care much for politics."

Marilyn considered this. "Me too. So, we really could be in trouble," she whispered. "Good night, Bo."

"Good night, Marilyn. Wait for me and I'll follow you out."

She nodded and raised her window while Bo made his way to his car. He followed her to her apartment building and went to pick up Daisy and the kids, praying Robby hadn't text them, so he didn't have to listen to any comparisons to his being a knight in shining armor or some kind of superhero.

**

Marilyn kicked at the tire of her car before trudging back into the lobby of her apartment, her phone to her ear. She'd been too excited about Bo rescuing her the night before to do anything about her car at that point.

And in the morning, well, she really had no excuse. She considered getting a bus pass.

Daisy answered on the third ring. "Hey you!"

The baby began wailing so Marilyn had to hold the phone away from her ear.

"Hey Daisy!" she shouted. "I need to cancel your lesson today!"

"What?"

The dancer wondered why she didn't text instead. After a bit of shuffling on the other end of the line, Bo's deep voice came through. "Hey. Baby's misbehaving." He chuckled. "What's up?"

"Oh. Um, my car won't start again, so I didn't want Daisy waiting. I'm going to call a mechanic, or maybe a tow truck." She mentally ticked off the tiny nest egg she started to build and wondered how badly this would tear into it.

Wouldn't be the first time. Probably wouldn't be the last time.

"Oh." His tone made clear the disappointment. "Hold on."

After a brief pause of silence, Bo returned. "I'll pick you up. Daisy doesn't want to miss. Then I'll help you work out your car situation. Maybe you can get it scheduled for while we're away?"

Marilyn's mouth hung open as the baby wailed for a second and then Bo's tender voice said, "Shh... Bo got you, sweetheart."

Marilyn gulped. Her knees were so weak she realized she started leaning against a wall for support. She searched for words.

"I can work out the car situation. You don't need to come and get me!"

He grunted as he "shh'd" the baby until her cries turned to soft whimpers and Marilyn heard nothing at all.

"I'm sure you can handle it. But Daisy is looking forward to dancing and she's my boss, so I want her to be happy. All right? I'll be over around ten."

What else could she do?

"OK." Marilyn exhaled. "See you soon."

**

Marilyn watched Bo look up at her building and yank his phone out of his pocket. As he started typing, she skipped closer praying this didn't get weird and inevitably ruin the image she had of the bodyguard.

"Right here, Muscles."

He looked up with flushed cheeks. "Hey. I never asked which apartment."

Marilyn didn't say. "Why would you let Daisy talk you into coming all the way out here?" Her eyebrows raised in surprise as he opened the door and waited for her to hop inside. "It's so far out of the way."

Bo lifted a shoulder, indicating the trip didn't put him out. "Daisy enjoys her time with you. She really missed dancing after her accident so when Robby hired you… anyway, don't knock it." He slammed the door and hustled to the driver's side, got in, and started the car. Marilyn hadn't been in such a close space with him before.

She danced with him and appreciated his size in that realm, but here, even in an SUV, Bo's body ate up all additional space. He leaned into the armrest as if the driver's seat were child-sized.

As he started the car and glanced in her direction, he grinned. "Besides, I'm not going to lie and say I'm upset having to come out for you."

Marilyn's stomach fluttered. "Really? Well, you do know how to make a girl swoon."

He chuckled. "You heard the baby. I had to get out of there." He nudged her. "I'm kidding."

"You're too funny."

Bo drove in silence for several long moments, drumming his hand on the steering wheel to the beat of a song playing softly on the radio. Marilyn watched him with interest. He was a puzzle. A huge man who didn't appear to worry over anyone's opinion of him, outside of his employers and family, that is.

"Is it going to be weird when we show up and they know… I mean, that you asked me on a date?"

Bo raised an eyebrow. "Even if I'm ashamed to admit it, I believe you asked me on a date."

She leaned closer. "You conned me into an entire weekend."

He snickered. "I only asked for one thing. You pushed it to a whole weekend. Probably a long one if I had to guess. Friday through Monday?" He shook his head. "You must really like me."

Bo poked her. "You fell for it. Maybe you really like me."

He turned his attention back to driving, likely so he could consider his answer. Or maybe so he could change the subject.

"I'll make myself scarce and take care of Nicolette while you two work."

Marilyn gave this a moment's consideration. She was a decent enough flirt, but she could guess Bo probably made a mess of that kind of thing and could be too shy to flirt in front of his employers anyway.

"That's fair." She sat back, satisfied with this resolution. "So where are we going on our date? I need to know how to dress."

"I'm not sure. Definitely dinner."

"That's a good start. I like to eat."

Bo glanced at her with a wink. It appeared to be the extent of his ability to flirt. She'd take it for now. But if this date went well, Marilyn already decided to work on making his cheeks flush.

"Will you be wearing your glasses?"

Bo coughed and his cheeks began to turn. She grinned. Mission accomplished.

"You like my glasses?"

Marilyn bit her lip. "I do."

"Well, I guess I'll start wearing them all the time. Just not if we dance again. Too much of a pain."

Now Marilyn couldn't hold back. She shifted in her seat to face him as he steered through the gates, waved to the security guards and kept going down the long driveway toward the house.

"But you would dance with me again?"

He shrugged. "Sure."

"Excellent. You pick the restaurant, and after we're going dancing."

Bo parked the car. "Dancing? Really?"

She nodded.

He dropped his head and slipped out of the car, barely making it to Marilyn's door as she popped it open herself.

"You don't want to dance with me?" She hated how disappointed she sounded. "You said you did."

He raised an eyebrow as he reached behind her to close the door. "What I want is for you to stop getting ten steps ahead of me. Stay on the beat."

Marilyn punched him, fully aware of Robby and Daisy peeking at them through the front window like two concerned parents.

As if they spotted her catching them watching, the curtains shifted and the couple disappeared.

"I better get to work," she muttered, shouldering her bag.

Bo started walking with her toward the house. "I'll tell Daisy you're here. When you guys are finished, come back to the house with Daisy and I'll take you home before I pick up Alice."

Marilyn nodded and they walked in companionable silence until they reached the back of the house. To her surprise, Bo squeezed her arm, his warmth sending tingles down her spine.

"I'm kind of glad you're having car trouble. I like carting you around."

Marilyn's jaw dropped, but he left before she could reply.

**

"I updated your schedule for next week. I'm taking Daisy and Robby to the interview with Rolling Stone. You can sit tight with the baby. Oh, and I sent you some resumes to go through for a nanny."

Bo's gut tightened as he looked at Jazz. He bounced the baby in his arms and turned slightly away so the other man wouldn't see his face.

"Sorry, man. I know you got it. I tried to tell Robby, but he gets something in his mind and that's that."

Bo turned around, one hand on the baby's back to hold her in place on his shoulder as she slept, the other pointing practically in Jazz's face.

"I figured this would happen if he found out I'm going on a date with Marilyn. He thinks I'm not focused. He thinks I'm going to mess up."

Jazz chuckled. "You're connecting the wrong dots."

Bo snuggled the baby close. "Really?" He paused. "I can't lose this job."

Jazz whistled. "No one said you were. No way I'd let that happen anyway. It's all good, man." He nudged Bo. "Make yourself indispensable, tell Robby there's not one nanny in the bunch who will do better than you will, and keep on showing him. He'll lose interest. It's the current bug up his butt."

The words brought little solace.

"I'm cancelling the date." He tried to hand the baby off to Jazz who held his hands up and away.

"I'm not helping. You want to cancel the date, you do it without me." He started out of the kitchen, muttering the entire way.

"Idiot."

Bo's gut twisted. He and Jazz got along so well. He shook his head.

"Right back at ya."

**

Marilyn counted Daisy off, watching as she finished the latest spin.

"There it is! You got it." She stopped the music as Daisy beamed, wiping the sweat from her face. Before the accident that changed her life, she'd been a dancer. When Robby hired Marilyn, he showed her a video of his soon-to-be wife in her element, flying across the stage in a way that said she felt the music to her soul.

A horrible car accident ended it all. Or so, at one time at least, Daisy thought. But not her husband. For all of his rock and roll bravado, Robby never doubted she'd dance again, and he intended to see it through for her. Marilyn smiled, still in awe over what true, honest love could do for people.

Watching Daisy now, wheelchair or no, anyone would be a fool to miss her amazing skill, rhythm, and passion for movement.

Marilyn offered a silent prayer of gratitude she got to be part of this reawakening in her friend.

"You're killing me!" Daisy laughed. "And I love it!" She exhaled loudly. "Now, before someone interrupts us or we're forced to get back to the rest of our lives, I want the scoop on you and that bodyguard of mine who's been smiling like a complete fool lately."

Marilyn couldn't think how to answer that. "I wish I knew what to tell you. I mean, he's clearly enamored of me, but he's also scared to death."

Daisy moved closer. "He's intimidated. You're a gorgeous, confident woman."

Marilyn sat on a weight bench as they continued talking. "Maybe that's it. But he can be hard to crack."

Daisy rolled her eyes. "Tell me." She pursed her lips. "But I'll admit some of that is my fault. He works so hard and doesn't ask for a thing. It makes it easy to forget I haven't made any effort to get to know him better. I've been trying – and I'm going to keep at it until he gives me something."

Marilyn chuckled, but she sobered quickly. "He's worried that if we date, you guys will be upset."

"Bah!" Daisy tossed one hand in the air. "No way. Robby will tease him, and I'll pump for information or tell him what to buy you, but I don't get involved in people's relationships if I can help it." She sighed. "He should know better!"

The comfort this brought dissolved quickly when Marilyn considered there were other obstacles in her way where Bo was concerned.

"Daisy. I should probably tell you something."

The petite blond flinched. "Yeesh. That's ominous."

Marilyn nibbled at her bottom lip. "I hope it's not. But the thing is, dancing isn't working out for me. I mean, not as a career and definitely not the way I dreamed it would."

"What are you talking about? You're amazing!"

Marilyn appreciated the effort, but she wanted to get this out. "Oh. Well, I, um, haven't made any firm decisions yet, but I'm considering quitting this craziness and just going to college."

Daisy stared at her. "How old are you?"

"I'll be twenty-three in a few months."

Daisy waved one hand in her direction. "Twenty-three? Really? You're a baby."

Maybe to some that could be true, but for Marilyn she sometimes wondered if she passed her good years already—the ones ripe with possibilities—and sailed straight into disillusionment. Perhaps she'd too long chased a dream that wasn't meant to be.

"I've been at this a while," Marilyn said. "One crappy off-off-off Broadway show, four months in my own studio space, only to be kicked out unexpectedly, and one car problem after another." She met Daisy's eyes. "This job with you is about the only stable thing outside of waitressing right now. And I'm glad for it, I am. But maybe the universe is trying to tell me something."

Daisy tossed the towel she'd been holding. "I highly doubt that. Nothing really worthwhile is ever easy." She paused. "So, what does this mean with you and Bo? Because if you're only flirting with him, I might come on like a mama bear and rip your head off. He's strange sometimes, and not my type, but I am certain you won't find a better, more faithful and trustworthy man."

Marilyn sighed dreamily. "Yeah. But I'm kind of a loser. He needs someone better. Someone successful."

Daisy poked her arm. "Stop. Let's go inside and find out if Fernsby has anything good cooking. Then I'll make that sweet bodyguard drive you home and help you get your car situation figured out."

Marilyn nodded, wondering how the conversation turned so quickly.

"But first." Daisy turned to look Marilyn in the eye, clutching her hands to keep her planted on the weight bench. "Don't make any plans to go anywhere, OK? Not until we talk again."

"OK." She followed Daisy out of the gym and toward the house, grateful for a friend and a few days to reconsider her decision.

**

Bo glanced down at his clothes again, not sure he should have let Daisy talk him into the tie. She swore between that and the glasses it would be a lethal combination.

Robby just pointed and laughed.

Bo ignored them both as he wrestled with the few things he thought he knew about dating. Would he remember? Would he do something stupid?

His first date in two years. Of course, he'd do something stupid. Poor Marilyn. He really should call this whole thing off.

Bo fussed with his hair. He tried to tell Daisy this didn't matter. It's only one date. But she clucked over him like a mother hen until Bo locked her out of his room and refused to speak with her again if she made any comments about his looks or the date he continued to downplay as 'a friendly evening'.

Daisy insisted he sounded like he stepped out of the eighteen hundreds and now claimed he was 'courting' Marilyn.

Perfect. He needed to be teased by her too. Already Robby and Jazz scarcely missed an opportunity to pick on him about the whole thing.

He couldn't stop thinking he might be making a mistake. But then he ran into Daisy on his way to put Nicolette down for her nap. She was giving Marilyn the house tour, and whatever the woman saw in his care of the baby must have melted her. He didn't miss the way she sighed as he whispered,

"Hey. I need to put her down."

To him it might have been another day, another task, but Marilyn even mentioned later in a text,

You're so good with Nicolette. It's precious.

And later, because Daisy took so long dragging the woman around the house, he had to take Marilyn first to get Alice before he could take her back home, which of course meant he talked them both through taking care of her useless car.

That must have struck her too, because she also said,

You're phenomenal with Alice too. Robby and Daisy are lucky to have you.

He hoped they saw it that way. And maybe that Marilyn saw that she, too, could be lucky she found him. Of course, he could be reading too much into everything.

And a little voice reminded him he still worried over who Marilyn might be deep down. If she was still the kind of woman who'd prefer Zeke or Titus's big personalities to a mild-mannered wimp like himself then this whole thing would probably end before it even began. Still, his gut told him different.

He desperately wanted to believe.

Bo prayed he could get through this night unscathed. It had been so long since he'd been on a date, he worried he'd come on too strong or too weak, or worse, say something stupid.

Instead of taking the elevator, Bo hustled up the stairs to Marilyn's third floor apartment. He jerked his head from side to side, exhaled, offered a silent prayer, and tapped on the door.

It swung open immediately and Marilyn stood before him as he'd never seen her. Her dark, curly hair hung in ringlets down past her shoulders and her make-up, though light and natural, bespoke of care for this moment, for him and his impression of her.

And that dress would probably do him in if he kept staring. Having seen Marilyn only in sweats and dancer's clothes, Bo wrestled with the stunning woman who looked up at him with that ever-present mischievous sparkle in her eyes.

"You're fast," he muttered.

Marilyn grinned. "You come up the stairs like a tank."

"Oh." His cheeks burned as he continued staring, holding out a small bouquet of flowers out like some kind of offering. He kicked himself as he wondered if Daisy was right to say he'd started 'courting'.

"You look beautiful, Marilyn."

Her eyes lowered as she accepted them. "Thank you." She exhaled and lifted her chin to meet his gaze.

Bo gulped.

Marilyn's pale pink dress was tasteful and made her chocolate eyes pop, her lashes longer than he ever noticed before.

"Are you, um, ready, or…?" Bo kept his hands tucked safely in his pockets to keep from reaching for her. No telling what kind of fool he'd make of himself if he let his hormones take over. He also had no intention of scaring her off if he could help it. He only wished he didn't feel like a fifteen-year-old on his first date.

"I'm ready." Marilyn smiled. "Come in a sec. I'll put these in some water and get my coat and purse."

Bo stepped inside the small, but neat, apartment and waited as his date disappeared.

A redhead sat on the couch, her nose in a book, her interest clearly not on him. Still, he wouldn't be rude.

"Hello. I'm Bo Sutton."

The woman exhaled, stuck her finger on the page to hold her place and looked up at him. Her demeanor changed as her eyes went wide and she gave him a rather obvious once-over.

"Oh. Hello." She apparently caught her faux pas and lowered her eyes again. "I'm Sonya. Don't worry about winning me over. I don't have any pull with her if you were hoping to get into my good graces."

Bo's smile slipped. "Wouldn't dream of it." He paused. "It's nice to meet you, Sonya."

She nodded but kept reading as Marilyn reappeared.

"Sorry." She glanced at Sonya. "'Night."

"Yep. Have fun, kids."

Bo stepped into the hallway and Marilyn followed, tugging the door behind her. She grinned up at him.

"We're, like, best friends if you couldn't tell."

He chuckled, at ease with how this night would go. "Let's go, Twinkles."

**

Marilyn wondered if she'd ever been on a better date in her entire life. Bo opened doors, asked her preference on everything from the music in the car to the temperature, to whether she'd like dessert at the end of the meal. He listened attentively and maintained an easy way of talking with her that made her laugh many times.

And every time he talked about Alice and Nicolette, she swooned.

Full-on. No-holds-barred—swooned.

As hard as Marilyn fought, she couldn't deny she started falling hard for this man, this thoughtful, kind superhero who'd be as perfectly-suited to wearing a cape to save the world as he would khakis while rocking a baby to sleep. How would she ever get through an entire weekend with him without ending up head over heels in love?

If only she could tell what he might want from all of this.

"So…" Marilyn took a last sip of coffee. "This was delicious. Have you been here before?"

Bo nodded. "When Robby takes Daisy on a date either Jazz or I have to go to keep the press away. And with Daisy we need to be especially careful because taking care of her safely make a fast getaway difficult." He paused as he wiped his mouth and set his napkin on the table.

"So, one of us comes along and keeps an eye on things. We're careful and we try to be subtle." He shrugged. "Sit at a table not too far away, eat a good meal. It's a bit awkward and weird at first, being a third wheel on someone else's date. But it's a job and I'm used to it now."

Marilyn noted the pleasure in his eyes when he spoke of his job. She'd not once caught him complaining—a feat in today's TGIF world.

"Did you ever think you'd be doing this? Working for celebrities?"

He scoffed. "No. There were times I couldn't figure what I should be doing. I'm really grateful I found this job. It's like God moved everything out of the way so I could find it."

Marilyn beamed, leaning her chin on one hand. "I'm happy for you. It's something special to find the perfect job."

Bo met her eyes. "So…are you ready? I mean, to go?"

Marilyn found his occasional lack of confidence endearing. She nodded, waiting as he stood to help her from her chair. He grabbed her purse and held it out.

She bravely tucked her hand into his arm as they started out of the restaurant, making it almost like a real date.

They started toward the car and Bo gently took her hand and laced their fingers together, sending tingles up Marilyn's arm. They shared a beautiful moment as he paused walking simply so he could look into her eyes.

"I'm so glad you asked me tonight."

"Me too."

Marilyn had never had a date as wonderful as this. And certainly not with a man she respected, admired, and who treated her so well. "Ready to dance with me again?"

Bo gulped. "I think so. Just point me in the direction and we'll be off."

"All right. I'm ready to Fred and Ginger this night away. Let's go!"

**

Bo flipped Marilyn over his shoulder, no longer shocked when she ran back at him for another lift. The woman was an insatiable bundle of energy on the dancefloor. And for as much as Bo hated to admit it, he caught onto swing dancing much faster than expected.

And now the entire dance hall circled them, watching and clapping along until the song ended.

Never would he have dreamed he'd be dancing for an audience and loving every second of it. The beaming woman in his arms sure helped make him think anything might be possible.

Marilyn jerked Bo's arm and they took another bow before she hauled him toward the bar. He ordered two waters, paid, and led her to a small table off to the side.

"Well, Mr. Sutton, you are almost too good at this."

He smirked. "You don't weigh a thing. Makes it easy to toss you around."

"Ahh… perhaps. But there is technique involved." She paused, pointing at him. "I realize you poo-pooed it before, but I seriously think we can do that lift I mentioned."

He nudged her. "You've been planning that all along, haven't you?"

Marilyn raised her eyebrows and looked away, as if trying to play coy and innocent. "Maybe I have, maybe I haven't. But I really think we can." She grabbed his arms and gave him a playful shake as their eyes met.

Bo could stare at her all day long if that wouldn't make her think he might be some kind of freak. But try though he might to tear his eyes away from hers, he couldn't manage it. Marilyn Darby was magic.

"You're so handsome." Her words didn't register at first, so Bo stared as he tried to process them. He jumped when her hand flew to her mouth, her cheeks turning pink. His own warmed too as he looked away.

"I didn't mean to say that out loud," she whispered. "Sometimes I forget to filter."

Bo scooted his chair closer so he could easily take her hand. "It's all right. I'll take the compliment. Thank you."

"You're welcome."

He tingled with the sensation of their joined hands, relishing the feel of being her protector, her tiny fingers warm and soft as they fit together with his own. It was one thing to hold her and toss her around on the dancefloor, and Bo definitely enjoyed that, but it might be quite another to share an intimate look, the touching of hands. He couldn't remember the last time he'd done that.

And then he remembered. Not since Frannie.

Summoning all his courage, Bo studied their hands. "You're amazing, Marilyn. And if it makes you feel better about saying what you did, I think you're the most beautiful woman I've ever met." He paused, kicking himself for laying his feelings so bare. "This is really fun. I mean, it's been a perfect date."

She nodded in agreement, leaning toward him as if they shared a glorious secret. "Definitely top five."

Bo's hand gripped hers. "Well, I guess I'll need to work on the next one to make sure it's number one."

"Does this mean you're asking me on a second date, Mr. Sutton?"

He cleared his throat, wondering how he'd fallen so fast without a safety net. He still didn't know if he could trust this woman with his heart, but he couldn't stop himself from confirming the answer to her question. He wanted to believe in her. He needed her to be safe, different from Frannie, the kind of woman he dreamed of.

"I am asking you on a second date. Will you go out with me again, Twinkles?"

She held his gaze for some time before answering.

"Very well. I accept."

**

Marilyn couldn't believe the car display showed it was nearly midnight when Bo pulled up to the curb outside her apartment building. After dinner and dancing, they'd taken a short walk before reluctantly agreeing it might be time to go. They held hands, talked, and laughed the entire time.

She couldn't remember being this giddy in her life. It must be how infatuated teens felt, full of inexplicable emotions crashing together and all because of someone she barely knew.

Would Bo try to kiss her? And if he did, how would she reach his lips when they stood over a foot apart!?

Marilyn watched him walk around the car. Everything about the bodyguard made her tingle. She admired his strong features and even his hair, still slightly mussed from dancing. But she especially loved his grin as he caught her checking him out.

She flushed when he opened the door.

"Well, here we are, Twinkles." Bo held out his hand. She took it and stepped from the car as he closed the door.

"Same time next week?" she asked hopefully. "I'm off Saturdays."

He met her eyes. "Perfect. One week to date until we fool the families." His gaze never wavered as he stepped closer to her, his hands on her arms.

Marilyn's heart constricted as she prayed he didn't think she'd been pretending all night. Had he been pretending? Surely no one could be that good.

"By now you should appreciate how I am about rehearsing." She hoped it sounded light. "Practice makes perfect and soon this dating thing will be a solid habit for us." She flinched. "That sounded less weird in my head."

Bo chucked her playfully on the chin. "You aren't the woman I thought you were."

Marilyn softened. "Who did you think I was?"

Bo closed his eyes briefly. "I guess since you were dating Zeke when we met, I figured you were…"

He let the sentence fall off, but she understood, even if she wished she didn't. He thought she might be a woman of no character, one who'd sleep with a man she wasn't married to in order to get what she wanted, which in her case was the possibility of having free dance space in his gym.

"You…?" She stepped back, grimacing. "I'm not like that. I wouldn't… I didn't…" She couldn't imagine why he'd bother to take her on a date if that's how he saw her. But defending herself against such a charge seemed impossible. She could say anything but had no real evidence for her character.

"Hey." Bo grabbed her hand and jerked her back, leaning down so she found no choice but to look into his eyes.

"I was wrong. I understand that now. And I'm sorry." He squeezed her hand. "I wouldn't have agreed to go out on a date with you, and I certainly wouldn't have invited you to meet my family if I still believed those things about you."

Marilyn exhaled, still embarrassed. "I met Zeke when I first got to New York. He was a smooth-talker and I was naïve, but I figured things out quick when he dumped me because I wouldn't…." She winced, kicking her toe at the pavement, still unable to look into Bo's eyes. "I kneed him pretty good and ran off."

The words burned as much as the memory. "I haven't dated anyone since."

"Really?" Bo's gentle voice urged Marilyn to raise her head and look into his eyes. "I'm proud of you."

Her cheeks flushed. "Well, I don't want to be stupid again. I want to succeed in work, and I figured just steering clear of any relationships—at least for now—would be wise."

Bo's eyes darkened in a way that made Marilyn's pulse kick up a notch. He exhaled as he leaned closer. "Thank you for telling me."

Marilyn stupidly nodded.

"Twinkles." Bo closed his eyes, leaning so his forehead touched hers. Marilyn inhaled, drunk on the moment, his cologne, their attraction for one another, and a host of emotions raging through her.

Before he said anything, Bo groaned, clutching her hands even tighter as he raised his head slightly. "I really want to kiss you, but I...hate to presume..."

Marilyn lifted to her toes. "Me too."

He urged her to step closer, as if relieved by her admission. He brushed his lips gently against hers. Maybe she shocked him by giving such quick permission. But she didn't care. His hands went from her arms to her back and she sighed dreamily into him before looping her arms around his neck.

For a moment the world stopped. There were no job or money problems, no parents to contend with—only Marilyn and Bo and too many wonderful, perfect emotions to untangle.

"Wow..." Bo lifted his head enough to look into her eyes. He brushed a stray strand of hair from her cheek. "You're incredible."

"So are you."

His lips met hers ever-so-softly one more time before he took her hand. "I'm sure this is the best date of my life."

Marilyn elbowed him in the gut. "Don't set the bar so low. We'll top this one in no time."

Chapter nine

"Bo!" Daisy's voice rang through the upstairs, catching the bodyguard on the way to his office.

"Yeah?" He paused midway down the staircase, turned, and started back up. He reached the top step and started toward Daisy who pursed her lips in a rare display of annoyance.

"The elevator isn't working again! I'm stranded! Did you call?"

Bo frowned as he leaned down to look at the display which bore its typical malfunction message. "It's on the list for Monday," he said. "By the time I realized I couldn't fix it yesterday and with today being Sunday, not much else I can do." He tried a few buttons and resetting the entire system before turning to Daisy.

"I'll take you down the old-fashioned way for now. Then later Robby can cart you around. You know how he loves that." Bo scooped her up and started down the steps to find her extra wheelchair.

The first time Bo had to carry Daisy had been awkward. But now, with helping her daily, he never flinched at serving her needs when Robby had work or other obligations and couldn't be around, and thankfully she didn't mind asking for help when she needed it.

Daisy patted his shoulder. "I'm dying to hear how your date went but I don't want to be nosy." She barely suppressed her amusement. "But Robby did say your car didn't get back inside the garage until well after midnight. That's a good sign. Right?"

Bo's stomach fluttered as he thought of his evening. And then his cheeks flushed as he recalled their perfect kiss. He hoped his boss didn't notice given she could turn her head and see his goofy lovesick look.

"I wouldn't know. It might be." He chuckled as she groaned in frustration, whacking him for good measure.

Bo reached the bottom of the staircase and located Daisy's chair. He set her in it, waiting as she got comfortable and led him to the kitchen. He'd barely slept for thinking about Marilyn, dancing with her, and all the laughs they shared. They had a lot in common and even when she gave him a hard time, he enjoyed it.

He only had to keep stuffing the worry away that she might leave New York and go home to a life she had no interest in actually living.

Bo would use the weekend to convince her that sticking around would be best for everyone, especially them. He'd win her over.

Daisy got her coffee and went to the table where Alice sat holding Nicolette who started to fuss. Bo stole her away and she immediately calmed.

"For heaven's sake you'd think she's your kid," Daisy muttered.

Bo grinned, cuddling the baby closer for good measure as he wondered if one day he would have his own family after all. At one time he believed it could happen, and now, with Marilyn…

"How was your date, Bo?" Alice asked, a teasing lilt in her voice.

Bo coughed as he corralled his thoughts away from marriage and babies and back to the moment of work and responsibility.

"That's the million-dollar question he isn't answering." Daisy and her stepdaughter shared a look of sass and pursed lips.

"All right." The bodyguard groaned. "But you both gotta promise to not be all weird about it, especially with Marilyn. I wouldn't want her to think we're talking behind her back."

They dissolved into a fit of shared giggles.

"We'll make no such promises," Daisy said. "We're weird about everything. And we're asking her too, so don't think we aren't talking about both of you behind the others' back!"

The bodyguard grabbed a cup of coffee for himself before answering their amusement.

"We had a good time," he said. "Made a date for next week." He didn't share anything about their weekend. He'd prefer to discuss that privately with Daisy because heaven knew he'd struggle to get the words out.

"Ohhhh…" the women cooed in unison as Robby entered through the back door, covered in sweat and clearly just back from his workout. Jazz followed shortly behind.

"Got in kind of late last night, lover boy." Robby playfully slugged Bo. "Must have been some date with old Twinkles."

"Robby!" Daisy squealed as he leaned over her in further dramatic evidence of his affections, nuzzling close into her neck until she squeaked again, louder than before. She half-heartedly tried to push him away but the singer only grinned and did as he pleased.

"Yeah, angel?"

"Ugh! You reek!" Daisy might protest but no one in the room believed for a second she wanted anything other than her husband's devoted attention. Still, she made her best effort to remain serious as she pointed at him.

"You need to get ready for church! Hurry up!"

Because he'd never been a fan of being ordered around, Robby smooched his wife again with a cocky grin. "They'll hold the service until we get there. Pastor Tate knows the drill."

Daisy rolled her eyes. "They will not hold the service until you get there. This isn't one of your concerts and the congregation isn't made up of your fans."

"Everywhere I go is made up of my fans." He patted Nicolette's backside. "Right, baby girl?"

"You do stink, Rob," Bo chimed in, moving away from him.

Robby chuckled as he and Jazz left the room, heading in opposite directions to clean up for church. He talked a big game, but Robby only did what his wife wanted of him.

Once Robby's loud footsteps bounded up the staircase, Daisy shook her head and held out her arms for the baby. Bo handed her over to be fed.

"I'm glad you had a good date." She smiled at him. "You two make a nice couple. Maybe we can go out on a double sometime."

Bo grinned. "And make Jazz tag along as security? Sign me up."

"I heard that!" Jazz yelled from the next room. "And no way!"

Everyone howled. Bo took a swig of coffee as Alice put her dishes in the dishwasher.

"I'll go get dressed so someone doesn't get on my case too." She patted Daisy's shoulder with affection as she hustled from the room.

"Grab that burp cloth for me please."

Bo did as told before starting the dishwasher. "So, uh, since Marilyn is without a car, I considered loaning her mine so she can get around. If you don't mind my using the SUV for a few days since I mostly run it anyway for all of your stuff."

Daisy shrugged as she finally got a burp out of the baby. "Fine by me. That's awfully nice of you to take care of her too. She'll appreciate it."

Bo wasn't so sure the independent woman occupying most of his thoughts would agree. But he also couldn't imagine letting her fend for herself when he had the means to help.

"You don't think it's overstepping? She can get pretty sassy when she doesn't want to do something."

Daisy resumed feeding the baby. "I guess that's something you need to figure out with her. Ask her. One thing about Marilyn that's true, she'll tell you straight-out what she's thinking."

**

Marilyn tucked her legs under her as she applied to her first college ever, per the link her mom sent earlier in the week.

Did she want to go to Princeton and live with her parents? No. She probably wasn't qualified anyway, but at least if she said she applied it might hold off the questions and 'encouragement' for a while.

After her date with Bo, Marilyn realized that for every question she asked before, she only gained several more.

And she returned to the same conclusions. He was another reason she didn't want to leave New York, or her dreams, behind. But how would she make them happen? How long would she fight for something that showed no signs of becoming hers?

A sudden knock on the door made her jump.

It was after eight on Sunday night and while her roommate would be at her study group for a while, Marilyn decided to take full advantage of using the living room without fear of interrupting Sonya, who preferred—no, required—quiet at all times. Since Marilyn rarely stayed home, it hardly mattered. Tonight, she meant to enjoy the small apartment on her own terms for a change.

She went to the door and peeked through the peep hole, surprised to find Bo shuffling from one foot to the other in the hallway.

"Hey." She yanked the door open. She skillfully avoided him at church that morning, mainly because she didn't want to embarrass him in front of the family, or put his or her own job in jeopardy. While it seemed likely the Grants wouldn't care one way or the other about it, everything was so new between them that Marilyn figured a quick 'hello' should be enough.

Bo appeared to agree as he didn't prolong their interaction either. Marilyn only wished she didn't hear the giggling between Daisy and Alice as she walked away.

"Hey." Bo coughed, averting his eyes briefly before turning back to look at Marilyn. "I wasn't sure how to go about talking to you this morning. I'm sorry if it was rude."

They regarded each other awkwardly, both apparently unsure of this thing between them. The day after a great date and they acted as if they only just met.

Marilyn kicked herself to say something. "It's fine. I wasn't sure what to say either. I hope they didn't give you a hard time."

Bo shrugged, his eyes on the ground near her feet. "Not more than usual."

Marilyn felt like a teenaged wallflower at a junior high dance. Her hair probably even stuck up. She prayed the spinach from her dinner didn't sit lodged in her teeth.

"Um.." Bo reached into his pocket and yanked out a set of keys he held out to her. "Since the garage didn't know how long you'd be without a car, I brought mine. Figured you can use it until you get yours back."

"What?" Marilyn tried to follow his thinking. "I'm not taking your car."

Bo jerked his head toward the staircase. "Jazz followed me over and he'll give me a ride home. Daisy said she doesn't mind me using one of theirs for the week until you get yours back. I only thought…"

Marilyn leaned against the doorframe, surprised, touched, and annoyed by Bo's ridiculous push to take care of her this way.

"What? That I needed a superhero to swoop in and help? You work for Daisy- you do this stuff for her, not me." She raised an eyebrow. "There's a thing around here called a bus.

And another called a taxi. I'm capable of figuring out how to get where I need to be." She left out that it was inconvenient, unsafe, and cost money she didn't want to spend. Those weren't his problems.

Bo held out his keys again. "Take the keys, Marilyn. It's safer and it's fine. I even filled the tank for you."

Of course he did. He wouldn't be perfect otherwise.

Marilyn waved her hands between them. "I'm not at the point in whatever we're doing to steal your car."

Bo clenched his jaw. "It's not stealing if I'm giving it to you." He exhaled loudly while jingling the keys again. "Take them. I don't want to make Jazz wait."

Marilyn folded her arms over her chest. "You shouldn't have made Jazz come at all. If you called me, I would have declined your… generous offer."

Bo stared at her, his annoyance evident in his narrowing eyes. "Why are you being difficult? I'm trying to be nice!"

"You don't work for me, Bo." Marilyn raised to her full height, which did little to remove her from Bo's enormous shadow. "You don't need to make my life easier."

His forehead wrinkled as he considered this. "I realize we only had one date." His voice went softer. "I like you. You need help. I don't see a reason not to."

Now Marilyn paused. She winced, both hopeful and irritated and not appreciating the turmoil this brought. She'd been on her own, figuring out her finances and frustrations for so long that having anyone take an interest, let alone someone she'd only known such a short time, brought questions.

"Why?"

"Why?" Bo paused. "Because that's what I do. It's who I am." He held out the keys again.

Reluctantly, she accepted them. An uncomfortable feeling of owing him something in return settled into Marilyn's chest. But what?

"Thank you."

Bo lowered his head, beaming in his success. "You're welcome."

Marilyn shifted feet. "What do I owe you? I mean, of course I'll fill the gas tank and get it cleaned."

Bo squeezed her arms. "Your thank you is enough." His phone buzzed and he yanked it from his pocket.

"Jazz is getting antsy. I better go."

Marilyn watched him head for the stairs. "I appreciate this. It's really unexpected and so nice of you."

He turned before hitting the first step. "No problem, Twinkle Toes. I'll see you tomorrow?"

She dipped her chin in agreement. "Sure. Tomorrow."

**

Bo finished cleaning up the latest diaper blow-out, complete with a bath for Nicolette and a shirt change for himself, all while Daisy worked with Titus in the studio.

He prayed Robby didn't get back before...

"Did you go through the resumes I sent you?"

Bo lifted Nicolette to his shoulder and turned, trying not to bristle when he faced Robby. "Not yet."

He jerked his thumb over his shoulder. "I left Jazz down there to keep an eye on things while I found you. I don't like her being alone with him."

Bo didn't mention that while he didn't like Titus either, the more time he spent in the man's presence the less of a threat he considered him. He also didn't mention that by now, Robby ought to trust his wife who would never, in a million years, consider cheating.

"Sorry. She exploded and I had to take care of it. I'll head down and relieve Jazz."

Robby nodded. "Go through the resumes, dude. You can't be pulled in so many directions."

Bo bit his tongue. Arguing with Robby never did any good. The man made up his mind and the conversation ended. This wouldn't be different. Besides, Bo dropped the ball. He should have had a diaper bag with him that included a change of clothes for both he and the baby.

"Sorry. I'll handle it."

Robby winked. "Darn right you will." He rubbed his hand gently over the baby's soft hair as Bo walked by.

"Don't sweat it, dude. I'm not mad. I'm only trying to make your life easier. Pretty soon this one is going to be even more work. She needs someone." He paused. "So, go through the resumes and we'll talk, huh?"

Against the knot in his stomach, Bo nodded.

"Sure. I'll send Jazz up."

He raced down to the studio, hating that he seemed incapable of speaking up for himself.

**

Marilyn stared at the man behind the counter.

"How much?"

The mechanic rolled his eyes to heaven. "It's all right there in the bill. Your car is nothing short of toast. We did what we could." He pointed one greasy finger at the paper in front of her. "It's all itemized. Car ought to last you a solid couple of months until you find something else—maybe a year if you get lucky."

Marilyn's mouth felt as if it filled with cotton balls. "Is there any chance I can make payments? This is going to wipe out my savings."

The man had the audacity to laugh. "The car stays put until you can pay the bill." He closed his hand over her keys, which sat between them on the counter.

Marilyn glanced back at Bo's SUV, which sat right outside the window. A few days remained until they went on their next date. She wanted to get his car back to him by then.

Now…

"Thanks so much for your help," she muttered. "I guess I'll be in touch."

**

Bo stared at the text, disappointment pooling in his chest. After a week of missing Marilyn numerous times, he'd been looking forward to their second date.

But this text killed it.

I'm sorry but I need to break our date. I got the chance to cover someone's shift and I couldn't turn it down. You can come get your car if you need. I'll take a cab home.

Bo struggled with a reply. He missed his car, but he didn't exactly need it. He tapped out his answer.

No worries, Twinkles. I'll get it sometime this week or when we go on our trip. Call if you don't get in too late.

He hoped she would. He needed someone to talk to, someone outside the house where he spent so much time. He worried about his position, and beyond that his family and how they'd react to him after so long. And how could he help Marilyn with her family issues?

It all seemed too much for him to handle.

But Marilyn never called.

And Bo wondered if their weekend would be a horrible bust.

**

Marilyn emerged from the shower exhausted and ready to fall into bed. She survived a fifteen-hour day and not eaten since breakfast, unless one counted a granola bar and a can of off-brand soda. She, personally, did not.

Bo text her twice and she only once had the chance to get back to him. He was so sweet it made her sick to think she couldn't make time for him. They barely knew each other, and she agreed to go away with him for the weekend.

Her mom would flip if she ever figured the truth.

"Hey." Sonya followed her grunt with a thud to Marilyn's bedroom door that had to have been her foot hitting it.

"What?" Marilyn didn't move from where she fell on the bed.

The door opened and Sonya entered, carrying something that smelled heavenly. Marilyn didn't open her eyes.

"Is that Chinese food? Do I smell egg rolls?" One eye popped open.

Sonya looked only slightly less annoyed than usual. "I almost asked the guy to leave because I didn't order anything and I doubted you did either, but he insisted some huge man ordered this and paid for it too."

She stepped closer, holding out the bags. "Sounded like that new guy who's been coming around here, so I figured…"

Marilyn opened both eyes and shoved to sit. "Bo?"

Sonya lifted her eyebrows and tore a piece of paper off one of the bags and held it out to her. "There is a note attached."

Marilyn took it.

"Did he do something wrong?" Sonya pressed, clearly intrigued.

The note read: *Sounded like you were having a long day. I thought I'd send you something delicious and nutritious to end your day well. (you can share with Sonya if she's home) XO- BO*

Marilyn warmed at his concern, especially when they hadn't been together in days, stuck only with texts and a quick phone call. She shot off a quick text to thank him, with a promise to call in a half hour when she finished gorging herself on the food he sent.

He text back immediately: *Take your time. Enjoy it.*

Marilyn stood and grinned at her roommate. "Let's eat and I'm calling to tell him how wonderful he is."

For the first time in the two years they'd lived together, Sonya actually looked amused. "Forget studying. Food first!"

**

A short time later, Sonya insisted she was full and had to get back to her work of studying for another exam. Marilyn could barely keep her eyes open, but she slipped back into her bed, satisfied by the delicious meal she hadn't expected, as well as the decision she made to take Bo home to her family.

They'd adore him, which would easily take the focus off her weak life.

He answered on the third ring.

"Hey, Twinkles," he whispered. "Got a full stomach?"

He wasn't even in the room and Marilyn's cheeks burned. "Yes. It took all I had to roll myself into bed." She paused as he chuckled. "Thank you. That was so unbelievably sweet of you."

"That restaurant is fantastic," he whispered. "I'm glad you liked it. Daisy and Robby swear by it. I'm pretty sure we keep them in business."

"Why are you whispering?"

He chuckled again. "Baby duty. Robby and Daisy wanted some alone time so…" he paused. "She's almost asleep, but it takes forever. She's a demanding diva exactly like her father."

Marilyn imagined Bo cuddling Nicolette as he rocked in a rocking chair or paced around the house or laid on his bed.

She sighed dreamily.

He groaned lightly. "I'm only doing my job. Don't go making me into something I'm not."

"But it's the sweetest thing in the world- a big man taking care of a wee little muffin. You're so good with her." Marilyn snuggled under the covers with a yawn as she imagined Bo cuddling the baby. "How did your day go?"

"Busy – lots of dirty diapers and teenaged drama." Bo paused. "Are you excited? Big weekend coming up!"

Marilyn didn't hide her feelings, the safety of being on the phone giving her needed courage. "I'm nervous." To finally admit it aloud didn't bring relief, but questions.

"Aww. Nothing to worry about, Twinkles. It's going to be fun. I'll buy you food, my mom will talk your ears off, my sister will ask a thousand questions, and Lincoln and Asher will stare at you because, well, they're not very good with women."

Marilyn grinned. "Runs in the family?"

"Hey!" Bo's protest was followed by a baby fussing. "Dang it, now look what you did."

Marilyn giggled. "Oh! I'm sorry!"

Bo's voice returned a moment later, this time stronger and not a whisper. "I'm only kidding. I laid her back in her crib and she always does that. The last protest before sleep."

Marilyn yawned. "I feel her pain."

"Go to bed." Bo's deep voice became tender with these words. "You need to rest too."

Although she didn't want to stop talking, Marilyn wasn't sure how much longer she could keep her eyes open either. "OK. I'll see you soon." She paused, not sure how to say it without going overboard.

"And thanks again for the late dinner. I loved it. It made my day."

"Happy to do it. Good-night, Twinkles."

"Good night, Muscles."

**

"Daisy?" Bo found his boss in the kitchen working on her delicious chocolate chip cookies. That meant she and Robby had a spat and she intended to smooth it over. The singer went nuts for her baked goods.

Daisy didn't look up from the recipe. "Hey- hand me the eggs, would you?"

Bo grabbed the eggs and set them on the counter, anxious to get this conversation over with, but well aware this might not be the best time. He forged on with his plan anyway. "Baby should be down for a while yet."

"Excellent." Daisy continued working. "I'm good here if you want to take a break."

Bo dragged a stool out and settled on it. "I actually wanted to talk to you about something before I get Alice from school." He cleared his throat, wishing this was already over with and he could get on his way.

Daisy cracked an egg. "Shoot."

Bo inhaled and exhaled slowly to center himself. He'd reviewed this conversation so many times it shocked him she didn't already guess what he'd say.

"Bo?"

He shook himself and looked at his boss who regarded him with an amused twinkle in her eye. "You good?"

"Yeah. Sorry." He drummed his fingers on the counter. "So, you know how I'm going away this weekend?"

Daisy shrugged as she reached for a wooden spoon. "Your cousin's wedding? Sure."

"Right. Anyway…"

Spit it out, idiot.

"Um, I asked Marilyn to go with me. She said yes." He coughed. "And I'm going with her to an engagement party for her sister. So, we're leaving tomorrow, and we'll be back late Sunday or sometime Monday." He cringed. "Is that all right? It's kind of a long time for me to be away. I didn't want to presume."

Daisy stopped stirring and looked at him. "What? Really? You've been out on one date, Bo. You don't think a weekend together is a little… um, fast? Not to mention presumptuous?"

His stomach tightened as if he'd come clean to his mother on this. "It's terrible fast," he admitted. "But it didn't start like you're thinking. It all kind of rolled together and got out of control."

Daisy waved the spoon slightly as if to urge him on.

"Anyway, I wanted you to understand that whatever happens, or whatever is going on this weekend or even into the future with me and Marilyn, I swear I'm devoted to my position here. I'm not looking at those resumes Robby wants me to review for nannies because… well, I'm sure I can do all of it. Just like I've been."

Daisy's blue eyes softened. "Bo."

"I mean it, Daisy. I do. After this weekend, I swear I'm committed here. You won't need anyone else. Please give me this."

She nodded slowly. "OK. I will." She paused. "No one doubts you here. You're exactly what we need. Robby just worries you take on too much and might not be there the way I need you if you're pulled over to take care of the kids too."

"That will never happen. I can do all of it." He stood, needing to get some aggression out on the bag in the gym. "Yeah?"

"Sure. Of course." She paused. "Bo?"

He turned to her. "Yeah?"

"You're doing a fantastic job. We're not worried. I promise."

Bo didn't want to get between the husband and wife, but he also understood he had a better shot at this conversation with Daisy than with Robby. "I like taking care of the kids. If you don't think I'm shirking my responsibilities with you, I'd like to keep doing it. I'll look through the applications Robby and Jazz sent me, but I don't really know if we need someone for that yet."

"Yeah, I keep telling Robby I don't want another full-time person in this house. I mean how many people do we really need to make us function?"

With the million different directions the couple often went, and the engagements, events, and work in general, Bo understood it took a village to keep a celebrity couple together. But he believed he could be that village with Jazz's help.

"Not sure. Maybe with some reshuffling we can make this work. If you're open to it, I'll keep thinking. Sound good?"

"I'm fine with that," Daisy agreed. She went back to work on the cookies. "And by the way, you better behave yourself on a weekend with Marilyn. No funny business. Got it?"

Bo sobered. "Yes, Mom."

"Ha. Ha."

Bo trudged up to his room, wondering if he'd done the dumbest thing imaginable.

Chapter ten

Marilyn rolled into the Grant's driveway at eleven in the morning, nearly an hour later than she meant to get there. She hoped this didn't upset Bo. With clashes in schedules, they'd not talked for several days and his texts remained professional not personal, which left Marilyn in a state of perpetual concern.

Their date had been so perfect. Their conversations golden.

And if she dreamed again about his lips or the tender way he held her in his muscular arms, she might explode.

She prayed they hadn't taken ten steps backward.

A suitcase sat outside at the edge of the expansive porch. Did she go to the front door? Did she text him? Marilyn's experience with this sort of thing remained on the far end of useless.

She exhaled.

The front door opened, and Marilyn climbed out of the SUV as Bo grabbed his suitcase and came toward her, beaming.

"I just text you." He dropped his suitcase near her feet and pulled her into a huge hug that made her squeal over his attention.

Marilyn whacked his shoulder. "Geez! They're probably watching!"

Bo set her back on her feet, looking sheepish. "Sorry. I'm happy to see you."

She patted him on the arm. "Me too."

He lifted the tailgate and slid his suitcase in beside hers. She handed him the keys.

"Thanks for loaning me your car. I really appreciate it."

"No problem." Bo led her to the passenger side and opened the door, appearing to be at a loss for words. "How's your week gone?"

He met her eyes and gently took her hands.

"Good." She flushed. "You even won Sonya over."

Bo winked. "Well fancy that." He held her gaze for a moment before leaning down to brush his lips over hers. "I'm hoping it won you over too."

Marilyn pushed her hands against the solid muscle of his chest. "You're well on your way. Get that movie lift down and we'll talk."

Bo threw his head back as he howled. "OK, OK, we'll work on it. How's that?"

Marilyn grinned wickedly and moved to the opposite side of the driveway. She gestured with her hands to make her point clear. "So when I come at you, you'll really need to bend those knees to get me up and roll with the momentum."

Bo's eyes went wide. "What? I didn't mean now! Not on the pavement! Don't be crazy, Mar!"

She rolled her neck, followed by her shoulders. They were doing this. Now. "Strong arms, Muscles. Strong arms."

"Marilyn." Bo gulped as he cast a quick glance toward the house. "They're watching."

"Then let's give them a show!" She bent her legs slightly indicating she was about to charge. "Here I come!"

Before he could think or protest any further, Marilyn raced across the driveway and leapt, certain the bodyguard wouldn't let her down.

And, of course, he didn't.

Bo easily lifted her over his head, only offering a low exhale as he held her above him. "Happy now?" he muttered as cheers erupted from inside the house.

Marilyn beamed as she looked down into Bo's deep eyes. "Ecstatic."

"Well, then I guess we accomplished something important." He lowered her slightly for a feather-light peck on her lips before setting her gently in front of him.

Marilyn giggled victoriously and grabbed his hand. "Now bow for our adoring fans." She leaned into him and whispered. "We're doing that again later. It was more fun than I thought it would be."

Bo groaned as he followed her lead. "I'm never going to hear the end of this…"

Marilyn allowed him to drag her back to the car where he opened the passenger door. "Everyone here been giving you a hard time?"

His lips curled upward. "No worse than usual." He hustled to the other side of the vehicle and hopped in, tipping his head toward the house.

"Wave to the family before we go or Daisy will start texting me and if I don't answer her, Alice will start."

Marilyn looked up to find Bo rubbing the back of his neck. He jerked his head toward the house again where Daisy, Robby, Jazz, and Alice all watched them like a family seeing their loved one off.

"Aww… they love you!"

Bo groaned as they both waved, making Marilyn feel like a teen going on her first date. He backed up the car, turned around, and tooted the horn before pulling away with a last wave.

"They're certainly... caring, aren't they?"

Bo lifted his eyebrows on an exhale. "That's one way of putting it."

Marilyn leaned back in her seat, tilting her head to look at him. "Better give me the rundown so I don't say the wrong thing to the wrong person. I'll do the same for you before we go to my family's."

Bo smiled. "Be yourself and you should be fine. Except you probably shouldn't mention Daisy or Robby. I need to have that conversation with my parents first. I'd hate for it to slip out and cause a fuss."

Marilyn nodded. "Fair. I can do that."

Bo cleared his throat, his eyes still on the road as he appeared to mull something over. Marilyn couldn't decide what to say so she watched the scenery pass, aware she stupidly set her hand on the center console, a breath from Bo's own hand.

"I realize I already thanked you for coming with me, but it really does mean a lot." The warmth of his hand enveloped hers as he laced their fingers together. She turned her attention to their hands, loving the way they felt together.

Supported. Fitting. Perfect.

He caught her eye for an instant before again turning his attention to the road. Marilyn smiled as their hands remained together.

"You're welcome." She squeezed his hand. "How are you going to tell them? And when?"

Bo snorted as he drove. "Haven't figured that part out yet, but I'm open to suggestions."

It wasn't as if the dancer had a clue either. She didn't know his family, but she couldn't imagine how they could get upset with him. He was so kind and caring, surely they'd understand why he'd not been open sooner.

"I imagine we'll catch up with them today, right? You wouldn't want to say something at the wedding and ruin that time—or at least make it uncomfortable." Marilyn squeezed his hand. "I'd do it today—as soon as possible. Just get it over with. Maybe since your mom is understanding and your dad is tough they'll balance each other out?"

Bo glanced at her. "Maybe. Part of me wants to turn the car around and forget the whole thing."

Although Marilyn understood that sentiment, she'd also grown tired of running. "No way. If you can get me through my audition, I can get you through this."

Bo clutched her hand. "I sure hope so, Twinkles."

**

The trip to the hotel went faster than Bo expected, largely because of Marilyn's ongoing, easy chatter. They sang together, laughed, paused for lunch and a little sight-seeing, and, whether Bo liked it or not, they just got closer. This trip would be fun even if he noticed himself falling deeper into his feelings for the dancer whose spunk made him think they could have a future together.

Until the part where he had to tell his family the truth of what he did for a living reared up again. But he could ignore that for now.

"You don't have to carry everything." Marilyn trailed behind him with her purse and the long garment bag with his suits, while Bo carried her bags and his.

He grinned at her over his shoulder as they slipped into the elevator together. "What kind of man would I be if I let you carry your own bag? It's bad enough you've got my suits."

"I don't want you to wrinkle." She lifted her nose in the air. "Then I'd be ashamed to be seen with you."

Bo snickered. Leave it to Marilyn to worry about wrinkles. "My fans appreciate it."

The doors clicked open and Bo kept grinning stupidly as he started out, only realizing too late that his mother and sister were staring at him with open mouths from the hallway.

Marilyn bumped into his back when he stopped cold and stared back at them, awash with emotion.

Two years meant he missed more than he realized. His chest filled with anxiety, fear, and relief. He might throw up.

"BO!?" Emma shrieked.

She'd gotten taller, lost her braces, and grew further into herself. Bo gulped, now understanding what 'overcome' really meant.

His sister was beautiful.

Bo dropped his bags in time to catch Emma as she leapt into his arms. He closed his eyes and hugged her tight against him, grateful for the practice of that earlier lift Marilyn insisted on.

"Hey, Ems." He set her on her feet and turned to his mom. "Ma…"

Tears rolled down her cheeks as she yanked him close and buried her head against his chest. Bo blinked as he fought the tears filling his own eyes too.

"Bennett." His name muffled against his shirt, but he felt it, deep inside. Whatever his fears might be, his mother would forgive him. She'd have his back. She only wanted him in her life again, like it used to be.

Marilyn's hand pressed warm and supportive against his back, leaving him overwhelmed.

The tears now clung to his lashes. He deserved none of this.

"Missed you, Ma." Bo held her tighter. "You look so great." He released her and stepped back, looking between his sister and mother again.

"You both look amazing. It's so good to see you."

"You're huge!" Emma squeaked. "What do you eat?"

Bo raised an eyebrow. "You got a boyfriend? I eat little sister's boyfriends. For lunch."

Emma groaned and slugged him. "Knock it off."

Marilyn slipped her hand around his bicep and stepped closer, a reminder he needed to make appropriate introductions. He left the luggage lay on the floor and wrapped one arm around her.

"Mom, Emma, this is my girlfriend, Marilyn Darby." He paused. "Marilyn, my mom, Robin, and my sister, Emma."

Marilyn extended her hand, but Robin wouldn't accept that formality. She pulled Marilyn into a tight hug instead.

"My word, you're beautiful. It's wonderful to meet you! I can't wait to hear all about you and Bo and…"

Emma offered the same treatment, hugging Marilyn too, who glanced at Bo in surprise. He forced his lips together to fight the amusement welling up inside him.

"It's wonderful to meet you both too." She stepped back beside Bo, perhaps for her own protection, slipping her hand around his arm again.

"What are you doing with him?" Emma muttered with a wink. "You're way too pretty to be with this slug."

Not to be outdone, Marilyn gave it right back. "I felt sorry for him. Poor thing." She shrugged easily, glancing up at him with a sweet expression of light flirtation.

Bo grimaced. "Hey! Maybe I felt sorry for you, Twinkle Toes." He tweaked her nose and she squeaked.

Everyone laughed.

"We were on our way to get something to eat. Your father's at the pool already. Can we count on you two for dinner? Asher and Linc should be around. But it would be nice if we could all catch up tonight."

The note of hope in her voice caught Bo in his gut. He nodded stupidly, grateful when Marilyn took over the conversation for him.

"We'd love that! I'm dying to meet everyone. And I know Bo wants to visit." She squeezed his arm. "Right?"

Again, he nodded stupidly, still working to process the scene in front of him.

Marilyn sneakily elbowed him as she held out her phone. "Why don't you put your contact information in here, Robin, and you can text me with the details of where to meet you?"

Bo's mom readily accepted this invitation, and he couldn't help but notice she beamed the entire time, once again revealing to him how magical Marilyn could be.

"Bennett's father mentioned seafood earlier, but I'll let you know what he decides after we chat." Bo's mom handed the phone back to Marilyn and gave her another hug.

"We're glad you came." She looked up at her son who struggled to breathe. She patted his chest as if she somehow understood. "We have a lot to talk about, don't we?"

Bo nodded. "Yeah."

She patted him again. "There's time. I'm glad you're here." She turned to Emma and tugged on her sleeve. "Let's go find out about lunch, sweetie."

Emma winked at Marilyn who winked back. She leaned close enough to whisper loudly to ensure Bo heard too, "Make sure you get him to make you scones sometime. Nothing in the world like his scones."

Bo gave his sister a playful shove. He watched as his family got into the elevator before lifting his bags and Marilyn's from the floor.

When the door closed, he looked down at her and leaned close to press his lips to her forehead. "Thank you. A thousand times for that."

He stepped back and looked into her eyes.

Marilyn grinned, a wicked twinkle in her eye. "My lips like to be thanked too."

Surprised by her boldness, Bo leaned down to brush his lips to hers. "Thank you, Marilyn's lips."

She squeezed his arms. "Thank you, Bo's lips. Let's try that again later."

**

Hours later Marilyn clutched Bo's sweaty hand as they made their way down to the hotel restaurant where they'd meet the bulk of his immediate family for dinner. To say her man was nervous might be the understatement of the year.

"Sorry." He yanked his hand free and wiped it on his pants again. Marilyn nudged him into a quiet hallway, several feet from the restaurant entrance.

She held out her bare arm, flexing. "Do you need to punch me? I can take it."

Bo looked into her eyes, his own now dancing with amusement, not fear. A win in Marilyn's mind.

"You want me to punch you, Twinkles? You can't even move the bag and I shoot it across the room."

"Hey!" She punched him. "I can move the bag. I just choose not to."

Bo chuckled. "OK. You can move the bag." He glanced around. "Apparently, there's a fantastic pizza place not far from here. Any chance you'd be interested in that instead? I feel like pizza."

Marilyn cocked her head to one side. She couldn't fault him for bolting. After all she, too, would avoid her own family at any cost.

But they were adults. They could do this.

She tapped her lips as she considered a plan. "We need a code word."

Bo's eyebrows lifted. "What?"

"Like if things get bad, a code word or phrase that we need to get out of there. I might not realize it and there's no need to make it ugly, right?"

Bo took Marilyn's hand. "No. Right. So, what should the code be?" He paused, grinning as he looked into her eyes again. "I got it." He snapped his fingers. "Titus."

Marilyn giggled, though she didn't follow his line of thinking. "Why Titus?"

Bo shrugged. "Because he annoys me. You'll realize I'm upset if I say his name."

Marilyn exhaled in exasperation. "We can't use Titus!" She whacked his arm. "We'll use something that's less likely to come up."

Bo rolled his eyes. "Why would Titus come up?"

"Your sister's probably his biggest fan."

Bo pursed his lips. "I'll kill her."

"Bennett Oliver."

The bodyguard stilled. Marilyn schooled her features as she waited for him to catch up. But instead of taking things seriously, his lips curled.

"I like that."

Marilyn stared at him. "You like what?"

He pulled her close. "I like when you say my name."

Marilyn squirmed in his arms, while at the same time not making a real effort to escape him. Why would she?

"Now is not the time for this. Your family is waiting!"

But Bo didn't listen to any of her protests. Instead he lowered his head and pressed his lips to hers. "I think you're amazing, Twinkles." He held her tight and kissed her until Marilyn got dizzy.

Finally, Bo lifted his head and grinned. "Code word is dizzy. Because that's what you're doing to me." He laced their fingers together.

"Let's go, Twinkles."

**

Bo entered the hotel restaurant, grateful that Marilyn walked beside him for support. He could be brave. All that closeness in the hallway boosted his confidence so he felt he could do anything, including deal with the father who likely wouldn't be nearly as happy to see him as his mother and sister had been.

That code word might actually come in handy.

"There they are. Showtime." Bo ground the words out through his teeth. Marilyn gripped his hand.

"Remember, dizzy."

Against his nerves Bo snickered anyway. "I'm not sure I'll ever forget being dizzy where you're concerned."

Her cheeks darkened and she elbowed him in the stomach.

"Bo!" his mom's voice reached him above the restaurant's din. She stood and waved her arms as if he could miss the three large tables pushed together in the center of the space to accommodate their family.

He pulled Marilyn along, allowing his mom to hug them both, presenting them to the rest of the family as if they were some kind of sideshow attraction.

Before Robin could make the introductions, his brothers stood and clapped him on the back, hugging him and Marilyn too. Bo shot them each a glare to remind them of their place, even as a sudden idea struck him hard.

He'd been so worried about what Marilyn knew, and that she not share his secrets before he wanted that he'd not even considered mentioning Frannie to her.

Worry pooled in his gut.

His family would say something stupid. He knew it. All the good he'd done, all the work to let himself go and enjoy a new relationship would disappear in a puff of smoke when she realized he hid such an important part of himself from her.

Could he steal her away and tell her now? He couldn't figure how he'd drop a bomb like Frannie and then go on with dinner as if everything was the same. Once Marilyn knew the truth, things probably could never be the same.

He wanted to puke.

In desperation, Bo leaned toward Marilyn and whispered, "Dizzy." He jerked his head toward the door.

She rolled her eyes and started to pull out her chair. Reluctantly he nudged her aside and pulled it out for her.

"I'm serious," he whispered.

"I'm going to slug you," she shot back.

Bo frowned but placed two firm hands on her shoulders as she sat next to Emma.

"So, I don't need to do this a million separate times for all of you," he began loudly. "This is my girlfriend, Marilyn Darby. Marilyn, that's Lincoln and Asher, you met Emma already."

Marilyn waved to everyone as he continued.

"And that's my sister Hailey, her husband Paxton and their little girl, Cara."

Bo cleared his throat as his eyes fell finally on the head of the table, the spot he avoided from the second he entered the restaurant.

He looked down at Marilyn. "And that handsome guy at the head of the table is my father, Joe Sutton." He paused, turning his attention back to his dad, grateful his mother seated them as far apart as possible.

"Dad? This is my girlfriend, Marilyn."

Marilyn smiled as Bo slipped into the seat next to hers. He took her hand as she spoke. "It's lovely to meet you all. Bo's told me so much about you."

A few pleasantries were exchanged as Bo tried to focus on the stunning woman next to him, who already had fallen into a companionable conversation with his sister. Marilyn could be friends with anyone, he assumed, and despite his initial misgivings about her, he realized she might be the perfect person to be at his side in this.

It didn't hurt that her long dark hair fell in beautiful waves past her shoulders. Or that her dress showed off the benefits of the hard work of her dancing career. She looked stunning. But it was more than that. Bo hoped this trip wouldn't be overshadowed by the family problems they'd both been running from for so long, but that instead they'd get the chance to become closer to find out if maybe, just maybe, he could be ready for a serious relationship again.

A nudge to his gut brought him back to the moment. Everyone laughed as he rubbed the tender spot while looking at Marilyn.

"What's that for?"

She grinned and leaned into him. "Your father asked you a question."

Lincoln chuckled. "But you were too busy staring at your girlfriend to listen."

"Not that we blame you," Asher offered with a wink he aimed at Marilyn. She returned it.

"Right back at ya!"

Marilyn shifted in her seat and looked up at Bo and patted his cheek. "We should visit with your family again. It's good for my confidence."

Bo met her gaze, wishing he could stare into those eyes forever. Reluctantly, he forced himself to turn his attention to his father. "Sorry. What did you say, Dad?"

"I asked how your job's going?"

He would ask that. In front of everyone no less. Bo didn't want to play this game.

"It's exceptional." Marilyn beamed up at him, trying to communicate something he didn't quite understand with her wide eyes. "Isn't it, sweetie?"

The endearment caught Bo in the chest. Sweetie? She would pick the same moniker Frannie gave him. He'd squelch that later. For now, he squeezed her hand hard enough to let her know he didn't appreciate her help. She frowned, probably wondering what she'd done.

"Work is great, Dad." Bo's phone buzzed in his pocket and he slipped it out, surprised that Daisy's name popped up.

He slipped his fingers free from Marilyn's and pushed his seat back. "In fact, there it is now. Excuse me."

**

Bo disappeared so quickly Marilyn didn't get a chance to regroup. She smiled stupidly at his family who now mostly stared at her in either fascination or annoyance.

Like so many things, it might be a toss-up.

She glanced down at the menu, grateful the waitress showed up at that exact moment.

Bo returned in time to offer his order and menu to the server.

Marilyn leaned toward him. "Everything OK?"

"Yeah. My boss had a question." He paused, reassuring her with a look. "I took care of it."

"So. Bennett. Marilyn just started to tell us about her job."

Marilyn thought this through and was happily prepared to offer her most impressive synopsis of her work. She winked at Joe Sutton.

"I actually have a few jobs. I'm currently building my clientele for a dance company, so I do private lessons for people who aren't able or don't want to join a traditional dance class, and I teach basic classes too—mostly preschoolers. Outside of that I waitress a few nights a week for extra money. I'm almost at the point of being ready to put a down payment on a studio space I've had my eye on for a long time."

Joe nodded silently.

"I've always wanted to learn how to dance." Robin's tone sounded dreamy and wishful.

Marilyn appreciated her effort at helping this conversation along. "Well maybe me and Bo can teach you a few things at the wedding." She nudged him, unaware of the way he frowned beside her.

"Earlier today we even got a new lift down, didn't we?"

"Bo dances?" Lincoln howled as he and Asher proceeded to tease their older brother.

"OK, knock it off," Robin snapped. "Why can't he dance?"

"Because men his size don't dance, they play football," Joe snapped.

Marilyn reached over to grip Bo's hand. "He wanted to help me get ready for an audition, so he learned enough to catch me properly and spin me around." She looked up at him, only then becoming aware of his annoyance. She winked, ignoring it.

"But I found out how good he is and I've been teaching him a few things." She leaned into him. "And you promised to dance with me at the wedding."

Bo groaned but made no acknowledgement of her words. Marilyn rummaged through her mind, trying to figure what she said or didn't say that had him looking so distraught.

"If he won't dance with you, I will!" Lincoln offered.

Marilyn winked at him before turning back to the rest of the family. "Don't worry." She leaned forward and scanned the table as if they all now shared a secret. "I'll make him dance for you. Like a sweet baby show pony."

Everyone howled and she leaned into Bo again, careful to look up at him in adoration so he'd understand she was only kidding.

His upset appeared to dissolve and he leaned down to whisper, "You're in trouble, Twinkles."

She batted her eyelashes, relieved that whatever had Bo upset appeared to have gone away. "Aren't I always?"

**

The meal went smoothly after that, with Marilyn holding her own against Bo's loud, but welcoming family. He cursed himself for waiting so long to visit. But at the same time, he relished being bold enough to make this relationship happen—whatever it might be now or might become—because Marilyn was everything Bo ever dreamed he wanted.

Eventually the group began to disperse, and dessert plates were collected. Everyone but Bo's mother, father, Marilyn, and Bo went back to their rooms.

Joe leaned back in his seat, his eyes focused entirely on Bo as the waitress set a drink in front of him.

"Been a long time, Bennett. You made your mom's day coming to this."

Bo nodded, grateful his father spoke first. He said a silent prayer for peace as he replied. "Yeah. Life's been crazy the last few years. It made getting away almost impossible." He looked at his mom as he continued. "I missed everyone."

She smiled. "We sure missed you too."

Bo reached for Marilyn's hand under the table. He glanced at her and they shared a moment, one he expected to mull over later.

She cared about him. She wanted this to go well. He smiled, warming when she leaned into him.

"Your mom's behaved herself all night but I'm not sure she can keep something to herself any longer." Joe glanced at his wife, shrugging his shoulders. "Go ahead, Robin."

Bo looked at his mother, surprised when her gaze reflected not love and warmth but concern and maybe sympathy.

He gulped as she turned her attention to Marilyn. "We're glad you came, honey. I just… I think maybe there are things you need to know."

Bo's mouth went dry. Surely she wouldn't unload the Frannie debacle like this. She had too much class.

"Mom…" he ground out.

She raised one hand. "Bennett. I'm going to speak and you're going to listen." She slipped her phone free and tapped it a few times before handing it over to him.

Daisy filled the screen, followed by a picture where he stood in the shadows behind her and Robby.

Bo cleared his throat. He'd bought time on Frannie, but not the truth of his job.

"Emma found that when she went looking for tickets for the tour. She swore it was you and wanted to ask, but I said it couldn't be." His mom raised her eyes. "I mean, what would you be doing hanging out with rock stars?"

The photos were grainy and for all that Bo tried desperately to keep his face and name hidden, he should have been aware that regardless of his care and hopes to stay clean and out of the spotlight, his position would shove him there anyway.

He turned his eyes away as Marilyn accepted the phone and handed it back to his mom.

"Mrs. Sutton," Marilyn began after a long and painful silence passed where Joe drank, Robin worried her hands, and Bo stared at them both.

He squeezed Marilyn's hand.

"I got this." He paused as he sat up straight in his chair. "I'm not CIA or a spy. I'm a personal assistant to Daisy Grant. I live with her, Robby, their daughters, and another bodyguard. I help them with everything from appointments to security to baby duty. That's what I do. We only wrapped up a tour a few months ago." He sighed, grateful to have the truth out, while at the same time nervous for how his parents would process this news.

His mom's mouth hung open and as usual his father showed no change in expression. He sipped at his drink as the waitress brought another.

Marilyn squeezed Bo's hand this time. He rubbed his thumb over her skin as he tried to breathe, grateful for her support, but wondering if it would be enough to see him through this moment.

The silence stretched on from a beat to a minute.

"You're a personal assistant to a celebrity couple? Since when?" Robin asked. "Why wouldn't you tell us?"

Bo gestured toward his father with his free hand. "You saw the look on his face. That's why. It's not a 'manly' job, Ma. He's going to be humiliated in front of his friends. It's bad enough I don't play football. Now this. I mean, the bodyguard part, that's something- but the changing diapers and scheduling interviews part, that's another."

Joe's cheeks reddened. Still, he said nothing.

Robin looked from her husband to her son. "This is what you've been doing since you got out of the military?"

Where should he begin? "Not immediately after. No. Only the last year."

Keep it simple. They didn't need to fuss over his string of lame jobs that came before the one he'd been born to do. It would only make things worse if he gave them too much information at once.

Marilyn moved closer to his side, her small body almost entirely against him as if her mere presence would hold the family together. "Bo is phenomenal at his job."

Robin looked at her in surprise. "You knew about all this?"

Marilyn nodded. "I did. And I truly don't understand the problem. He's incredibly devoted to his work and to Daisy and Robby. They all adore him."

Robin lifted her eyebrows.

"So, tell me, son," Joe snapped. "What else have you been doing the last few years? What else got ahead of getting a real job, taking responsibility for yourself, and coming home to visit your mom every once in a while?"

Bo didn't respond. There would be no winning. He slid his chair back, releasing Marilyn's hand as he did.

"I've always taken responsibility for myself and I haven't asked you or anyone else for a thing, Dad." He paused. "For the last year I've wondered if I should tell you about my job and how I'd even do it. I stewed over it for so long I couldn't find my way clear."

He glanced at Marilyn as he stood. "But when I met Marilyn, I realized I made a mistake. I'm proud of my job. I'm proud that I'm practically the only one who can get Daisy and Robby's baby to sleep at night. I love what I'm doing and I'm good at it. So, guess what? What you think about it actually doesn't matter. You don't have to like it or even approve of it."

Bo held out his hand to Marilyn who slowly shoved back her chair and stood. She took his hand and they walked out of the restaurant together while Bo wondered if it would be appropriate to just start driving home now or wait until morning.

Chapter eleven

Bo didn't say a word all the way back to their rooms, which were side by side and connected by an adjoining door. Understanding that he needed time to process the emotional explosion, Marilyn said nothing either.

She squeezed his hand, not wanting to push him to talk. He squeezed back, waiting as she unlocked her door. She held it open with her back and turned to him, arms open. He wrapped her up close, pressing her tight against him, his nose finding her hair.

"I'm glad you're here," he whispered, inhaling before he continued. "I'm sorry you had to witness that. They're ridiculous."

Marilyn shook her head against his chest. "No, it's fine. We knew it might not go perfectly, but you did fine."

Bo stepped back, one hand toying with her hair before he dropped it slowly, he head down. "I think I need to be alone—to think. I'm sorry." He released her and went to his own door and slipped inside as she watched, saying a silent prayer for him, his parents, and their entire family.

**

Bo stared out the window for so long he lost track of time altogether. And still, he found no answers.

A light tapping on the hallway door dragged him from his stupor to look through the peephole where he found Emma in her fuzzy pjs, eyebrows drawn together in worry.

He yanked the door open but couldn't feign happiness, even for his little sister. "Hey kid, you shouldn't be consorting with the enemy."

She pushed her way inside and closed the door. "I'm sorry I outted you to mom and dad. I should have asked you first."

Bo loosened his tie as she flopped into the chair he vacated, making herself right at home.

"Marilyn knew about it?"

"Yep." Bo sank onto the bed. "She's Daisy's dance instructor." He would not revisit their real first meeting story. While he assured himself he'd let his worries over her go, a tiny bit deep down still hung tight. What if she really was like Frannie? Maybe once she got what she wanted out of him, or when she realized he'd only ever be this strange combination of housewife and muscleman, she'd bolt too.

Marilyn could do better than tie herself to Bo. Maybe at that very moment she realized it too.

Bo forced these things aside. Not much good they'd do right now anyway, before he handled the matter in front of him.

Emma considered this new information about her brother's girlfriend. "That's neat she gets to teach Daisy. Now I really like her."

Bo blew out an exhale. "Me too." He shouldn't have left Marilyn to worry over him. He'd check on her after he talked to Emma.

He looked at his sister. "How ticked are mom and dad?"

She shrugged and put her feet on the bed next to him "Mom's crying. Dad's staring at the television. I think we're all supposed to sit at the same table at the reception so that should be interesting."

Bo ran one hand over his hair. "Yep. Sorry."

"For what?" Emma bounced out of her chair and landed next to him on the bed. "I can't believe you work for Robby and Daisy Grant! Holy heck, Bo! That's awesome! Tell me everything! You're practically famous."

He snorted at his sister's innocence. "Not even close. But they are pretty great."

"What are they like? Are they nice? Does Robby walk around without a shirt on? Oh my goodness—all those tattoos! How do you get to look at that every day!? It's not fair."

She froze in the midst of her joy, turning to him, mouth hanging open.

"Oh. My. Gosh. I want to meet them!" she paused, grinning wickedly. "Can I come and visit you? I bet they have a thousand rooms in their house- they probably wouldn't even know I was there for a week!"

Despite his worries and hurt, Bo cuddled his sister close. "Settle down, kid. I'll tell you all about it."

**

Marilyn took a long, hot bath, and painted her nails. She itched to talk to Bo and make sure he was OK, but at the same time she could appreciate his needing space. Family did that to you sometimes.

Finally, after surfing the channels on her television, she had enough. She lifted her phone and text him. Whether he answered or not didn't matter—but at least he'd know she was there for him if he needed to talk.

I'm praying for you and your family. I hope you're feeling better.

After ten minutes of not getting a response, Marilyn lay back on her bed and prayed again for peace and wisdom, not sure what else to do.

A light knock on the door separating their rooms made her sit up. Nervous tingles raced up her spine as Marilyn hustled to the door and threw it open. Bo held up his phone, his expression unreadable.

"I figured I'd come over instead."

"Sure." She widened the door and he entered, leaving the door between their rooms open, watching him for any signs of a change in his demeanor.

"How are you doing? Did you talk to your mom or dad?"

Bo sat heavily on the chair on the opposite side of the room. "No. I doubt we'll be talking for a while. Emma stopped." He laughed. "She wants to come and visit me to find out if Robby walks around without his shirt on."

Marilyn smirked wisely. "Well, she is fifteen. Can't blame her. I'd be thinking the same thing."

Bo looked at her, lips pursed. She snickered, grateful to see some of his normal behavior returning already.

"If I was fifteen and didn't know him and love his wife…?"

Bo nodded. "Better."

Marilyn sat near him. She reached for his hands and held them tightly.

He looked into her eyes and Marilyn recalled the moment they shared at dinner. Maybe she still had a lot to work through with her family too, but she fit with Bo. He felt it too if that look in his dark eyes meant anything.

"You're gonna be OK," she determined, a confidence in her voice she hoped would convince him too. "And we'll have fun tomorrow. You said what you needed to and now they know. If they have questions or want to talk about it, you're open to that. The ball is in their court."

Bo released her hands so he could stand and pace. "We don't need to do this. I can mail the card to my cousin and…"

"Oh no you don't." Marilyn stood too and went to him. She poked him hard in the chest.

"Ow!" Bo stepped back, rubbing the spot. "Why do you always do that? That and elbowing me in the gut really gets on my nerves."

Marilyn folded her arms over her chest. "Why do you always wimp out when things get hard?" She didn't wait for his response. "You can go to that wedding and you will. Not for your parents. But what about your sister who looks at you like you hung the moon? You need to go for Emma and Lincoln and Asher."

Bo surprised her with a smile. "You sure became one of the family quick enough."

"Yeah, well, I like yours better so I'm defecting from mine."

Bo grimaced. "Yours must be terrible."

Marilyn lifted an eyebrow. "Worse. I'll tell you all the dirt on our way there." She paused. "But for now… are you OK?"

Bo silently pulled her into his arms. He rested his chin on the top of her head after pecking her softly in the same spot, the intimacy of the gesture comfortable and right.

"I'm better now. I'm glad you came, Twinkles."

"Me too." She paused, not sure how to push, but knowing he needed it. "And you're going to dance your shoes off tomorrow."

Bo stepped back and looked down at her. "You're really going to push me, aren't you? Dancing doesn't fix everything."

She squeezed him. "It can if you let it. It can if we're in it together." She lifted one shoulder. "Besides, now that we've bragged about it, we need to show off a little at least."

He groaned. "You bragged. I didn't."

Marilyn boldly stepped closer and pulled him in again. "Yeah? Well, you should. Because you're a talented dancer and an even better man, Bennett Oliver Sutton."

"You're crazy." He paused. "Hey, what's your full name? No fair you knowing mine and using it against me all the time."

"Ugh." Marilyn winced, closing her eyes as she said it. "Yours is so much better. Mine is Marilyn Autumn Darby."

"Marilyn Autumn? That's a beautiful…" His voice drifted off as he put it together.

Marilyn stepped back and looked up at him as he tried not to chuckle.

"That's right. You're the BOS and I'm MAD. Apparently neither of our parents considered initials like they should have."

Bo howled until he gasped for air. Marilyn folded her arms over her chest as she waited for him to get control of himself.

He swiped at his eyes as she exhaled. "Better?"

"Sure. I'm better." He reached for her again, squeezing her close. "I promise I'll only call you Twinkles unless you really get on my nerves, then maybe you'll be Mad. OK?"

"Fine. But don't expect me to call you 'boss'."

He smirked with a wink. "Wouldn't dream of it."

**

The next day, after sneaking away from the hotel for breakfast and touring the area, Bo dropped Marilyn back at her room so they could get ready for the wedding, which graciously was only streets away and would make for a nice walk. They'd had a fabulous day and not once run into any of Bo's family. He still needed time to mentally prepare for how to handle sitting with them for the entire evening.

Marilyn mercifully didn't bring anything up about them all day.

Bo showered and dressed quickly, anxious to see Marilyn's dress since she'd been teasing him about it and how it would make it "sooo easy to show off on the dancefloor all night". He chuckled to himself as he fussed with his tie. She still assumed he would dance all night with her.

Truth be told, he would do practically anything she asked.

When their agreed-upon time to leave for the church finally came, Bo tapped on Marilyn's door, waiting only seconds for her to open it.

"I've been ready for twenty minutes!" she squealed, her mouth forming an 'o' as she stared at him from head to toe.

Bo didn't begrudge her since he planned on doing the same thing. Her dress was miraculous. A pale green, it hugged in all the right places and flared in the rest. He imagined twirling her fast and hard, so the skirt stood straight out as they crossed the dancefloor together.

Marilyn finished ogling him and twirled around so he could get a better look. "Perfect for swing dancing, huh?"

He nodded. "You look amazing. Stunning. Gorgeous."

She stopped twirling and met his eyes. "Thank you." Her voice sounded breathless, like she might be afraid to believe him.

Still, she held his gaze.

"I'll let the lack of glasses slide for now." She winked. "There won't be anyone else I'll look at the entire night."

Bo pulled her close, relishing the way they fit together. Reluctantly, he pulled back. "We better go or we'll be late for the wedding."

**

Marilyn proudly held Bo's hand as they entered the church together. He nodded and said hello to several people, but didn't introduce her as he appeared to simply want to sit and be left alone. She didn't pry, wondering if he'd let her in on any of his past on his own when he was ready.

Emma spotted them from several rows up. She winked at Marilyn who did the same in return before nudging Bo. He grinned at his sister and stuck out his tongue.

It didn't escape Marilyn's notice that neither of Bo's parents seemed the least bit interested in him or where he sat.

"Hey." Lincoln and Asher slid into the pew next to Bo, bumping him roughly so he had no choice but to urge Marilyn to scoot down.

"Hello…" Asher winked as he leaned across Bo who elbowed him.

"What?" the younger Sutton squeaked, elbowing him back.

"Hello boys." Marilyn emphasized the word 'boys' as she bit back her amusement.

"Enough." Bo rolled his eyes.

Asher winked again to prove his point.

"Man, are Mom and Dad pissed at you." Lincoln whistled low and shook his head. "You're the black sheep now, not Wyatt."

Bo slugged his brother. "I've been the black sheep for years. And watch your language. We are in church."

"Ugh." Lincoln groaned. "Did you hear they invited Frannie? I'm going to slug Ricky."

Bo stiffened at these words. Now curiosity might kill her. But Marilyn didn't ask. She wouldn't, when it looked as if Bo wished he could crawl out of his skin or run out of the church altogether.

Who was Frannie?

Asher whacked Lincoln. "Mom said not to say anything because she probably won't come."

Lincoln hit him back. "Knock it off. The service is starting."

But Asher didn't quit. He leaned over and poked Bo. "Think you can get me a date with Carli Cross? I figured I'd ask her to prom but if you know her, hey, maybe she'll actually say yes."

Marilyn leaned over and smiled at the boys, both of them adorably smaller versions of their older brother.

"You two need to sit with us at the reception."

"Yeah?" Lincoln asked. "Why?"

"So, I can make sure your brother doesn't sneak off and kill you for annoying him."

Bo glanced at her. "Like you know how to do that. Remember I didn't like you much when we met, Twinkles."

She grinned. "I'll never forget, Muscles. It's a badge of honor."

"Man, do you got a sister?" Asher asked longingly.

Marilyn lifted her eyebrows. "Sadly yes. But they're both older and spoken for."

The organ began playing at that moment and Bo glanced down at her with something she couldn't quite discern in his eyes. She smiled but he didn't, turning his attention to the back of the church as everyone stood and watched the bride coming down the aisle.

All except for Marilyn who wondered over Frannie and why Bo suddenly seemed so distraught at the mention of her name.

She squirmed. They really should have spent more time getting to know each other before taking this trip.

**

Bo couldn't pay attention to anything that happened during the service. Nothing made any sense as soon as he realized Frannie might show up somewhere. In fact, she could be sitting behind him right now, watching the back of his head and wondering how he'd finally moved on without her when she worked so diligently at destroying him.

Of course, she moved on without him first. She didn't earn the right to be hurt.

Bo lifted his arm and stretched to put it around Marilyn's shoulders. He told himself it might be because of the day's romance and how well things were going between them, not because Frannie might see him and wish she'd been different when she had the chance.

Unaware of his torment, Marilyn snuggled into him, resting her head in the crook of his shoulder as if she'd been meant to reside exactly in that position. Bo kissed the top of her head, wondering how to tell her about Frannie. And worse, how to handle the humiliating story.

He should have told her already. He had plenty of chances and he'd blown all of them because he'd been too focused on his parents, his job, and falling in love with the frustrating dancer who occupied everything since he met her.

What responsibility did he have to her, really? Their weekend started as a farce, and while it morphed into something deeper, neither had been bold enough to delve into what it might be. Maybe they were both too scared of ruining the magic that seemed to be happening to dig into defining their relationship.

He should have worn the glasses. It would be easier to tell her the truth if he could convince himself she might think him handsome enough to forgive.

"Hey, Muscles, you getting up?" Marilyn nudged him to stand as the service ended.

Bo stood, pressing his lips to her soft hair as he did. He tried not to look around the church. He didn't want to know if

Frannie came, and if she did, he'd rather do anything but see her again.

Could they skip the reception?

Lincoln and Asher tumbled over each other to get out of the row first while Bo clutched Marilyn's hand and followed behind.

"I should probably tell you something before we get to the reception," he began as they made their way out of the church.

Marilyn looked up at him. They walked leisurely, slowly separating from the people outside the church. She didn't say anything.

Bo licked his lips, wondering where to start. Hating to say this at all, let alone right after a wedding ceremony.

"Bo Sutton!?"

That voice.

Bo froze.

Frannie ran down the sidewalk toward him, her husband dragging behind.

Everything happened in slow motion.

And it happened too fast to stop.

Just like a horrific train wreck.

Bo crushed Marilyn's hand until she squeaked. "Bo? What's going on?"

But he couldn't even muster the strength for an apology as he turned toward the woman he hoped to never in his life see again.

He should have expected this. After all, she and Bo, along with the bride and groom had all grown up together. But he'd never given it any mind. His mom said Frannie moved, got married, this was his family not hers… there were a million and one reasons she shouldn't be running toward him now.

And yet here she came, barreling toward him in heels and sequins.

"Gosh, you walk fast, but you always did, didn't you with those long legs of yours!" She tossed her stylish blond hair over one shoulder.

Uninvited, she sidled up to Bo in a hug that made him want to run away and loofah for an hour. She smelled like she always did, too much perfume and hair product. Bo coughed and looked away to collect himself at the memories this brought.

He'd been a fool then, but found himself a worse one now. He didn't tell Marilyn about this part of his past, and by the confusion in her eyes, he understood he made a huge mistake.

Frannie stepped back and gestured toward the supermodel beside her.

"You remember Bradley."

Bo nodded in the man's direction, careful to keep his expression neutral even as he watched Frannie giving Marilyn a lengthy once-over.

"Well…" Frannie dragged the word out, which set Bo's teeth on edge. He lifted an eyebrow, still saying nothing.

Marilyn jerked on his arm as if to remind him of her presence. He clutched her hand, aware he had to say something, but unable to make himself speak. Frannie, again, beat him to it.

"It's nice you came. I didn't think you'd make the trip. Your family said you haven't been home in years."

Again, Frannie looked him over, followed by a quick glance in Marilyn's direction. She always worried about appearances, so whatever she noted apparently didn't set well because her lips pursed in that way that indicated Marilyn fell short of her high-brow interest or concern.

"Been a few years for us too. I imagine you figured you wouldn't see me again."

Bo's nostrils flared. He wouldn't give her the satisfaction of anything. Not a damned thing.

Again, Marilyn squeezed his hand, eyes wide. Bo exhaled.

"Well, Frannie, if you'll excuse us…" He started to turn away, but Marilyn jerked on his arm and at the same time extended her other hand toward Frannie.

"I'm Marilyn Darby, Bo's girlfriend. It's a pleasure to meet you… Frannie?"

Bo's stomach clenched. This couldn't be happening

Images of the devil on one shoulder and the angel on the other filled his mind—one with Frannie's face, the other with Marilyn's.

Frannie's lips curled into a vicious grin. "Bo…" She made his name sound like a dirty trick. "I figured you'd given up forever after I left you at the altar."

If this revelation shocked Marilyn, she sure didn't show it. Instead, her own mouth formed a sweet smile as she moved even closer against Bo's side, clinging to him possessively. "Oh honey, don't give yourself so much credit. I could hardly get his attention for all the girlfriends he had when we met." She clung to his arm as she laced their fingers together, squeezing hard enough to let him know this façade would end and he'd pay heavily.

Marilyn batted her eyelashes at him, sweetness and venom at war in her gaze. "Who knew he'd be waiting for me? Would you believe we've been together six months already?" She looked up at him, mouth smiling, eyes on fire.

Oh no. He was a dead man.

**

This bombshell demon-woman left Bo at the altar?

While Frannie might have a pretty face, her sour expression and bitter tone told a different story. How had someone as sweet as Bo fallen into her trap?

Marilyn clung to Bo to make a good show of things, but more so she could remain upright and not pass out with a mix of anger and shock.

They had hours for him to bring this up and yet he only appeared to be worried about his dang parents and their reaction to his job.

Apparently Bennett Sutton didn't have one skeleton in his closet, but a whole crew of them having a rave.

And for how great Marilyn thought things had been going between them, she'd not known a darned thing. He must be the world's best actor.

She tried to breathe, working to give him some kind of reason for keeping this to himself. How could he presume it wouldn't come up with his family? And if it did, it would have made Marilyn look like a fool, and worse, would have exposed their ruse—fading though it might be—for everyone to see.

It all amounted to one of a few options- Bo didn't care, didn't trust her, or didn't plan to stick around after he got what he wanted from her.

Just like Zeke, and Lucas before him. Only out for themselves and what she could do for them. Well, she signed up for this, so she'd play her part and do it well. She'd bear no guilt at the end of the weekend.

But he better keep those powerful lips away from her from now on.

Bo squeezed her hand, likely relieved she continued playing along. She tugged on his arm. "Let's go, Muscles."

Marilyn glanced at Frannie. "It's been lovely meeting you. Maybe we'll catch you two at the reception."

She dragged Bo down the sidewalk, wondering how far away they had to get before she dropped his hand and bolted for the hotel alone.

"You're amazing," Bo said gratefully.

What did he mean by that? She wanted to kill him!

Marilyn's cheeks burned. "Don't you dare speak to me." They turned a corner and crossed a street where she dropped his hand, now sure they were out of Frannie's scope of vision.

Bo gaped at her. "What...? Marilyn, seriously."

Marilyn power walked most of the way to the hotel, stopping only to look both ways before crossing. Bo silently kept up, saying nothing until they reached the hotel. He pulled her off the sidewalk and toward the garden area where a few people milled around.

"I'm sorry." He grasped her arm tightly. "I didn't know she'd be here, and I couldn't find a reason to bring it up—at least not this early into things."

Bo rubbed his forehead, effectively shielding his face from Marilyn as he continued.

"Getting left at the altar is pretty humiliating in case you didn't guess that already."

Marilyn scoffed and looked away, tugging her hand free of his electric touch. "Don't worry," she snapped. "I'm not going to out you or this stupid fake relationship. But if you don't mind, keep your lips to yourself for the rest of the weekend and stop messing with my head."

She turned her back to him and pretended to study an array of wildflowers in the landscaping. She felt Bo's warmth against her back, followed by his hand on her shoulder.

"I didn't mean to mess with your head. I'm… not so good at sharing things about myself- especially this. It was awful, beyond awful. Don't you think it's bad enough I've got family problems, and a horrible relationship past too?"

He didn't say anything for a long time. "Marilyn. I've dated Frannie and you. That's it. You want me to humiliate myself? There it is. Two girlfriends and I'm thirty-two years old. Only a handful of dates between those two experiences because I don't trust people."

Marilyn's shoulders sagged. She felt for the guy. She did. But what about her feelings? She had a part in this relationship too. And she had enough of men using her over the years. They were all the same.

This one only hurt worse because she'd been sure Bo might be different. He'd been so sensitive and kind and caring already that…

Well, she needed to accept that he must be like all the rest. And that's why she didn't bother with relationships. Good thing she already started Plan B with her application to Princeton.

Her stomach soured.

Slowly Marilyn turned and looked up at him.

"Being left at the altar is a bit of an important detail. One you could have shared."

Bo nodded. "It is. And I should have. You're absolutely right."

When he didn't deny his part in the problem, Marilyn lost her will to fight. "So why not tell me?"

He raked one hand over his head. "Come on. I don't know much about your past either except for Zeke and the gym—and that's not much really. This is still new for both of us."

While true, Marilyn didn't intend to turn the conversation back to her own past. "Fine. But before we go in there, I want the rundown on what happened, so I'm not blindsided again. With our luck the bride seated us right next to Frannie and whatever his name was."

Bo looked deeply into her eyes. "I don't know if I could be sorrier for all this. Really."

The sincerity in his voice caught her in the deepest part of her chest. Marilyn stared at him, hating the way she melted, her defenses fizzling out.

"I accept your apology. Now, tell me about Frannie."

**

Tension radiated from Bo's neck and shoulders all the way down his spine. He could not, by his own stupidity, lose the first good relationship in his entire life. Marilyn deserved better, but he didn't know how to stop this, wallowing in his fears until he nearly drowned felt like Bo's normal.

He glanced around the gardens and spotted a bench on the far side. He tentatively held out one hand. Marilyn looked at it briefly before giving in. He pulled her to sit with him so they could talk privately.

"Frannie lost a bet and had to take me to a dance in high school." He began with no pretense. The story, now having been told too many times among his family and friends to count, was sadly, one of the main reasons he never went home. Even now at the wedding, he ducked his head ten or so times to avoid the looks of pity from well-meaning relatives.

Marilyn's eyebrows knit together. "Wait a second. She lost a bet?"

Bo nodded, aware how ridiculous it all sounded. "Yeah. I wasn't exactly the most popular kid in school, Twinkles. Everyone expected me to play sports, but I never quite managed the finesse that sort of thing needed. So, I worked as the equipment manager for the basketball team when I was bigger than some of the players. And I…" He looked away, recalling how embarrassed his dad had been.

"I acted in school plays. I loved that."

Marilyn nodded. "OK. Go on."

"So, of course Frannie was the stereotypical 'golden girl' everyone either strived to be or be friends with… or in most guys' cases, they wanted to date her. I didn't even go there, I silently worshipped from afar. I'm not stupid. I didn't even think of asking anyone on a date in high school."

Bo exhaled and watched as several couples made their way into the hotel. He leaned back in his seat and continued, careful not to look at Marilyn. He didn't want any pity on his behalf.

Truth be told, he wanted to go back to New York and forget he ever tried to do this.

"Frannie and her friends had a good time making fun of me, picking on me, the usual stuff high school kids do. I took it, I didn't care. I had a few theater friends who didn't judge and that satisfied me enough. I got excellent grades and planned on joining the military after—figured getting into military intelligence would be fun and use some of what I liked to do best—computers, research, that kind of thing."

Marilyn listened intently, smiling at him in all the right places to keep him going. "Sounds like I would have liked you in high school."

Bo shrugged and continued. He didn't want her pity, he only wanted to get this out and go home where he could be appreciated for a job well done—and only as the person the Grants knew him to be, with no worry he'd be the loser he'd always been.

"Things would have been different for sure if I met you first."

Marilyn nodded. "Go on... what happened?"

"I'm still not entirely sure how the bet started, but it involved her asking me to Winter Formal. She was nominated to be the Queen of course and the guy she dated was supposed to be King. But the next thing I knew I found her crying on the bleachers after a game while I collected drink bottles and whatnot. I couldn't very well keep doing my job and not find out the problem, so I sat next to her and listened while she griped about her relationship problems."

His gut twisted over how stupid he'd been. Or maybe it was naivety. He had no experience with girls or dating—how could he know he'd been played?

Marilyn placed her hand on his arm and squeezed, the gentle pressure reassuring him. "You're always sensitive to what people need. That's a gift, Bo."

He grunted. "It's not always. She lured me right in and before I knew it, I was entertaining the masses by thinking she wanted to be with me. She kept up the joke until the end of senior year when she dumped me in a grand production that had my tail between my legs running to the Army recruiter's office to get the heck out of town."

Marilyn leaned her head against him. "I'm sorry."

He exhaled. "Me too. Because that's not the worst of it. When she realized college wasn't the same as high school and she'd become a little fish in a big pond, she ran back to the easy mark. Me." He paused. "I was stationed in Kansas when she started texting and writing. I forgave her. I guess when you aren't looking into someone's eyes it's hard to tell they're lying."

He forced himself to do better, to say the worst part of all. "I got leave and went home, proposed, and she accepted." Bo gulped. "I meant it to be a quick thing so she could come back with me and we could start over. But she got cold feet or… well, I don't know. I stood at the altar like an idiot for an hour waiting for her. She never showed."

Bo leaned forward and rested his elbows on his knees. "And that was that. I finished up my commitment with the Army, decided it wasn't for me after all, and ended up connecting with Daisy through Jazz because he worked out at my gym."

He glanced at Marilyn, wondering if he'd ever been so transparent before. "And that's it. That's Frannie."

"And you haven't dated anyone else?"

Bo shrugged, looking away. It was ridiculous to be thirty-two years old with his pathetic track record.

"I've been on a few dates since, nothing even close to serious. I never stuck it out beyond a second date. Plus, I moved a lot, that kept me from getting bogged down."

Summoning all his courage, Bo sat up and shifted so he looked directly into Marilyn's eyes. But he didn't find pity or even sympathy there. Something else filled her eyes and the expression on her lips.

"Well, if you don't mind my saying so, Frannie is an idiot. She had a thoughtful, kind, sensitive man—something every woman searches years for—and she used it and blew it. She's an idiot. I'm sorry you went through that."

Bo stared at her. No one ever said anything like that before. Anyone familiar with the story always wondered how he could be so stupid and naïve.

And even if he promised to keep his lips away from hers the entire weekend, Bo couldn't fight the force that pulled him closer to her, his arms wrapping around her until she pressed against him.

"Thank you," he whispered between kisses. "You're amazing, Mar."

**

Marilyn's head swam with the information Bo shared. She wanted to stay in his arms forever, despite her earlier directive for him to keep his lips to himself for the rest of the weekend. But she also wanted to punch Frannie's lights out for being so horrible.

Still, she would take the high road. As long as she didn't run into the woman in the restroom alone—then she made no promises. She'd put the fool in her rightful place.

Not a very Christian attitude. Convicted, Marilyn cleared her mind and prayed quickly for a kindness toward Frannie she didn't believe she could feel.

"Bo…" She leaned back slightly. "Should we… maybe go inside?"

He shrugged, his cheeks pink. "I'd be just as happy to take you out for dinner somewhere without all these people."

While she understood, she also couldn't imagine his time with his family should end merely with them realizing the truth about his work. He had things to do.

"We should try again with your family. Shouldn't we?" She took his hand and stood, trying to tug him to his feet.

"Why are you always right?" He muttered as he finally stood.

Marilyn grinned as they started walking. "I'll remember you said that if I'm ever wrong."

Bo chuckled as they went inside the exquisite hotel lobby, following the crowd to a huge ballroom with a sign that read 'Sutton- Harper wedding'.

Marilyn located their table number and they entered the crowded room. It would work in their favor that the wedding appeared to involve four or five hundred people, which would mean running into Frannie, if she decided to come, might be less likely.

"Over here." Bo directed Marilyn toward a large table where his sister and brothers were sitting, playing some kind of game with a folded piece of paper and some napkins.

"Yeesh," Lincoln moaned. "Where have you two been? We're bored out of our gourds."

Bo held the seat for Marilyn, and she scooted in, waiting until he sat before she said, "There's always a huge gap between the wedding and the reception. You walk slow or go somewhere else and you don't end up sitting and waiting as long."

Asher sipped at his iced tea. "It's been an hour already. I have a life to live."

Marilyn snickered at the drama of a teenager as Bo took her hand under the table.

Emma nudged her from the opposite side. "So, Bo won't say much, which I guess isn't shocking since he hardly says a word about anything. Will you tell me what Daisy and Robby are like? I'm dying here!" Her rapid-fire words made Marilyn giggle. She exchanged a glance with Bo, who shrugged.

"I told her Robby wears a shirt most of the time."

Marilyn turned her attention to the teens, all of whom waited in rapt attention for her assessment of the celebrity couple.

"I've never seen Robby without a shirt, Emma. But I'm not around him a lot. I mostly work with Daisy."

"What's she like?" Lincoln asked, nosing his way into the conversation. He leaned against the table and rested his chin on one hand as he listened, his dark eyes wide with interest.

Marilyn smiled. "She's one of the sweetest people you'd ever meet. Normal, honestly except for that amazing singing voice. Robby's a nice guy, quirky and kind of immature sometimes but he's a good man. I like them both a lot."

Bo squeezed her hand. "Me too. I mean, Robby seriously tries to get under my skin all the time, but I think that's who he is."

"And they definitely are relationship goals," Marilyn chimed in. "I don't think I've ever seen a couple so in love."

Bo grunted. "It is embarrassing to be with them sometimes. I take them out for dates to work security and pretend I don't know them. Yeesh."

The Suttons approached and the mood of the table shifted from light and fun to tense. Lincoln and Bo both straightened while Asher flicked his paper triangle over a goal set up in front of Emma. She caught it and sent her brother a death-glare.

"Hi Ma." Bo tried breaking the tension by acknowledging them first.

Joe nodded curtly as he sat beside Emma. Robin managed a weak smile as she followed suit.

"Wasn't that a lovely wedding?" she asked, her focus on Marilyn.

"Indeed. The bride's stunning."

Robin smiled silently at her son. He smiled back.

Marilyn reached for her water and took a small sip. It was going to be a long, long night.

**

Bo pushed the remainder of his dinner around the plate as he worked to avoid his father's eyes. Marilyn carried much of the conversation with his siblings and mother, which effectively kept him out of the spotlight during the meal.

He'd be thinking for a long time about how to repay her.

"Well," Robin began. "Marilyn, you are a delight. I'm sure glad you and Bo met."

Marilyn looked up at him. Despite their earlier argument, her eyes held no signs of any lingering frustration with him. Bo gently stroked her cheek as his chest filled with relief. "I'm glad too." He grinned. "And that you didn't let me get away with being such a jerk."

"Ohh… that sounds like a good story." Emma plopped her chin on her hand and waited anxiously for him to spill the details.

Bo huffed. "No way, little sister."

Joe cleared his throat. "I'm going to get some coffee." He stood and left the table, not bothering to offer to get any for the rest of the group.

Bo looked at Marilyn. "Would you like some coffee? Or anything else?"

"Sure. I'll take some coffee. We'll need it for the cake and cookies." She winked. "And we'll need that for energy for dancing."

Bo groaned as he stood. "You aren't still holding me to that dancing bit are you?"

Marilyn leaned back in her seat, feigning shock. "Of course. It's really the only reason I came."

"Ugh…" he leaned down to peck her forehead. "Fine. We'll dance. I'll be right back."

Bo slowly made his way to the bar, hoping to avoid his father who stood at the end of the short line.

They sized each other up for a moment before Bo spoke. "I am sorry for lying to you and Mom. I should have told you sooner what I do. I'm not ashamed of it."

Joe frowned, turning to the bartender. "Two coffees please." Bo waited as the man served his father before placing his own order as well.

Once they had their drinks they moved off to the side, but didn't start back to the table.

"You know, son, you always assume things about me. Just because we aren't the same doesn't mean I don't value the person you are. Did I want you to play sports? Sure. But it's not the end of the world you didn't." Joe paused. "You assume I'm going to be hard and that's all you see. Maybe try assuming I'll understand instead sometime, and you'll find something different."

Bo's mouth opened as his father's words hit.

"I like your girl. Don't lose her."

And with that, Joe started back to the table, his son woefully behind on everything.

Chapter twelve

An hour later, the band started playing music perfect for Marilyn to dance to. She batted her eyelashes as she nudged Bo who'd been entertaining his siblings with tales from the tour. He glanced at her, and she could tell he understood what she expected of him.

"Yes, Twinkles?"

He clearly intended to make her speak the words.

She refused. "Muscles." Marilyn held his gaze until he smirked, the amusement rolling into a chuckle that rumbled deep in his chest.

"Would you like to dance with me, Marilyn?"

She beamed, gasping as she pressed one hand to her chest. "Why, Bennett Oliver, I wondered if you'd ever ask!"

He stood, exhaling loudly as he extended one hand to her. "Sure, you did. Besides, if I didn't ask you, you'd ask Lincoln."

Marilyn winked at his brother who howled.

"I might." She grinned. "But I'm not sure he can toss me around like you can."

"Hey!" Lincoln held up a skinny arm and flexed. "I got guns."

Bo hit his younger brother, making him wince.

"You're not even close to what she needs, bud." He tipped his head across the room where a cute college-age girl eyed their table.

"She looks like she could use a partner. Go turn on that Sutton charm and get out there." Bo squeezed Marilyn's hand.

"Shall we?"

She allowed Bo to lead her to the floor where he first pulled her close. "I need to come up with something else, but you're totally amazing." He spun her outward in time with the music and back again, so her hands were back in his.

"I'm here for this. I might be nuts, but I am."

She giggled. "Me too, Muscles. And if we're nuts—I'm not sure I care. Let's dance!"

**

After spinning and flipping Marilyn around the dancefloor so many times they both were getting dizzy, Bo was grateful when the band decided to slow down. He pulled Marilyn close against him, appreciating that now they could fade into the background with the other couples on the floor, rather than remaining a main attraction who stole the attention from the bride and groom.

Marilyn rested her cheek against his chest and Bo wondered why he ever worried about bringing her, and worse how he could even consider her a 'fake' girlfriend.

He desperately wanted this to be real. By the end of the weekend, he intended to make it so.

Bo lay his cheek against the soft hair on top of Marilyn's head, inhaling her sweet shampoo. In a moment like this he could forget the Frannie debacle, and that she'd been seated at a table only feet away from his own. Bo caught her and her new husband watching him and Marilyn several times, but it didn't trouble him. Why should it? He had the best woman in the world in his arms. And he intended not to blow it.

He'd be smart. He'd be careful. But he'd also put aside all his worries and trust Marilyn. What did it matter, since his heart left him ages ago when he laid eyes on her?

"Thank you," he whispered, his words making her lift her head so their gaze locked.

She stared at him, eyes wide as they swayed slowly together, the other couples morphing to a blur that didn't matter to their moment. Bo's heart tumbled.

He would not fall in love so fast. He'd be smart. He'd be careful.

Marilyn's eyes danced in amusement. "What are you thanking me for now?"

Bo exhaled, clinging to a small bit of hope that he wouldn't hurt her or get hurt himself. "For doing this. You really shouldn't have come." He spun her around.

"Hmm... a free trip with a handsome, sweet guy? Yeah. I'm an idiot. You should probably run away."

Bo leaned down to brush her lips with his. "You kind of are an idiot for giving me a chance, Twinkles. But I'm lucky for it."

"You are indeed." She held his gaze. "But I'm glad I came. I hope it helped."

He kissed her again. "More than you can possibly know."

**

As the night wound down, Bo realized they might not talk to his family again before they left early the next morning. While it might be tempting and even easier, he couldn't leave, still wondering what their assessment of his job might be, or what they thought of the man he became over the last few years apart from them.

As much as he didn't want to do it, he leaned down and whispered to Marilyn, "Let's go talk to my parents. I... imagine we still need to say some things."

She grasped his hands tightly. "I think that's a good idea." Her warmth and encouragement gave Bo the courage he needed to lead her from the dancefloor, toward the table where his parents sat, chatting intimately.

"Hey, guys." Bo yanked out Marilyn's seat, waiting for her to sit before he followed suit.

"We're leaving pretty early tomorrow," he continued. "I wouldn't want to go without saying our good-byes."

His mom nodded, her eyes bearing the sadness they assumed the night before. "Make sure you say good-bye to your sister and brothers too."

"We will."

Marilyn took Bo's hand under the table, reassuring him with her touch that all would be well.

"I'm sure the tour will go through Alabama next year," Bo began. "If you'd want to come out to a show."

Robin managed a smile, though it appeared to take a bit of effort. "Emma would certainly like that."

Marilyn leaned into him. "No doubt this one will get you all backstage if you want. Just don't tell the boys or you'll never hear the end of it."

The tinge of worry on his mother's brow softened as she smiled at Marilyn and again Bo filled with gratitude for her presence beside him. She made all of this, horrible as it might have been, completely bearable and most of all, better.

They shared a smile.

"Good. We'll set it up." Bo exhaled. "I wanted to apologize again for not telling you about where I was and what I do for a living. It wasn't fair to hide it and definitely not for so long." He couldn't bear to look at his father, so he trained his eyes on his mom instead.

"I love you. I'm sorry."

Robin's eyes filled with tears as she stood and came to him, arms open. "I love you too, Bennett. Always."

Bo stood and wrapped his mom tight in his arms, grateful for her forgiveness.

"I still want to smack you," she muttered. "But that doesn't mean we can't move on." She stepped back, hands on his arms as she looked up at him.

"You never, ever need to worry we'll be proud of you. I realize the man you are. I know you're happy and doing good things." She glanced at Marilyn and winked. "And because of all that you earned the love of a perfect partner." She reached out with one hand and Marilyn took it, the women sharing a moment.

Marilyn blinked back tears and his mother did the same.

Oh, Lord, he was in trouble.

In that moment, Bo understood the magnitude of what he'd done.

He claimed Marilyn to himself, and now his family, but most of all, he dropped deep into something he never experienced with Frannie—complete trust of a person who could, and just might, rip out his heart and break it.

And for all that it mattered, he couldn't make himself care at all.

**

The next morning Marilyn woke with a start, late again. She hustled to dress, glanced at her phone and found Bo text her earlier, saying he'd meet her at the café downstairs for a quick breakfast. They planned the night before to try and find a church before heading off to Princeton.

Bo even left it open that they could get hotel rooms if she felt too drained after dealing with her family to head home.

The man might be close to sainthood for that.

Marilyn dragged her suitcase toward the café, wishing she put on some make-up and fixed her hair. But at this point, she remained under no delusions about her time with Bo. They had fun, sure, but did he want more? She should have held firm on the 'no kissing' thing but when he twirled her around the dancefloor or rubbed her sore feet, she couldn't find the gumption to fight even a sliver of happiness.

She sure hoped he could pull out the magic with her family and make that painful part of the trip less so.

Marilyn scanned the small crowd in the café, surprised to find Bo at a tall table talking to his father. She slipped back a step, watching and definitely not wanting to interrupt the conversation. Both men's eyebrows were furrowed as they frowned and gestured through their conversation.

The night before, when Robin so easily forgave her son, Joe merely watched from the sidelines, silent and stern. He thanked Bo for his words, and graciously said good-bye to them both, but there wasn't much love lost, even when Bo, again, tried to engage his father in conversation.

Marilyn encouraged him later that he'd done what he could and shouldn't have any regrets. What else could she say?

But now she couldn't tell if Bo was angry or merely serious. She watched for a few seconds, thinking herself hidden behind a large plant.

But Bo sensed her presence. He raised his eyes and met hers, beaming as he stood and gestured for her to join them. She offered a quick prayer and dragged her suitcase into the café. Bo grinned, his feelings open for anyone to guess as he relieved her of her luggage, which he shoved out of the way.

"Morning." His deep voice rumbled with an emotion Marilyn couldn't quite name. "How about a muffin and coffee?"

She glanced at his father. "Sure. If I'm not interrupting."

"Not at all." Bo slipped away to the counter, leaving her with Joe.

"No one else is up as early as we are. It was always that way." He sipped his coffee.

Grateful for the man's willingness to start the conversation, Marilyn smiled. "Yeah, I'm not much for early mornings but we wanted to get to church if we could and then we need to get to Princeton for my sister's engagement party."

Joe grunted. "Yeah? Lots of weddings. Is there one coming for you?" He jerked his head toward Bo who waited for his order.

Marilyn felt her cheeks warm. "Oh. We haven't really been dating that long."

Joe nodded, and Marilyn figured he asked to be polite and not out of any real interest.

"You guys doing OK?" she asked gently, unsure if she should prod or mind her own business. But she'd never been very good at minding her own business. She'd always been a prodder.

"I do think we're OK. It's good he came." He reached over to pat her hand. "It's even better he found you. You two were something else on the dancefloor last night. Almost made me want to get out there."

Marilyn laughed. She recognized the gleam in his eye as the same one she noticed many times in Bo's too. "Well, any time you and your wife want lessons, you give me a call."

"Who's getting lessons?" Bo set down her coffee and muffin along with a handful of creamers. He grinned. "Extra since you drink it white."

She rolled her eyes. "You're awful."

"You're so welcome." He kissed her head for good measure before sitting down across from his father, Marilyn between them.

Joe pushed to his feet. "I'm going to go get everyone moving." He looked at Bo. "I'm glad I caught you before you left."

"Me too, Dad."

Joe eyed Marilyn warily as she stood and gave him a hug. "I'm glad I got to meet you, Joe. I appreciate you welcoming me into the family. This was a lot of fun."

Joe squeezed her before letting her go. "I'm glad you came. We all are. Maybe think about coming to Alabama for Christmas…?" He looked at Bo who stood and gave his father a hug too.

"We will." The men shared a look that revealed peace had been restored between them.

"Tell everyone again we said good-bye." Bo sat beside Marilyn.

"Will do." Joe left the café and Marilyn turned to Bo, jaw dropped.

"What happened? Last night it went from tense to bearable and now it's downright warm!"

Bo took a sip of coffee. "I came down here to think about things and he showed up. We started talking and… I guess it kind of came out and we're better. Not great, not good. I don't think we'll ever be close. But at least we're better. It's out there. I said what I needed to, and he gave me some things to think about. I guess I haven't always been fair with him. I didn't try hard enough to understand him."

Marilyn swelled with pride. "Takes a big man to admit he can do better. I'm proud of you."

Bo scooted his chair closer and brushed his lips to hers. "I couldn't have done it without you."

Marilyn nodded as Bo stood and tossed his trash. "We should get going. I found a church about ten minutes out if you want to go."

She smiled at his consideration. "I'd love to go to church with you, Bo."

**

Bo held Marilyn's hand through the entire service. He always went to church growing up and when he moved into Daisy and Robby's house, he was relieved they shared his faith as well. Their church in New York had a huge congregation and might be less personal but the message remained spot-on and challenging and recently Bo even started occasionally attending a men's Bible study when his schedule allowed.

This church, one they picked at random, consisted of a tiny, but welcoming congregation that made an effort to meet the new people in the middle row. Bo and Marilyn shook so many hands they could hardly get out of there.

But it felt good being together. It felt right.

And it also felt serious in a way that was beyond Bo's comprehension. To have a gorgeous woman he now admitted to falling in love with beside him as they worshipped and praised God together meant he might be in over his head. They would soon have a lot to talk about whether he was ready or not.

It dawned on Bo that he'd rarely been able to convince Frannie to go to church with him. It should have been a warning sign, but he'd been too blind back then, thinking himself fortune simply because the angels blessed him with a beautiful woman who wanted to be with him.

He wouldn't fall for the trappings of perfection again. He'd analyze the situation, tread lightly, be careful.

Take it slow. Keep your head on straight.

"OK. Ready." Marilyn slipped out of the bathroom and took Bo's hand. They walked silently to the car and minutes later they were on the road, now heading toward what Marilyn only describe to Bo as 'doom'.

"It's only going to take us about an hour and a half to get there," he began. "Do you want to text your parents, or do they expect us?"

"They can't ever be sure what to expect where I'm concerned." Marilyn kept her eyes focused out the window on her side of the car. "But I told them we'd be getting there sometime around lunch or after. Honestly, it doesn't matter. They'll be annoyed with me regardless, so you can stop at any sights or to grab a bite to eat."

She waved her hand around. "Take as long as you want so we can prolong the agony."

Bo cleared his throat. Given how hard he tried to keep his personal life hidden, he'd shown unbelievable trust and transparency in sharing his problems, not to mention being left at the altar, with Marilyn.

Now it was her turn. Did he dare push to delve into her issues? He couldn't imagine how to help if he didn't.

"It might be a good idea for you to tell me what we're walking into. I mean, so we don't end up with a Frannie situation."

Marilyn reached over and took Bo's hand from where it rested on the center console. She laced their fingers together. "I never have any idea what I'm walking into with my family. There's no fiancé left at the altar or ongoing battles. For us it's a 'crisis du jour'- depending what my mom suddenly finds important this week. Then she'll point out all the ways my sisters and brother are fulfilling that, and not-so-subtly point out the ways I'm not."

She sighed heavily. "Right now, it's probably that I'm bouncing between embarrassing jobs—ones they can't brag to their friends about."

Bo considered this. "What did you tell them about us? Is it the truth or did you spice me up so I'm exceedingly impressive?"

Again, Marilyn looked out the window. "I don't need to spice you up. They're glad you have a steady job. All my father will worry about is that maybe he can pawn me off on you so I'm your responsibility and not his. Or that maybe you'll talk some sense into me and get me into college."

She paused, thinking. "So, decide how many cows I'm worth. I'm sure he'll offer a dowry of some kind. And don't be stingy. I'm worth a few good heifers."

Bo didn't find this amusing. He rubbed his thumb over her hand reassuringly. "Hey."

Marilyn glanced at him. He lifted an eyebrow. "I'm going to make them wish they never looked down on you. It's high time your family remembers who you are, and how much you matter."

She smiled, but it didn't quite light her face the way he wanted it to. "Thanks."

Bo turned his attention back to the road as Marilyn looked out her own window again. Tension radiated from her.

"So, you said your mom is a brain surgeon. What's your dad do?"

"Defense attorney. Brother is a doctor too; his wife is a college prof. His twin sister is the business owner, and she married a lawyer. Up next is the bride to be, Rosemary. She's the computer genius working to stop human trafficking. She's marrying an engineer for NASA."

Marilyn batted her eyelashes. "And then there's me. A mere out of work circus performer. Imagine their shame."

Bo jerked her arm. "Hey. Don't do that. Who cares what they think?"

She leveled him with her frown. "Says the man who's been hiding from his family for years because of his job."

Bo exhaled. "Geez. That only means I know from whence I speak, Mar."

She shrugged. "Don't worry about it. We'll be fine. We'll get there, get dressed for the party, endure that madness as quickly as possible and after a respectable hour or two we'll beg off and head home."

"In and out?" Bo glanced at her doubtfully. "Really? That's counterproductive."

Marilyn looked away. "That or I barf all over and you run me to the hospital."

Bo's eyebrows furrowed. "Is there something you aren't telling me?"

Marilyn snorted. "Nope. No matter how hard I try to describe this, I'm incapable of it. You'll need to experience it for yourself."

She glanced at him. "And with that, I'll apologize right now. Because it's not a matter of if they'll be terrible. Really, it's a matter of when and how. Prepare yourself. We're heading into battle."

**

Bo pulled into the long driveway that led to the Darby residence shortly after two o'clock. After Marilyn encouraged him to stop at a diner for lunch, followed by ice cream for dessert, and finally a little shop she 'had' to check out, he asked how much longer she meant to stall their arrival.

She yanked him into a park where she sat him on a bench and talked his ears off before finally, reluctantly admitting she'd do anything to go back to New York.

Through no small amount of effort, Bo managed to get her into the car and talked into going to the engagement party and seeing her commitment through.

"Marilyn." He aimed for the sternest voice possible. "Imagine using this visit to mend some fences, to speak up for yourself and define your own future. We'll talk you up and show them how successful you are already."

But she only pursed her lips and punched him. "OK there, Pollyanna. We'll try that."

So, he gave up and figured it would play out however it did. He'd do his part to keep it positive.

With this in mind, Bo set the parking brake and looked into her eyes. "If this gets bad, we don't need to stick around. You're an adult and you can leave any time you want."

She nodded silently.

Bo offered a small smile. "Remember the safe word."

"Titus?" Marilyn made a hopeful face.

He chuckled as he brushed a thumb over her cheek. "I'm pretty sure we agreed not to mention Titus. We went with 'dizzy' instead."

"Oh. Right. Sorry."

"Hey." He nudged her, waiting until she looked at him. He shoved up the sleeve of his tee shirt and flexed his humongous bicep.

"I got these too if we need 'em." He held her gaze, willing her to believe in him, in herself, and most of all, in them.

"Nobody puts Twinkles in a corner."

Despite her obvious fears, Marilyn did reward his efforts with a laugh. Bo took her hand, waiting as she worked to process something or maybe dig up the courage to move.

She glanced at the imposing house before them. If Bo didn't already live in a celebrity mansion and surrounding compound of outbuildings, he might have been intimidated. The two-story home looked almost like a hotel with a manicured lawn, fountain in the circular driveway, and a crew working on setting up tents on the back lawn.

Clearly, they were expecting a major turnout and intended to display their wealth as ostentatiously as possible.

"Well." Bo exhaled. "How about we pray first?" He took her hands in his and began. This moment was new. They'd not yet prayed together but he desperately wanted to do this for her after all she'd done—intentional or not—for him.

"Dear Lord, you know what we're facing. You understand the situation and the history of it all. We ask for your wisdom and peace in all we do today. We ask that you guide us. Bless Marilyn and her family with relationship, real relationship that they can build on. And thank you for the newness of that in my family."

He squeezed Marilyn's hands before continuing.

"And whatever this is now or is meant to be, please guide us in your will, not our own. Amen."

"Amen." Marilyn met his eyes as she brushed away a tear.

Bo swallowed hard. While he meant every word, he'd not expected her to be so moved by the sentiments he shared. "Hey…" He reached out to caress her cheek. "Why are you crying?"

She shrugged. "I always cry when I pray. I can't believe God would ever want to hear from me. I'm overcome that he does."

Darn if that didn't break whatever bit of resolve Bo had left inside him. He leaned over and brushed her lips with his. "You're killing me, Twinkles."

Her eyes sparkled. "I'm working on it."

He chuckled. "Someone keeps looking outside at us. I'd say we better get in there before they call the cops on me for mauling their daughter in the driveway."

Marilyn reached for the door.

"Don't you dare." Bo hopped out of the car and opened it for her. "Come on. Let's go show these people how amazing you are."

**

Marilyn stopped on the porch, wondering if, after having been gone so long she should walk right in or ring the bell. She opted for the bell, aware of her parent's preferences for propriety.

A maid answered. Since she was new or another in a string hired by the family's revolving door policy- 'don't want anyone getting too comfortable in the house!'- Marilyn hadn't ever met her.

"Hello. I'm Marilyn Darby." She didn't look at Bo, figuring he'd think it strange she had to announce herself at her own parents' home.

The maid ducked her head and stepped back, gesturing to Marilyn and Bo to enter. "Yes, Miss Darby. Of course. I'm Angela. I recognize you from the pictures in your father's office. Please. Come in. They're expecting you!" She smiled as Marilyn exchanged a look with Bo, who kept his hand on her back as he guided her into the house.

"The family's resting before getting dressed for the party."

Marilyn slowed her pace, despite Angela's apparent eagerness to deliver her to the family. "Um, Angela?"

"Yes, Ma'am?" The woman turned, waiting.

Marilyn twisted her hands together, worrying over everything that would come next. "Well, I wondered if we're dressed all right. And if anyone else is here or just my parents?"

Angela nodded, as if she understood the concerns. "You look stunning, Ma'am. And your parents were joined a few minutes ago by David and Rachel, and of course Donna and Paul flew in yesterday." She paused. "Miss Rosemary and William haven't yet arrived. Is that all?"

Marilyn admired the woman's precision, and her ability to distract the youngest Darby from her fate. She exhaled. "Yes. Thank you."

The warmth of Bo's hand on her back should have been reassuring. But it only served to remind Marilyn how embarrassing this would be. Having witnesses would send him packing.

And who could blame him? Even she didn't want to be in that house.

"Here you are." Angela opened the back door onto the patio and Marilyn stepped out, Bo at her side.

"Well!" Marilyn's father pushed to his feet, offering a nod in Angela's direction as he moved toward his daughter. "You finally made it home." He hugged her quickly before offering a hand to Bo.

"Peter Darby."

"Bo Sutton." He shook her father's hand but kept his other hand firmly on Marilyn's back as if to show them all he joined her team and wouldn't be persuaded otherwise. For a moment Marilyn wondered if he intended to punch her father if things didn't go well.

The idea made her press her lips together. Her strait-laced father surely hadn't ever been in such a situation with someone towering over him as Bo did, all muscles and strength. That the bodyguard was also a proper, respectful, Christian man didn't matter in that moment. Marilyn felt protected, supported and strong enough to survive this with Bo at her side.

She smiled up at him before turning her attention to her family again.

"Good to see you, Dad." Marilyn turned to her mother who set her iced tea down and approached almost cautiously.

"Marilyn." She opened her arms and hugged Marilyn so tightly tears sprang to her eyes.

"Yeesh, Mom." Marilyn's voice caught in her throat. "Go easy or you'll squeeze my brains out."

Grace swatted at her playfully, her own eyes filling with uncharacteristic tears her daughter noted as she gulped.

"I'm not apologizing for hugging my beautiful daughter." She pointed at her. "*You* should apologize for not coming home for so long." She patted Marilyn on the back before turning her attention to Bo, who apparently found the reunion amusing. She wished she could tell him where it would go. It truly would be anyone's guess at this point.

"Grace Darby."

Bo shook her hand. "It's a pleasure to meet you, Dr. Darby. I'm honored to be here."

Grace's eyebrows lifted at his attention to the detail of her title.

Marilyn rolled her eyes, her elbow connecting with his gut to indicate he was a suck-up and could wind the charm down a few notches.

David and Rachel caught the intimate exchange. Rachel snickered. David exhaled loudly and pretended not to notice.

Score one for Marilyn and this whatever-it-might-be relationship.

"Good of you to come, David. Rachel." Marilyn tipped her head in their direction.

"Welcome home." Rachel nudged to her husband who nodded in agreement.

"Yes. Welcome home, from two hours away when you could have come home a thousand times since last you were here gracing us with your presence." Her brother lifted his eyes. "Been busy off-off-off-off-off Broadway?"

Marilyn exhaled while Bo tightened his grip on her waist as he leaned forward to shove his hand in David's face. Reluctantly, the man shook it.

"Nice to meet you, David. I'm Bo."

Rachel's eyes went wide as Bo's arm nearly grazed her nose.

Marilyn frowned as she watched the exchange.

"Yes. Lovely to meet you." David forced the words out and averted his eyes from his sister. He, too, appeared to be both impressed and concerned by Bo's size.

But it would take more to intimidate the incomparable David Darby.

"Please. Make yourselves at home." Grace spread her arms wide. "Can I get you something to drink?"

"Iced tea please." Marilyn sat on the love seat lounger, patting the empty cushion beside her. Bo took it, gently sliding one arm over her shoulders and inching slightly closer.

Her guard. Her protection.

Marilyn stole a millisecond to lean into him, patting his leg in appreciation of his care.

"Iced tea is fine." He laced his fingers with Marilyn's, doing that thing with his thumb to remind her they were in this together.

She wanted to curl up in his lap or maybe escape together. But she only just arrived.

And the bombs would soon drop. She couldn't let her guard down, not even with the safety of Bo at her side.

Even he might not be man enough to stop the drama once it started.

Marilyn exhaled, a prayer firm in her mind that she could do this and get out of there before anything bad happened.

**

Bo accepted his iced tea from Marilyn's mother and took a sip. So far, the family seemed a bit too proper, a little too distant, and not at all in close relationship. Not that he had any room at all to judge, but at least Emma, Lincoln, and Asher stayed close even if the older siblings went their own ways and Bo continued wrestling through his problems with his parents.

But nothing volatile appeared to be on the horizon with the Darbys. Everyone except David appeared to be on their best behavior—and even he could be described as condescending but harmless. Bo wondered when he'd need to be concerned, because even with Marilyn's limited description of the family, nothing earth-shattering had been mentioned.

"So, Bo? What is it you do for a living? Bodybuilder? Gym rat?" David truly had condescension down to a science.

Bo wouldn't bite, aware this would likely make someone like Marilyn's brother angrier. He didn't care. What a loser to belittle his own sister and her boyfriend.

Might as well put the man in his place.

Bo didn't miss a beat as he rattled off his resume. "I have a degree in physical therapy with a special emphasis on working with the physically disabled. I did a bit of time in the Army, was honorably discharged when I saw that wasn't my path, and now I'm a special assistant to Daisy Grant—but really the job entails security, scheduling, and a whole host of things you can't really define day to day."

Rachel's eyebrows lifted, her opinion apparent. "You work for Daisy Grant?"

Bo glanced in her direction. "Yep."

Marilyn placed her hand on his arm and leaned her head against his shoulder. "He's amazing. Works almost twenty-four-seven and loves every minute of it."

David remained silent. Bo wanted to punch him.

"That's certainly impressive." Peter lifted his iced tea in a mock toast. "Bet with a record like her husband has, you get to witness all kinds of legal matters up close and personal. Remind me to give you a card to pass along, should he ever need it. I wouldn't mind a foray into entertainment law."

Bo cleared his throat. Apparently, everyone had an angle. "Sure."

Rachel nudged her husband as if reminding him to behave or try harder. "And how are things going with you, Marilyn? Last time your mom said she talked to you, you had a big audition. How did that pan out?"

Marilyn tried to sound unaffected by her disappointment. She failed, at least to Bo's astute ear. "I didn't get the part."

Bo patted her hand. "But she did get an opportunity to do choreography for Titus Black."

She met his gaze, communicating her gratitude, but not elaborating to her family.

"Wow. Titus Black? You two are hobnobbing all over the place!" Rachel appeared to be the only culturally aware member of the family. Bo liked her, reminding himself she clearly married into the family.

Grace set her glass down, eyebrows knit together in confusion. "Who's that?"

Rachel didn't miss a beat. "He's a singer. Quite popular with the college set. I hear about him almost daily. Had a whole group of students skip class last semester just to go to his concert."

Grace lifted her eyebrows.

Rachel shrugged even as her husband rolled his eyes. She glanced at Marilyn. "Well, I'm impressed even if they aren't. It must be exciting to live among the rich and famous."

"They're just people." Bo might once have agreed with Rachel, but now that he saw behind-the-scenes every day, the glitz faded to a once in a while event that held little excitement.

"It's part of the job. It's a façade."

Rachel sipped her iced tea. "Of course. But exciting just the same."

"Anyway," Marilyn continued. "Whether it's exciting or not, I've been choreographing some pieces for Titus's concerts for next summer. I'm working with his back-up singers, so that's been fun."

No one spoke.

Bo cleared his throat, searching for anything he could say to cut through the awkward tension of a family who didn't appear at all to care about anything that might be important to Marilyn.

"You have a beautiful home, Mr. and Dr. Darby. Thank you for inviting me."

"We're delighted you came, Bo. How about I give you the tour?" Grace stood and gestured for him to follow. He looked at Marilyn, trying to pull her with him.

But Dr. Darby had other plans. "She'll be fine for a few minutes, Bo. Feel free to enjoy the tour."

Not sure what else to say, Bo reluctantly followed Marilyn's mother out of the room, along with Rachel who shot after them, peppering him with questions about his celebrity connections.

Bo prayed earnestly for Marilyn to make it through the firing squad alone.

Chapter thirteen

Marilyn drew a deep breath as she sat back on the lounger, painfully aware of the absence of Bo's support. How did her family so smoothly manage to yank her security away within minutes? They'd probably been training for this.

"So, you're still piece-meal on working?" Her father didn't mince words. "A few hours waitressing, a few teaching classes at someone else's studio, and now filling in riding Bo's coattails with Daisy Grant and her friends?"

"Whoa." Marilyn raised one hand, nausea rolling over her. "You put all that together without my saying it? Smooth, Dad. Real smooth." She started to stand.

"I picked up the same thing, sis." David sloshed his ice cubes around his glass. "So…?"

What fool notion made Marilyn believe she could do this? "Well, you're both way off. I got the gig with Daisy on my own. In fact, Bo and I didn't even get along at first."

David exchanged a glance with their father. "But you wisely realized your sinking ship and jumped on his?"

"Oh my word." Marilyn pushed to her feet. She could find Bo and get out of there and be home within two hours.

She took a step toward the door.

"For heaven's sake, Marilyn, you just got here."

Marilyn didn't sit. "You're right, I did. And already you're starting in on me. Just like old times." She put her hands on her hips. "I should go make sure Mom hasn't pushed Bo to sign a contract to marry me or something."

David smirked. "Might be a good move if she could swing it."

"Shut up," Marilyn snapped. "I'm not marrying him."

Peter sighed loudly as he set his glass down. "Sit down. No one is trying to upset you. We're only talking."

Marilyn reluctantly fell back into her seat. "Well your talking is upsetting me."

"My sincerest apologies." Peter's tone did nothing to soothe his daughter's nerves. He continued. "We're only curious how everything is going since you haven't been here in some time to keep us updated."

Marilyn didn't buy this at all. "Things are fine. I have a place to live, I never go hungry, and I'm happy. Anything else?"

David glanced toward the door Bo had gone through. "He actually doesn't seem horrible. Probably ought to get that marriage thing down quick before he discovers what a hot mess you are."

Marilyn groaned. "I can take care of myself. I do not need a man to do it for me."

Her father's old-fashioned notions just didn't quit. "Marilyn. On three or four random incomes, taking care of yourself is harder than it needs to be. Why don't you at least consider Princeton? We can make sure you get in given that your mother is on the board and knows everyone over there."

Before she could consider her words, she burst out, "Will you leave it alone already? I applied last week."

Her father's eyebrows lifted in shock. "Really? It's a wonder you didn't mention it already."

David snorted and Marilyn shot him a bitter look.

"Bout time," he muttered anyway.

Her father sipped his drink, obviously working on absorbing the news. Or maybe he didn't yet believe her—fair, since she'd made promises before and not bothered following through.

"Your mother will be thrilled."

Marilyn wished she could eat her words. Given she applied in a crazy moment of weakness, before this glorious time she'd spent with Bo the last few days, she couldn't imagine now actually going through with it. Still, maybe it would shut her parents up for the rest of the day. She'd think of something before she had to tell them the truth.

David smirked at her again. "What's Bo think? If he's looking at you and thinking marriage he might not want to wait or move so you can finish school." He rolled his eyes. "You really shouldn't have put it off. What a waste of your time."

Marilyn frowned. "I'm going to get dressed for the party. Thanks for the... hospitality."

She stormed out of the room and hustled up the long staircase toward her old bedroom where she slammed the door and yanked out her phone. She flopped on the bed, grateful when she saw Angela had laid out her dress and toiletries while she 'visited' with the family.

Marilyn text Bo.

Inquisition over. I went to freshen up for the party. I'll meet you down in the foyer in an hour. Angela can show you where to change.

He wrote back immediately.

You OK?

Been better, but not at code word status yet.

Hang in there, Twinkles. I got your back. They don't win— you do.

**

Bo double-checked his tie and splashed on a little extra cologne before glancing between his glasses and contacts. Given Marilyn's state, he figured he might as well put his glasses on for her sake. He frowned at his reflection. Only a few days and already he was making decisions that centered around making Marilyn happy. Foolish, perhaps, but how could he help it? His frown dissolved quickly, as his lips moved into a stupid, lovesick grin. She was amazing and if it was in his power to make this trip easier for her, then so be it.

Glasses it would be.

Marilyn's mother and sister-in-law nailed him with questions for the better part of forty minutes under the guise of giving him a tour of the expansive mansion. The house was impressive, sure, but he would have much preferred walking around the grounds with Marilyn alone. He prayed she would be all right and not angry he left her to the wolves.

Bo made his way down the front staircase, relieved to find Marilyn already at the bottom waiting for him. She looked breathtaking in a blue wraparound dress and silver heels, her hair half-up and curling around her face in waves.

"Whoa..." he pulled her close. "You look amazing." He leaned close to her ear. "You doing OK?"

She nodded, even if her expression said otherwise.

He took her hand and kissed her knuckles. "So... what now?"

Marilyn tipped her head toward the back door. "Most everyone is here, so if we head for the food and drinks, we should be in good shape. We can offer Rosemary and William our congratulations, stick for maybe an hour and then we'll head out. Deal?"

Bo smiled. "Deal. If we're out that quick, we can even stop for a round of ice cream on the way home."

Marilyn laughed. "You really can sweet-talk a girl. Let's go."

She dragged him through the house and outside where the party was already in full swing, complete with a band and waitstaff walking around with trays of appetizers and drinks. He yanked on his tie, wondering whoever thought such bondage made any sense whatever.

Marilyn smirked as she swatted his hand away. "You look great, so stop fussing." She winked. "Nice touch with the glasses by the way."

Bo leaned close. "I hoped it might take your mind off things."

The tension in Marilyn's shoulders eased as they lowered. "You should have made them the huge, black-rimmed ones with a fake nose and mustache. But this will do."

Bo allowed Marilyn to guide him carefully through the guests, navigating around and away from her family every chance she could find. He couldn't blame her, really. The questions had been daunting for him, he couldn't imagine what they felt like to her, especially when they came from people whose approval she so desperately wanted.

"What did your dad talk to you about while they dragged me around the house?"

Marilyn didn't look at him, instead snagging two appetizers off a passing tray. She handed one to him.

"The usual." She began eating her stuffed mushroom while surveying the crowd.

"And what's that?" Bo began eating as he waited for her answer.

"My birthday is next month. He didn't mention it directly, but I'll be twenty-three and that, to him, is criminal. I should have a job by now. One job that pays all my bills. And of course, there's an added bonus if he can brag about what I do."

She sighed. "But telling the upper crust crowd that your daughter is a dancer—unless of course she's headlining a Broadway show—a real one—might as well be saying I work in the red light district if you get my drift."

Bo looked up to heaven as he spoke. "Are you putting words in his mouth or did he say those things? Because after I talked to my dad… I mean, I realized maybe I assumed things that weren't entirely fair and definitely weren't true."

Her head jerked as she turned to him in surprise. "He's said it enough that now he doesn't need to. It's articulated by osmosis. The weird light that glows complete disappointment in his eyes." She leaned close and pushed up to her toes to whisper, "Look closer next time."

Bo groaned but didn't respond as a woman approached them. She moved in a way that said she didn't need anyone's approval.

"Marilyn, you actually made it this time. So glad to see you." She air-kissed her on each cheek before stepping back to look up at Bo.

"Rosemary. Congratulations." The sentiment wasn't heartfelt or emotional.

The woman smiled at Bo and he recognized a similarity in the sisters in the slight upturn of their noses.

"Bo Sutton." He extended his hand to her. "Congratulations on your engagement, Rosemary."

She made no effort at warmth or welcome, her words failing to find the mark of sincerity. "It's nice to meet you."

Bo nodded. "And you." He looked around. "Where's the groom?"

Rosemary's left eyebrow popped up. "When he and my father start talking business it's impossible to separate them." Again, she looked Bo up and down. Satisfied, she turned her attention back to Marilyn.

Neither sister seemed sure what to say. Bo held one hand to Marilyn's back. "So, uh, do you live in New Jersey, Rosemary?"

She nodded. "For now. I'm assuming I'll move to Florida with William for his work since I can work anywhere. We haven't entirely decided as yet."

Bo nodded, pressing his hand firmly into Marilyn's back. She almost lost it. He could press his hand as hard as he wanted to, it wouldn't force her have anything else to say to her sister.

That's how pathetic this situation was.

"William and I talked about coming to New York for a few shows." Rosemary smirked as she sipped her drink. "We'd be happy to support you if there's something you're in right now?"

Marilyn elbowed Bo in the gut. "I'm getting dizzy."

Bo exhaled as he looked away. Apparently, he expected her to make a better effort at relationship with her family. What did he know? Marilyn straightened her spin, intent on ignoring his opinion on the subject.

The couple stared each other down, a silent battle brewing. Finally, Bo's expression softened and he leaned close to whisper, "Come on, Twinkles. You gotta try if you want this to get better."

Marilyn hated how right he was. She nodded as he gently kissed her head before stepping away.

"I'll get you a drink."

Marilyn turned back to her sister, wondering why she bothered with a code word if Bo wasn't going to let her use it. They'd talk about it later.

Rosemary's sour expression returned. "So? Are you in any shows?"

"I'm focused on teaching right now so I'm not in any shows. But it's nice of you to ask." Marilyn paused. "Congratulations on your nomination."

Rosemary waved her hand in dismissal. "It's a formality. I won't get it even if the honor will certainly earn us additional grant money."

"Hmm…" Marilyn nodded, glancing down at her sister's hand. "Can I see your ring?"

Like every bride in the world, Rosemary's face lit up and she held out her hand. "William insisted on this monstrosity. I would have been fine with a plain band. But far be it from me…"

She continued on, filling the silence with details of the engagement and marriage plans that held no interest for Marilyn, who nodded politely in all the appropriate places to be polite. The older sister didn't notice the younger's eyes scanning the parameter for her date.

Finally, Bo returned and shoved a drink into Marilyn's hand, making her wonder what happened since he disappeared, his upset clear in the way his jaw worked while his eyes avoided hers.

"Still dizzy?" His tone held a hard-edge Marilyn never heard from him.

She shook her head but said nothing.

Rosemary smiled, missing the tension. "Well. It's lovely to meet you, Bo. I'm glad you both were able to join us. Please excuse me while I go rescue my fiancé."

Marilyn waited until her sister was gone before she turned to Bo.

"What are you doing?" she snapped. "You were supposed to get me out of there when I said the code word."

His scowled openly now, shooting daggers at her with his eyes. "I'm guessing you'll be less dizzy once you get your acceptance to Princeton. Bet that clears everything right up where your family is concerned, huh?"

Marilyn wished she could slug him for getting so mad before talking to her first. She set her drink on a table nearby, balling her hands into fists. "Oh, for heaven's sake, Bo, I was going to tell you. It's nothing."

His expression said he either didn't believe her or didn't care. He huffed and turned around as her parents approached them.

Great.

"We'll talk about it later." Marilyn grabbed his hand, intent on continuing the charade of a happy couple. "But trust me, I'm not going."

Bo snorted, his touch cold and unreceptive, though he didn't pull away from her, mercifully allowing her to maintain the ruse of their relationship at least for a few more moments.

"Whatever," he growled low enough for her ears only.

Marilyn gulped as she watched her parents get closer, worried more about the man beside her who now felt further away than ever. She wasn't sure how she'd managed to ruin this, but she promised to fix it as soon as possible.

**

Bo wished he could drop Marilyn's hand and get out of there. But a strange sense of propriety kept him from embarrassing the dancer, no matter how much he wanted to.

He worked all afternoon to help her navigate her tense family situation. He tried to steer conversations in her favor and make everyone happy with kindness and an overall polite demeanor, but nothing appeared to work, probably because she didn't make any effort. Bo couldn't force the stubborn woman to try, but he sure didn't intend to be the reason this blew up either. He figured if he left Marilyn and Rosemary alone, maybe at least they could hash something out and move ahead.

But when he went to find a drink, he'd been pulled into a conversation with David, Rosemary's fiancé William, and Peter.

At the core of the discussion was everyone's joy that Marilyn applied to Princeton.

Bo's heart froze in his chest. When did she apply? Why didn't she tell him?

The value the Darbys placed on education might be admirable, but in Marilyn's case it only told Bo they didn't know her—nor did they want to if they persisted in pushing her toward an education she didn't want. That she would do their will made Bo nauseated.

His stomach rolled again as he realized Marilyn's own family didn't believe she could get into Princeton on her own merit. To hear Peter tell the story, his wife already made several calls on their daughter's behalf.

Bo forced himself to smile in all the right places, but his stomach clenched tight as his mind continued working him over.

Maybe this was Marilyn's plan all along.

If she truly intended to go to college and get a 'respectable' job, that would mean she would leave New York—and him—behind. And that meant she never felt any of the things Bo believed she did.

Frannie's fool made a grand return, this time as Marilyn's moron.

Sure, she threatened to make this insane move weeks ago, but they'd come so far, Bo couldn't imagine she'd follow through. Didn't this weekend mean anything to her?

Bo refused to let himself be played. If Marilyn meant to use him, he would make a firm and final exit from her before she ever got a chance.

He squared his shoulders. Maybe he reacted hastily and lost his game face for a few minutes. But Bo could hold it together for a while longer, and once they got into his car for the ride home, he intended to let her have it.

He couldn't believe he'd been 'Frannied' all over again. Just like his fiancée, Marilyn got what she wanted, had her fun weekend, and probably entertained herself all the while. Now she'd go take on a life she swore she didn't want. Regardless, her plans didn't include him.

The bodyguard breathed slowly as Marilyn squeezed his hand. Who knew or cared what she'd been clamoring on about as her parents made a beeline toward them? Nothing she said mattered now. It all amounted to a bunch of lies anyway.

"Bo?" Grace slipped her hand onto his arm, urging him closer. He didn't look at Marilyn as he pulled his hand free, willing to let her mother take him wherever she pleased so he could escape his so-called girlfriend's presence again. He tried to listen as Grace continued, his mind still laser-focused on his crumbling relationship, one he probably never should have claimed.

"I just told Peter about your experience with rehabilitating spinal cord injuries. Would you mind sharing some of that with him? He's terribly intrigued."

Bo most wanted to get Marilyn out of there and demand an explanation. He tossed her a cursory glance. "I'll keep it quick. And then we should probably get going."

He wished he didn't see the confusion and hurt in her eyes because it only made him wonder if he'd been mistaken. But one thing was sure, Bo refused to let himself be taken for a ride like Frannie ever again, so if he erred on the side of caution, so be it.

**

Marilyn watched as Bo disappeared with her father into the crowd of people. Her mom turned to her.

She was beaming.

BEAMING.

Marilyn gulped. Even if she hadn't told her mother a thing, she knew the news already traveled to her. And she could guess what came next. Grace wrapped her arms around Marilyn and hugged her tightly.

"Oh sweetie, your father told me your amazing news! I already called the dean to make sure your application gets top priority. He said he'd get right in touch with the provost. Of course, he was thrilled…" She emphasized the word, drawing it out as if some major feat had occurred. "He was thrilled to do it. He understands the family dynamic and all—and what a great student you will be."

Marilyn's mouth went dry. She'd finally gotten the accolades she'd been after and instead of the elation she'd expected, her stomach turned over itself.

"Wow. You called already? Huh."

Grace paid her no mind as she continued skipping down her joy-filled fantasy of a daughter finally doing right. "I didn't want to bring up our agreement again. You seemed so set on digging your heels in."

She stole a sip of her drink before continuing. "What a relief to find you've come to your senses."

"Well, I…" How did Marilyn put a stop to this? "Mom…you might be getting ahead of yourself here."

Grace squeezed her daughter with one arm, ignoring her protests entirely. "What does Bo think? Is he upset you're moving two hours away?" She held her daughter's gaze. "I'd hate to see you lose him, especially when he seems like a completely decent man, and so different from--- what was his name?" She waved her hand. "That one was a loss. I wouldn't want the same thing to happen here."

Marilyn knew full well who her mother meant.

Zeke.

Lying. Cheating. Useless Zeke.

At the time she'd been dating him, her mother raved about his entrepreneurial spirit, encouraging Marilyn that maybe that success would rub off on her. When the relationship ended—her parents were most disappointed that she lost such a great opportunity, not that she'd been hurt.

"We didn't get to talk about it yet." She paused. "I'm sure Bo will be fine with it. We'll figure it out."

Grace tucked a strand of hair behind Marilyn's ear. "Of course. I'd guess he'll be so busy soon with his own job and touring and whatever that it's the perfect time for you to take care of your future. People do long-distance successfully all the time. I mean look at your sister and William." She leaned close to Marilyn's ear.

"That rock is no joke, let me tell you. Maybe you'll get one of your own soon too."

Marilyn lifted to her toes to try and find Bo but unfortunately, he'd gone MIA.

"Oh, he's fine," Grace assured her, patting her hand. "Come on. Let me fill you in on what to say when the admissions office contacts you."

**

Hours later Bo managed to peel Marilyn away from her family who were so over the moon about her going to Princeton he could scarcely fathom the changes in their demeanor. Even David gave his sister a hug before Bo yanked her toward the car.

He smiled and waved to everyone, playing the supportive boyfriend, all while trying to make his heart stop hurting as the awareness settled in.

He'd been lied to, he'd been used.

He never should have bothered with dating again. The fact that they didn't even like each other at first, and more that he barely trusted Marilyn, should have been reason enough to stay away. But no. He'd gone and let himself be charmed by her balance of sass and sweet like some kind of hormone-driven teenager. Maybe if he kept his lips to himself this wouldn't have happened.

He wondered if he was any better than Zeke.

"I'm sorry," Marilyn began as he started the car, giving one final wave to her parents who beamed with pride at their wayward daughter who'd finally agreed to do as they wanted all along, her own desires be damned.

Bo ignored her apology. "Put on your seatbelt."

"What? Oh." Marilyn's voice barely registered as an embarrassed whisper. She focused on snapping the belt and sitting back in her seat.

Bo pulled out of the driveway, fuming at everything. Of course, she wanted to go home. She wanted to be absolved of her agreement with him. She got what she needed from him and now she could be free again to live her life as she pleased.

No more dates. No sweet kisses or earnest prayers together. No more anything.

Bo focused on the road the same way he did when he pretended he didn't hear Daisy and Robby making out in the backseat or arguing over some personal thing he shouldn't be privy to.

Marilyn rode in silence for several miles before Bo ventured a look in her direction. In the dwindling light he noted her frown, worry wrinkling her forehead. He couldn't help himself.

"What happened back there?"

She glanced at him. "Does it matter? The weekend's over."

The words were a sucker-punch to Bo's gut.

"So that's it? You only intended to do the weekend?"

She didn't say anything, and Bo didn't push. He continued driving quietly, mulling over everything. His heart couldn't be trusted. He let it get in the way before and now he stood to lose himself again. He clung to his resolve. He refused to lose his position with the Grants while he pined over Marilyn, or worse tried to fight for something that wasn't meant to be.

And to his chagrin, it also seemed to be something she didn't want.

Bo kept his voice deliberately even. He could give her credit for her role in helping him—as he asked—and he could let her go. Just like that.

He gulped.

Maybe.

"I'm glad you came," he said. "I'm sure it helped me get things straight with my family."

"Bo…" Marilyn's voice cracked.

"Don't." He forced his eyes to stay on the road. He'd give anything to get out of that car and away from her. Sitting so close meant he kept stopping himself from reaching over and holding her soft, tiny hand the way he did before. Now, he could only get them home safely and hopefully never, ever think about her again.

As if that could happen.

Bo breathed slowly. Inhale. Exhale. He reminded himself that whatever she had to say didn't matter. It couldn't. She meant to leave. He'd only been a nice distraction from her plans, her reality.

"Don't what?"

"Don't bother explaining." Bo swore he wouldn't be this stupid again. He'd focus on work, faith, cooking, driving, planning… anything but relationships. Even if giving Marilyn up and walking away were the right things, Bo's chest constricted as he imagined a world where he couldn't dance with her anymore.

Marilyn's soft voice interrupted his internal bleeding. "I should have told you I applied. I'm sorry. It was just a stupid moment of weakness. That's all. I'm not serious. And I'm not going."

This brought no comfort. Bo remembered another time that Marilyn got what she was after by doing things that seemed beneath her. He bit his tongue as he tried not to bring up the way he met her, the way she played his former boss until he relented, letting her have a space in his gym for her dance studio—the same one he promised earlier to Bo.

And then Bo had to listen to all the ways Marilyn would thank Zeke for it. His stomach rolled as he tried to forget his former boss's coarse words.

When Bo saw Marilyn in church he figured she'd changed, and he could trust her. Heck, she even denied that scandalous behavior to his face. But now he wondered if anything she said could be true. Maybe all women were the same, like Frannie—out for themselves no matter the cost to anyone else.

Bo scoffed. "Your family thinks you're serious and you didn't exactly correct them. Why is that?" The hurt burned deep in Bo's gut.

Marilyn shifted in her seat and looked directly at him, eyes full of fire. "What did you want me to do? Ruin my sister's engagement party just so I could set the record straight? And how was I supposed to do that?"

"You wouldn't have had to say anything if you didn't lie about it in the first place. If it even was a lie. And I'm not so sure it was."

"Would you listen to yourself?" Marilyn wrapped her arms around herself, pushing back into the seat, looking small and almost afraid of him.

"I'm sorry if they gang up on me and remind me incessantly what a loser I am. Maybe it was nice for two seconds to have them be proud of me." She snorted. "I'm weak, but maybe I'd be stronger if I had someone to believe in, someone to believe in me all the time not just when I get some big award." She turned away in a huff, stewing.

Bo understood manipulation. Frannie trained him well for this moment. He was not about to cave like he used to, years ago. "I've done nothing for you to question."

"Nothing but lie about being engaged."

Now she pushed too far. Bo fumed. "Didn't we get past this? Stop being ridiculous!" He slapped the steering wheel.

"I'm being ridiculous?" The fire between them smoldered to an intense burn. "So, explain to me how you aren't like every other guy who lies and cheats and steals, Bennett Oliver Sutton." She poked his arm to punctuate her sentence.

Bo struggled to follow her logic. "I didn't lie to you! And I have never cheated or stolen in my life, so don't even think you can compare me to whatever idiots came before me."

Marilyn folded her arms over her chest. "Don't make it sound like I had a million boyfriends before you," she snapped. "The fact that you're so mad over nothing tells me everything."

Bo fought to rein in his anger. No one brought this out of him. "I'll bet it does." He paused, steaming. "And how do I know you didn't have a million boyfriends before me? Besides, even if you didn't, I know at least one of them and he's not exactly a ringing endorsement for the choices you've made."

Marilyn whacked his arm. "Don't you dare do that. We talked about him and put it behind us. If you're going to dredge it up again, I'm absolutely done."

Bo hated himself for it, but he couldn't stop. "Zeke Fullerton is a bottom feeder. I saw the crap he pulled on the daily. And if you dated him, don't tell me you weren't part of it or didn't know about how he really was."

Marilyn sucked in a breath as Bo jacked the brakes to stop the car at a red light he nearly missed.

Great. Now he'd done it.

"I can't believe you'd say something like that!" Her voice cracked.

The light turned green as Bo muttered, "I can't believe you think I'm this stupid."

Marilyn shifted so she looked away from him. "I have absolutely nothing else to say to you."

Bo grimaced, gripping the steering wheel so hard his knuckles turned white. "Excellent. I imagine anything else I'd say would only get me in trouble anyway."

It would be a very long two hours until he got her home.

**

Marilyn slammed the door to her apartment, not caring that it was after midnight and she'd probably awaken her roommate who never took kindly to such things.

She was in misery and so should everyone else be.

Bo didn't speak to her the entire way home. Fine. She didn't plan to ever speak to him again if she could help it.

He proved himself. He wanted something. He got it. And then he found a way she could be the one in the wrong.

Exactly like every man before him, but especially the one that, apparently, he'd been upset over this entire time.

Stupid Zeke Fullerton. While it might be true Marilyn fell for the man's slick, charming ways and believed every ridiculous promise he made, Bo appeared to forget the part of the story where he dumped her the minute he realized she had no intentions of sleeping with him just to secure her perfect studio space.

Besides, how did he think he was any better? Sure, Marilyn dated Zeke for a few months, but Bo apparently stayed in his life, in his gym, for a year before she came on scene. Why didn't he leave if Zeke was so terrible? She should have expected he'd be every bit the same person her former boyfriend had been.

Selfish. A user. A façade that didn't remotely resemble the real, inner man.

She'd never forget that when he pulled up to the curb he looked straight out the front window as he spoke. "I'm glad I didn't make a fool of myself trying to define this relationship before I realized the truth."

"And what is that?" Marilyn pushed open her door and waited for his venomous words, for his anger to sting.

"That this was a game to you. I'm not good at games. So, congratulations. You win."

"I win? I WIN?" Marilyn nearly fell out of the car as she tried to stem the tide of anger. "I didn't win a thing but a reason to steer clear of conniving, selfish men in the future. Good-bye, Bennett."

Marilyn tossed herself onto the bed and finally dissolved into the tears that threatened the entire way home. Truth be told a few of those wayward tears escaped and she managed to cover by laying her head against the window and carefully brushing them away.

She hoped he would be different.

Bo Sutton. A caring, considerate, compassionate man remained a fantasy because that's all someone like that would ever be.

The magic disappeared. And Bo would never be a superhero.

And Marilyn would always be alone.

She sobbed until her door opened a crack and Sonya stood framed by the weak hall light.

The stoic med student said nothing as she entered the room and sat beside Marilyn, placing one warm hand on her back and patting her gently.

"I don't know what that man did but I can't say I'm surprised," she muttered. "A man can't look that good and actually be good too. The stars don't align like that."

Marilyn sniffed. She'd never even been sure Sonya liked her much, so to receive any compassion at all was not only shocking but welcome.

"I wish they did." She sniffed again as tears continued falling. "He was perfect. He kissed like… and he…" she moaned. "Oh, who am I kidding? This was always going to happen. They're all the same. And good things don't happen to me."

Sonya shoved to her feet. "Come on. I'm a medical professional and I can write prescriptions and everything. I got exactly what you need."

"You can't write prescriptions yet. You're still a med student." Marilyn managed to sit up, still wondering if she'd been run over by a truck. She was empty and her stomach rolled over and over again.

"OK maybe not, but I went grocery shopping today and got a ton of ice cream." She wiggled her eyebrows. "Can't hurt. Come on."

**

Bo slipped into the house unnoticed and hid in his room until morning. He didn't sleep. He tossed and turned all night, hating himself for the way he spoke to Marilyn, and for being so stupid and careless to even consider dating again.

It ended the same as before. While it could be his fault or Frannie or Marilyn's, it didn't matter. Work and restoring a relationship with his family would be his focus. Maybe he'd bring Emma out for a few weeks. She and Alice would have a great time together and it would help build a bridge with this family.

He dragged on a pair of pants and a clean tee shirt, praying the entire time for a way to gently say positive things about the weekend but to also be capable of shutting down any expectations about himself and Marilyn.

It was over. And that was it.

The sound of Nicolette fussing in the next room offered the perfect buffer and return to his job. Bo opened his bedroom door and hustled down the hall, glad to get there first and take care of her diaper so Daisy and Robby could keep sleeping.

"Hey! You're back!" Alice exclaimed as she entered the nursery. She threw her arms around him from behind, filling him with joy and a resolve that he made the right choice to do this job with all he had.

"Hey!" He finished diapering the baby and turned to give Alice a full hug. "Missed you, kiddo."

"We missed you too. I think Robs might fire Fernsby. He likes your cooking better."

Bo ruffled her hair. "Come on, let's get you some breakfast and get you off to school."

"Sounds good to me." She followed him happily down the staircase and into the kitchen.

"So, how was the trip?" Alice took the baby from him as he set about making coffee and starting breakfast.

"Did you dance your feet off with Marilyn at the wedding? What's her family like? Did you take any pictures?"

Bo chuckled despite the pit in his stomach. "One question at a time."

Alice groaned. "Fine. Did you dance?"

Bo cracked several eggs into a bowl. "Yes, we danced. Quite a bit actually."

Alice swooned. "I bet you two are amazing together. I want to see you dance and toss her around and do that lift again like you did in the driveway before you left. It was so romantic!"

Bo didn't answer. Instead, he tried to change the subject. "So, what happened around here this weekend? Daisy only called and text once each."

Alice shrugged. "Same old same old. Warren came over with the kids and we all played. Fernsby made chicken ala king on Sunday, and Robby took me and my friends for ice cream last night. That's it." She paused. "Oh, and Carli Cross came over. She fixed my hair and let me do her nails. She's really nice."

"That's good."

Alice wiggled her eyebrows. "She was really disappointed you weren't here. Said she wants you to be in her next video."

Bo forgot his upset. "Nope. Daisy better have shot that one down."

Nicolette started fussing so Bo grabbed the carrier and set it on the table before going back to the eggs.

"You can strap her in, and she'll be fine. Give her the pacifier."

The elevator caught Bo's attention and he knew Daisy would be in the kitchen in seconds. He'd been able to discourage any questions from Alice, but he wasn't sure he could do the same with his boss.

She'd want the whole story. And if he wasn't careful, she might get it from Marilyn.

Chapter fourteen

Marilyn stared at the check with no small amount of disappointment. Now she'd have no car, but at least the money she got from selling it would provide her with extra to put toward the studio space or a car. She hadn't made any decisions yet. She only knew for sure she'd be taking the bus for a few weeks.

"Thanks." She left the garage and walked three blocks to the dance studio. After that she'd take the bus as far as she could to get to Daisy's for a lesson. She could walk ten blocks.

She didn't care. Her entire body felt empty. She'd tell Daisy she needed to find someone else to work with. Even if Marilyn decided to stay in New York, she couldn't, no she wouldn't, have the strength to see Bo again. Maybe ever.

But she couldn't deliver that news through a text or by a phone call given how good the Grants had been to her. It was a conversation to have in person, no matter how difficult it might be. She respected Daisy and this was part of being an adult. She hated it, but she'd do it anyway.

Already Marilyn had come up with the names of three dancers she could confidently recommend for the job.

She glanced at her phone as she entered the dance studio. She realized it might be futile but part of her still wondered if she might get a text from Bo. But there was nothing but silence.

**

"Marilyn text me to say she's coming late today." Daisy entered the gym behind Bo, still trying to pry information out of him about the weekend. So far, he'd been tremendously tight-lipped, steering the conversation to different subjects or work as skillfully as he'd always done. But Daisy was getting frustrated.

"That's fine." Bo shrugged. "I checked your schedule and Robby's, and everything looks pretty clear. Tomorrow's a little crazy but today you got some wiggle room."

Daisy watched as he wrestled to move a weight bench from the center of the dance space.

"Do you want to be in a Carli Cross video?"

Bo frowned. "No. Stop asking already. I'm tired of hearing about it."

"I told her that, but she still wants to talk to you."

"For real, Daisy. I'm not interested. At all."

Daisy watched him work before she continued. "I've behaved about as long as I can. How was the weekend?"

Bo finished getting the bench where he wanted it and shrugged. "Fine."

Daisy continued looking at him as he headed for the door. "Fine? That's all you're going to give me? Are you and Marilyn serious? What did you think about her?"

Bo held up his hands as if in defense. "Yeesh. She's..." For as much as he wanted to say beautiful, talented, and perfect, he couldn't. Not now. She hurt him and he gave it right back.

He met Daisy's eyes briefly before he managed to speak. "The weekend went fine, but we agreed it's not a good idea. I mean, us, together. So, that's that."

Daisy's expression softened. Bo couldn't handle any questions or advice on how he could fix what they'd both broken. He decided that heading her off completely would be the only way.

"You don't need to say anything. I'm not sure I should be talking about it." He paused. "We're too different. We want different things."

Daisy moved toward him. "I don't get it."

Bo exhaled. "Me either. But don't worry about it. She's fine. I'm fine. We're professionals so we can both still do our jobs for you like before."

Daisy nodded silently. Bo noted the disappointment in her eyes. He opened the gym door.

"If you don't mind, I'm going to go take Nic off Jazz's hands so I'm not here when Marilyn shows up. There's no reason to make it worse."

Daisy nodded again and Bo hustled toward the safety of the house, intent on diving head-first back into his job to fill the emptiness in his soul.

**

The walk from the bus stop nearest Daisy's place didn't look so far on a map. But two miles felt like forever, especially with the wind and dropping temperatures. As she hustled, Marilyn yanked her phone out, aware she wouldn't make it on time. She text Daisy quickly that she was running late and then actually broke into a run.

She threw open the gym door minutes later and tossed her bag aside. A glance in the mirror told her she sunk to 'hot mess' status.

"Hey!" Daisy exclaimed from across the gym where she'd been doing some kind of arm exercises on a frightening-looking machine.

"Hey." Marilyn exhaled, wondering what Bo told her and at the same time, what she should say about the weekend. She wouldn't volunteer anything and opt for a 'less is more' approach if pushed to do so.

"Take your time. You look... cold?" Daisy moved closer.

Marilyn rubbed her hands together. "It's chilly today."

Daisy squinted at her. "Your cheeks are awfully red for only walking around the side of the house."

Marilyn kicked off her shoes and started warming up. "I had to take the bus today."

"What? The nearest stop is like three miles away!"

Marilyn laughed. "I hope I didn't hold up your day any."

"No." Daisy started stretching too, abandoning the machine she'd been working on. "I'm pretty free today if you, um, need anything or want to talk."

While Marilyn appreciated the effort, she also couldn't be a fool about where Daisy's allegiance would lie. Bo lived in her home. He deserved to keep his position and reputation intact. As always, Marilyn would be the expendable one.

"I'm good." Marilyn forced her racing pulse to slow down. "It's probably better we don't talk about anything until after the lesson."

"I don't need a lesson if you need a friend."

The words were so genuine, and unbelievably needed, that Marilyn's lip actually quivered.

As she and Sonya gorged themselves on ice cream late into the night, Marilyn finally admitted to her roommate she started to fall in love for the first time in her life. Bo seemed so perfect that to find him as bad or worse than every other guy she ever thought about committing to rubbed her insides raw.

A tear slipped out and Marilyn swiped at it with a wry laugh. "I'm sorry. I'm not going to be stupid about this and I'm also not about to drag you into the middle."

"You aren't dragging me, I'm shoving myself." Daisy moved toward her. "Sit." She gestured to the bench nearby. "We can forego the lesson today. What happened? He wouldn't tell me anything except you two aren't dating."

Marilyn sniffed. "That about sums it up." She shook her head. "It's not my place to say anything. He's not a bad guy. It's just… not a good fit. Anyway, I should tell you that I'm probably going to be making some tough calls in the next few weeks and… I don't think I can keep coming here. After all this… it's probably not a good idea anyway."

Daisy lifted an eyebrow but didn't say anything.

"I can text you the names and contact information for a few dancers who would be fine to take over and work with you."

But Daisy's head cocked to one side. "What if I don't want to work with anyone but you?"

Marilyn raised her eyes. "I'm sorry. I might be going back to New Jersey. My mom can get me into Princeton and that's…" She tried not to choke on the words. "That's probably best. It means a degree and stability and makes better sense than trying to force this dancing thing when it's not meant to be."

"Says who?"

Marilyn scoffed. "Everyone." She pushed to stand. "Let's dance. I'd like to enjoy our last lesson if we could." She swiped at her still-wet eyes and forced a laugh. "There's no point in crying over something I can't do anything about."

"You mean Bo or dancing?"

"Either. Both." Marilyn plugged her phone into the speaker system. "I'm sorry about all of this. I'm honored I got to work with you. I really would keep going if I could swing it."

Daisy watched as Marilyn went to the center of their makeshift dancefloor. She said nothing as her wheels appeared to be turning.

"Let's pick up where we left off last week."

Marilyn counted them off and they started the routine as she tried to pretend Bo wasn't just a short distance away in the house, probably cursing the day he met her.

**

"You are a miracle worker." Jazz watched as Bo got Nicolette into her seat after getting her to sleep on the heels of a nearly hour-long battle.

Bo grinned as he fastened her securely and covered her with a soft pink blanket covered with teddy bears. He gently rocked the carrier a few extra times before going to the sink to start the dishes.

"No running Robby around?"

"Nah. He's in the studio for the next few hours with Titus."

"Titus?" Bo lifted his eyebrows. "Did I come home to the Twilight Zone?"

Jazz grunted. "Close. Daisy finished the lyrics, but some part of the song wasn't working so she batted her eyelashes and Robby didn't get much choice but to do as his wife wanted him to."

Bo laughed. He'd seen Daisy wrap her husband around her pinkie finger several times. For all that Robby fooled the world into thinking him the 'sexiest man alive', a man who bowed to no one and did whatever he wanted, he met his ultimate match in Daisy.

"Good for her."

Jazz's phone buzzed next to the baby and Bo shot him a glare.

"You wake her, and I swear I will kill you. Like a freaking gladiator."

Jazz silenced the phone. "Daisy wants me to take Marilyn home." He looked up at Bo, who turned his back and focused on the pan he'd been scrubbing.

"You don't want to do it? I can handle the baby for a while."

Bo didn't doubt he could. He wondered whether Marilyn needed to pick up her car now or if she might buy a new one. He'd been surprised when he saw her practically running up the driveway, clutching her coat tightly around her against the cold breeze.

Despite the worry filling his chest, he reminded himself that he didn't get to take care of her needs now. She'd do it on her own as she'd done before he met her.

"Bo? You want to take Marilyn home?"

He didn't look at the bodyguard as he spoke. "I better not."

Jazz's silence made Bo curious. He turned and lifted his eyes to heaven. "I don't need advice or for you to solve anything. Just make sure she gets home if that's what Daisy wants you to do."

Jazz whistled. "What happened?"

Bo rinsed the pan that minutes earlier had been clean enough to use again. He scrubbed his fingers off trying to avoid this.

"Not a thing."

"Bull. Your fault or hers?"

That really was the million-dollar question, the one that kept Bo up all night. He didn't trust her not to be like Frannie and she didn't trust herself to cut ties with her family if need be.

"We're both guilty. And I'm not talking about this." Bo wiped his hands on a paper towel as he looked at Nicolette, half-tempted to pinch her or drop something so she'd wake up and he could escape this conversation.

Jazz pushed to his feet. He patted Bo on the shoulder as he passed, heading outside to get the car for his next responsibility—the one that should be Bo's but never would be again.

**

Marilyn climbed into the SUV and fastened her seatbelt as Jazz slammed the door and went to the driver's side. She told Daisy she didn't need a ride home but arguing with the woman was futile and Marilyn finally gave up.

Jazz fussed with the radio until he appeared to be satisfied with the selection. "You got everything?"

"Yep. I told Daisy I could..."

Jazz snickered. "You don't tell Daisy anything. She gives the instructions. It's no problem. I can use the drive—especially since princess will be wailing again in the next half hour or so."

Marilyn nodded. "Oh. Well, thanks."

"No problem." He waved to the security guards at the gate as they let him through while Marilyn wondered what this sort of life must be like. Her phone buzzed in her bag and she grabbed it, not surprised to find her mom calling.

She groaned. "I'm sorry- do you mind if I take this? It's my mom. Again."

Jazz waved his hand. "Don't keep her waiting on my account."

Marilyn pressed the button and held the phone to her ear. "Hey mom. Calling already?"

"I had a few minutes before I head into surgery."

"Mmmm…?" Marilyn didn't doubt what this was about. "Can you make it quick? I'm in the car right."

"I don't like you driving and talking."

"I'm not driving. What do you need?"

Never one to waste time or mince words, Grace dove right in. "Well, your father and I—the whole family really—are simply over the moon about your boyfriend. Really, Marilyn. He is a fine, fine catch for you."

She spoke as if Marilyn had risen above her station and the family would now be forced to come up with a tempting dowry to seal the deal.

Marilyn didn't correct her. There would be time for that.

"Ma."

"You are quite welcome. He couldn't be more supportive of you going to college and handling your relationship long-distance for a time. I'm not sure he could have said anything more glowing about you. I'm thrilled for you two."

She bet her mom would be willing to work with the lawyers to make certain Bo didn't get away. Marilyn rubbed her forehead.

"He said all of that? Really?"

"Really. Now, I won't keep you. But if you get a phone call or an email from Dr. Boris Clark, do make sure you answer or respond immediately, Marilyn. The man owes me a favor and since we missed some deadlines, it's going to be a trick to get you in on short notice. But from what he said you could start as soon as next semester."

Marilyn gulped. "That soon, huh?"

"Oh. I need to go. They're ready for me. Call me when you hear from Princeton." The phone went dead, and Marilyn tucked it away.

"Princeton, huh?"

Marilyn glanced at Jazz who looked sheepish. "Your mother got a loud voice."

"You have no idea."

Jazz didn't say anything as he drove. Finally, Marilyn couldn't take it. "So, I told Daisy today would be our last lesson."

If this surprised the bodyguard, he didn't show it. He kept his eyes on the road. "Yeah?"

She nodded. "I'm afraid it will be weird now... and on top of that I might move back to New Jersey. To go to Princeton."

"What for?"

Marilyn fussed with the hem of her sweatshirt as she spoke. "Well, I've been in New York for four years already and nothing's going my way. I figure it's time to grow up and…"

Jazz chuckled. "I meant, what are you going to study."

Her cheeks warmed. "Oh. Right. Business. I guess." Her tone remained so flat there appeared to be little possibility of finding any passion in this pursuit.

"Right. Business. So, you're done with dancing?"

She shrugged.

"Did he wreck you that bad? I'll knock some sense into him if you need."

Marilyn laughed. "No. This doesn't have much to do with Bo. It's an ongoing family thing."

Jazz considered this. "Your parents want you to go to Princeton?"

"Something like that." Marilyn watched some kids playing at a park, their hair flying behind them as they ran after their kite. She wished she could be so free.

"Huh. And you're how old?"

"Twenty-three in a few weeks."

Jazz nodded again. "Twenty-three, living on your own, paying your bills... by all accounts you seem pretty happy—unless I'm missing something?" He glanced at her. "Is there some kind of 'you don't get your part of the family fortune if you don't do our bidding' attached to this?"

"Not exactly."

Jazz lifted his eyebrows as he turned the car into a space in front of her building. "Sorry. Not my business. I shouldn't pry."

"Nah. It's fine. Everyone in your house will be talking about me leaving at some point. I only wanted to thank you for how kind you've been. I really enjoyed working with Daisy and getting to know all of you." She reached over and squeezed his arm.

"Thanks for the ride home."

"No problem. You ever need anything you call us." He paused. "Sorry things didn't work out with you and Bo."

Marilyn managed a watery smile as tears welled up in her eyes. She leaned against the door. "Yeah. Me too. But that's OK. It was good for a little while." She urged her bag back onto her shoulder and slammed the door, waving as Jazz drove away.

**

Bo stood in the shadows, watching as Jazz drove from the house with Marilyn in the passenger seat.

Did he imagine that the light that once radiated from her in the spring in her step and the bounce of her curls now seemed to be extinguished? Had he done that?

A swift and hard 'whack' to the back of Bo's head made him gasp and turn to find Robby frowning at him. "What the heck did you do, idiot?"

Bo rubbed his head and started to walk away from the window and his boss. "I need to go check on the baby."

Robby grabbed his arm and swung him back to the room. He shoved him at the couch where Bo half-fell into a seat. Robby folded his arms over his chest.

"Daisy's with Nicolette." He rolled his wrist as if to get the conversation going. "Talk. Now."

Bo stared at him. "Daisy said, heck, you said, my personal life is none of your business!" He couldn't believe he'd be forced to tell anyone what happened. He also couldn't imagine where he found the gumption to push back against his employers.

"I changed my mind. Talk." The singer lifted an eyebrow.

Bo groaned. "I'm never dating again."

Robby smirked. "From the sounds of it you hardly dated ever."

"How would you know that?"

Robby flopped into a chair nearby and put his feet up. "Because I'm not stupid. You acted like you never met a woman before when you were with Marilyn. First the fighting like you were on an elementary school playground, then the junior-high-level flirting." He paused to smirk. "All that blushing made me sick."

Bo's nostrils flared as he imagined taking one shot at the singer. He wouldn't do it, but imagining it took his blood pressure down a notch.

As if he understood, Robby kicked Bo's leg with the toe of his favorite sneaker as he continued.

"And finally prom, almost like you were getting your crap together, but no. You dumped her for some stupid reason like a man about to head off to college."

"You're not even close." Bo looked away. He drummed his fingers on his leg, hoping this inquisition ended quickly. Maybe Daisy would need him, and he could escape. He ventured a look toward the door.

"She's not going to call for you until I say so."

Excellent. Now Robby graduated to mind-reading.

Bo frowned.

Robby smirked again as he leaned forward, resting his elbows on his knees. "Now that you moved through the ranks in a weekend, let's get you up to speed on being an adult in a relationship." He closed his eyes. "Shoot." He started laughing, opening his eyes and still grinning as if he amused himself silly.

"Who would have ever thought I'd be solid enough to give anyone relationship advice?" He howled as he yanked out his phone and tapped a few keys before slipping it back into his pocket.

"I'm reminding myself to tell Warren about this later." He cleared his throat. "All right. I'm going to help you not lose a woman you're clearly in love with."

Bo scoffed and started to stand. "I'm not…"

"Sit." He waited as Bo slowly settled back into the chair again. "If anyone in this house knows what it's like to be a moron when it comes to relationships, it's me. Now. Are you going to use this perfect resource that's sitting right in front of you?" He winked. "Or are you going to be a fool who loses something that could be amazing?"

The bodyguard glared. "I'm not in love with her. And she's definitely not in love with me."

Amusement shone in Robby's green eyes. "OK so file this away for later. It could come in handy."

Rock and roll legend Robby Grant intended to fix Bo's relationship problems. This couldn't get any worse. Bo slumped back in the couch and rubbed one hand over his face as Robby spoke.

"Does your chest hurt when you look at her? Do you think about her all day long?" He poked Bo in the leg.

"Answer honestly or I swear I'll get Warren and Jazz in here to take care of you."

Bo didn't look at him. "Maybe."

"Do you check your phone eight to ten thousand times a day, hoping she'll call or text you? Did you—even once—imagine yourself married to Marilyn with little kids running around?"

Where did a rock legend get such a spot-on checklist of love?

Bo looked away. "Maybe."

Robby shoved to his feet. "That's love, dude." He punched Bo's arm. "Let's go. We got work to do."

**

Marilyn avoided five phone calls from her parents and a few from the rest of the family as well. What would be the point? They won. She officially accepted her offer to go to Princeton and would start in the spring semester. Even if the idea currently turned her stomach and brought on a gag reflex she never before had, she repeated her mantra.

This would be for the best. It made sense. She needed to be an adult.

She suffered for four years with no reward at all. This would at least give her stability and peace of mind.

Or so she kept telling herself.

As she walked to the bus stop after picking up an extra shift at the restaurant, Marilyn tried to look important and rough so as to not be trifled with. It was getting dark with fall on its way out, winter in the wind. She hadn't talked to Bo or Daisy in two weeks.

Her phone vibrated in her pocket and she tugged it out, not intending to answer until she saw the name on the display.

Robin Sutton? What could Bo's mom want?

Marilyn sighed. Probably to chew her out. Should she answer?

Nope. Marilyn started to tuck the phone away when it stopped vibrating, but immediately it started again.

If Robin was anything like her own mother, this could go on all night. She pressed the button and held it to her ear.

Who knew what Bo told her and the rest of the family?

"Hello?"

"Oh, good, you answered!" The light southern lilt of Robin's cheerful voice offered brief hope as Marilyn danced from one foot to the other under the bus shelter. It would be at least ten minutes before her chariot would arrive.

"Yep. How are you?" Marilyn had no idea what to say.

"I talked to Bo this morning and you'll be glad I read him the riot act."

Marilyn didn't need Bo's mother doing anything of the sort, or worse, deluding herself into thinking there might still be a chance for the couple.

"Mrs. Sutton."

"Don't you Mrs. Sutton me. I'm not taking your side either, missy."

Marilyn stood straighter and held the phone a bit further from her ear. The woman sounded enraged. Politely. But still enraged.

"I'm sorry…?"

"You should be sorry. If I had a nickel for every person who came up to me at that wedding and asked when it would be your turn, well, I can tell you I'd have more money than Robby and Daisy Grant!"

Marilyn coughed but said nothing. Perhaps if she let Bo's mom get this out of her system she could hang up and move on with her life.

"You listen to me," Robin continued.

As if Marilyn had a choice?

"Everyone has problems. You don't think Joe and I went through our share when we first got together?" She whistled. "I nearly ran away for how enraged he made me. I couldn't imagine marrying a man like that."

"Mrs. Sutton. I'm not sure what Bo told you, but…"

"Bennett? That boy didn't say a word. But a mother knows. I can hear it in his voice. He might not realize it yet- or maybe he can't admit it, but he loves you. He misses you. Don't be stupid. You can't go to Princeton!"

She meant business.

"You were made to dance! And you were meant to be with my son. I'm sure of it."

Marilyn gulped. "No one said I planned to completely quit dancing. It just might not be my career now," she muttered. "I can't keep living like this. I had to sell my car because fixing it cost more than it was even worth."

Yikes. She never meant to say that.

"You sold your car? Oh honey… I'm sorry."

Marilyn kicked at a pile of garbage inside the shelter. "Yeah. Me too. Look, I appreciate you calling—your family was so wonderful to me and I'll never forget the fun we had."

"But?" Robin didn't budge. She probably guessed what came next.

"But I can't do it. Bo needs someone else. Not me. I'm sorry if that hurts him, but it's for the best."

"Marilyn. Whatever you think is wrong doesn't amount to a hill of beans against the feelings you two obviously have for each other." She paused. "Now. I'm going to hang up and let you think about what I said. I'll call back in a few days."

The phone went dead in her hand before Marilyn could even say good-bye.

She tucked it back into her bag as the bus rounded the corner and made its way toward her.

She'd be thinking about Robin's words and encouragement all night as she stuffed boxes full of nonessential things into her closet in preparation for her move. She'd take the first load home at Thanksgiving and the rest at Christmas when she moved back with her parents.

Ugh.

**

Bo increased the weight on the machine and resumed his workout. No one was up yet, and he had a full day of running Alice around, supervising Daisy and Titus, and acting as security during a Robby/ Daisy weekly date. On top of all that he should call his mom and sister back, but he couldn't find the strength.

He grunted as he cranked out a few additional reps, pushing his frustration over Marilyn into his biceps. If he could physically hurt, maybe his mind would steer clear of the chest pains that plagued him over that sassy brunette who'd taken up residence in every dream he now had, each one worse than the last.

Would she leave and he'd never see her again? It had been two weeks since they came home from the weekend disaster that split them and she only came for one last dance lesson with Daisy, who tried to stay out of it, but mentioned Marilyn wouldn't be back and she'd soon start interviewing instructors for herself and Alice.

That was that then.

"Brought you a present." The gym door closed behind Jazz who carried a screaming Nicolette against him.

"Daisy's not up yet and Robby told me to find you."

Bo dropped the weight and pushed himself to stand. "I'm gonna need a shower, man." He bounced the baby, shushing her until she quieted.

"Calm her down and I'll handle it after that. Kid hates me."

Bo chuckled as he continued his work. Already the baby's eyes were droopy and nearly closed. "She fights it so hard but once she realizes she'd be better off just giving in, she's done."

Jazz snorted. "That sounds familiar." He didn't elaborate but Bo felt the dig regardless. Jazz tipped his chin toward him. "Heads-up that Lil mentioned there should be quite a few paparazzi hanging around the restaurant for date night, so get your game face on."

Bo rolled his eyes. He loved his entire job, but he could honestly do without the photographers at every turn. "Should we both go? Just in case?"

"Nah. I got Alice duty anyway and starting the security clearances for the next round of shows. I'm pretty swamped. You got this."

Bo shrugged. "All right. Close this place down and turn off the lights. I'll put her down and you can keep an ear out while I get a shower. Meeting around nine?"

"Sure. My office this time."

"Got it." Bo slipped out of the gym, confident he could get Nicolette down, shower, and start breakfast for everyone in under thirty minutes.

**

Marilyn couldn't imagine why Titus Black would call her. She text him to say she didn't have access to Daisy's gym and so needed to put an end to their working together.

Burning bridges didn't suit Marilyn at all, especially not when she spent so much time and energy building them in the first place.

Still, she should answer so he didn't hate her. She couldn't exactly afford to make enemies of one of the music industry's biggest names.

"Hey Titus."

"Sweetheart, why would you text me and break us up like that? You're killing me!" he exclaimed. "We still got work to do!"

In spite of her ongoing agony, Marilyn couldn't help but be encouraged by this attention, even if Titus would probably always assume the world should revolve around him. With looks like his, she could hardly blame him.

"I'm so sorry, but I'm not working for Daisy anymore and while I do teach at a small studio, I don't think there will be any chance at privacy for us and…"

He cut her off with a noise that sounded like he refused to believe her. "Blah, blah, blah. I need time and so do my girls."

"Well, I can't go back to Daisy's."

"Did that lousy muscle-man hurt you? Because I got security too and they will not hesitate to take him down a peg if you want."

Marilyn rolled her eyes. "I don't need you to beat Bo up for me, Titus. We're not children." She stuffed another book into a box bound for her old bedroom. Her mom promised to send a moving van three weeks from now to get the bulk of her things, so she stepped up her game and tried to pack something each day.

A stack now lined one wall of her bedroom, a sad reminder that things were getting real.

"Well, I gotta do something!" Titus exclaimed. "I need you. Besides, I might have some work for you. You'd do a video for me, wouldn't ya?"

One thing remained true of Titus Black, the man never took 'no' for an answer.

"I would do a video for you, Titus, but…"

"But what? It would pay through the nose! Come on." He paused. "Tell you what. I'll get my manager on it and text you the details and the song and everything. You come up with some kind of dance and he'll let you know the plan in a day or so? All right? We'll get the contract to you once we got the details."

In spite of her annoyance over her bleak future, Marilyn's stomach sparked with a twinge of excitement over this idea.

"Nothing over the top and I'm in. I don't take my clothes off or make out with you. Got it?"

Titus howled as if he never heard anything better in his life.

"Not that I wouldn't love to do all those things with you, darlin', but I am not stupid. Even if old Bo and you broke up, I'm not about to throw anything in his face and risk my nose being broken." He paused. "Wooo! You're something. I gotta go. I'll get back to you."

"OK. Thanks, Titus." Marilyn hung up, fully believing he'd forget about her in five minutes.

**

For whatever reason, Robby insisted on driving Daisy on their date, so Bo contorted himself into the back seat, letting the man have his way. He didn't listen to the conversation in the front seat, focusing instead on his hand tapping on the window next to his head as he stared out at the passing scenery.

His phone buzzed. He didn't look. His mom and sister had taken to calling him all dang day and they apparently conned Lincoln and Asher into making pests of themselves too. Bo's patience waned quickly. He'd even considered changing his phone number.

But when the phone buzzed again three times, Robby must have had enough.

"For the love of all that's holy, answer the dang thing or shut it off."

Bo frowned as he looked at the screen.

The texts were from his mother, sister, and Lincoln. He scrolled through them, imagining them all sitting at the dining room table, plotting to drive him bonkers.

The phone buzzed again.

This one was from his father.

Bo silenced the phone in case anything else came through.

He scrolled through the texts.

Praying you can get past yourself to apologize. She's worth it.

When can I come and visit you? Mom said maybe over Christmas?! YEA!!

Don't be stupid. Marilyn's hot.

You're better than this, Bo. Get your head out of your backside and apologize. Do something romantic. And bring her to Alabama. Your mom wants dancing lessons.

Bo grunted as he shoved the phone back into his pocket. Only then did he notice Robby parked outside the Italian restaurant where Marilyn worked. He closed his eyes and drew a breath, praying for patience.

"Are you kidding me, Rob?" He muttered, now sure why Robby so desperately wanted to drive.

The singer chuckled. "She's not working. I checked."

"It's my fault, Bo." Daisy shifted in her seat to look at him as Robby hopped out of the driver's side to get her wheelchair. "I keep talking about their amazing ravioli. Robby got sick of listening to it."

Bo looked away. "You two are so weak." He hopped out of the car, grabbed the keys from Robby and locked the vehicle as the singer set his wife in her chair.

"Let's get this over with," he muttered, trailing after them into the quiet restaurant. They were seated immediately in the same quiet space they'd been in before, only now Bo didn't have the distraction of the baby to keep him busy.

He got comfortable at a table nearby and started scrolling through the nanny applications Jazz reminded him to finish. He didn't like any of the women who'd applied so far and did his best to make this known.

But even Robby wasn't budging. So, he did what he'd been asked.

"Can I get you something to drink?" The waitress she held her pen over her notepad.

"Yeah. A peach iced tea please."

"You got it, sweetie." Her tone indicated interest, either because of his connection to Robby or because she actually found him attractive. It did nothing for him. Bo turned his eyes back to his work.

Once he placed his order a short time later, Bo admitted there were at least two potential candidates for the nanny position. He didn't like it. But he couldn't lie either. He'd talk to Jazz about them tomorrow.

He studiously kept his eyes on his plate as Robby and Daisy fed each other, cuddled, and all-around annoyed him with their amorous behavior. His eyes kept finding their way to the small opening that allowed him to peek into the rest of the restaurant and to his chagrin, Robby was right--- Marilyn didn't appear to be working tonight.

It was just as well.

He'd only get hurt if he stupidly tried to ask forgiveness. And he couldn't stomach any further humiliation.

Chapter fifteen

"That's enough, Titus!" Marilyn shrieked, desperate to get the man back on track. Already he'd dragged the whole thing out by fussing over the strap on his guitar, the way his hair looked at a certain angle—which of course required a stylist to spend thirty minutes making it back to his liking—and then there was Marilyn's role.

He'd not been entirely forthcoming with the character she'd play. And that meant she fought with him for a ludicrous amount of time for lying to her.

After that, she yelled at his director, agent, and the stylist who insisted she wear a glorified bikini for the video.

Marilyn told them all she'd give the money back that she'd been paid.

And Titus, grinning the entire time, said jeans and a low-cut tee shirt would be fine.

They settled on jeans and a high-neck tee shirt.

Marilyn tried not to care that apparently, she wasted hours choreographing a routine she'd never use because the director did, in fact, want her to be Titus's love interest in the video.

And that meant he already kissed her twice.

She wanted to barf.

Titus roared in amusement again as he tugged Marilyn closer. "Come on, sweetheart, a few hours and we'll be on our way if you play your cards right. Just do what the nice director says."

Marilyn ground her teeth and went back to her mark.

The only good thing about this job was the pay. She'd be able to get a decent used car for what she'd make for two days' work. And that meant she wouldn't need to take the train or a bus back to New Jersey. It wasn't much but there was some solace in the freedom this would bring.

And hours later when the director yelled, "That's a wrap!" Titus pulled her in for a huge hug.

"You're going to be a star now, Marilyn Darby. Mark my words."

Marilyn rolled her eyes. "You're full of it." She shoved him away and started to collect her things.

"We're going out to grab some food. You should come. My treat!" Titus wiggled his eyebrows and Marilyn shrugged. Why turn down a free meal?

"Sure. Sounds good."

**

Apparently, Titus Black's idea of 'going to grab some food' after a long day of shooting a video was vastly different from Marilyn's. He led the entourage through the back entrance of a club Marilyn read about on social media but hadn't herself ever ventured into. She wished she'd dressed better for the fun. But her favorite jeans and tee shirt would have to do.

Titus looped one arm casually around her as they slipped by several photographers, all of them snapping pictures and shouting questions so fast Marilyn was both blinded and struck dumb as to how to even begin a response.

Titus leaned close to whisper, "Ignore them. We're goin' upstairs. That's where the party's at."

Marilyn almost groaned. She should have gone home.

As she sat watching the rest of the group dance and entertain each other while popping back appetizers from a generous buffet set up on the far wall, Marilyn slipped her phone from her purse and stared at the numerous texts that she unintentionally ignored throughout the day.

There was, of course, the daily text from Robin Sutton: *Marilyn, sweetie, I hope things are going well. I'm working on Bo as hard as I can, but you need to make an effort too. Don't let him get away!*

Followed by one from Daisy: *I miss you. I hope all is going well.*

One from Robby: *We'll double your salary if you come back. Daisy misses you.*

Marilyn warmed at that one. Robby had been generous beyond belief already. Even if she could come back, she'd be out of bounds to think she deserved more than she'd already been paid for her work, especially when she enjoyed it so much.

But the last text stopped her cold: *Are you OK?*

She nearly dropped the phone. Why would Bo care? And why now? He didn't care. He made that abundantly clear already by his angry words and, later, his complete silence.

Her phone buzzed again.

Daisy: *What the heck? Are you dating Titus?!!*

The text preceded a picture that could only have been taken minutes earlier because it showed Titus with his arm around her as they walked into the club. The shot made it look like Marilyn leaned into him, listening, as he whispered sweet nothings into her ear.

Marilyn froze.

She pecked out a quick text to Bo.

I'm fine.

Let him think she started dating Titus. What did she care? Even if a thing like that made no sense at all to anyone who knew Marilyn, apparently the image Bo painted in his mind of her would make her just the sort of woman drawn to flirty, relationship-phobic celebrities.

But then she text Daisy: *Of course, I'm not dating Titus. I did a video with him. And now we're with a hundred people eating dinner.*

Daisy text back immediately.

Someone is sure you've lost your mind. He's pacing like a tiger. It's very entertaining.

Marilyn frowned as she text back: *Let him pace.*

And then she turned off her phone and put it back in her purse.

Bo Sutton lost his chance to say one word about her life when he gave up so easily on them.

And yet the tiniest part of Marilyn's heart wondered if there might be any hope left. After all, if he was jealous and checking on her, he probably hadn't completely given up either.

**

Weeks went by and Marilyn sank into a pattern of waitressing, teaching, and planning to move home with her parents who were thrilled at the prospect but also laying down ground rules as if she was still a teenager.

Bo could visit, but he would not sleep in her room. And he'd need to confine those visits to weekends only—after all, she had to focus on her work first.

And of course, they expected her to be home at a decent hour on school nights.

She started taking only every fifth or sixth call from them because otherwise it gave her a headache. She really needed to break the truth to them.

Daisy checked in now and again but the questions about Bo subsided completely. Marilyn wondered if he moved on. The idea made her nauseated.

As she packed the last of her boxes, leaving only essentials out to get her through her last week at the apartment, Marilyn surveyed her work. She could fit most everything into her new-to-her car, the rest she could get later when the moving van brought it.

The defeat of it all weighed heavy. Reality stung. She planned to leave the one place she dreamed her whole life to be living and working. Was struggling for four years enough? She wondered if she might be on the verge of something amazing, and that, if she'd only waited a few weeks or another year it would finally happen.

But she could play that game forever. There had to be a cutoff. And even Marilyn couldn't imagine working three or four jobs in her thirties simply to make ends meet. Worse, she wouldn't go back to school ten years from now and try to make a go at a new career.

Why did everything need to be so dang hard?

She sank onto the bed and stared at the ceiling. Her phone rang and she reached for it without looking.

"Hello?"

"Hey sweetheart, turn on channel fifteen." Titus didn't trouble himself with pleasantries.

Marilyn sat up and flipped on the television, clicking to the station.

"We're famous." His confident voice jarred her as much as watching the two of them on her television screen, cuddling and dancing in his latest video.

Marilyn snickered. "Well, you're famous. I'm just a little thing that…" Her mouth dropped. The editor sure took a good deal of powerful liberties with what really happened on that set. Marilyn gulped as another shot of she and Titus looking to the world like a couple in love filled the screen.

Bo would hate her. She gulped, even as she wondered why she cared. This experience already paid handsomely, and she felt like she could breathe again.

Beyond that, the dancing looked amazing. Marilyn had seen videos of herself before, but this…the pit in her stomach grew. Could she truly give this up? Like it or not, dancing wiggled its way into the core of her being. Maybe her parents were wrong after all.

A wave of nausea rolled over her as she considered sitting in a classroom for the next four years. A classroom where she'd have to sit still, take notes, and pretend to care about things like math and writing that, on a good day, helped her take a nice long nap.

Her skin began to crawl.

"Ain't it fantastic?" Titus shrieked. "Like I said, we're famous. Get ready for your phone to start ringing. And by the way, you're welcome, darlin'."

He hung up before she could say anything else.

Her phone rang immediately with an unknown number.

"Hello?"

"Marilyn Darby? This is Alex Dobbs. I'm an assistant for Marty Martin. We saw your Titus Black video and…" as he went on, Marilyn wondered how they acted so fast. The video still played on channel fifteen for the first time ever from what she could tell.

Who were these people?

But as soon as she hung up with one person, another called immediately. She finally dialed Daisy's number and prayed her friend would be available.

"Marilyn! I miss you! What are you up to?" Daisy's cheery voice brought the dancer back to reality. It would be all right.

Marilyn couldn't imagine where to begin. "Hey Daisy, I'm so sorry to ask this out of the blue, but can I come over? Like, now? That stupid video just came out and my phone is going nuts. I need help! Can I get Lily's number or some advice or… something?"

Daisy laughed. "You're in luck. We're in for the night. Come on over."

**

Bo spun the stroller around and headed back to the house. He clocked over four miles before Nicolette finally dropped off for good.

"Yeesh, what a rough one." Alice shook her head. "My feet are about to fall off. They better not have another baby like this one."

Bo chuckled. "I thought they were adopting?"

Alice shrugged. "They talk all the time." She paused. "What's going on with the nannies? Did what's her face work out? Marguerite?"

The exotic beauty unfortunately knew only about anything outside of nannying. Clearly someone made a resume for her and never considered her actual skill set, which wasted most of Bo's afternoon. But since Daisy and Robby had been locked up in meetings together most of the day, likely about the next tour, he still hadn't had a chance to tell either of them yet.

"Nope. Marguerite is not going to get anywhere near Nicolette. I scheduled a meeting with Robby and Daisy tomorrow so we can talk about shifting some responsibilities around. I think I can hack most of what they need without too much trouble."

Alice smiled up at him. "Good. You're a perfect man for the job."

Bo snickered as they walked around the security gate and started up the long, tree-lined driveway.

"What would you think of having my sister come out for a while? I figured I'd bring it up with your 'rents tomorrow."

Alice grinned. "That would be cool. I really want to meet her!" Her expression grew serious as she pointed up the road. "Whose car is that?"

Bo looked in the direction where she pointed. It didn't surprise him that he didn't recognize the car. Daisy and Robby often had guests unannounced. If the person got by the security gate, likely all was well.

He shrugged. "Not sure. Probably someone with the tour."

Alice followed him around the house. He carefully extracted the baby from the stroller, but for whatever reason she started fussing. Alice grinned and slipped inside, leaving the door open for him. He followed her slowly, bouncing the baby to get her to quiet down.

Jazz filled a coffee mug. "Hey. Good walk?"

"Yeah. Until she woke up again, the stinker."

Jazz chuckled. "Daisy's in a meeting in her office. You mind taking this to her? I gotta get Robby over to practice. He's already late."

Bo slipped the baby snugly over his chest and put Nicolette inside so his hands were free. Jazz's eyes danced in amusement.

"One word and I'll slug you. It looks stupid, but I'm not carrying hot coffee and the baby at the same time."

Jazz handed him the mug. "Fair enough." He patted Bo on the back and hustled off after his boss. Bo left the kitchen and rounded the corner down the long hallway toward Daisy's office.

He tapped lightly on the door and opened it, eyes trained on Daisy and her desk. "Jazz said he had to scoot so he asked me to bring you this…"

He set the mug on the desk and glanced at the woman sitting across from Daisy.

Marilyn Darby.

Bo's mouth went dry as he tried to process this assault, cursing Jazz, aware the other assistant knew full well what he'd done sending Bo in that room.

But for all the work he'd done to convince himself he didn't trust Marilyn or need her in his life, Bo struggled to keep his eyes and mind away from her mouth, her hair, her eyes.

He straightened slowly, one hand firmly on the baby's back to hold her still. "Marilyn." His voice squeaked like a pre-pubescent schoolboy.

Smooth.

Bo cleared his throat, ignoring the amusement in Daisy's eyes.

He remained focused on Marilyn. Her dark eyes went wide as she stared. She recovered quickly and averted her gaze. "Hello."

He tipped his head at her, not sure what else to say as he backed toward the door. "Call if you need anything else, Daisy. I got my phone. I'm going to put Nicolette down."

"Sure."

He pulled the door closed and nearly collapsed against the wall outside.

He'd been fooling himself for weeks.

Marilyn Darby had somehow, miraculously gotten under his skin. And if he didn't talk to her tonight, he realized he might never get the chance again.

Whether it mattered or not, Bo was in love with her and he'd be an idiot to miss his chance. He'd say something. Anything to fix this.

Why did his mom always have to be right?

**

Marilyn had already been in conference with Daisy for an hour before Bo poked his head inside the room and delivered her coffee.

What was it about looking at him with a baby strapped to his chest that made her heart stutter? She exhaled slowly, hating herself for wanting to run after him and beg him to give them another chance.

Daisy grinned as Marilyn's phone buzzed yet again. "Are you all right?"

"Yeah. Fine. So, what were you saying?"

Daisy sipped her coffee. "Just that I left Lily a message to get back to me as soon as she could to help you out. If she can't take you on, I'm sure she can recommend someone who'd be suited to field these calls for you."

Marilyn nodded, trying to keep her eyes on her friend, but they betrayed her and trailed to the door.

"The man wears a baby like no one else, doesn't he?"

"What?" Marilyn's eyes snapped back to focus on Daisy. "I… guess I didn't notice."

"Sure you didn't. Even Robby can't pull that one off." Daisy paused. "Listen. What you need to decide—pretty quickly too—is whether you want the life of a Princeton grad, or the life of an independent dancer. Neither path is better or worse, but they sure are different. And with the opportunities being thrown at you now, well, you could quickly build up the money you were saving for your own studio space and really get rolling."

Marilyn exhaled. "I'm nearly packed. I'm leaving in a few days."

Daisy shrugged. "You aren't fully packed. You're still here." She paused. "And if your roommate has someone else moving in, there's a guest house here for you until you find a place."

Marilyn shook her head. Thankfully Sonya hadn't found a roommate yet and planned to keep looking. Her parents were footing the bill anyway, so she wasn't in a hurry.

"I don't need to leave."

"I never hired a dance teacher. I'd take you back in a minute."

Marilyn appreciated the genuine sentiment. "I know you would."

Daisy moved toward the door. "Looks like you got a lot to think about. Maybe come by tomorrow? Hopefully I'll hear from Lil and we'll make some moves."

Marilyn followed her out the door and down the hall.

"I can't thank you enough, Daisy."

"I'm happy to help." She winked. "That video is awesome by the way—even if it left a certain someone with steam coming out of his ears."

Marilyn rolled her eyes. She still couldn't process what seeing Bo again did to her insides. But she was an adult. She could handle anything.

She leaned over and hugged Daisy. "I'll come tomorrow around ten. I at least owe you a dance or two for this."

"You sure do." Daisy smiled. "I swear I'm minding my own business…"

Marilyn sighed. "But…?"

"But Bo's not busy tonight. You might talk to him."

Marilyn couldn't imagine what to say. "I probably should think about it. I tend to say whatever pops into my head and I'm not sure that's a good idea where he's concerned."

Marilyn headed outside and started around the house, surprised when she ran almost directly into Bo, who blocked the sidewalk with his huge body, legs planted as if he'd never move again, arms folded across his chest, and a bag with 'happy birthday' dangling from his arm.

He cleared his throat. "Before you go… I, uh, got you something."

**

Marilyn stopped walking a few feet away from him, her mouth hanging open in a way that made Bo want desperately to pull her into his arms and fix everything they stupidly broke.

"I saw your video." He stepped closer and held out the bag to her.

"I'm not dating Titus." Her tone wasn't defensive, but matter of fact. "Those video people made it look like things aren't the way they really are."

Bo shrugged. He figured as much but hearing her say it settled some of what troubled him. Some, but not enough. Regardless, he still hated seeing her in another man's arms.

"That's not my business." His eyes met hers. Marilyn wasn't blind. He tried to mask the pain, but the bags under his eyes probably spoke volumes about his current state.

"You're beautiful in the video. It's the perfect chance for you to shine—exactly like you always do. The way you deserve." He briefly closed his eyes as he spit out the words.

"It's like I kept telling you, Twinkles. You were made to dance."

Marilyn's cheeks reddened. "Thank you."

He lifted the bag again as an offering, relieved when Marilyn slowly took it. "Why would you…"

He shrugged again. "I remembered your birthday. I got it when we were... I mean, during our weekend away."

"Oh…" She peered into the bag and lifted out tissue paper, followed by a pink tee shirt with the message 'My Dance, My Rules' on it. She lifted her eyes as she tucked the shirt back into the bag.

"It's perfect."

Bo nodded as he stuffed his hands into his pockets. He'd tossed out an olive branch, foolishly thinking it would break the ice.

But this ice needed a drill. A big one.

He didn't look at her as they spoke at the same time.

"I'd love to talk to you, Twinkles…"

"Bo, I've been thinking…"

They laughed and looked into each other's eyes.

Bo cleared his throat. "Mind if I go first?"

She gestured for him to continue.

He exhaled. "I bought that shirt because you're a strong woman in every way—heck, half the time I can't tell if I'm even leading when we dance together."

Marilyn chuckled, but didn't look at him. They'd had that battle multiple times. She told him that he needed to be the man in their partnership. He hadn't taken kindly to her words.

"So, when you dance, it's your rules." He raised his eyes. "But in your life, you let everyone else tell you what to do. Well, at least your family anyway. Why are you letting them lead when you already know the steps, the music, the tempo?"

Marilyn straightened her spine, and Bo prepared for her to snap back at him. But he wasn't finished.

"Do you want to go to Princeton? Because if so, you should go." He paused. "But don't do it because they want it. Go because it's what you want. No one else. Not me, not them, no one else."

She balled her hands into fists and stalked closer to him. "Spending a weekend with me doesn't make you an expert on how I operate or what makes me tick."

For all that he wanted to shake her, Bo folded his arms over his chest instead. "I'm only calling it like I see it. You'll tell me off or yell at Titus but you can't even find the guts to tell your parents that just because you're made to be a dancer doesn't make you less than any brain surgeon or lawyer or anyone else."

Marilyn's lip quivered, making Bo wonder if he pushed too far.

"I need to go."

Bo closed his eyes and stepped aside, gesturing to let her pass. She raised her head and stomped by him, making it nearly around the house before he said,

"I'm sorry for ever thinking you're anything but amazing and perfect for me, Marilyn. I love you."

Chapter sixteen

Bo choked as the words he thought he buried bubbled out. He couldn't take them back now.

Marilyn's dark curls stopped bouncing as she came to an abrupt halt on the sidewalk. She didn't turn around, her head sinking as if she stared at the ground.

Summoning the resolve to see this through, he stepped closer. He'd come this far. He might as well go down in flames.

He didn't stop until he stood right behind her, his shaking hand lifted as he tried to keep himself from touching her hair.

"I don't want to make this complicated." He set one hand on her shoulder. "And I didn't mean to say that."

She turned slowly and looked up at him, tears clinging to those long eyelashes. "So why did you?"

He exhaled. "I told you I'm not very good at communicating." He paused. "I want you to be happy, Twinkles. If you need to go to Princeton to make your dreams happen, then go to Princeton. I don't want you to regret anything. But I don't want to regret anything either."

She nodded but still didn't say anything. Bo's stomach knotted. He'd thrown out the 'I love you' like a fool and stood here to deal with the consequences, which meant that she didn't love him in return.

And she'd be leaving.

They stared at each other for a long, painful moment.

"I don't want to go." She closed her eyes. "I've been afraid to say it out loud." She laughed as she waved her arms around.

"My whole life is all packed and ready to stuff into my car, Muscles."

He brushed a lock of hair from her forehead. "It can be unpacked. If you think you want to stick it out here." He didn't add that he could be part of that package. If she chose to stay, it had to be for her and no one else.

"I'm sorry, Marilyn. I got so mad about you caving to your parents because our weekend was going so well that I planned to talk to you on the way home about being exclusive. I mean, us dating—seriously dating. But when they said you were going to Princeton and you agreed, I guess I… I felt like you used me to get what you wanted. Same as Frannie."

He stepped back, taking his hand away and running it over his head. "I went back to how it felt with her. She used me. I figured you got your rehearsal, your weekend, got your parents off your back, and now would do whatever you wanted and cut me out. I should have talked to you. It wasn't fair."

Marilyn stepped closer. "I'm sorry too. I wasn't fair to you either." She squeezed his arm briefly, sending a current of electricity between them.

"This might take a while. Is there any chance we could talk somewhere private?"

Bo scrambled, his mind landing on the perfect place. "Sure. Come on."

**

Minutes later Marilyn sat on a weight bench in the gym, while Bo sat on another nearby. She never expected to share this with a man, or even want to. But if Bo could blow her mind by saying he loved her, whether he meant it or not, she could tell him the truth.

She set the gift he'd given her beside the bench along with her purse.

"The whole thing about Frannie blindsided me. Until that moment I figured things were pretty good. I thought, maybe like you did, that we might even want to date—beyond the weekend."

Bo nodded, his eyebrows knitting together. "I'm really sorry about that. I was wrong—for not telling you about Frannie, and before that, for thinking it would be OK to use you to pretend to be my girlfriend. I treated you badly because I completely misunderstood you, I judged you and then used you." He lowered his head, his shoulders sagging.

"I'm so sorry for being a jerk, Marilyn. You deserve better."

Marilyn appreciated his words, but the feelings the situation raised couldn't be ignored. Maybe she wasn't good enough for Bo. His failing to tell her he'd been engaged—while a shock—could be explained away easily.

As for the rest, Marilyn had enough time to think it through and she could see why he'd believe she might sell herself short for a relationship with Zeke, creep though he was. As a handsome, suave, older businessman, he'd shown her a world of power, wealth, and extravagance the likes of which seemed more like a movie than real life.

They had fun, but when she asked him to go to church, Zeke laughed. When Marilyn tried to get him to dance with her, he played along in a half-hearted way that told her he humored her, but just barely, using the opportunity to touch her in ways she could now see were less about dancing and more about his own entertainment.

Zeke's focus remained where it had always been—himself. He believed being seen and worshipped by an adoring public largely comprised of women made him the man he was. Nothing Marilyn said would ever change that.

Whether he cheated or not, whether he understood her feelings on intimacy before marriage or not, their relationship likely would not have lasted.

"When I met Zeke, I couldn't imagine how someone like him would want to be with someone like me." She didn't look at Bo. She couldn't.

"He's so engaging it just, I guess it swept me up. I was young and stupid—not that it should be an excuse." She shrugged. "I figured if I got to New York and in the first week I already had an amazing boyfriend and a job that I was going somewhere. Unfortunately, it only meant that I needed to get my priorities straight and grow up."

Marilyn laughed wryly. "I figured it out pretty quick but picking up the pieces took longer." She ventured a look at Bo whose features softened as he appeared to search for something to say.

Might as well go for broke. He needed to hear the whole thing.

"Zeke didn't respect me. He didn't understand why I would ever wait until I was married to…" She averted her eyes, turning her focus to her hands because looking at Bo when she said it would be too embarrassing.

"… to be with a man. He wanted to convince me how wrong I was, so for a while he just played the perfect gentleman, so he'd get to be my first." She coughed. "When he saw that wasn't working he lost his patience, started seeing other women on the side but kept going with me too, figuring I guess if he was patient enough he'd get his way."

"You don't have to do this," Bo began.

But she did. So, Marilyn continued.

"I was too dumb to believe he'd be like that. Why not just let me go?" She swallowed. "But he didn't. He took me out for a romantic dinner, tried to get me to drink, then thought if he had me alone in a beautiful place all to himself, I guess he thought he could work his magic."

Marilyn shook her head. That was enough. She didn't need to get into the details of him ripping her dress and trying to touch her when she didn't want to be touched. She hurt him, she protected herself, she survived. That's all that mattered. And until Bo, she assumed she was fine—not only that she recovered mentally from the trauma, but that she'd accepted moving on and focusing on her career, leaving any consideration of relationships and dating until later, when she settled more.

She squeezed her eyes tight, anxious to get through the last part, praying Bo wouldn't hate her or think less of her, but that he'd understand.

"When I met you, some of that stuff from Zeke was dredged up, but not for the reasons you might think."

"OK…" Bo appeared to be following along, sticking somewhere between concern and curiosity as he listened.

"I guess what happened made me think I didn't have much to offer, or that a man would only want me for the physical side, not for who I am." She shrugged.

"You were at Zeke's gym, and now you work for a rock star and you're... you..." She waved her hand over his body as if that explained everything. "So, even if I wasn't scared of you, I definitely didn't presume you'd be interested in me since we couldn't stand each other, and then when I did think there could be something between us, I wondered if you'd only want one thing too..." Her eyes flicked over him. "I knew I wouldn't be able to fight you the way I did him."

Bo's shoulders rounded. "Marilyn, I swear I'd never in a million years even try to take advantage of you."

She exhaled. "Oh, I know, it's just that, I felt more for you than I thought I'd ever feel for anyone. I didn't think I could resist that and then I'd make a different kind of mistake, one I wouldn't be able to blame anyone but myself for."

Marilyn wouldn't blame him for wanting to take back that whole 'I love you' thing now. The very thing he feared of her might even be true. She breathed deeply, grateful she'd not made any promises to stay because now she'd have to leave with her tail between her legs, a scandalous, wanton female who admitted she felt an unacceptable attraction for a man who turned out to be entirely too good for her.

"Maybe the city, maybe being an adult on my own, is still too much for me."

"Hey." Bo took her hand, swirling his thumb over her skin, reminding her of when he'd done the same thing weeks earlier.

"Thank you for trusting me with that. I don't imagine it was easy to say."

The dancer shrugged, still unable to look at him for fear of the pity, or worse the disgust, she'd likely see there.

"I completely understand where you're coming from."

His words, sincere and with no hint of judgement struck Marilyn. She slowly raised her eyes.

Bo smiled. "I'm not a robot, Twinkles. I might be able to restrain myself and be a gentleman, but that doesn't mean I'm not wrestling with the way I feel about you." His eyes softened as he held her gaze. "I meant it when I said I love you." He squeezed her hand.

"That doesn't stop because you level with me about your feelings. And I'm not here to judge you for what happened with Zeke. That whole thing is on him, not you."

The tenderness in Bo's voice might have been genuine but Marilyn didn't believe she deserved it. The whole debacle still embarrassed her.

Bo sighed as he continued. "I didn't date for two years and when we reconnected, even if I played tough about it, I wanted to know you, I wanted to date you. That's only been confirmed the more time we spend together." He paused, looking away for a breath. "I just, I got gun shy, with no experience on top of that." Bo scooted his weight bench closer to hers until their knees were almost touching.

"And of course, you're strong and confident and amazing and I guess I panicked, but I swear, that whole Zeke stuff, and what you told me now, it doesn't matter."

Marilyn nodded, grateful for his strength, honesty, and his hand again in hers.

"Don't buy into the lie that you aren't enough. You're perfect as you are. Zeke's an idiot and he's probably still alone—will be for a long time if he can't see other people for who they really are. Your family is packed with idiots if they miss it too."

Marilyn's heart swelled but a shadow of doubt held her back. The battle felt all too real and powerful for her to keep fighting.

"I miss you." Bo's voice caught, raw and exposed in a way that made Marilyn want to meet him halfway.

Tears of hope filled her eyes. "I miss you too."

Bo scooted closer. "Regardless of anything else, do you think we can, I mean." He raised his eyes. "Would you go out with me again?"

Marilyn held his gaze. She wanted to say yes more than anything in the world.

"I…want to. I'm just so scared."

Bo lowered his head, exhaling. "Marilyn. How many calls have you gotten since that video went live?" His voice turned serious, making Marilyn wonder over the turn in the conversation.

She offered a wry laugh. "I had to turn my phone off. That's why I came over, to get some advice and help from Daisy about what to do."

Bo grinned. "I know everything that goes on here. Titus called us and told us to check it out. Said he'd make you a star." He paused. "What did Daisy say?"

Marilyn squirmed. "She called Lily. We're waiting on her."

"You realize what's going to happen, don't you?"

Marilyn shook her head.

"You're going to get so many offers you won't know what to do with them all. For dancing, acting, maybe modeling—you name it. And if you still want to go to Princeton and get a degree, fine, whatever, but if you go now it's because you want to, not because your parents can find any reason to think you're not successful." He grinned.

"And on your terms too. Fancy that."

Marilyn's stomach fluttered. "You think?"

He leaned forward. "I'm sure. So? What do you want, Marilyn Autumn Darby? Because right now—it's on you to decide. School. Me. Everything. It's yours if you want it."

Their gaze held.

"I love you." She closed her eyes, wondering how they'd gone from one conversation to another and now came back again.

Bo's dark eyes softened. "I figured that out, Twinkles, but it's sure nice hearing you say it out loud." He beamed. "And I love you too."

He leaned closer and brushed her lips with his, the light scruff of his unshaved cheeks tickling hers.

"I've been so lonely," he whispered. "I've missed you so much." He kissed her again, finally scooting over to her bench so he could wrap his arms around her.

"Does this mean you'll stay? Or do you want to go and try college?" Bo tucked a strand of hair behind Marilyn's ear.

Peace filled her. "I want to talk to Lily and get some advice before I say one hundred percent for sure. But I think I'll stay."

His eyes lit with his smile.

"But," she continued. "How do I tell my parents? Will you come with me?"

Bo laced his fingers through hers. "I'll be right by your side, Twinkles."

**

A week later, Bo held Marilyn's hand as they sat next to each other having coffee and dessert with her parents the day before Thanksgiving. He helped her unpack her boxes and get her apartment in order, even managing to make friends with Sonya, a feat that only solidified his 'superhero' status further.

Now, as Bo held her hand, Marilyn felt peaceful and courageous. She had so much good to share with them, even if they were upset she decided against getting the degree, they'd get no choice but to congratulate her on the career that now looked beyond promising, thanks to Titus and a string of wonderful opportunities her agent, Lily's friend Dominic, was navigating on her behalf.

"Thank you for having us this weekend." Bo set his napkin on the table, again squeezing Marilyn's hand. "We're excited to be able to spend some time with you."

"We're delighted you came." Grace leaned back in her seat and lifted her coffee cup.

You got this, Marilyn. Just do it.

"So, Mom. Dad. I have news."

Peter Darby lifted his eyebrows as he refilled his coffee cup. "Good, I hope?"

"Yes. Very good. So, when I worked with Daisy, I connected with a musician who's doing really well in the industry. He hired me to be in his video and to help with some choreography for his shows. Anyway, long story short the video came out and I got so many calls I had to get an agent to field all the offers."

Her father's eyebrows shot up again. "What kinds of offers? Is this some sort of scandal?"

Marilyn laughed. "No. Offers to choreograph for different musicians, and multiple offers for modeling and acting too. I've got engagements and work set up all the way through summer, with things happening every day."

Grace's eyebrow twitched, which told Marilyn she could be walking on thin ice and better get to the 'good' news soon.

"That's lovely. But how will that work with classes?"

Marilyn drew a deep breath. "I'm not going to college."

Her mom gasped and her father slowly set his mug down.

"Are we doing this again, Marilyn?" Peter scrubbed a hand over his face. "Your mother went to no small amount of trouble to get you into Princeton. Again."

"I realize that. And I'm grateful but I'm sure you understand it wasn't ever my dream to go. I was at my whit's end and I latched onto a lifeline. But now…" she squeezed Bo's hand again and he returned the favor.

"Now Marilyn saved enough money to sign a lease for studio space." Bo beamed at her. He'd been with her every step of the way and together they found a perfect space for her business. Now, they were getting things set up for classes and even instruction at local nursing homes and rehab centers too. Soon, Marilyn would need to hire additional teachers.

"You're sure about this?" Grace asked. "I don't think I'll be able to get things rolling a third time if you change your mind."

Marilyn stood and went around the table to her mother. She leaned over to hug her tightly. "Mom. You and Dad are amazing people. You're the reason I found dancing and got to take classes all my life." She sat slowly.

"But having parents who are so successful, not to mention Donna, David, and Rosemary too, always made me wonder if I'd never measure up. And for a long time, because I was measuring against the wrong things, I didn't." She glanced across the table at Bo.

"I realized I'm made to bring joy to people with dancing. So, while I'm getting the business set up, I'm going to work on degrees in physical therapy and business. That will help me do what I want to do with dancing. But I'm going to do some of it online and the rest local to the studio. So, I won't be in New Jersey."

Marilyn raised her eyes to look between her parents, hoping to assess their mood and opinion. To her surprise they exchanged a look before Grace said, "I'm not sure we've ever been prouder of you than we are right now."

Marilyn's mouth fell open.

Her father smiled. "You don't need to be us, Marilyn. You only need to be you—the best you. If that means Princeton, fine. If that means community college, fine." He paused. "I apologize if anything else ever came across. If so, we've done you a disservice. All we want is for you to make and keep a solid plan. One that will make you happy, and not leave you struggling. This sounds like the perfect plan."

Marilyn hustled to hug them again before returning to sit beside Bo who slipped one arm around her.

"I'm proud of you too. You're going to be so great in all of this."

Peter cleared his throat and the couple turned to him.

"I only have one request."

"What's that, Dad?"

He smiled again. "Please don't avoid us again. Promise you'll come and visit again."

Marilyn exchanged a look with Bo. "You got it, Dad."

**

Later that night, Marilyn sneaked down the hall to Bo's room and tapped on the door, glancing around for any witnesses. In case.

Seconds later the door opened, he grinned, and tugged her silently inside.

"You looking to get us in trouble with your parents?" he asked as he pulled her into his arms.

"Nope. I only wanted to see you before I went to bed." She leaned her head against his chest, unable to look at him as she spoke.

Bo pecked her hair. "I'm glad you did. I always want to be with you."

"I know." Marilyn closed her eyes as she continued. "I wanted to thank you for being you, for putting up with me, and for believing in me."

"Hey." Bo stepped back and reached under her chin to lift her head, so she had no choice but to look at him. "That's what being in love is. I'm not going anywhere."

She beamed. "How about out back with me so we can do the lift again?"

Bo's mouth dropped, likely at the strange turn of their conversation. "Now?"

Marilyn sighed. "Come on. I'm the circus performer. And even if my parents are happy with my decision, they surely don't expect me to behave all the time." She grabbed his hand and pulled him toward the door.

"They're all in bed. We're good."

Bo groaned. "Wait, I need shoes."

Minutes later, Marilyn tugged him out into the chilly November air where her breath escaped in puffy clouds.

She happily dragged Bo into the yard to the exact spot where the moon still offered light, but the security cameras and floodlights didn't reach.

"You're going to break your neck doing that lift out here!" Bo exclaimed, folding his arms over his chest. "No way. Come on. Back inside." He turned and started to walk, clearly assuming she'd follow along. Of course, she didn't.

"Boooo…." Marilyn used that tone. The one that made him turn, roll his eyes and step closer.

"Once only."

Marilyn giggled. "You better toughen up, bud, or Nicolette will be walking all over you in a few months."

"She already is." He shook out his neck and rolled his shoulders. "It's cold out here. Come on. Let's go so we can get back inside."

"And you'll kiss me?"

As usual he pretended to be put out by the request. "Yes, of course. As much as you want. If I don't freeze to death out here first."

Marilyn grinned, loving the way she could talk this man into practically anything she wanted.

She ran at him, thrilled with the rush of being lifted so easily over his head. But this time he didn't stop at that. He spun in a circle too, keeping perfect form the entire time.

"This is why I love you." Marilyn held his gaze as he lowered her slowly to her feet before leaning down and pressing his lips to hers.

"I love you too."

The sound of a man clearing his throat stopped them cold. Marilyn stepped back and Bo reached out with one arm to protect her as they both squinted into the light coming from the house.

"Marilyn."

"Oh shoot," she whispered, nudging Bo. "Hey Daddy. We were…" She dragged Bo closer where they found both of her parents in their pajamas, shivering but laughing at the same time.

"Oh, we saw what you were doing." Grace winked at Bo. "Impressive lifting."

Bo coughed as his grip tightened on her hand. "My apologies, Mr. Darby. Dr. Darby. We, uh…"

Marilyn snickered. "I made him come out with me so we could try the lift again."

"Yes. Well, remember there are security cameras, dear. And behave yourself." Peter glanced at Bo before shaking his head. "And for all that's holy, you don't even need to ask my permission to marry her. I can't think of a man who'd put up with this nonsense besides you."

Her parents went inside, and Marilyn looked at Bo with her mouth dropped. "What. Was. That?" She punched him.

"Ow!" he rubbed the spot. "You're getting really good at that."

"Oh, I know." She put her hands on her hips. "Did you ask my father's permission to marry me?"

Bo stepped back, his hands up. "No! Not yet! I don't know what he's talking about!"

Marilyn understood that but she liked making him squirm. "Really?"

"Yes! Really, Twinkles. Besides, I haven't been alone with the man since we got here!"

She stepped closer and wrapped her arms around him while he did the same to her. "Good. I believe you." She paused and looked up at him. "Thanks for trying the lift again."

Bo shivered. "Sure thing. Can we go inside now?"

Marilyn shook her head. "One thing, Muscles."

"What's that?"

She held his gaze. "I love you."

He beamed as he lifted her off her feet for a sweet kiss. "And I love you too, Marilyn. And believe me, if and when I ask you to marry me it's going to be because it's right and perfect and not because your dad thinks it's time."

"I won't be fifty, will I?"

He snorted as he set her back on her feet. "Maybe. I guess you'll have to wait and see."

Epilogue

Bo grinned at Marilyn as he drove the familiar roads of Easton, Alabama. They were mere minutes from his childhood home where everyone would be waiting to celebrate their arrival and visit for the family reunion.

He laced his fingers with Marilyn's, lifting her hand to his lips. "Thanks for coming, Twinkles. This week's going to be a blast."

They managed to get away from their responsibilities only by Bo's meticulous planning, harping, and attention to detail. If he left it up to Marilyn, they'd still be in New York praying it all worked out.

And he loved her for it anyway. He needed her free spirit to keep him from being a killjoy.

"I'm excited to visit with everyone. Your parents want dance lessons. Lincoln and Asher said they'd do it too."

He groaned. "Don't fall for it. Those goons only want to touch a girl for the first time in their lives."

Marilyn giggled as she squeezed his hand. "Don't be jealous. You're the only one I want to dance with."

Again, Bo kissed her hand. "Yeah. I've had to remind Titus. That man's looking to meet my knuckles up close and personal."

His precious girlfriend's cheeks only flushed as she nudged him. "You won't hurt him. Without him we might not even be here right now."

Bo grunted, but he couldn't argue. In the weeks after they got back together, the truth came out. Robby, Daisy, and Titus all schemed to get Marilyn into the video, make Bo jealous and jerk them back together.

He loved his extended family as much as they, apparently, loved him and Marilyn too.

She giggled. Bo knew the drill, but he liked to tease and gripe anyway. She'd been in another video for Titus and two for other artists as well. Her business, while still growing, was thriving and she continued teaching Daisy and sometimes Alice too. So far, she enjoyed her classes, but wasn't looking forward to the weeks ahead when Bo left to tour with Robby and Daisy.

Eventually she hoped to hire enough teachers to fill in so that she could go on tour too, even if it would be for short spans of time. Being away from Bo, according to Marilyn would be 'the worst time of her pathetic life.'

He sighed. She could be a bit over-dramatic about her love for him. And he wouldn't have it any other way.

Besides, the idea of being away from Marilyn all summer did sometimes make Bo occasionally want to quit his job or find a way to bring her along on the tour. But he wouldn't tell her that—it would give the woman entirely too much power when already she ruled his heart and head as he never imagined would be possible.

And that must be the reason Bo fought so hard to get a week with her now. Because once the summer started, they'd unfortunately be apart more than they were together.

It turned his stomach.

"There it is." Bo turned into the driveway of a large home that sat back from the main road on twenty-five acres of land that had belonged to his family for decades. The wraparound porch on the old farmhouse had been recently painted and Asher sat on the swing, reading, while Emma played a game with Lincoln in the yard.

Bo warmed at the sight of his family running full steam toward his rental as he parked beside the garage.

"You're here!" Emma shrieked as she yanked Marilyn's door open and dove into her arms.

"Finally! We're starving!" Lincoln muttered as Bo climbed from the vehicle and pulled him into a hug. The younger man groaned.

"I'm only glad you're here because Mom said we couldn't eat until you came."

Bo ruffled his hair. "Our flight got delayed and we had to get our luggage. What's for dinner?"

"Chicken wings!!" Asher shrieked as he approached and hugged them. "Come on! Mom and Dad are in the kitchen."

**

Hours later the meal ended, and the family sat around the expansive porch watching the sunset as they ate dessert. Bo vanished with Lincoln and Asher after he scarfed down three slices of his mom's apple pie, while everyone else refilled coffee and lemonade and chatted about the family who would be joining them later in the week, and before that, all the sight-seeing, and things that needed to be accomplished.

Marilyn remained certain she stepped into heaven.

Robin grinned at her with a wink. "We are thrilled that you were able to come, sweetheart. I can't wait to take you into town to do some shopping. Bo said you like funky bags for your dancing stuff. There's a great little store we can go to that I think you'll like."

Marilyn smiled. "That sounds fabulous."

"Can we get ice cream?" Emma asked.

"Sure, honey."

Joe refilled his coffee for the third time. "We're serious about that dance lesson. Don't forget to get that in."

Marilyn stood and held out her hand. "We got plenty of room right here, Joe. Let's do it."

His expression said he hadn't expected her to call his bluff, but to his credit, Joe Sutton stood and took her hand. "I'm not sure I can do any of those fancy flips you and Bo do."

Marilyn laughed. "We won't start off with flips." She jerked her head toward Robin. "Come on, dear. We'll need you for this."

Robin stood and took her husband's hand, but before Marilyn could begin any instruction, a tractor pulling a wagon interrupted as it loudly rambled their way.

Bo drove with Lincoln and Asher in the back, each holding the end of a huge sign covered in sparkling lights that read, "I love you, Twinkles. Will you marry me?"

Marilyn's jaw dropped. She gasped as her hand flew to her mouth and tears filled her eyes.

Emma squealed.

Robin squealed too.

Bo parked the tractor near the porch and hopped off, leaping over a low fence to stand before her, dropping quickly to one knee as he held up a ring.

But Marilyn didn't even look at it as Bo held her gaze with his own.

"Marilyn Autumn, when I met you, I thought there probably wasn't another woman in the world I'd be less likely to ever want in my life."

She sniffed. "Aren't you proposing?"

He chuckled. "I am. So, shut up for a minute and listen."

She nodded.

"But then I got to know you." He shook his head. "You're beautiful. You've shown me who I am, and who I want to be. But more than that you've shown me that I'm nothing without you next to me. I want you there forever. You're the dancing partner I never even knew I needed. Will you marry me, Twinkle Toes?"

Marilyn smiled as Emma and Robin squealed again. "Yes! Of course I will!"

Bo stood as he slipped the ring on her finger and lifted her into his arms. "I love you. I love you like I never even realized I could."

Marilyn kissed him right back as his family whooped and cheered around them. "I love you so much. You're my superhero, my best friend, you're everything. I love you."

Bo leaned closer and whispered only for her to hear, "Let's make it a short engagement, huh?"

She raised to her toes as he leaned closer, their lips meeting once again. "I'm game for a short engagement, Muscles. Next week?"

A chuckle rumbled in his chest. "Whatever you want, Marilyn. Whatever you want."

"I want you."

Bo met her eyes and kissed her yet again. "You got that, Twinkles. Forever."

About the author

Find out more about Kimberly M. Miller

https://kimberlymmiller.com/

Check out Kimberly's other books either through her website, or on her Amazon author's page.

Enjoyed any of Kimberly's books? Please leave a review!

Made in the USA
Middletown, DE
31 July 2022